Praise for
In the Shadow of the Oak King
The First Volume of the
Dragon's Heirs Trilogy

"Powerful and vivid. . . . Jones has a remarkable talent for presenting the realities of Dark-Age life in Britain. . . . [a] high level of enjoyable storytelling."

—*Washington Post*

"Oh this is a wondrous tale, aptly told and full of ancient marvels. . . . a delicious retelling. . . . If you like the tales of King Arthur, are a fantasy fan and enjoy good stories, this book is for you. If not, you need to read it anyway."

—*Lincoln (NE) Journal Star*

". . . adventures aplenty."

—*Kirkus Reviews*

"This lively extension of Arthurian lore, the start of a projected trilogy, takes accurate cognizance of the various peoples of fifth-century England   Jones' version of Camelot in its early years is appealing; readers will look forward to later volumes."

—*Publishers Weekly*

Books by Courtway Jones

In the Shadow of the Oak King
Witch of the North

Published by POCKET BOOKS

WITCH OF THE NORTH

Second book in
the story of
DRAGON'S HEIRS

COURTWAY JONES

POCKET BOOKS
New York   London   Toronto   Sydney   Tokyo   Singapore

POCKET BOOKS, a division of Simon & Schuster Inc.
1230 Avenue of the Americas, New York, NY 10020

Copyright © 1992 by J. A. Jones

ISBN: 0-671-73406-7

First Pocket Books paperback printing March 1994

10 9 8 7 6 5 4 3 2 1

POCKET and colophon are registered trademarks of Simon & Schuster Inc.

Cover art by Teresa Fasolino

Printed in the U.S.A.

ACKNOWLEDGMENT
AND DEDICATION

People say to me that writing must be a lonely occupation. I have not found that to be true. I have a lot of help. This time Lilian Fuller Jones, my resident wise woman, checked plotting and other basics. She enlisted our daughter, Kathryn Courtway Jones, a behavior analyst, to review the manuscript for psychological reality before I released it to Brent Locke and Carroll L. Riley for comment. Brent is a novelist with the kind of ear Hemingway called a "built-in shit detector." Cal is an anthropologist, who is not sure the St. James Bible isn't an early draft. Next in line was Knox Burger, who was an editor for years before becoming an agent. He's tough. When he was unsure, he showed my work to his partner, Kitty Sprague. We both listened to Kitty Sprague. My friends, Harry and Nancy Leippe, made individual contributions, Harry with his art and Romano-Celtic lettering and Nancy with her computer expertise. (I once erased my whole dictionary.) At Pocket Books, my editor Claire Zion and her consulting editor, Dudley Frasler, polished the manuscript to book standards and carried it through the mysteries of publication.

With all this company, how could I be lonely?

It gives me pleasure to acknowledge the contributions of these excellent people and to dedicate this book to them.

DRAMATIS PERSONAE

One of the most difficult things about trying to base a book on Malory's *Le Morte D'Arthur* is that Malory made nearly everyone in his story related to everyone else and chose names for his characters that seem much alike. It might help to think of these folks as being from different tribal groups even though some of them, like Arthur, are related to at least two, and sometimes three, such units. Arthur had relatives (father's side) from Armorica, in what is now Brittany in France (Lancelot and his kin), relatives from among the Gaels through his mother, Igraine the Gold, and among the Britons through his father, Uther Pendragon.

The names used here come chiefly from Malory, except for a few minor characters I either made up or gleaned from other sources on the Arthur myth. The following list identifies most of those who appear in this book.

BRITONS OF THE ISLES

Arthur	High King of Britain, son of Uther Pendragon and Igraine the Gold (baby name: Bear)
Brastius Red-beard	Warden of the North
Cador	Duke of Lyoness

DRAMATIS PERSONAE

Ector	Arthur's protector as a child, Kay's father
Gorlais	Duke of Cornwall, husband of Igraine the Gold, father of Morgan
Hilda	Lady of the Lake
Brother James	Sexton for Duke Gorlais
Father John-Martin	Priest for Duke Gorlais
Kay	Arthur's seneschal, son of Ector
Lot	King of Lothian and the Orkneys, husband of Morgause
Myrddin	Arthur's tutor, master smith, guardian of Nithe
Nithe	Hilda's daughter, friend to Arthur and Pelleas, Myrddin's ward
Sam	Horse master for Morgan
Samana	Arthur's first wife, daughter of Cador
Susan	Lady-in-waiting to Morgan
Abbot of the Usk	Foundry master on Usk River
Uther Pendragon	Arthur's father, High King of Britain

BRITONS FROM OVERSEAS

Balin	Knight, Hilda's killer
Bors	Cousin of Lancelot
Ector de Marys	Cousin of Lancelot
Lancelot	Queen's Champion, son of Ban

DRAMATIS PERSONAE

GAELS

Aggravain	Son of Lot and Morgause, enemy to Guenevere
Gahoris	Son of Lot and Morgause, killer of Morgause
Gareth	Son of Pelleas and Morgause
Gawaine	Son of Lot and Morgause, cousin and close friend to Arthur
Igraine the Gold	Wife to Gorlais and Uther, mother of Arthur and Morgan, sister to Morgause
Julia	Lady-in-waiting to Igraine and priestess of the Great Mother
Moira	(called Big Red) Wife of Drake
Mordred	Son of Arthur and Morgause
Morgan	Daughter of Gorlais and Igraine the Gold
Morgause	Wife to Lot, mother of Gawaine, Gaheris, Aggravain, Gareth, and Mordred
Uwayne	Son of Morgan

PICTS

Accolon	Son of Urien and youngest stepson of Morgan
Brusen	Mother of Pelleas, sister to Pellinore, wife to Pelles
Drake	Son of Urien, oldest stepson of Morgan

ix

Elaine	Mother of Galahad, lover of Lancelot, daughter of Brusen and Pelles
Galahad	Son of Lancelot and Elaine
Grance	The Lion of Grance, guardian of Guenevere
Lamerok	Son of Pellinore, lover of Morgause
Pelleas	Son of Uther Pendragon and Brusen, High King of the Picts, lover of Nithe
Pelles	Old king of the Strathclyde, husband to Brusen, father of Elaine
Pellinore	High King of the Picts, brother of Brusen
Urien	King of Gore and husband of Morgan
Viki	Adopted daughter of Pelleas

SAXONS AND JUTES

Horsa	Jute Chief, father of Rowena
Guenevere	Queen to Arthur, daughter of Rowena
Jerome	Cousin of Guenevere
Rowena	Queen to Vortigern, mother of Guenevere

FOREIGNERS

Cornu	One-time slave of the Romans, shield bearer for Gorlais and Morgan

INTRODUCTION

Most scholars are agreed that Geoffrey of Monmouth invented the story of King Arthur in the thirteenth century, building on tales of a hero, or heroes, who lived before his time. His book was immensely popular and attracted imitators who added to the legend until Sir Thomas Malory brought the body of texts together as *Le Morte D'Arthur* in the fifteenth century.

Today most readers are familiar with at least the main outlines of the story and can identify the six major characters: Arthur, Guenevere, Lancelot, Merlin, Mordred, and Morgan la Fey. Few, however, have read Malory. They would be surprised to learn that he portrays Arthur as passive to the point of idiocy, Guenevere as vain and hysterical, Lancelot as conceited and snobbish, Merlin as devious and cruel, and Mordred as brave and charismatic. They would probably recognize Malory's portrayal of Morgan la Fey as vicious, scheming, and manipulative, much as her reputation is today. Malory had a low opinion of women.

When I was old enough to read the story for myself I was not yet old enough to understand it; I know I didn't like parts of it. I didn't like reading that Merlin foretold a baby born on May Day in the year of Arthur's crowning would rise up to depose him. Since the baby's identity was shielded from Merlin's foreknowledge, he counseled Arthur to have all the babies born to noble houses collected and drowned. It was done. I was also uncomfortable with whatever it was Guenevere and Lancelot were up to, something I strongly suspected was one of those things my parents would disapprove of, but didn't talk about, at least while I was around. I thought then I could have managed the story better. I wanted my heroes and heroines to be strong.

Many years later, after retiring as an anthropologist and community developer, I reread Malory (Keith Baines' presentation of the Winchester Manuscript) and I found myself with much the same feelings. I was sure I could do better by the characters. I started reading everything, both fiction and fact, that I could find on the period when the story was supposed to have taken place, the generations immediately following the departure of the Roman legions from Britain in the early fifth century. Happily, I found the correspondence from John Steinbeck to his agent and to his editor that is printed along with his unfinished "The Acts of King Arthur and his Noble Knights." Steinbeck evidently stopped writing the book when his correspondents evinced disappointment with the work in progress he had submitted. They had wanted him to use the Malory framework and develop new insights into the story. That's what I decided to do.

I encountered a number of problems, mostly arising out of the fact that Malory wrote in the fifteenth century about the fifth century, in thirteenth-century terms. For example, he has men riding around on huge horses while clad in full thirteenth-century armor, something that obviously had not come into being in the fifth century and had gone out of style in the fifteenth.

My anthropological background helped me to find some solutions. There remain some problems. Malory features Saracens in his story. Saracens did not exist until after the rise of Islam (seventh century) and were but little known in England until after the Third Crusade (twelfth century). They were certainly not in existence in Arthur's fifth century. I substituted Picts for Malory's Saracens. Picts were as troublesome in the fifth century as the Saracens were later. Unfortunately, no one, including anthropologists, knows much about Picts!

Again, Malory has druids in his story, and so do I. I am sorry to report that no one knows much more about druids today than they did in Malory's time. For the most part, however, I was able to keep anomalies to a few that were mechanically useful, like inventing copper coinage with Arthur's likeness to facilitate a market economy in my story, when markets were probably restricted to barter after the Romans left Britain.

The murder of the innocents to protect Arthur's throne and the betrayal of Arthur's trust by Lancelot and Guenevere are here, but handled differently from Malory's account. He was an old cynic, who probably had it wrong, anyway.

Other than that, I have tried to keep events within the compass outlined in Malory's work, though I have added a few themes from other places. Even the giants of Geen are to be found in Malory in a tale of Arthur killing one on the top of Mont-Saint-Michel, for example. And, I admit I have given everything else a twist to make the story come out the way I wanted. So be it.

WITCH OF THE NORTH

Part I
The
Captive Bird
453~468

In Rome, Leo I, the greatest administrator of the early Catholic Church, is establishing the primacy of the Bishop of Rome over the other bishops. In Britain the first act of the tragedy of Le Morte D'Arthur is about to begin when Uther Pendragon, High King of the Britons, falls in love with the wife of one of his noble followers.

CHAPTER I

What is this, Shield-maiden? Only three out of six in the heart?"

I squinted up at my father, splendid against the clear sunlight of autumn, looking tall in his chariot, though in truth, I was as tall as he. His driver, Cornu the Horned, crouched at his side, holding in the mettlesome ponies while my father watched me at practice. I had not heard them come up through the soft turf of the meadow where the archery butts were erected.

Looking back at the target with three arrows in the gold and three evenly spaced along the lower portion of the thin black ring bordering the center, I sighed and shook my head. Carefully I shot four more arrows to complete the ring, all truly in the narrow band, and glanced up at my father out of the corner of my eye. I said, "I don't think I'll ever get the hang of it!"

My father laughed suddenly, his rich voice drawing glances from where the women were working, washing clothes in caldrons set on tripods over peat fires down near the spring. I knew their eyes lingered over the sight of the handsome figure in the blue tunic that brought out the color of his eyes. My mother had dyed the cloth with that in mind. The dye was woad and hard to come by, though, and I wore brown or hunter green like my mother. A gold torque gleamed about my father's throat, but no more brightly than his silky dark hair. Oh, he was beautiful!

"That's all very well, Shield-maiden," he said, "but you should always aim at the heart. Never be satisfied to miss."

"I never miss what I aim at, Sire," I said. It didn't need Cornu's exasperated lifting of his eyes toward the heavens to tell me I had made a mistake in answering my father so. Royal dukes did not permit such irreverence in underlings, perhaps especially in daughters. Nevertheless, I was a shield-maiden, and I spoke the truth to everyone, just as my father bade me.

"I think, Cornu, we will need proof of that boast," my father said. "Jump into the wagon, Shield-maiden, and we will go coursing."

Coursing! Shooting from a light hunting wagon at full gallop: my father wanted proof, indeed! Even so, I felt a thrill that at last I had his attention. He'd see how faithfully I had practiced.

At the far end of the meadow were the rabbit warrens, a tricky place to run horses, with holes everywhere ready to snare a carelessly placed hoof. Even Cornu was concerned, judging from the frown creases that appeared between his eyes.

On the way, my father indicated a stump here, a bush there as targets, and I confidently aimed and shot at each and every one, hitting them with ease. I was ready for the rabbits and loosed an arrow at one even before my father pointed, willing it to stand still for me. I hit it, too, and Cornu pulled up the horses, and I jumped out to claim my trophy. The creature was not dead! The arrow had pierced one of its hind legs, and it thrashed around in agony. I stood hovering over the injured animal. Dropping my bow, I sank to the grass, reaching out a hesitant hand toward the poor thing. It was in shock, shuddering horribly when I touched it. Warm blood stained its soft fur, and I lifted my hand to look where it had smeared on my fingers. Tears came unbidden.

"I didn't mean to hurt it!" I blurted out as my father and Cornu came to stand behind me. I held up my bloody hand to show them, before wiping it on my skirt, wanting to rid myself of the evidence of my recklessness.

4

"Hurting is not the goal of hunting," my father said softly. "No skillful man merely wounds an animal if he can help it. The old hunters say pain sours the meat."

I nodded. I was not ready to be a hunter. Just then I hoped I never would be. In the meantime, however, I had to deal with the result of my boasting. "Heal it, Cornu," I pleaded. Cornu knew how to cure animals; he cared for my father's hawks and horses with his own hands.

Cornu knelt and lifted the rabbit, remarking, "It is young. It will heal if we can set the bone before shock kills it." He broke the arrow off short, near where it had entered, and carefully drew it out. He then used the two pieces of arrow shaft to splint the break, working with speed and skill to immobilize the leg, tying the pieces of arrow shaft with the bowstring. He used his teeth and one hand to work, carefully cradling the animal in his other huge hand while I watched breathlessly.

"Here," he said, giving it to me. "It must be kept warm. Hold it against your belly while we drive back." And I did, barely noticing that he brought my bow with him. I little cared.

When we reached the horse yard, my father gave over the ponies to a stable lad to unharness, a task I should have handled. I realized I was not acting as a proper shield-maiden, but I could not help it. My father walked off with an odd look on his face, and I knew he was musing on my behavior.

"I never even thought," I told Cornu, after my father had gone. "It was just a target, nothing more."

He nodded, without speaking, which was one of the best things about Cornu.

I went to bed early after eating little, avoiding my mother's searching questions. There was much to think about, but it could wait until morning.

Voices raised in anger, coming from my parents' room, awakened me. My own small room adjoined theirs, a nursery, really. Had there been other children after me, I would have been moved to a room upstairs, replaced by a sibling.

"I won't have her learning your witchy tricks!" my father shouted.

"If you want a boy so badly, why don't you breed one?" my mother's shrill voice replied. My father didn't respond, but slammed the door as he left, and for a time the only sound was that of my mother's quiet weeping. I fell back into a troubled sleep, resolved not to learn any witchy tricks, whatever they were. I would be a warrior queen, like Boudicca. I was sure she didn't do witchy tricks.

The next day both Cornu and my father were gone. No one told me why. There was no way to escape my mother's sharp eye, so I spent the day with her, rather than in the woods as I had planned. The dreary rain made being indoors attractive anyway, for my mother's room was warm and pleasant with braziers at either end to stave off the chill. Stools were placed conveniently for her women to sit on while they worked. A tall loom dominated the room, set to catch the light from the high, arched windows. It glowed with the colors of my mother's weaving.

She set about teaching me to knit, and I found it an easy skill to master and fun as well. I decided, after talking it over with her, to knit a pair of long stockings for horseback riding. Rubbing against the hair on a horse's sides in the winter's cold would rub flesh raw within hours. Men could wear trousers, but women were doomed to don long dresses, which had to be hiked up around the hips even to sit a horse properly. Even in the summertime women's clothes were a bother, for bare legs got plastered with horsehair glued on with sweat. Most women were content to ride in wagons to avoid the discomfort, but not me.

My father was gone ten days or more; I lost count. I finished my stockings, learning to turn the heels and produce a foot as shapely as anyone could, even Julia, my mother's personal attendant and the most skillful of her ladies. It did occur to me that I was being praised above my deserts, perhaps to encourage my acceptance of a woman's tasks with more forbearance than I had previously shown. It didn't matter. Without Cornu and my father, there was no one else to play with but the women, so I took the praise as my due.

When a page came to announce that my father had returned,

I put on my new stockings, intending to show them to him. I knew he would approve.

"Word came to me at Dimilioc that Uther wants us to celebrate Beltane with him," my father announced as he entered my mother's workroom. He was dressed in woolen travel clothes, plaid tunic and trousers.

Dimilioc. So, that was where he had gone. He had left no word, and my mother worried, though you could not guess it from her demeanor. Dimilioc was his other castle, some sixty miles south at the tip of Cornwall. We spent winters there, departing from Tintagel as soon as the first snowflakes began to fly. We were always rushed, for my mother loved Tintagel, and loathed leaving it. With Trewarmett Hill just to the east, Tintagel reminded her of her girlhood home in the Scoti mountains.

I remembered overhearing the words with which my mother had sent him away, and I suddenly felt shy about running to greet my father, much as I wished to. He seemed not to notice, however, and watched my mother closely instead.

"London is not a place I would choose to bring a young girl like Morgan at such a time," she replied calmly, continuing with her weaving as if his absence had been unremarked.

"London? Who would go to London for Beltane? Not even Uther would expect it! Besides, Beltane needs woods for couples to hide in from the light of the bone-fires."

"Where, then?" my mother asked in a tone of suppressed exasperation, while I wondered about what the couples were doing while they hid.

"Why, Exeter, of course," my father replied. "It's the nearest Roman city to our lands and has woods at every edge."

"I thought Uther was a devout Christian," my mother observed. "Why does he hold a Beltane feast? After all, it honors the Great Mother and entreats her to bless the fields and flocks with fertility."

"The folk expect it," my father replied heavily, shaking his head. My father was a devout Christian, too, though my mother was not. My father deplored the pagan festivals, but as a ruling lord he was obliged to participate if he would not lose the allegiance of his own people. He was commiserating with Uther!

My mother glanced ironically at me, but repeated her objection, "Morgan is too young to go."

"Then she shall stay here and be chatelaine," my father said, smiling at me. "You must go, however," he told my mother. "Uther particularly requested your presence, to see whether there were grounds for the tales that hold Igraine the Gold the most beautiful woman in Britain."

My father took inordinate pride in my mother, rewarding bards lavishly when they sang praise songs of her in his hall. I grimaced. Where she was tall and round and golden, with hair that reached to her waist, I was tall and lean and dark, with black hair I kept short with my belt knife to avoid tangling it in my bowstring. I was near puberty, but only near, and could not see it would bring much change in my appearance. I feared only that it would bring an end to my days of pretending I was a boy, playing with Gawaine and the village children in boys' games.

My cousin Gawaine usually joined us at Dimilioc for the winter. His health was delicate and his mother worried when he stayed in cold Galloway during that season. I missed him. It would be months before winter yet.

"I don't want to stay behind," I whined. I hated when I did that, like a child! I started again, "No one will bother me at Beltane. Why would anyone wish to?" Perhaps I sounded more forlorn about being plain than I truly felt, for both my parents laughed in sympathy, bringing them closer in their feeling for their ugly daughter. For that, at least, I felt grateful.

I waited until I had my father alone to show him my new stockings. "I made them myself," I told him. "They are woven tightly enough to turn arrows, I think, though Julia told me that is not a desirable trait in knitting."

"Sounds useful, though, but doesn't it itch wearing them inside just now?" he asked, a twinkle deep in his eyes.

"Not at all," I lied out of embarrassment, longing to draw them off. "I could wear them to Exeter." This last was said to test my father's commitment to making me stay at home while he and mother went to the Beltane party. He knew what I was up to.

"Your mother said you were not to go, and I agree with her. In a few years it might be more appropriate, though to my mind the unbridled lechery surrounding Beltane makes attendance undesirable at any time."

I thought to myself that being a Christian didn't sound like much fun. "Do you have to go?" I asked.

"We have been summoned by the High King," my father said. "He is counting on us to bring enough supplies to feed all who attend."

"Can he demand that?" I asked.

"No, but he offered to count it against next year's taxes, one measure now for two then. It would be foolish not to comply."

"How long will you be gone?" I asked.

"We can travel about twelve Roman miles a day with the oxen. We'll need four heavy wagons to carry the grain Uther has requested. That will be three full days' travel, one way. The festival will take another four days, and with marketing and one thing and another, I expect we will be gone a fortnight."

"Why do we have to pay taxes, anyway?" I asked, still grumpy, though I knew the answer.

"I've explained that before," my father replied somewhat sharply. He didn't like paying taxes. "When the Romans pulled their legions out of Britain in my grandfather's time, they left representatives behind to collect taxes. They warned they would be back to exact a heavier toll if we resisted. It's easier and cheaper in the long run to pay taxes than to fight. Think of the loss of lives and treasure that would result if the Romans actually brought the legions back to Britain once again."

"Queen Boudicca wouldn't pay taxes," I said stubbornly.

"Boudicca? Where have you heard of that rebel?" my father asked in sudden, deep anger. When shock sealed my tongue, he answered his own question, "Like as not some idle tale told among your mother's women!" he snorted. "Hear me, Shield-maiden, she was in rebellion against legitimate authority and no proper person

9

to emulate. If you hear such talk again among the women, you must tell me!"

I nodded, happy not to have to lie. Only Cornu spoke to me of Boudicca, knowing my need to learn of shield-maidens of old. She was my hero! Still, I would not betray Cornu's friendship by telling my father about our discussions. I would not speak of her again to anyone but Cornu! I didn't like it when my father yelled at me. He didn't raise his voice, but it was yelling all the same.

I changed the subject. "Why does Uther want us to travel so far?" I asked, unreasonably, for I knew Exeter wasn't far. My father usually indulged me. Why not this time? I resented being left behind. Besides, I was irritable because my new stockings did itch badly. It was too warm for wool stockings, as my mother had warned me, but I had wanted to show them off. Now, since my father suggested that as well, nothing could induce me to remove them, no matter how uncomfortable I felt while wearing them. He was supposed to praise me!

"When Uther calls us to muster, along with the other nobles who recognize his rule as High King," my father observed, "it is to prove his right to do so, mostly. If it were not inconvenient for us to comply, it would prove nothing." It made no sense to me, though I had come to realize adults often thought that way.

Since I had not won my father over, I decided against trying to convince my mother that I should go with them. My mother was harder to get around than my father. My one chance would lie in the nature of father's objection, that it was a pagan ceremony. My mother was a trained priestess in the rituals honoring the Great Mother, and she might change her mind. I knew, however, that nothing I said would bring her around. She made up her own mind about things.

That evening I took off my stockings and was idly scratching my legs in her workroom, where she was hastily sewing up new gowns for the trip, working with her ladies. I asked, "Will Gawaine be at Exeter?"

"No, but I expect his mother and father will," my mother replied absently.

"Why is Gawaine's father a king and mine only a duke?" Gawaine was my favorite cousin, but did tend to speak overmuch of "my father, King Lot."

"Only a duke?" my mother responded. She frowned as she jabbed her needle into the cloth with unaccustomed ferocity. "Your father, Gorlais, was born into the family who gave Cornwall its kings for generations before the Romans came. His people traded tin for Roman luxuries for two hundred years before Claudius brought his legions to live among us. Your father is still acknowledged king by Cornishmen. Duke is just a Roman military title, awarded by some past emperor to whoever was the head of your father's family then."

"And Lot?" I asked.

"Gawaine's father, King Lot, was merely a strutting warrior until he took the eye of my sister Morgause," my mother said with asperity. "Morgause is a true queen, the head of the Scoti clan Merrick. Lot is a king by courtesy only, as her contracted husband."

"Why is Aunt Morgause queen, and not you?" I asked. My mother rarely was willing to talk about such things, and I didn't want to miss the opportunity of finding out more about her people. Besides, it might put her into a good humor, and let her change her mind about my going along.

"She is older than me by several years, though it isn't a topic much discussed in her presence," my mother replied with a fond chuckle.

"Gawaine says he will be king after her," I said darkly.

"Does he? As a matter of fact, until she births a girl of her own, you are next in line to be head of the clan, not Gawaine. Only women may become clan heads among the Scoti. Morgause seems only able to throw boys."

"Me?" I asked, astonished.

"Yes, and it is something I'll have to talk to her about when we meet in Exeter. Your father has been reluctant for you to undertake the training all girls of our clan are expected to go through, and in particular girls from the royal line, but it's beginning to look as if it may be necessary."

11

"I'd have to leave home?" I asked.

"Yes. I know your father hopes to avoid that. He hopes I will relent and allow you to become Christian, as he is. If you were, you would not be allowed to learn the women's mysteries and would be ineligible to be heir to Morgause."

"Gawaine won't be a king, then?" I asked, wishing to be sure on that point. He made such a thing out of his father's title.

"Not of the Scoti, at least," my mother said.

Well! That was very satisfactory. I had one more question. "Who is father's heir?" Almost immediately I wished I had not spoken, for a look of pain crossed my mother's face.

"If your father had a son, it would be he," she said. "Males rule among the Britons. As it is, his brother's son, Mark, stands next in line." With that she compressed her lips and I knew enough not to intrude upon her further. Mark! He was my least favorite cousin, a whining sneak who was forever telling on Gawaine and me, getting us into trouble. No wonder my mother hated the thought.

I felt this might be another factor in the estrangement I felt growing between my parents. I had been uncomfortable thinking I was the cause of their discord, and it relieved me that there might be other reasons.

"Will I truly be chatelaine while you are gone?"

"Yes, but you are not to do anything foolish," my mother admonished. "Julia will stay here to keep an eye on you."

I liked Julia. We were cousins; she was the daughter of my mother's younger sister. Nevertheless, I frowned at the thought of her being a watchdog over me. When I glanced at her, I saw her pull a wry face and knew she was thinking the same thing. And of course, my sharp-eyed mother saw us both.

"Beltane is no better place for a girl like Julia than it is for you," my mother said calmly. "Worse, for she has reached puberty, and pretty as she is, I would be unable to keep her by my side without more diligence than I like to exert." Julia looked down and blushed.

12

She was pretty, a more fit daughter to a woman such as my mother than ever I could be.

"Do you have some particular thing in mind you wish to do as chatelaine?" my mother asked me, returning to the subject of my interest in that position.

"Yes. You know cook's girl?" I asked, coming to the point.

"Jennie? Of course. What about her?" my mother replied.

"She and Rob, the groom, would like to get married. They are afraid to ask Father, for he will just tell them to go to the priest, and Father John-Martin will say no."

"What makes you think that?"

"The steward has already spoken to the priest for himself. You know he gives special meals to the priest whenever he requests," I added confidently.

"No, I did not. On whose authority?"

"Oh, I don't know; Father's, maybe," I replied, not wishing to be drawn off on that subject. The kitchen was my mother's responsibility, and the request should properly have gone through her. "Maybe he just did it on his own," I added, not caring if steward got into trouble. I was cook's friend, not his.

"The steward wants to marry Jennie? Why, he's twice her age," my mother objected.

"He's been watching her since his wife died, maybe for longer," I said. "Jennie's just turned fifteen, and cook wouldn't hear any suitors before that. Now, she's worried."

"I see. Why didn't she come to me?" Mother asked.

"She would never do that," I said, amazed. "Not when it's for Father to say."

"But she came to you."

"Of course. I could speak to you, and it would be all right. Don't you see?"

Mother looked at me, and for a moment I thought she was distressed, at least until she began to laugh. I joined in, uncertainly. I felt better when she helped me make a plot to let Jennie marry whom she chose, and I must say, it made missing Exeter almost worthwhile.

My father spoke to me about my duties at some length before he and my mother left for Exeter. "I want you to remember who you are, Shield-maiden," he said. "You come from a noble house and must act accordingly. Do nothing petty that would diminish you and your family in the eyes of other people.

"You do not have to account to anyone for your actions, but if you choose to explain them, do not lie. It's much the same thing as being a warrior. Depend on your skill and your strength. Winning by trickery only causes others to fear and despise you. Be worthy of trust."

I wondered if he was referring to Mother's "witchy tricks." Did that mean he no longer trusted my mother? I tried to be noble after he and my mother left for Exeter, but I doubt I was fooling anyone by my good deportment over the next few days.

They had been gone less than a week, and I was brooding about this in Mother's workroom when Julia came running in to tell me riders were approaching the castle. We ran out to the gate together, and Julia asked the porter if he could make out who they were. I couldn't imagine raiders coming on horseback, but no friendly visitors were expected or my father would have told me.

"It's the duke," the tower sentry called down. I ran through the gate by myself, down the narrow causeway that connected the castle to the mainland, and was waiting for them when they came up.

My mother was in her light wagon, driven by Cornu, which was unusual in itself. Cornu was much the best driver of any of Father's men, but his dignity demanded that he be on horseback when he wasn't driving Father's chariot. Father helped Mother alight, but did not speak to her, though she clutched at his arm and looked at him beseechingly. Receiving no kind look in return, she fled up the causeway to the shelter of Tintagel. My father hugged me tightly in greeting for a moment before bidding me to follow my mother.

"Don't venture outside the walls until I return," he said. "We will have harsh war before the moon is full again, and you will not be safe in the woods any longer. Promise me so I need not worry about you."

It was hard. I liked to spend most of every day in the woods with Cornu when he wasn't too busy. There was always something different to see there, and he could explain almost everything. The great trees kept the frequent rains from wetting us, and I had learned to move as quietly through them as any wild animal. I would not be surprised by an unfriendly intruder.

"Promise me," he insisted.

"I promise, but I don't understand," I said reluctantly. "Where are you going?"

"To Dimilioc. Uther will have to come there to fight. Tintagel's citadel is impregnable when guarded by a few honest men, but is not a place for battle."

We lived in the ward at cliff-edge with easy access to the fields that supported us. The citadel on the tiny sea-girt promontory attached by a razor-edge of land to the ward was hard enough to climb when no one was hindering you. My father was correct in calling it impregnable. No one lived there in peacetime and only Cornu much frequented it, keeping his falcons where there were no dogs to make them uneasy. The top was only a few hundred yards across.

"Uther? You fight the High King?" I was shocked. My father had condemned Boudicca for being rebel to her lord.

"Uther, the oath-breaker," my father corrected me bitterly.

I truly didn't understand, but I knew safety only in the presence of my father. "Can't I come with you this time?" I pleaded.

"No, Shield-maiden. You must stay here and look after your mother," he said, and he kissed me good-bye before remounting. Cornu had surrendered the wagon into the hands of stable serfs from the castle, and was on his own horse, waiting. "One more thing," my father said. "Rely on Father John-Martin for guidance in my absence. He will watch over you in my place." He wheeled away, calling, "Pray for me!" over his shoulder. I watched, ready to wave, but he did not look back.

"Why is Father so angry with Mother?" I asked Julia when I

could get her alone. Julia had been in attendance on my mother, helping to bathe her and put her to bed, exhausted after the trip from Exeter. They had made it in less than two days, not stopping for rest!

"Hush! Keep your voice down or you'll get me whipped," Julia scolded. Then she whispered, "I was told Lady Igraine went off with King Uther after the feast and didn't return until daybreak. Your father was waiting for her, and she had no explanation to turn his anger."

"But doesn't everyone do that at Beltane?" I asked.

"Not the wives of royal dukes, silly, only young unmarried men and women. It was most indiscreet of my lady to be so wanton," Julia said confidingly.

"But if it was my father who was wronged, why does he expect war?" I asked.

"I was told the king could hardly keep his eyes from your mother's face at the feast, and was obviously so smitten by her beauty that he will follow anywhere to reclaim her."

"He would drag his kingdom into war to steal the wife of one of his nobles?" I asked unbelievingly. "What kind of king is he?"

"The High King; he's very handsome," Julia explained.

"What excuse is that? Why doesn't he get his own wife?"

"Well, he seems to want your father's," Julia observed practically, "and there's going to be trouble over it, more than we have seen in our short lives."

"Can my father win a war with Uther?" I asked fearfully.

"They say your father sent to Ireland for help, and your mother's sister Morgause left Exeter in anger and may rally the Gaels, but either will take time. Perhaps when help reaches Dimilioc it will be over," she concluded, and she nodded wisely. I could see she had been talking to the guards, some of whom had made the trip to Exeter and had been left to defend Tintagel when my father rode on to our winter castle in Dimilioc. Julia was very pretty, as my mother had said. In fact, I was jealous of her, for she looked more like my mother's daughter than I did, being small but round and golden like her. Everyone liked Julia and talked to her, especially men like the guards.

My mother shut herself up in her room, and I did not see her. I spent my mornings in the chapel on my knees, imploring my father's God to succor him. Father John-Martin, the old priest, watched me. I could feel his eyes on me and sometimes his hands. I always knew when he was close. He never bathed, saying cleanliness was a vanity. He smelled worse than father's dogs after a day's hunting in the wet brush; the dirty wool of his habit reeked of old sweat.

He petted me as Gawaine liked to do, not as my father did. The priest's sexton, fat Brother James, would cover his mouth with one hand and snicker whenever he saw the two of us together. It made me uncomfortable, though there was no fault in me that I could see. I suffered the priest for the sake of my father, whose last command to me was to pray for him.

A few days after my father left, I dreamed he had returned. I awoke in my room hearing voices murmuring through the door to my mother's room, a sound that had often given me comfort as a child when I woke at night in the dark. Voices! My prayers had been answered as the priest had promised. My father had returned.

I jumped from my bed and ran to the door, opening it into a bright light emanating from a wealth of candles that lit the room. Before my eyes were fully adjusted to the glare, a thrown boot crashed into my face and fell at my feet. The man who had thrown it was sitting at a small table with my mother, who was naked in the warm night. The man had tossed a light plaid that belonged to my father over his shoulders, but wore nothing under it. Dazed, I touched my forehead and looked at my fingers to see what caused the wet sensation. It was blood! My anger flared, but before I could protest such treatment, my mother was half kneeling before me, clutching my arms and assessing the extent of my injuries.

"That was not needful," she said in an exasperated voice, glancing over her shoulder at the man, who had arisen now and was watching the two of us.

"I was surprised and did not realize it was only a child," the man replied in an apologetic voice. I glared at him, and seeing this, he added, "Keep her quiet or we'll have the watch down on us."

"This is not what you think it is, darling," my mother said in a coaxing voice. I had not formed an opinion on what it was until then. I already knew that people often say what they wish were true as if it were really true. This was something she wished were not true.

"Where's my father?" I asked, looking past her at the man. Though I had never seen him before, I could guess who he was. I thought I recognized him from the description I had been given: a big, handsome, red-haired man who wore a seven-colored cloak and a torque with dragon heads. There was such a torque on the table and such a cloak lying across the bed. This was Uther, the High King.

"Your father is in Dimilioc, where I want him," the man said in an insolent voice.

"Well, I want him here!" I retorted, stamping my foot.

"I have come to take his place," the man responded.

"No!" I stormed, as my mother patted me, shaking her head at Uther's words and trying to turn me and thrust me back into my own room.

"You'll be sorry!" I shouted, glaring at him so fiercely that he stepped back. I twisted away from my mother's grasp, ran into my room and slammed the door. A very few moments later someone entered through the hall door, holding a rushlight torch. I looked up as a very tall man placed the torch in a wall sconce and sat on the edge of my bed. He wore a hooded cloak, but had pushed the hood back so I could see he had a long full beard, streaked with gray, like Cornu.

"Let me see where you have been hurt," he requested in a deep, kind voice. "Ah, no," he muttered, seeing the cut on my forehead from which blood was seeping into my eyes, mixing there with tears and spilling down my face. I blinked it away, rubbing my hand across my face, discovering my nose hurt, too. I watched as

18

he patted his chest and sides, bringing forth several small containers from concealed pockets. One he opened and sniffed before speaking further.

"I wish to put this salve on your cut," he said. "It will soothe it, stop it from bleeding and help keep it from festering. With luck, you won't even have much of a scar."

I let him administer to me. He sounded just as Cornu did when he worked on an injured horse, concerned, but confident he could help. It worked with the horses, too.

The cut on my forehead felt better almost as soon as he covered it with his salve. He clucked over my nose, but said it wasn't broken. It had already stopped bleeding but felt swollen and clogged up inside, as if I had a cold. It hurt a lot.

"What's your name?" he asked in a conversational voice, not an adult to child one.

"Morgan," I said. "Morgan of clan Merrick, daughter of Igraine the Gold and Gorlais, Duke of Tintagel and Baron of Dimilioc. My father's really King of Cornwall, but doesn't like to use the title," I said. "He says kings are common, except for the High King."

"You're Princess Morgan, then," he said.

"I guess," I said doubtfully. "Do you know my father?"

"Oh, yes," he replied, fixing a bandage on my cut, and winding a strip of white linen around my head to hold it on.

"What has happened to him?" I asked.

"Why, nothing, that I am aware of," he replied. "Your father is under siege at Dimilioc, but this night's work will lift it and he can come home, or I will regret my part in it as long as I live."

"Does he know you're here?" I asked.

"I hope not, or he might do something foolish. He is safe as long as he stays within his walls."

"My father never does anything foolish," I blurted. It wasn't true, but I had to say it. My father was good, truly good. Since he had no falseness in him, he was often unable to see it in others even as well as I could. I looked carefully at this man. I was surprised to sense he was much like my father, a truly good man, but one whose experience in life had given caution. I could see the gray in his beard and hair glitter in the rushlight.

"What's your name?" I asked.

"I am called Myrddin, hereabouts," he replied. "Now, I want you to drink this, and you'll wake up tomorrow feeling much better."

He gave me a horn spoon full of some green-smelling liquid. It didn't taste too bad, and he was right. I was asleep before he left the room.

My mother gently shook me, and I opened my eyes to find her sitting on my bed. She was dressed, a warm shawl across her shoulders, though it was still full dark out. "Sorry to wake you," she said. "Myrddin told me he had given you something to make you sleep, but we must talk." She was smiling, but there was a wary look in her eye. I watched her as she brought a brace of candles and placed them on my low bed-table. "How do you feel?" she asked me.

"What is that red-haired man doing here?" I responded, ignoring her attempt to coax me into a better mood.

"We are negotiating a peace," she answered. "It will be all right now. Your father should be home in a few days."

"Who is he? What does he want?" I persisted.

"It's of no concern to you," she answered firmly. "It is between your father and me."

"It's Uther, isn't it? You gave yourself to him as you did at Beltane," I accused, hoping she would deny it.

"And, if I did, what of it?" she asked defensively, leaning back away from me. "I had my reasons. You are too young to understand what they were or to judge me fairly."

"But you enjoyed it!" I guessed, looking at her with narrowed eyes, trying to understand.

"Ah, that's what stings!" she said, rising and looking down at me enigmatically. "You may grow up to become one of those women who can permit a man to put his hands on her and take no pleasure in it, but I hope not. Of course I enjoyed it! It's true,

20

however, that I am negotiating a peace with Uther. I want your father to come home. The price was me."

"What were you 'negotiating' at Beltane, then?" I asked, greatly daring, aware that a streak of pride in my mother's character would permit only so much insolence. She looked at me closely, the smile now gone from her face.

"That was also for him," she replied finally. "Into most marriages comes a time when a wife decides to take a lover, to bring tension back into the relationship with her husband. Almost always she arranges for him to find out, although not, perhaps, quite as publicly as your father did. Still, I judged him to be a difficult case. We had become too comfortable. He would be taking a mistress if I let it go on much longer, that or take religious orders as his priest keeps urging him to do. I chose to risk what we had in the hope of getting something better. That is still my goal."

"Father won't like it!" I asserted in outrage.

"No, he won't," she agreed sadly. "However, I believe he will come to accept it."

I didn't know what to reply to this, so I pulled my blanket up over my mouth, letting only my eyes show.

"Very well," she said in a resigned voice. "I fear there may be times in the future when you will have to make choices as difficult as mine. I hope the people you love are more understanding of you than you have been of me."

I didn't take the covers off until after she had left, feeling confused and angry, partly at myself. I dressed, took my heavy cloak with the hood and my new boar spear from the corner and went down into the kitchen to fill a sack with cheese, apples and bread. I was going to find my father.

The spear gave me a feeling of reassurance. I had never used it and had only demanded it from my father in the hope that owning it would somehow make him give me a chance to hunt with him. Cornu had shown me how to use it. Boar hunting was dangerous, however, and my father's indulgence of me did not run that far.

It was still night, cold and damp. The moon shone fretfully

from time to time as clouds moved away from its face, but I shivered even under my warmest gray wool cloak. My winter cloak, lined with fur, was still packed with lavender and mint to keep out moths.

I found Myrddin in the stable and hid my sack and my spear before speaking to him. "I don't want to stay in my room," I said by way of greeting and to answer the question I knew he'd ask.

He reached out his arms to me, and I found myself weeping and being comforted by him as he patted me, saying, "I know, I know," over and over again.

Pulling back, finally, I asked, "What do you mean, you 'know'?"

"Why, how you feel, of course. Everyone within half a mile knows how you feel. Emotion flows from you like water from a spring."

I hadn't realized that! I didn't even know what he meant. "Everyone?" I asked, aghast at the thought that knowing eyes would follow me around. Now I was sure I was going to leave.

"Do you think what's happened here is a secret? Don't be childish," he said sternly.

He was right. There never were any secrets at Tintagel. My father used to say that even the stableboys knew things before he did. The daily life of the common folk at Tintagel was so dependent upon the actions of my family that if I were a serf, I would spy on the castle's gentlefolk, too.

"I'm not going to stay here," I told Myrddin. "I'm going to Dimilioc to tell my father."

"The roads are not safe in time of war," Myrddin objected. "I cannot take you to him for I have my ward with me, a girl of five. I'm taking her north for safety. Come with us if you want to leave," he urged.

"I cannot just run away," I objected. "I am a shield-maiden. My place is at my father's side."

"If he thought so, you'd be there now," Myrddin said reasonably.

"He told me to look after my mother," I replied darkly. "It's almost the last thing he said to me. At least I can tell him what's happened."

"If he said to look after her, then look after her. You said a shield-maiden doesn't run away." When I sighed, he released me, saying, "Help me with my oxen. I want to leave now, while it's still dark. I guided Uther here against my better judgment, but he can find his own way back."

His oxen were huge, bigger than anything my father had, and his wagon was small. "Why do you need such beasts?" I asked him.

"The wagon is very heavy," he replied. "I am a smith, and my tools and a good supply of metal stock lie therein."

Cornu was a smith, and sometimes let me help him with the bellows when he was making horseshoes. I thought it might be fun to go with Myrddin, but my duty lay with finding my father. I watched Myrddin out of sight, having told the gate guard to permit him to pass. He waved as he set off on the north road, and I felt more alone than ever. I remembered my father had not waved.

As soon as Myrddin passed from view I went back to the stables, picked up my spear, found my palfrey in the loose stall, saddled and bridled her and started for Dimilioc. I wondered briefly, as I tried to find a comfortable way to carry the spear, how I could kill a boar when I could not kill a rabbit? Anyway, I could not bear to leave it behind.

When I reached the gate this time, Father John-Martin and fat Brother James were mounted and waiting for me.

"We were told to escort you if you left the castle," the priest said, while Brother James smirked. Father John-Martin saw nothing amusing in it, overheated in his fur-trimmed robe, which looked suspiciously like one of my father's. I wondered how he had gotten his hands on it. Another time I would have asked him. Fat Brother James was in a brown cloak that was the same color as his habit. He seemed entirely a creature of darkness. He never washed, either.

I wondered whose orders he acted under, but knew he wouldn't tell me, if only because I was a female child. I said, "Come then," and led off at a brisk trot. They could keep up or lag behind as they would, but I could not allow them to slow me down. The cold mist soaked the palfrey's coat before we'd gone a mile, but I decided to continue as long as the moon gave sufficient light to see the road. Through the mist the moon appeared as if it were under murky water. Still, I wanted to be out of easy reach of Uther when he looked for me in the morning after the sun came up. He didn't seem to be the kind of man who put things off, and he hadn't liked me much.

The priest complained about the weather in a thin voice for hours before I finally stopped at a prosperous farmer's fence. At the yard gate I hailed the house, already wakened by the barking dogs. "It is Morgan, daughter of Duke Gorlais," I announced. "I need shelter from the rain."

After we waited for some moments, two people issued from the dimly lit house. "Come in, then, but who's that with you?" a woman asked, holding up a shielded lantern to throw light on my face, and then on the two who followed me. A man stood behind her holding an iron-tined pitchfork as I bent over to unhitch the gate latch.

"Father John-Martin from Tintagel and his sacristan," the priest answered. "Will your charity extend so far as to welcome us as well?"

The woman was flustered, and the man lowered his pitchfork to take the reins of Father John-Martin's horse as the priest followed me into the yard. A duke's daughter was one thing, but a priest was another!

We were shown to a shed where our horses could stay, but a few forkfuls of hay were all they were given. I took the fork from the man and fed the horses properly before following the party into the house. The dogs met me at the door and I spoke to them, telling them not to be so foolish with their growling. I reduced them to fawning with a few kind words, which surprised the farmer when he turned to see why the door was still open. Animals liked me.

We ate warmed-over porridge and stale bread, and I went to sleep in a corner of the farmer's main room with Father John-Martin's voice droning on about headstrong girls who needed to show more consideration to men of the cloth. Mostly he was still angry about my allowing Jennie and Rob to marry. I had asserted boldly that the match had my parents' sanction, and reminded him my father had ordered all castle dependents to accept my word as they would his own. The priest had performed the rites with an ill grace. I grinned at the recollection.

The farmer's wife was quite short with me the next morning, having heard more of the particulars of my behavior from Father John-Martin than were, perhaps, precisely true. The man was an artful liar. I was not offered breakfast and did not stay to eat my own food, but saddled my palfrey and set out as soon as the sun rose. Father John-Martin was angry about it, still complaining of my rash behavior and this new evidence of lack of respect until I turned on him.

"If my father were here, you wouldn't dare to use me so," I told him. "Be assured, I will speak of your lack of courtesy to his daughter. Remember, your company was forced on me. I did not request it."

"I did not request to come, either," Father John-Martin said bitterly. "By rights, I should return and report your own rude behavior to the king."

The king? I thought. "Well, return, if you have a mind to. I don't care. Doubtless, there is still a hot breakfast to be had for the likes of you at the house where we spent the night." He reddened, but did not reply, so I added, "Continue to follow me and I warn you I will stick a hole in you to let out the bad humors if I hear any more of this kind of talk," and I waved the boar spear at him. Perhaps he believed me, perhaps not, but he and Brother James fell far enough behind to be of no use should I run into difficulty, but never so far that I was out of sight.

That night we camped at two separate fires, and I sat dozing beside mine, huddled in my cloak. It was starting to feel damp in the continuing drizzle. My mother had woven it of brushed but unwashed wool so the natural grease would turn the rain, but even sheep got wet eventually. Wool stayed warm, however, even when wet through.

25

The next morning I came upon Uther's troops surrounding Dimilioc, camped out beyond bow-shot range. "I would speak to your commander," I said to the iron-capped sentry who challenged me with a wicked-looking spear. He called for a guard, and I was led to a red and blue pavilion on a low hill, away from the soldiers' brown tents.

"Brastius," the guard called, "here's someone asking to see you."

A red-bearded man in his early middle years opened a flap of the pavilion and looked me over. "Get down," he said mildly. "Come in." I did as advised, leaving my palfrey and boar spear with the guard who had conducted me.

"I am just about to eat," the man said. "Would you care to join me?" He was dressed in checked trousers and a plain tunic. His shoulders were covered with a four-color plaid against the morning air.

"Perhaps some other time, if I may," I replied, eyeing the hot food with longing and disarmed by the man's civility. "I am Morgan, daughter of Duke Gorlais, and I must see my father."

"He keeps late hours. He won't be up yet and there is less to eat there than here," the man said, motioning for me to sit beside him on the couch-bed. A low table had covered dishes, steaming in the chill. Well, I was hungry. I had eaten only cheese, cold bread and apples for two days.

"This is your father's beef," the man announced apologetically, lifting the lid of one of the dishes and spearing a juicy piece with his belt knife. "Doubtless, you have a better right to it than I do, but there you are. The least I can do is offer you some." He started to eat.

I laughed and helped myself. It was good.

"Daughter, you say?" he asked, looking at me sideways.

I nodded. My mouth was too full for speech. Did he think I was a boy?

"I wonder if I can guess why you've come?" he continued in a mild voice.

I put down the rib I was chewing on and glared at him.

"Bad behavior that. Running after another man's wife brings

26

nothing but trouble, as I told him. Would he listen? Has he ever?" and he snorted, shaking his head, ignoring me.

I picked up the bone and began chewing on it again, the hot juices oozing down my chin. We were in agreement.

As we concluded our meal we were interrupted by the guard conducting Father John-Martin and Brother James into the tent.

"Commander Brastius, I have dispatches from King Uther," Father John-Martin said. The priest looked at me sneeringly.

So! I thought, Uther was the one who had sent this man after me. How did Uther guess I would go to my father unless my mother had told him?

"This says Uther wants you to be allowed to see your father," Brastius told me, glancing at the missive he had been given. "Your father should be rising about now. If you look out the window, you can see his room from here."

I knew which room he meant. I wondered how he knew.

"I will go, then," I said. "I thank you for your hospitality," I added, with a grin, and saw he had the grace to look sheepish. As he had said, they were my father's cattle.

I stepped past the priest without looking at him, collected my horse and spear from the sentry and rode to the gate of Dimilioc. "Hail, the fort," I called out. "It is Morgan, daughter to your duke. Let me in."

As I waited, I looked back at the camp in time to see fat Brother James pluck at the sleeve of Brastius Red-beard. The commander glanced at him—first in impatience, and then with full attention. What could he have to say that would hold the interest of a man like Brastius Red-beard, I wondered.

A small door set into the great gate creaked open enough for me to pass through and was immediately closed, with a stout wooden beam dropping into iron braces designed to hold it shut.

"You are unexpected," said a voice I recognized, even in the dim light of false dawn.

"Ah, Cornu," I cried, tumbling off my palfrey into his arms. He hugged me tightly. I noticed with surprise how much taller I was than him, though he was so broad he could make two of me, at least. "Take me to my father," I pleaded when he released me, and he took my hand to lead me away. I wondered if he could see in the dark like the Picts, for he guided me without mishap through the shadow cast by the wall, to the door that led to my father's quarters. My father had risen and was dressing when I reached him. I was glad to see he had on the blue tunic my mother had woven for him for his last name-day. If he were still angry with her I thought that would not be so.

After greeting me, he asked, "What is amiss?"

"Uther is at Tintagel," I informed him, wondering how much I should tell him. It was not necessary to say more. He stood very still for a moment, looking at me in the rushlight, and then touched the bandage Myrddin had placed to cover my wound.

"Did he do this?" he asked gently.

"Yes," I said shortly. I would not tell him he hit me with a shoe when I walked in on him and my mother, naked, in my mother's room.

"Is your mother all right?" he asked again, as if dreading my reply.

"Yes," I said again, after some slight hesitation. At least she had not been hurt. Perhaps not saying more gave him the information he sought.

"You were brave to bring me these tidings," he said, still quietly.

"Father John-Martin and Brother James followed me here. They brought some message to Commander Brastius from Uther. Brastius even knows which room of the castle is yours," I finished indignantly. This amused him for some reason, and he laughed.

"I must go to her," he said. "You must stay in this room and bar the door after I have gone. You will be as safe here as anywhere, but I must get through the lines and go to your mother."

"She may not welcome you," I blurted out, aghast to hear him talk so, and thinking of no other way to dissuade him. Oh, how could I say such a thing?

He stopped for a moment, his fingers holding the straps to his shirt of chain mail. "Even so, I can do no less," he said. He knew! "Help me with this, Cornu, and get the rest of your gear on. We're going out," he commanded. I stepped away to the window and looked out. I could see Brastius' tent, the flap open and him standing in it. Without thinking much about it I waved, and he waved back, going in then and closing the flap. He had wanted to know if I was all right!

"Brastius is a nice man," I told my father. "Send a message to him and tell him you wish to leave. I'm sure he knows you intend to, anyway. If he gives you a safe conduct, he will honor his word."

"Brastius Red-beard? He would, indeed," my father said, "but I'm equally sure he is under orders to let no such thing happen. We will have to fight our way out."

"Take more people with you, then," I urged. "Take me. I have my boar spear. I will fight beside you!" I was near tears again. I thought bitterly that I had spent a lot of time lately crying. I used to be a happy person.

My words caught his attention, for he came and hugged me. "I am not sorry I had no son," he told me. "How could one measure up to you, Corbie Crow?" Corbie Crow was his baby name for me, because of my black hair and amber-colored eyes. He had not called me that in years. He smiled and walked away without a backward glance.

Now I was crying in earnest. "Oh, take care of him, Cornu," I begged.

"I will try, Princess," he responded. He was saying good-bye, too. He called me "Princess" only when I had to do something he knew I would hate. It was too much! I ran to my father in the hall and hugged him again to delay his departure. "They're waiting for you!" I cried. "You have no chance, just you and Cornu!"

My father spoke to Cornu, who came up right behind me.

"I fear Morgan is right, Cornu, and this effort is doomed. I excuse you from this duty. It is not your honor that is at stake."

"My honor is in my own keeping, my lord," Cornu said. "I freely choose to go."

My father turned and smiled at me. "What am I to do with such a man?" he asked me.

"Give him a chance," I urged. "Take a strong body of warriors

29

with you, one that has a chance to cut its way through the besiegers."

"There are so many more of them than of us that the two of us have a better chance of slipping through than a larger group might," my father reasoned.

"Slip through, then. I know a way that may not be watched," I told him.

"You, Shield-maiden?"

"Gawaine and I used to sneak out and visit the village at night, just for something to do," I told him, confessing to something for which I was sure to be punished later. That meant nothing now.

My father frowned briefly, and Cornu asked, when my father would not, "What way is that, Princess?"

"There is a tree around the corner from the kitchen portal that one can climb to reach the wall," I said. "We hid a knotted rope in the tree, one we could throw over the wall and climb down and then up, at need, without the gate guards being aware." Both Cornu and my father were listening intently. "From there we slipped down to the river and walked crouching near the water's edge until we reached the woods," I continued. "It was easy to move unseen."

"We will need horses," my father said, looking at Cornu.

"If we can get so far, I will steal horses," Cornu said. "Many of our own are in Uther's pens. They know me."

I felt a rising excitement. "Please, Father, let's do it," I pleaded.

"There is risk for you in it that I find unacceptable," he demurred. "Show us the tree, and Cornu and I will attempt it. You will stay here."

"Where it is safe?" I asked. "Where does safety lie, Father? With Brastius' men when they overrun this fort in anger on learning you have escaped?"

He considered but a moment further, then nodded. "Show us the tree, Shield-maiden," he decided.

Once in the yard I led them toward the chapel, saying, "If we are seen by the eyes of traitors, they will think we have gone to give thanks for my safe arrival," I said. It was the route Gawaine and I had often taken.

"And to think when Father John-Martin told me you were seen in the chapel with Gawaine, I believed Gawaine was leading you to a serious consideration of becoming Christian," my father murmured, causing me to blush in the dark. We had not been as unobserved back then as I had thought. I wondered if the priest had seen us slip out the back and over the wall, and if so, why he hadn't told my father. Maybe he had. Who else had he told?

We walked quietly into the chapel and slipped quickly out the back into the shadows. Our tree, a copper beech deemed too beautiful to cut though dangerously near the fortress wall, was not far away; and my father and Cornu followed me up into it with more agility than I had expected. I found the rope, still attached to a stout limb, and holding it, jumped lightly to the top of the wall, creeping on my hands and knees so I could use the corner to hide my descent down the outside wall.

My father and Cornu followed close behind me, moving as quietly as the experienced hunters they were. We slipped toward the riverbank and into the deepest shadows, wading in the shallows toward the woods.

I was exultant. We were winning free! I turned to grin at my father and never saw the man who struck me down, nor the ambush that had been laid for us.

I woke in Brastius' tent, with a splitting head, lying on his cot. He sat in a camp chair, his eyes intent on my face. The tension in his face eased as he saw I recognized him.

"Thanks to the Blessed One," he said with heartfelt sincerity. "I thought that fool's heavy hand had struck too hard a blow."

"My father!" I cried, trying to rise, only to have my vision fade in searing pain.

"Easy, my lady," he said, pressing me down gently. "You are not ready yet to hear about such things." His words stopped making sense, and I was lost in a terrifying nightmare of death and grief.

CHAPTER

II

awoke this time to see Gawaine beside me, his angular face filled with gloom. He was sitting on a low stool near my bed, looking through the open tent flap, and I guessed he would rather be outside. I stirred, drawing his attention, and he cut off my welcoming smile with an observation, "You sleep with your mouth open."

I began an angry denial and thought better of it, responding, "My nose got banged and it's swollen shut. I can't breathe through it." His face had grown stronger in the year we'd been apart, bonier, somehow. He was dressed in livery, red with white trim at the collar and cuffs of his long-sleeved tunic.

I had hoped to put him at a disadvantage, posing as an abused child, but he only said, "I thought it looked even bigger than usual."

That did it. "My nose is not big!" I objected. "My profile is an exact copy of my mother's. My father says . . ." Recollection came flooding back. "My father, Gawaine?" I queried, sitting straight up in bed.

Instead of responding, Gawaine gawked at me, and I realized I was naked. I clutched at the blanket, covering myself, to hear him ask, "What happened to you?"

"Nothing that wasn't supposed to happen," I grated. So, I was beginning to have breasts. What did he expect? "My father?" I prompted.

"He's a hero, Morgan, praised by all," Gawaine said, his eyes shining. "He took down a dozen men, he and Cornu."

"He's dead?" I asked shakily, sinking back into my bed.

"Of course, but what a death! The bards are already in competition, making songs for him." He shook his head in admiration, willing to die ten times over to earn such renown. Boys are such fools! My father was dead! I let Gawaine's voice wash over me as he told me the details, but didn't listen, thinking only of my father's kindness, and how alone I was. My mother no longer cared for me, and my father was dead! It was the sight of my tears that stopped Gawaine's flow of words.

"See here, Morgan, you're supposed to be a shield-maiden. I've heard you claim that a dozen times."

"Supposed to be? I am a shield-maiden!" I said indignantly.

"Well, shield-maidens don't cry!" Gawaine scolded, uncomfortable in the face of my grief.

"Who says?" I retorted. "Do you know any other shield-maidens?"

"No, but everyone says they're almost as good as knights," he informed me.

"Almost? They say almost? Hand me that shift, the one on the chest over there!"

"You're not supposed to get up. They say you bruised your brain, and I must say, you act like it!"

Ignoring my nakedness, I vaulted out of bed, swayed for a moment, dizzy, but beat off the hand he offered me and got the shift myself, pulling it over my head. I noticed in passing it was not mine, but it smelled clean.

"Who is it that claims to have killed my father?" I asked grimly. "We'll see what kind of a knight he is when faced by a shield-maiden sworn to vengeance!"

"Don't be a fool," Gawaine said scornfully. "No one brags of that. Who would claim to hold the blade that killed a man beset as your father was? He fell, was all."

"Fell? He was killed by Uther's men," I stormed. "If some other hand held the blade, at least he gave the order, he and Brastius."

"Red-beard? There, at least, you're wrong. When your father was carried in dead, and you and Cornu as good as so, Brastius had everyone involved flogged. He wept at your father's funeral rites, cutting his hair in grief."

"My father was betrayed!" I insisted. "We walked into an ambush!"

"But Brastius only wanted to capture him, not kill him," Gawaine urged. "Why don't you listen?"

"But how did he know?"

Gawaine brooded a moment before he said, "I think the priest told him, either him or fat Brother James. Brother James was always spying, you know. He caught me one time sneaking into the fort over the wall and said something dirty about playing around with village girls. He probably saw us and told the priest."

"And Brastius did not mean to hurt my father?" I asked again. "He was sorry about it?"

"Why do you think you're not in a cage, as Cornu is?"

"Wait, wait," I cried, wiping the tears from my face with both hands while trying to understand what he was saying. My head hurt. "Cornu lives? How could he be alive and my father dead?"

"After your father fell Cornu might have escaped, but he stood over your father's body and fought until he was clubbed insensible, struck from behind."

"Ah, I can believe that," I muttered. "What's this about a cage?"

"Brastius is going to send him to Rome to fight in the arena. They'll call him the Minotaur, because of his horns. Did you know his helmet doesn't come off? They think the horns are his!"

"My father said they don't do that anymore in Rome, and besides, that's just silly," I said with disgust. "I've seen him take his helmet off lots of times." I hadn't, though.

"Well, maybe, but Brastius says Cornu's a Pict. Maybe Picts have horns."

"A Pict? Cornu? Have you never seen a Pict, then?" I asked.

"I've seen lots of them!"

"Then don't be daft. Picts are short like Cornu, all right, but they're light-boned. Cornu would make two of any Pict I've ever seen." I found my boots under the bed, put them on and laced them up. "Take me to him," I ordered Gawaine.

"I'm supposed to find Brastius and tell him when you wake up," he said. "I can't just go off with you like the old days. I'm a page now! I serve King Uther. I'm supposed to do as I'm told."

"Do it then," I said with contempt in my voice. "I'll find my own way. Page! You look like an apprentice clown!"

"Clown? This is the uniform of a cadet officer!" he said in outrage. "Anyway, you're not supposed to go out by yourself," he said.

"There's no one to stop me, is there?" I asked, daring Gawaine to try. As an afterthought I looked to see if there was a guard outside. There was. He was stationed far enough away, however, so conversations in the tent would not be overheard. He was facing away, watching women with their skirts hiked up washing clothes down by the stream. I also saw Brastius Red-beard walking toward the tent with a young man who looked as if he might be my cousin Mark. What would he be doing here? I ducked back inside, lying down on the bed and pulling up the blanket.

"Red-beard," I whispered to Gawaine, and composed my face to appear weak and suffering. Gawaine snickered, but straightened up when I glared at him. He had assumed an expression of gravity by the time they came in.

"She is awake, Commander," Gawaine said, "but wants to get up. If I came to inform you she had awakened, she would have tried to rise and doubtless done herself an injury."

"Really?" Brastius asked, looking at me somewhat doubtfully.

"What have you done to my father?" I asked accusingly. I was not acting any longer.

"He tried to fight when ordered to surrender and was killed," Brastius said bluntly. "He took half a dozen good men with him, and wounded as many more. Whatever possessed him?"

"Perhaps he did not wish to live," I muttered, looking away. I thought of my mother with Uther, sitting naked in the candlelight.

I thought of myself leading my father into ambush. What could he have thought of that?

No one responded to my comment, out of embarrassment probably, so I asked, "What do you intend to do with me?"

"You are the king's ward. He sent word by the priest to hold you here after you had been allowed to see your father."

"I am no one's ward," I said, frowning.

"It is either Uther or me," Mark said, speaking for the first time. "You're not yet of age."

I never liked Mark. He was just enough older than Gawaine and me to try to tell us what to do when we spent summers together. We didn't permit it then, and I wouldn't permit it now. He was dressed as a warrior. He looked ridiculous!

"You, of all people? Whyever you?" I asked in astonishment. "And what game are you playing in war gear?" I added contemptuously.

"I am your father's heir," he said smugly. "I am now King of Cornwall."

I laughed bitterly. "Uther holds Tintagel and as good as holds Dimilioc," I said. "Where is your castle?" I assumed my mother would surrender Tintagel to Uther when she heard of my father's death, if only to avoid having it fall into Mark's hands. She didn't like Mark either.

"King Uther is welcome to Tintagel," Mark said, "but has promised Dimilioc to me. I have already offered him vassalage. I have been fighting beside Brastius here. Dimilioc is to be my reward."

"Traitor!" I stormed, jumping out of the bed to confront him. "Uther killed my father, your kinsman! What of the blood debt owed for him?"

"Traitor? I am not the one in rebellion against my liege lord! As for Gorlais' blood debt—you pay it!" Mark snarled. And turning from me, he bowed to Brastius and stalked out, furious.

Brastius made a face. "We cannot choose our relatives, Lady Morgan," he said. "Give me your word you will not run away, and I'll give you the freedom of the camp until such time as I

36

receive instructions from Uther as to your disposal. You can at least avoid Mark's visits if you're not restricted to this tent."

"Gladly," I said, "but I don't promise to obey Uther's instructions when they come. I don't admit he has any rights over me." Brastius nodded and, glancing at the chest where the shift had been, smiled briefly and left Gawaine and me alone again.

"He doesn't miss much, does he?" I sighed.

"No. He'll have you hunted down and chained if you try to escape, that I'm sure of," Gawaine said.

I was sure of it, too. "Take me to where they're holding Cornu," I told him as I rose once more, and we went seeking him.

Outside the pavilion we saw Brastius had had his men range their tents in orderly rows.

"We still have Roman discipline," Gawaine told me proudly. "The day we reached here, Brastius had us dig trenches around the camp area to protect us from surprise. He then had all the trees within bow-shot cut down for palisades."

"Who were you afraid of?" I asked. "Did you fear my father would come out and chase you away?"

"I could believe it," Gawaine said simply, reducing me to silence, tears aching in my throat once again.

We found Cornu in the center of the soldier's camp area. A number of men were standing in front of a cage, poking sticks at him inside as we came up.

"What is this? How dare you?" I shouted, pushing myself between them and the cage.

They stepped back, recognizing Gawaine in his page's uniform. "We're trying to see if it can talk," one of them explained.

"Talk? This is the King of Cornwall's shield-bearer!" I stormed. "How dare you treat him like some kind of animal!"

"We didn't hurt him any," one of the men muttered, inclined to argue. "Besides, everyone knows Picts don't feel pain the way people do."

I didn't respond, but they all turned away when Gawaine stepped up and glared at them. They were aware a king's page is a cadet officer, and they were just soldiers. Lud knows what they thought I was.

I turned to face Cornu and found him laughing silently. He looked all right, save the dirty bandage around his head. "Are they telling the truth? Are you all right?" I asked.

"Oh, yes, but not because they didn't try to do me injury."

"I'll speak to Brastius about it," I said.

"He offered me freedom in exchange for my word not to try to escape," Cornu said. "I wouldn't give it. These men may have been instructed to soften me up. Besides, they are angered by the deaths of their comrades."

"Well, I gave my word not to escape," I said, "but it won't stop me from helping you get out of here."

"What I need is a file," Cornu said. "I could break these chains, if I wished, but I can't bend the bars. They'll have to be cut out. This cage was built to hold bears." It smelled like it, right enough.

"Gawaine can get us a file," I said, "can't you, Gawaine?"

Gawaine looked startled, but responded bravely enough, "I could probably steal one of the armorer's tools, but it would be death to bring it to Cornu. You may not have noticed, but there are always eyes on us."

I looked casually around. It was true enough. Some of the watchers were insolent enough to wink as I caught their glances.

"We could do it at night, maybe," I said, in a tentative voice, "unless your duties as a page would prevent it."

"That has nothing to do with it," he flared. "Cornu is my friend, too." He was right. I had been unjust.

I nodded, and he continued gloomily after deciding that was all the apology he was going to get, "You must see it's impossible. There are fires at night, and men sitting around drinking and talking."

"The cage is in shadow," Cornu said hopefully. It hurt me to hear the note of pleading in his voice.

"Could we throw a file to him?" I asked.

"Do you throw that far and that straight?" Gawaine asked. "I know I don't."

38

"Ah!" I said. "We'll shoot it in tied to an arrow! I can do that, I know. But, you'll have to steal a bow and some arrows along with the file," I told Gawaine. He groaned, but as he had said, Cornu was his friend, too. He would do it.

Cornu smiled wolfishly. I could see the anger bubbling through him. "I would like to get out, for several reasons," he said, "not the least being the smell in here. I can't seem to get used to it."

I could well understand that. "I'll need a target, something to help me judge the distance in the dark," I said to him.

Cornu nodded. "I'll tie strips of my bandage between two of the bars, a hand's length apart. Shoot between the strips," he said. "Try for tonight or by tomorrow night at the latest. These men watch me to see if I'll fall asleep. I've heard them sneak up twice, just in time to keep from being hurt. As long as I'm faster than they are I'll take no harm, but I can't stay alert much longer." Then, to deceive his guards, he drove us away with shouts and curses, telling us not to come back. The soldiers laughed to see us go.

I told Gawaine, "We can't tail him. Go get the stuff, and bring it to the tent. We must do it tonight, for sure. I can't bear thinking of him in there. But first, take me to my father's grave. I have to tell him something."

There was a fresh mound of earth between the fort and the soldiers' camp that Gawaine indicated covered the remains of my father.

"Brastius buried him in his armor, with his weapons beside him," Gawaine said, hero worship naked in his voice. I didn't know if it was for my father or for Brastius, but thought it was probably for both, for the honor their actions had brought on all soldiers.

I knelt by my father's grave. "I prayed for you, as you asked," I told him. "Your priest and fat Brother James let me be tricked into leading you into ambush. They knew of the escape route over the wall Gawaine and I used to take! They will pay for their treachery, as will the one who sent them, I swear it on the head of Boudicca!" I could make no more binding oath.

I made a show of being weak as Gawaine helped me back to

the tent. I didn't wish to be watched too closely. I sent him away almost immediately afterward, as much to be alone with my grief as to arrange for Cornu's delivery. Stealing a file and a bow and arrows must have been more difficult than I would have expected with so much gear lying about, for I did not see Gawaine again until night had fallen.

I had composed myself by the time he poked his head under the tent flap, looking around to see if I was alone. "Come in," I whispered. "Don't be so conspicuous."

"Quick, hide these," he whispered back, giving me a small file, a bow and a quiver of arrows.

Putting them under my blanket, I sat in front of them.

He pointed at the tent wall and said loudly, "I don't see why you're so particular. My family is as good as yours!"

Brastius poked his head inside. I had not heard him come up. "Is everything all right in here?" he asked.

"She won't listen to me when I say I'm going to ask King Uther for her hand when she's of age," Gawaine said.

I was astounded! What was this? "Why, we're cousins, like brother and sister!" I objected. "We could never marry!"

"We come of noble stock, both of us," Gawaine asserted. "It's all right for such families, isn't it, Commander?"

"Once, perhaps, but not since the Romans came among us with their Christian ways. The church will not sanction marriage between persons so closely tied by blood, and whatever else my lord King Uther may be, he is a good Christian."

"Well, I'm not, and I'll marry whomever I please!" I insisted. Gawaine laughed.

Well! I glanced at him, realizing he had opened this conversation to keep Brastius from asking questions, and caught a sardonic look in his eye. Whatever made him think of this?

I stuck my chin up. "When I marry, it will be to a king, as befits one who is heir to Merrick," I announced. "I will be a queen in my own right." That for you, Gawaine!

"Quite right, Princess," Brastius agreed. "When the time comes, I am sure King Uther will have a suitable match in mind. Indeed, he may already. At least, be assured that, as his ward, you will be taken care of as a person of your status should be."

He was serious, and Gawaine was amused. I blushed in annoyance, and was furious with myself. I almost deserved to be laughed at.

Brastius had given me the private use of his pavilion, taking a common soldier's tent for himself. I was grateful. It gave me space to test the strength of the bow Gawaine had brought me. Gawaine said the owner had threatened death to the thief. It was a good bow, all right, but shorter and harder to draw than my own. I tied the file to an arrow, which made it almost too heavy to fly.

Gawaine had left with Brastius but returned that night, crawling under the tent in back, where he had loosened a rope. He looked grim. "If we don't bring this off now, there will be no point in trying later," he said. "The soldiers have been after Cornu all day. They talk of using firebrands on him next. Then he'll get burned every time he tries to defend himself. They're going to let him sleep tonight to provide more sport tomorrow."

"If he sleeps, he won't see the arrow with the file," I said, alarmed, digging the bow out from under the covers and stringing it.

"I know," he responded. "We'd better do it sooner than later," he added, but he looked a little unsure.

"You don't have to help with this, if you don't want to," I said to him. "I think I can manage it by myself." The thought that he might accept my offer terrified me!

He looked back at me amazed. "You never could!" he said. "Who would distract the guards while you shot the arrow with the file? Besides, Cornu taught me how to ride a horse," he added in an embarrassed tone and slipped back out under the tent.

I nodded and followed him as I did when we used to sneak out of Dimilioc, close enough to touch him and push if he hesitated or lost his nerve. I didn't think that would happen this time, somehow.

For once there was no rain, which was both a blessing and a source of danger. We could move more quietly but it would be easier to see us. We wore cloaks to conceal ourselves as much as possible and quickly moved under the cover of the trees.

There were no real guards about, for there was nothing to guard against. Besides, with the drinking that was going on I doubted that anyone was sober enough to stop us if they saw us. Dimilioc's stores had been distributed to Uther's troops after Dimilioc's defenders had surrendered their weapons. Among the spoils there were kegs of beer and mead, and even some jars of resinous wine from Greece. I didn't know how anyone could drink it, but these men didn't seem to mind the taste.

I didn't really begin to feel scared until we came to where we could see Cornu's cage. Then it hit me. We could get caught! What's worse, I needed a chamber pot so badly I wondered if I were about to disgrace myself like a baby. Some shield-maiden! I wondered if Boudicca had ever had to pee this badly.

My stomach lurched when I spied the two strips of white bandage Cornu had tied between two bars as he had promised. It meant he was counting on me to help him. Cornu! I had almost hoped not to see them so I wouldn't have to try the shot. The more I thought about it, the more impossible it seemed, aiming at a target that small in the dark with a strange bow and an unbalanced arrow. I'd never be able to do it!

Gawaine touched my arm, and motioned that he was going to leave me, as we had planned. If I were discovered, he had to be free to try to rescue both Cornu and me. Certainly, no one else would be interested. I waited until I saw him by the fire, begging a drink from the soldiers, and distracting them by whooping and jumping around to show them how strong he thought it was.

I drew in my breath, nocked the arrow, aimed and let it go, careful not to pluck the string, but to let the bow do the work. I saw a shadow fly true to the mark, grazing one of the strands of bandage, and heard the clunk as it struck the solid wooden cage back. Oh, yes! I saw the strips of bandage disappear and knew Cornu had the file. I'd done it. I barely repressed a shout of joy as I left the bow and arrows for Cornu to find and crept back through the woods, hugging myself. When I reached the edge of the woods where I could see my tent I saw men on guard. Oh, no! I'd never be able to sneak back in!

I realized again I badly needed to relieve myself and saw a way out of the trouble I was in. I squatted and peed noisily, as I had been aching to do anyhow, and sauntered back, wishing the guards a good night.

"I didn't see you go out," one said suspiciously.

"I wanted some privacy," I told him. "I wasn't particularly eager to draw attention to myself," I added, and brushed by them. I knew they wouldn't report it, for they would be punished for letting me out unaccompanied at night if it became known.

I dropped my cloak on the tent floor and crawled into bed without taking off my shift, not wishing to be found naked again by Gawaine or anyone else. Breathing deeply more out of excitement than because I was winded, I all but shouted, "I've done it!" I was in the midst of congratulating myself when I fell asleep, worn out from the hours of worry.

Next morning, I was awakened by Brastius, who came into the tent without ceremony, looked around quickly and rushed out again. No one brought me breakfast, so I went to the mess tent and got my own. From what the soldiers there were saying, Cornu's escape had been discovered, and he was being sought. Several of his tormentors had been found dead, their necks broken, and the soldiers spoke of killing Cornu when they caught him. I kept my face from showing any emotion, as if the subject were one of no interest to me.

I didn't see Gawaine that day, but on the next he came and told me Cornu had completely disappeared, adding to his reputation for being something other than human. Also, he said, Myrddin had driven into camp with his heavy wagon drawn by the huge oxen. Just now he was with Brastius, and Gawaine had been sent to conduct me to where they were.

"What has Myrddin to do with you?" Gawaine asked me.

"What's wrong with Myrddin?" I countered.

"Don't you know? He's a smith! He turns red rock into black iron, using fire. They say the rock runs like water!"

43

"You don't know anything," I said scornfully, and Gawaine walked the rest of the way to Dimilioc's gate in offended silence. Cornu had told me all about making iron when I watched as he forged horseshoes in Tintagel's smithy. I didn't see any reason to explain things to Gawaine. My father once said I was a princess and didn't have to explain anything to anyone ever, unless I wanted to. I then remembered he had also said I would be wise not to make a practice of such arrogance. I bit my lip in remembrance.

After my father's death, Mark had taken charge. He turned Dimilioc over to Brastius, who wisely disarmed its defenders but had not otherwise abused them. When we entered I went to where my father's people were quartered, brushing by the guards. Having Gawaine by my side helped.

I talked to the men in Cornish, a tongue little used outside of Cornwall. "You know me, Morgan of Tintagel, daughter of Gorlais. I speak for my father," I said. "I tell you in his name there is no dishonor in this for you, for there is no treachery in what you have done. I have freed Cornu, and together we will build a new kingdom where men will be honored as befits their due. When you hear of this, come to me, and I will honor you as men who have served my father."

The men listened in complete silence, but the sullenness left their faces, and I saw hope gleam in their eyes.

Mark came bustling up, shouting, "Stop this! What do you think you're doing?" and grabbed my arm roughly. I pulled my arm free and pushed him so violently he sprawled on his back. The men laughed derisively. Before he could retaliate, Gawaine thrust himself between us and glowered at him. "You touch her again at your peril, cousin," he growled. "She is the king's ward, and I am his page."

"I am my own keeper," I said hotly. "Remember my father!" I called to his men. "Remember my words; tell your children!" and stamped off toward the tower with the sound of their cheering in my ears.

As we entered and climbed the stairs, Gawaine told me there was talk that Cornu had been freed by sorcery, for his chains were

44

broken but the lock on the cage door was intact. I decided Cornu had filed through a bar of the cage, bent it out to escape, and bent it back so it appeared whole. No one would notice if the cut was covered with greasy dirt. If they put another bear in that cage, I bet he'd find it, though.

Brastius rose as I entered, and offered me his stool. He was dressed as a Roman centurion. Along with his uniform he had added an austerity to his manner. Perhaps the latter was due to the presence of Myrddin. Myrddin was seated on my father's couch-bed. "Welcome, Princess," Brastius said. "Myrddin has brought news from Uther. You are to be sent to your aunt, Queen Morgause, and sheltered there until such time as you come of age."

"Will Gawaine go, too?" I asked, smiling at Myrddin, who had not spoken.

"Indeed, he is to escort you there," Brastius replied, and I saw the smug look on Gawaine's face.

"I won't need protection," I said, irritated. "I came down by myself from Tintagel."

Brastius frowned. "Surely Father John-Martin and Brother James came with you."

"Never! They followed me, but they weren't with me. They came only to deliver Uther's message. They told you about how Gawaine and I used to sneak over the wall, didn't they?" I demanded.

Brastius did not reply, but he did not deny it.

"Don't you see?" I asked. "If they told you, they had told Uther as well. I think I was allowed to see my father because Uther knew he would leave the protection of Dimilioc and try to go to my mother when he heard my story. I was used by the false priest to lead my father into a trap! If Father John-Martin is still around, I will claim this to his face," I said. Anger washed through me again, as strongly as the first time it became clear to me what had happened.

"You think your father was lured to his death?" Brastius asked grimly. "My orders were to take him alive. You think the priest carried secret orders from Uther to some of his men to have Gorlais killed?"

"I know so," I retorted.

"Well, the priest has joined young Mark's household. You'll

have to talk with Mark, if you wish to pursue the question of his complicity, but know I would never plot to take a man in such a vile way," Brastius said.

"I don't claim you were part of it," I said. "Just Uther and the priest."

"Whatever that may be," Myrddin interrupted, "I am to take you to your aunt. Uther sent after me and had me return to Tintagel when it was discovered you were missing. At first he may have thought I had warned you to flee. I told Uther I had counseled you not to go to your father, but apparently you went anyway. So, he sent me here to seek you, and take you into my charge if I found you."

"You will take me to Aunt Morgause?" I asked. "Why can't I go home?"

"Uther said you cursed him, burned him with a flash of anger," Myrddin said, looking troubled.

Cursed him? I had not cursed him. I had only warned him he'd be sorry. He would, too! I said, "We'll go all the way to Merricks-hold, where Aunt Morgause lives?"

"Yes," he said, "but we will be some time on the road."

I remembered how slow the oxen were, and understood. "It's all right, if I'm in your charge," I said. "I just don't want Gawaine thinking he can order me around."

Myrddin nodded gravely, and Brastius smiled. Gawaine colored up, as I intended he should.

"I'm two years older than you!" he blurted.

"One," I replied, coldly.

"Sometimes two," he insisted.

"Fifteen months, no more," I said. "Besides you're just a baby. Girls grow up faster than boys. Ask anyone."

Brastius and Myrddin got up and left. "Be ready to leave, both of you, as soon as it is dusk," Myrddin called over his shoulder. Gawaine and I glared at each other until it became unbearable. Then we laughed until I started crying again. What was the matter with me? I fear my father would have been very disappointed in his shield-maiden. I wondered if Boudicca had ever cried.

CHAPTER III

I have to find something to wear if I'm going to move in with Aunt Morgause," I told Gawaine. "Will the soldiers let me go up to the family rooms?" My green dress had been washed and returned to me, and I'd given back the rough brown one I had been loaned. I needed more clothes if I were not to become as dirty as Father John-Martin.

"You'll be all right if you're with me," he said, absently, picking up his page's staff, a stout, peeled ash rod about four feet long and painted a royal blue. He was somewhat self-conscious about carrying it. So far I had resisted saying anything about it, contenting myself with glancing at it now and then with no readable expression on my face. He didn't know what I was thinking, but suspected I found it risible. Good.

The guard at the head of the stairs nodded at us as we went by. He raised an eyebrow and shook his head as I questioned him with my eyes: What was that racket?

At the entrance to my mother's room I paused a moment on seeing a half-dozen women scuffling over bits of my mother's finery. Her clothes chests were gaping open. Clothes were strewn everywhere, some ripped into pieces as claimants contested over choice items. These creatures were filthy! My mother was the tidiest woman in Cornwall, bathing daily winter and summer. Camp followers like these would never have been allowed in her rooms, much less

47

allowed to paw over her belongings. All the rage I had felt since finding her with Uther burst from me in one scream, "AAEEEAAAAH!"

I snatched Gawaine's staff from his hand and ran at the nearest, slashing at their hands, screeching all the while. The first one I hit dropped the gown she held, turned and rushed at me. I poked her in the stomach as if the rod had been a boar spear, just as Cornu had taught me. She sat down heavily, her slack mouth gasping for breath. I turned in time to strike a second woman across the shoulders, sending her sprawling.

"Out! Out! Out!" I shouted, herding the others toward the door. They pushed past Gawaine and the guard who had come up, dropping whatever they held, desperate to claw their way through the doorway. The woman I had winded was scrambling on all fours, and I aided her progress with several shrewd kicks, cracking her over the head with the staff as the last target within range while she scuttled by the men.

When I looked up I saw Brastius had joined us. Evidently my flaring anger had reached him way down in the guardhouse. "Who gave these sluts permission to pillage my mother's things?" I demanded.

"Uther said to move all stores out of Dimilioc, down to the last rag," Brastius answered, entering the room to confront me.

"Oh, rag it is," I agreed, kicking a torn gown toward him. He stooped to pick it up, frowning.

"I am sorry you had to see this," he said, in a tone of real regret.

"You'll be sorrier when my mother sees it," I threatened.

"I'm just obeying orders," he protested. "Uther said everything was to go."

"What excuse will he give to my mother, then?" I asked. "Do you really think he will take responsibility for this? I know my mother. She will have your head on a pike!" I kicked the other half of the torn gown at him.

"Uther is not one to let a female lead him by the nose," Brastius said, his own temper beginning to rise.

"Then he will learn," I prophesied grimly, "and so will you. You'll be lucky to spend the rest of your career on the northern frontier, fighting Picts!"

"Me? Warden of the North?" Brastius replied in disbelief. "Uther does not use his liege men so!"

"Ha!" I snorted. "It will happen." And I felt my anger wash over him as I walked to the door that led to my old room.

I was surprised to find that it was not despoiled yet. Gawaine followed me, looking subdued, as I sorted through my things, trying to find something I could still wear. These were mostly winter clothes, but a few lighter tunics had been made the last year and left behind, waiting for me to grow into.

I selected these, and an extra cloak, bundling them all up into a ball and thrusting it into a leather bag. I filled another with a few of my favorite winter things. They might be too small, but I didn't want them left for the camp followers, who, I knew, would be back once I had left.

"What did you do back there?" Gawaine asked, when I ignored him. He was looking over his ash rod, inspecting it anxiously for damage.

"You saw it," I replied. "Why ask?"

"I don't mean the shield-maiden bit, though that was splendid," Gawaine said in an enthusiastic voice, satisfied now that his page's rod had taken no hurt. "I mean filling the room with your rage. How did you do that? It was witchy!"

I turned and looked at him. "I don't know what you are talking about," I said finally, and picked up one of the bags, leaving the other for him to carry. I wondered, though. Myrddin had said something about everyone within half a mile knowing what I felt. Was this what he meant? Was this a witchy trick?

We brought the bags to Brastius' quarters to be loaded into Myrddin's wagon, and I questioned Gawaine more about Cornu.

"He got away. He even stole the war-horse that belonged to your father, and no one can find its tracks. They're both just gone. Men say it's sorcery, or worse."

"What's worse?" I asked, amused.

"They think maybe he's a satyr. They've heard him play his pipes at night, but when they've gone after him, they never find him. Not all who seek him return, either."

"You don't believe that," I said scornfully. "You helped him escape!"

"I know it's not sorcery," he said coldly, "but it is like Pictish sneakiness."

"Who says that?"

"Well, Brastius, for one."

"Well, he has to say something, doesn't he? He can't just say his men couldn't find a fox in a hen-coop, could he?"

Gawaine went away in a huff. Served him right. I didn't like what he said about me being witchy.

At dusk I left the tent, following the soldiers who came for my things. The weather was cold, that clear cold that comes in autumn before winter sets in. The leaves were turning red and yellow, a burst of color so much more glorious than spring's bright flowers, I wondered why the flowers were so valued.

I spoke to Myrddin's beasts, already harnessed, and they turned to look at me, recognizing my voice. I loved oxen, for their strength and patience and gentleness.

Myrddin came to us, leading my palfrey, followed by two people swathed in shawls against the rude gaze of the soldiers, a woman and a small child. He helped them into the wagon, and the woman turned to grin at me. It was Julia!

"Oh, Julia!" I cried, nearly pulling her back to the ground as I hugged her. "You're going with us?"

"Your mother thought I would do better with your aunt than with Uther," she replied. There was an edge to her voice, but I understood. She was very pretty. Mother wouldn't want her around to catch Uther's eye, fickle as he seemed to be.

The child with Julia pulled her shawl from her head and knotted it around her neck. A solemn creature she was, with wide-spaced gray eyes and black hair. She smiled at me shyly.

"Hello," I said. "I'm Morgan."

"I know," she said, "I'm Nithe. Myrddin said you are one of

us." And I suddenly was filled with a sensation of welcome and amusement. Was this stemming from the child? I stepped back in astonishment, and saw Gawaine, Julia and even Myrddin looking at her in surprise.

"Stop doing that," Myrddin ordered. "This is not the time nor the place for that sort of thing. There are churchmen about!"

She stuck her tongue out at him, but scuttled back into the interior of the wagon without saying anything, and without spraying that extraordinary sensation further about. I climbed in to sit beside her.

"Do I do that?" I whispered.

She grinned and nodded, snuggling up against me as if she had known me all her life. I was appalled! Is that what Uther had meant when he told Myrddin I had burned him with a flash of anger?

Our trip north was slow, but not boring, for as Myrddin drove the wagon he told us about the animals, the birds and the plants we saw on the way, when they were in season and what their uses were. The weather continued fine and the reds of the oaks joined the yellows of the southern maples. Gawaine spent most of his time on horseback, and I let Julia ride my palfrey. I wanted to listen to Myrddin talk. I also wanted to know what this thing was that Nithe did, and perhaps I could also do. Myrddin let Nithe explain it.

"I don't know how it is with you," she confided, "but I have a room in my head I can enter, a room filled with covered pots. The front of the room is all windows, and I can see out as well as with my own eyes." She frowned at this, as if it weren't quite right.

I tried picturing a room in my head, one fronted with windows. I imagined myself in the room looking out and realized what Nithe's problem was. When I looked out, there was no sense of windows at all, no confining space. I looked at her and nodded. "I understand now," I said. "Go on."

She looked at me gratefully and continued, "In the pots are my feelings. If I want to share one I take the cover off and tip the

51

pot, and the feelings flow out the window. I know that sounds funny, but that's what happens."

I shook my head. I didn't want to bother with that. All I wanted to do was to contain my anger so it didn't burn everyone within reach. I realized the room I had imagined was more like a cave, and something hot and dangerous lurked in the back of it. As long as I stood guard at the entrance, it couldn't get out and hurt people. That was the best I could do for now. Nithe was watching me anxiously. Myrddin seemed not to be paying attention to us, but there was a stillness about his silence that I knew came from concentration.

"Does that help?" Nithe asked doubtfully.

"Oh, yes," I said. "I understand what I must do now."

"I knew it," she exclaimed, clapping her hands. "Myrddin said you were like me."

"Did he? Then I grieve for you, little one," I said. "You are overyoung to carry such a burden."

She looked puzzled, but a wave of love and approval engulfed me, and I reached out and hugged her. I was also aware that Myrddin relaxed. Good. I knew I had to tame my cave-beast by myself, but at least now I might contain it until I came to know it better.

I awoke early and lay quietly in the wagon bed, between Nithe and Julia. Usually I rose as soon as I woke, but I didn't want to disturb the others. I tried to identify the birds who greeted the day's first light. The lark was easy, and the robin, but one bird puzzled me. It had a wider range of song than any one bird should have. There seemed to be a dialogue between two of them.

Julia turned to look at me, a question in her eyes, and together we sat up to see what was transpiring. Myrddin was sitting by the fire on a three-legged stool, with a linnet standing on his outstretched finger singing to him earnestly, then stilling to listen to Myrddin reply in kind. I laughed, and the linnet glanced at me before flying off. Myrddin smiled and called the bird back. The two of them continued their conversation until Nithe awoke and demanded breakfast, saying, "He'll sit there all day if you let him!"

The best part of the trip were the meals, morning and evening, when we were all together and could talk. Our staple was mixed oats and barley meal, boiled into a mush which we sweetened with honey. If mush was cold or lumpy it could be nasty, but Myrddin was a careful cook, and since there was nothing else available we didn't become bored with it.

Gawaine and Julia hovered around me, seeming to have some understanding between them that I was to be watched. What they thought I might do in my grief over my father's death, I do not know. I may have appeared distracted, and indeed, I was often thinking of my father and Uther and my mother and wondering what I should do next.

Sometimes I pretended to nap in the wagon to have private time for my thoughts. I missed my father so much! I was so distressed knowing I had led him into an ambush that cost him his life. What could be done about it? I had no brothers, no male kin on my father's side except Mark. He was no help! Who would exact the blood price and put my father's shade to rest? I knew. It was I, the shield-maiden.

I wondered if my father were watching me now, wondering how soon I could avenge him. It made me weep, knowing how helpless I was. Nithe always seemed to be aware of how I felt; she was sensitive to the feelings of others. She would pat my shoulder in sympathy at such times. It didn't comfort me much, but I pretended it did, so as not to distress her further.

We passed the road that led off to Tintagel early in the journey, and there found a group of men waiting for us. They were mounted and held spears; Gawaine bravely rode on ahead to confront them. Gawaine was behaving very well, I decided. I might have to tell him so. Myrddin unscabbered his long sword and laid it on the seat to be ready for trouble, should it come.

I looked intently and recognized my father's great war stallion. Then I saw the sun glint off the rider's horned helmet and said, "Why, it's Cornu!" And so it was. He and the others came to greet us, my mother's gillies, clansmen who had come with her on marriage to my father. They served her rather than her husband.

"Greetings!" Cornu called out as he rode into earshot.

"Greetings," Myrddin responded, and I stood up in the wagon and waved in excitement. Gawaine and Julia rode beside Cornu, talking excitedly at him. He nodded politely, but his eyes were on me.

"How do you fare, Princess?" he asked, concerned.

"I am well, Cornu, thank you. How is your head?"

"I mend quickly," he said, shrugging.

I remembered when my father had first brought him home, near death from the beating he had received from a mob which had wanted to burn him as a demon. I remembered how quickly he had recovered then.

His horned helmet with its furred crown, and his furred leggings cross-strapped to the knee, did make him look something of an animal, and his graying dark beard and thick hair added to his odd appearance. However, he looked no more a demon than I did. Just now he smiled broadly with the friendliest look imaginable. I loved Cornu. He was my best friend, and I couldn't remember when that wasn't true.

Cornu had been playing his flute, for he waved it to point out the small herd of mares that were following him docilely. His flute was longer and heavier than a true shepherd's flute, and was made from some dense, heavy material that allowed him to use it as a weapon, at need. I hadn't seen it with him in the cage, so he must have recovered it from one of the soldiers. I decided not to ask him about it.

"Those are my father's mares," I said. "You went back to Tintagel."

"Well, yes," he acknowledged. "Your mother thought you might want them for a dowry."

"Dowry!" I exclaimed.

"Well, maybe later," he said, smiling at me.

Gawaine frowned. "She's still a baby!" he objected.

Julia gave me a meaningful glance, and she looked down demurely. I giggled, voicing mirth for the first time in days, and I turned to pet the mares that Cornu had brought in, to hide my face. I was aware that everyone looked much relieved at my return to civil conduct except Gawaine, who merely turned red.

The mares following Cornu's stallion looked well, all leggy Roman stock. Acting as my father's bailiff for several years, Cornu had searched them out, traveling many miles. He'd traded rough stock for them, small, stout draft animals that were of more use to the farmers who took them in exchange than these lovely creatures could have been. Each one he brought back was petted, groomed and fed on oats until it gleamed with health. I didn't for a minute believe that my mother had given them to Cornu for me, however. Having spent so much time acquiring and training them, he would not dream of leaving them for Uther to claim and turn into wagon-pullers. Cornu had stolen them.

"Did Brastius Red-beard give you my father's stallion as well?" I asked, to show how little I had been misled.

"Well, no," Cornu drawled. "When I left the enemy camp, I went to say good-bye to my old friend here," he began, and he patted the stallion's neck. "He would have been upset had I not. I was well away before I found he'd followed me like a dog. I just didn't have the heart to take him back."

"I see," I said, and glanced at Myrddin, who was smiling to hear such nonsense. "Will you stay with me and take care of them?" I asked, finally. Perhaps my anxiety about being alone came through my words, for Cornu suddenly looked grim.

"I had a responsibility to your father which I did not fulfill as honor demanded," he said. "If you will have me, I will attempt to serve you more faithfully."

"Ah, Cornu! You are too good to me!" I protested and held up my arms to him. He reached down and swept me onto the stallion's back behind him, as my father had often done. I put my arms about his waist and hugged him, near tears again.

"Princess," the head gilly said, riding up and tugging at his forelock, "your mother has released us from service and we are going back to Merricks-hold to our families. When you become head of clan Merrick, we will be pleased to serve you as we did her these many years."

Gawaine gaped at him, but Julia nudged him sharply and he did not speak. I gathered she had told him he was not to be king of the Scoti as his father, Lot, was. Lot had married in. Someone should have told him years ago.

"May that time be long in coming," I said.

"Lud grant it," he agreed. After all, Gawaine was the queen's son, and I would become head of the clan only if his mother died or gave up the duty. The gilly held out a small leather sack to me. "Your mother asked me to give this to you, with her blessings," he said. "It was to be yours when you came of age, but she had no other parting gift for you."

I took the pouch and opened it, spilling a gold chain and pendant into my hand. The pendant was an enameled bird, a crow, with a yellow beak and amber eyes, caught in a fowler's net held by a golden hand. The chain was run through a loop at the hand's wrist. A corbie crow, my father's pet name for me.

I couldn't speak to acknowledge the gift, but was reduced to nodding my head dumbly. I slid off the horse and brought it over to Myrddin when he beckoned to me. He examined the pendant gravely.

"It is a costly jewel, Morgan," he said. "But more than that, it is a reminder of who you are. Only you can release the spirit of the crow from the net."

I but dimly understood him, but placed it around my neck and clutched it tightly.

"My mother never sent me a gift," Nithe said, "not once." I looked at her sitting in the wagon with her hands folded, gazing at me, her eyes on a level with my own.

"My mother is content to have me go, even though it is my father's murderer who orders it," I said firmly.

"And yet, she's thinking of you. Mine never does."

I looked at her coldly, and realized she was not playing a game with me. A tear escaped from her eye and coursed down her cheek unregarded. I realized she was trying to share my grief. Impulsively I stretched out my arms to her and hugged her. She clutched at me tightly, and sobbed as if she had been holding back her own

56

feelings for an endless time. I looked up at Myrddin seated beside her, and he was staring fiercely at nothing, blinking rapidly under some strong emotion.

"We are late, Princess," the head gilly said gently, breaking into what was fast becoming one of those orgies of feeling Gaels love so much. I was thankful he had interrupted. "We were told to collect Prince Gawaine and make all haste to join King Lot and his people. They are taking the young bulls to summer pasture."

"Just Gawaine? Not me?" I asked.

"No, Princess. Your mother, the Lady Igraine, hoped Myrddin might take you to New Avalon." He raised his eyebrows as he looked at Myrddin.

Myrddin shook his head. "There are compelling reasons why I cannot go there," he said. "Morgan can stay with me if she likes, for we are going to the Strathclyde as well, and will see Morgause there."

"I will take the girl to New Avalon," Cornu said. "I also spoke to the lady, and she asked it of me if no other escort could be found. She wants both Julia and the Princess Morgan to be taken there for training."

"What occasioned this change of plan?" Myrddin asked, frowning slightly.

Cornu looked embarrassed. "The Lady Igraine is pregnant," he said. "She had hoped after Morgan spent a few months with Morgause, she could induce Uther into having her daughter back at Tintagel. Now, with a child on the way, she thinks it better to have your return delayed by a year or so. Then she knows she will be able to prevail on him."

So! I was to have a sister or brother! I wondered if Gorlais or Uther was the father? How would Igraine know for sure?

Next morning we set out on our separate ways. Gawaine and the gillies rode east toward Exeter, where they could find the great northern road; Myrddin and Nithe followed the same route in the wagon at a slower pace, while Cornu, Julia and I went north on the road that skirted the sea. We could have made better time going east and then north with the others, but Cornu did not wish to pass through Uther's city of Exeter, where he might be taken and the horses returned to Uther's care.

I missed Myrddin and Nithe and, most of all, Gawaine. He was supposed to be my friend, but our relationship seemed to be changing to something else, though he hadn't said anything. It just felt that way. I would have liked to ask Julia about it, but felt shy.

Julia rode my palfrey, for she rode less well than me. I tried the mares, one after another, making friends with all of them. My favorite was a sweet gray with a face as delicate as a roe deer. When I rode any of the other mares she ran beside me, nudging me from time to time as if wondering what was wrong. I named her Cloud for her lightness of foot and soon chose her every day.

It took us weeks to reach New Avalon. Cornu said it was over two hundred Roman miles from Dimilioc. The trip was not tedious, for Julia sang to Cornu's flute, reminding me of home. It helped, somehow. Cornu knew the same kind of things about the country we rode through as Myrddin had known, and was happy to tell us about them. Julia was as interested as I was and asked as many questions. I was sorry when we came within reach of New Avalon.

We found the place to be a fortified farm on a small hill surrounded by apple trees. There was a cave at the foot of the hill where we were stopped by armed men guarding the path to the farm. The Usk River widened here to form a small lake which lapped at the cave's edge, making me wonder how damp it was inside.

"What is your purpose at New Avalon?" one of the guards asked, looking over the horses with more interest than I felt comfortable to see.

"Queen Igraine has sent her daughter, the Princess Morgan, and her cousin, the Lady Julia, to the Lady of the Lake for training," Cornu said.

"They are of an age," the man admitted. "If they will dismount I will take them to the lady. You will have to stay here with the horses," he added, speaking to Cornu.

Cornu nodded and took out his flute, starting a plaintive air I had not heard before. Someone had, though, for a woman came to the mouth of the cave, shading her eyes to look toward us, and started running with her arms outstretched, laughing. "Ah, Cornu!" she called.

When she reached Cornu, he leaned from the saddle and embraced her with one arm, lifting her to where she could throw her arms about his neck and kiss him soundly.

"Cornu, you faithless one! Where have you been? You promised to come back!" she scolded, laughing all the while.

"And here I am, Hilda," he protested.

"My dear, it's been years!" the woman said.

"You'd not know it to look at you," Cornu said. "There is no change in you."

"Is there not? I've become a positive hag, loaded with responsibilities since you left. Look at me!" And we all did. She was beautiful in the way my mother, Igraine, was beautiful, all gold and glowing with health. Her tunic was dyed woad-blue, like my father's, and complemented her blue eyes in the same way. I caught my breath to see it.

"My lady!" the guard exclaimed, scandalized at her behavior.

"Peace, Gilbert," she said. "This is an old friend whom I believed lost to me. Allow me some measure of joy in finding him once again."

"But he is a man, Lady," the guard said.

"Is he? I've often wondered if he were not some kind of minor god visiting earth." She was speaking half-seriously, it seemed to me.

Cornu grinned at the man wolfishly, and he backed away, making the circle sign of Lud with his left hand behind his back to ward off evil.

"And who have you brought me?" the lady asked, looking at me and Julia, standing together, gawking up at her.

"The tall, dark one is Morgan, daughter of Igraine the Gold, and the other girl is the Lady Julia, her cousin," Cornu said. "Gorlais is dead, and Igraine has been taken by Uther, the High King. Igraine sends these girls to you for protection."

The lady slipped out of Cornu's embrace to the ground and came to welcome us. "I know your mothers," she said. "You are as welcome here as if you were my own daughters," and she kissed each of us in greeting.

"Take them to the hostel," she told Gilbert, "and send down grooms for the horses. I'll be up later to settle you in your quarters," she told Julia and me. "First, I have much to discuss with Cornu that will not wait." And glancing over her shoulder at him, she strode off to the cave. He dismounted and followed her, dropping the stallion's reins on the ground, knowing he would not stir until the reins were lifted, and that the mares would not leave the stallion's side.

Well! He had not mentioned knowing the Lady of the Lake, Mistress of New Avalon, if that's who she was. The guard soon settled our minds about that.

"I don't know what the mistress is thinking of," he complained.

"Is it your habit to question her actions?" Julia asked tartly.

"Of course not," the man said, "but it's just not the kind of thing she does. Never have I seen her greet a man so. It isn't seemly in the Great Mother's chief attendant."

Julia sniffed. "I'll mention your disapproval to her," she said acidly. "I'm sure she'll take it to heart and mend her ways."

"It's not necessary," the man sputtered and fell silent. Julia glanced at me and winked. Sometimes she was really naughty.

We had not gone a dozen paces before Cloud nudged me with her nose. She'd followed me! "Wait!" I called, and Julia and Gilbert turned expectantly.

"I'll stay with the horses until the groom comes," I said. "Claim a bed for me, Julia! I could sleep for days."

She waved, and together they walked to the hostel, leaving me contentedly behind. I walked back with the horse, realizing Cloud had chosen me over the herd. This gave me more pleasure than anything that had happened to me in weeks; I had something of my own, something that loved me!

I had watched Julia work on Gilbert and saw him become

60

courtly under her smile. I'd never be able to do that, I thought with despair. I'd better work on being a shield-maiden.

The hostel appeared to be a pleasant, rambling building one story high, made of stone set in lime, with wooden doors and shutters. The shutters were open to let in the warm air but could be closed against the evening chill. It looked snug. The roof was of thatch and appeared to be in good repair.

A few moments later a small girl ran out the door toward some outbuildings, glancing at me from time to time. She soon appeared with several men in tow, urging them to hurry down to me. When they arrived she said in an outraged tone, "They won't pay any attention to me! I told them you were a princess, and they don't believe me."

One of the grooms smirked and said, "We're used to having princesses here. We treat them all alike."

"Do you mean you are insolent to them all?" I asked coldly. My father had told me to be civil to everyone, but to require it in return.

"Oh, no, ma'am," he replied, suddenly abashed, tugging belatedly at his forelock.

I ignored him, looking over the others he'd brought with him. One young man with an open face grinned at me and I motioned him over. "Do you like horses?" I asked him.

"Sure," he confided, reaching out confidently to pat Cornu's stallion. The horse would not allow everyone that sort of familiarity.

"Good. You're in charge of my animals when Cornu isn't around," I said.

"But he works for me!" New Avalon's head groom protested.

"That was true once," I said. "Now he works for me. He takes care of my animals and only my animals. You keep your hands off them. And him," I added as an afterthought.

"Well! We'll see what the lady says to that!" he blustered.

"And in the meantime, take the baggage from these animals and bring it to my rooms," I ordered.

He raised his voice to protest again, and I let my displeasure with his manner show. My beast peered out of the mind-cave; a flare of anger caught the head groom with his mouth open. His color drained away and, muttering to himself, he helped unload the spare horses, then scurried off up the hill with our gear, followed by all the grooms except the one I had chosen.

"Now," I said pleasantly to the lad, "we'll bring the horses to the stable. Lead the stallion, and the mares will follow." I turned to the girl, surprising an embarrassing look of naked admiration on her face.

"Would you like a ride?" I asked.

"Oh, yes, please!"

I helped her into Cloud's saddle and led the mare off behind the rest, talking to the beast in the kind of nonsense she liked best. She whuffled back at me in reply, understanding me very well.

I glanced up at the child. "What's your name?" I asked.

"Susan," she said, her eyes shining with pleasure. She was Welsh, a towhead, and her tunic was patched. I wondered who she belonged to, to let her go about so.

"Have you ever ridden before?" I asked.

"Oh, no!"

"Would you like to learn how?"

"More than anything!"

"Good. I'll speak to your people about it," I said. That way, at least, I could find out more about her.

The groom led us to an empty shed with a fenced meadow behind it. "Let me rub them down and give them oats and water," he said. "I'll put them in the pasture later."

I helped him unharness the animals and rubbed down Cloud myself, inspecting her legs and hooves carefully before leaving her munching contentedly.

"What's your name, lad?" I asked, aware he was probably older than me by a year or two, at least.

"Sam, Mistress," he said, watching me intently as he petted the stallion's flank. His clothes were in much the same condition as the girl's, clean but tattered. We clothed our servants better at Tintagel.

"Well, Sam, let no one touch these animals but yourself and my man, Cornu. You'll know him when you see him. He's about your size, only twice as big," and I grinned at him, leaving him a puzzle to work out.

He nodded and tugged his forelock. Susan led me up to the hostel. A woman in a simple blue tunic came to meet us. "Welcome, my dear," she said. "Did Susan help you see your horses settled?"

"Indeed, she was most useful," I said gravely. "I believe I will require her help quite often."

"Oh, but postulants are not allowed servants, I fear," the woman said doubtfully.

"Is that what she is, a servant?" I asked carelessly.

"She belongs to the house," the woman replied, more sure of her ground with this question.

"Ah. While I am here, she will belong to me," I said. "See to it she is issued a better tunic. I have some things too small for me she might grow into in time, but for now, she'll need new clothes if she is to wait upon me. And the same is true for the stable lad, Sam. I will require his service while I am here as well. Really, his clothing is disgraceful, and brings no credit to this place."

"But you don't understand," the woman dithered. "We have no rank here."

I stared at her curiously. "You have no rank here, perhaps. I am the High King's ward," I informed her. "I have rank." I looked at her with the kind of hauteur I remembered my mother using with tradesmen. "Now," I said, "I'd like to see my rooms, please."

"No one has rooms here except the priestesses," she said, scandalized.

"Oh, I'd be happy to share with my cousin, the Lady Julia," I said. "And Susan can have a pallet there. It will be best if she's within call."

"I'll put you in the guest room," she decided, flustered. "The Lady Hilda can deal with you." And she led us off to a pleasant room fronting on the house's atrium. It had a dressing room and separate sitting room, which I thought would do very well and said so. She grunted in disparagement, so I dismissed her airily, telling her to bring the baggage in as soon as possible as I wanted to bathe and change. She left talking to herself.

"I'm hungry," I said to Susan, who was speechless with awe.

"No one talks that way to the chatelaine, not even the Lady Hilda," she said. "She's going to kill you!"

"Why would she do that?" I asked in surprise.

"But you paid no attention to her!"

"Should I have?"

"Everyone does!"

"She only had to say no," I remarked. "About that food?"

Julia was already eating in the hall Susan led me to. It was a separate building, connected to the main house by a roofed walk.

"We eat here, close to the kitchen," Susan said. "The lady is afraid of fire because of the straw roofs, and insists we restrict it to this building. If the kitchen burns, that's all we lose." That made sense.

The lady did not come to us that evening. Julia was amused by Susan's story of my encounter with the chatelaine and predicted the Lady Hilda would be harder to handle.

The next morning she waited on us in our rooms before breakfast. "Pardon me for my neglect of you. I see the chatelaine has placed you in the guest quarters. It was very fitting she should do so. We'll have you moved to the dormitory after breakfast." She smiled, and continued. "Cornu and I had so much to talk about it took longer than I realized. It really has been a very long time since I last saw him."

"Do not concern yourself unduly, Lady," I said. "These rooms will do very well for us, if we decide to stay."

"I'm afraid the postulants live in community," the lady said.

"I am not a postulant, Lady. I am a guest. I am sure Cornu told you the circumstances which led to my being here. Though he did not say so, I am also sure he brought you presents from

64

my mother and from the High King to defray my expenses while here."

"I see. And if we ask you to subject yourself to the same discipline the postulants do, to keep jealousy down, what would you say?"

"I will do anything you require that befits my rank," I said, "but I will start each day and end each day here in these rooms with my chosen companions. If this is not acceptable, I will leave."

"But where would you go?" she asked with genuine interest.

"I do not know. I will decide that question if it becomes necessary," I said.

"Cornu told me you were only eleven," she mused. "You talk with the assurance of a woman twice your age."

"I am twelve," I said with dignity. "I am a shield-maiden, Lady. I must have respect, or I have nothing."

"I see. Very well. If you change your mind, I trust you'll let me know instead of just running off. I don't want to have to try to explain your absence to those who sent you here."

"Shield-maidens don't run away, Lady," I said in a stuffy voice. I was quaking inside, but if I was going to take care of myself and not be an object to be moved about at the pleasure of others, I had to make a start at independence right away.

She nodded and led us down to breakfast. Julia shook her head, but did not contradict me. It was a start.

We were welcomed into training with an initiation ceremony. Julia and I, dressed in long white shifts, faced the Lady Hilda. Her double handful of priestesses were ranked behind her; behind us stood the other postulants, half a hundred, at least, dressed in white robes. The ceremony was held in the sacred grove where the Great Mother's spring was guarded day and night, and the chill made me shiver.

"What name do you wish to take while you are here, Princess Morgan?" the Lady Hilda asked me.

There was no doubt in my mind. "Call me Boudicca," I said. Silence greeted my choice, and I doubted if many knew who she was.

The Lady Hilda did, however. "It will be a challenge to live up to her reputation," she said gravely. "And who will you be, Lady Julia?"

"Choose for me, Lady," Julia said.

"Very well. You shall be called Mavis," she said.

Mavis meant songbird in Gaelic. It was very fitting, I thought.

"Now," the Lady Hilda said, "You both know the Great Mother has three guises: maiden, mother and crone."

I didn't know that, I thought. I sneaked a glance at Julia and she smiled encouragingly at me.

"No one but the goddess can be all of these things all the time. Your training here will be in one of these aspects, depending on your wishes. If you choose the maiden's guise, you will be trained as a lay priestess in the rituals surrounding fertility, both among the folk and in the flocks. It is the duty of a queen to lead her people in the spring ceremonies," she said with a meaningful glance at me. "If you choose the guise of mother, you will be trained in midwifery and healing. If you choose the guise of crone, you will be trained in the rituals to assuage grief. With your lovely voice, my dear, you would bring much comfort to bereaved families," she said, and she smiled at Julia.

"I choose the guise of mother," I said firmly. "I like healing things."

"Things?" the Lady Hilda said faintly.

I realized I had made an error. Nevertheless, it was my choice. "Things," I said. "I want to help animals and birds that have been injured."

There were snickers, but the Lady Hilda frowned at the source of them. "Birds and animals are under the protection of the Great Mother. Helping those in trouble cannot be anything but pleasing to her." But not for a princess, I thought. Thus admonished, the giggling ceased. I felt my face go hot with embarrassment. I'd have to show them what it meant to laugh at a shield-maiden.

The following day we started routines which did not vary as long as I lived at New Avalon. In the morning we were given exercise. In the afternoon there was training in our area of specialization. And at night there were stories and singing.

I soon excelled at the physical games we played, particularly at stick fighting and knife wielding. I practiced with the other girls at first, then with the priestesses, and then with the guards as I became too adept to find challenge among the women. Even there I ran out of volunteers.

"I've had enough, Lady," Gilbert complained to Hilda after one morning's exercise period. "She hits too hard." He was rubbing his ribs where I had caught him a shrewd thrust when he was fooled by a feint to the groin.

"I have said you should hit back," I protested.

"And I would if I could, believe me, and take pleasure in it," he retorted grimly.

So, in the end, only Cornu would work with me. He lived in a hut in the woods, and Susan and I would seek him there each morning for instruction. In addition to advanced lessons in knife and stick fighting he told us about other things, like falconry. He had once been a slave to a centurion and responsible for the care of the legion's mascot, a golden eagle. He'd run away after the eagle died, to avoid punishment, though the bird's death had been through no fault of his. The experience left him with a love of all birds and a hatred of all things Roman.

I learned all I could of midwifery and curing herbs and potions in the years between the time I was twelve until I turned seventeen. When I'd exhausted what the priestesses knew, again I worked with Cornu, whose mastery of the healing arts far exceeded what the women knew. It made trouble for me when I was tested before the priestesses at the conclusion of my training.

"Cornu is an observer of nature," I said in answer to one question posed me. "He helps birds and animals who have been hurt. He does not practice midwifery, nor have we discussed it. I do not know what he knows about it. I have respected the silence enjoined on me about the women's mysteries." It was true.

"Very well," the examining priestess said. She was the head of the midwifery trainers, an old woman with a bitter tongue and a bad eye. "There is still one test to determine the quality of your faith in the Great Mother." A black cockerel was brought in to

67

her, trussed and squawking with terror. In the middle of a screeched protest, the priestess cut the bird's head off and drained its blood into a cup. From a pocket in her robe she brought forth a small sealed jar and extracted a spider from it, black and wriggling, and dropped it into the cup of blood. I noticed the cup had a nick on one of its two handles.

I loathed spiders. They were the one living thing I could not abide to touch. I watched the woman suspiciously.

"The Great Mother can change this bloody cup to wine, and the spider to a cherry, if you but believe it so," she said. "You must prove your faith by drinking from the cup, blindfolded. We will see if the Great Mother accepts you."

I looked at her steadily, not believing her. This could not be a part of the ceremony. There was an air of sly triumph on her face and one of self-justification on the face of her assistant, a woman I had not bothered to treat with respect. She was a fool, but not so great a one as I, it seemed.

"We shall see, indeed," I said, pride stiffening my back. "Give me the blindfold," I demanded, and tied it on myself. I stretched out my arms, expecting to be given a cup of wine, the only excuse for the blindfold being to hide the switch. As I took the cup, my hand encountered the nick in the handle, and I smelled the blood as I brought it up to my face. I dashed it away in revulsion and suddenly was struck on the head with something that broke and splattered. Almost immediately I felt hundreds of tiny creatures crawling on me, on my shoulders, down my neck and in my hair.

I tore off my blindfold, and saw my hands were covered with dozens of tiny spiders. The priestess was sneering at me. Unbidden, my cave-dweller came out, and I blasted the woman with such a wave of hate and horror that she wilted before me, falling senseless to the ground. I ran through the grove to the sacred spring, tearing frantically at my hair, and plunged into the Great Mother's sacred pool. I ripped off my shift, staying under the frigid water until I thought to burst my lungs, rising to shake my head in sick panic. I went under again and repeated the writhing in the water to rid myself of the clinging motes, and once again.

I suddenly knew myself free of the creatures and dashed from the water in an agony of fear that they might crawl on me again. Hilda was there to receive me, along with Julia and the keeper of the sacred pool.

"She immersed herself three times, Lady," the keeper said, excitement giving her voice an almost girlish lilt.

I was shuddering uncontrollably. Hilda took off her cloak and wrapped me in it.

"It was baby spiders in my hair," I said. "I want to shave my head to make sure they're all gone."

"Hush," she said, putting her arms around me. "They could not have survived the cold water. They are gone."

"Why would she do such a thing?" I asked.

"The spider in the glass is a form of ritual execution," Hilda said. "It is called for only when the secrets of the women's mysteries have been revealed to those not entitled to share them, and never without a trial. It was completely unauthorized. The priestess has been punished for her presumption."

"What could you do to her that would pay for this?" I asked.

"Not me," Hilda said, "but the Great Mother. The priestess is dead. She used a sacrament for her own ends. The baby spiders were her own invention. They were not poisonous."

"Only an invention? She fell under my rage. If I killed her, it would have been for that!" I retorted, the feeling of something crawling in my hair still fresh in my mind. Suddenly I knew the truth. "And I did kill her, didn't I?"

"No, you did not."

"I did. I willed it," I insisted.

"You have immersed yourself in the Great Mother's spring and lived," the keeper said, the excitement gone from her voice, replaced by a quiet authority. "The Great Mother may have worked through you, but it was her will that was done, else you, too, would be dead for profanation."

"We will need a teacher of healing," Hilda said to me. "Would you consider staying with us? You have more lore than any of the priestesses, thanks to Cornu. Before you decide, you must know word has come that Uther has died, naming Arthur, his son by Igraine, as his heir. She may want you to come to her, instead."

I shook my head. "If my mother had wanted me to return, she would have sent for me," I said. "Nor do I wish to stay here. When the bloody cup was given me, none of the women standing around sought to prevent it. When the spiders were loosed upon me, no one of them came to my aid. If I were to become your teacher of healing, I would drive them all away. Were you aware that half the lore they teach is in the art of poisoning?"

Hilda's face betrayed the shock she must have felt to hear that. It was her turn to shake her head slowly.

"Ah, Lady, you have spoken to me about my temper. Do you really think I have the right temperament to be a priestess?" I asked.

"It is difficult, as I know to my sorrow," she said.

"You, Lady?"

"Oh, yes. I had to struggle with mine when I was your age. Those of us who spew forth anger are said to have dragon blood, you know."

"No, I didn't know. How could that be?"

"The old story goes that a sea dragon came to land and took human form, making love to various women as occasion presented, before returning to the sea permanently after one refused him. His descendants are said to be cursed with tempers as hot as a dragon's breath."

"Are there many of us?"

"No, not many. My uncle, Myrddin, whom you know, is one, and my daughter, Nithe, another. I was forced to send her away from here because her temper was so disruptive."

So, this was Nithe's mother! And Myrddin was Nithe's great-uncle! It explained much. I understood why Myrddin couldn't come with us to New Avalon. To bring Nithe into contact with her mother, when Hilda's duties as the Great Mother's chief priestess would prevent her from taking the child, would have been cruel. She seemed serene when she told me that, and I came to understand what Nithe meant about her mother's not thinking of her. I guessed she had made her choice between being a mother and being a priestess and had come to terms with the consequences. I didn't think I could have done that. I didn't think I wanted to.

"Now you know why they call us witches," Hilda said sadly as she watched me thinking through my choices.

I nodded, for I did. I also realized that I would have to leave New Avalon, which I had come to love. I would never be able to hold in my anger after what had happened; as with Nithe, it would be too disruptive to the community for me to stay. The worship of the Great Mother was not for me, any more than Christianity had been. I wondered if I would ever find a religion compatible with my rebellious nature. I sighed. It was time to go to live with my Aunt Morgause, whether she was ready for me or not.

CHAPTER IV

Julia elected to stay at New Avalon to complete her training as a priestess. "My place is here, at least for a while," she told me as we took some private time for good-byes. "It was my dream you would remain as well. Hilda has told me she thinks you made the decision right for you in leaving, though she had counted on your being here as much as I."

"She understands me," I admitted. "I would never be happy here. Worse, I would be a danger to the community. I wonder if I shall be happy anywhere."

"When you know what you want from life it will be easier for you to answer that question," she said, smiling.

Susan, on the other hand, had never considered life apart from me. "You need me, Morgan!" she explained. "Who would get you up in the morning if I weren't there?"

Who could resist an entreaty like that? The same was true of Sam. I had spent less time with the boy than Cornu, but he assured me of Sam's fidelity. "Besides, the herd has grown so, I can't take care of it by myself, now can I? I can't even count them!"

That was nonsense. Our six mares had all conceived that first year, and four of that crop were fillies, now able to bear young themselves. We had fourteen mares, eight geldings and eleven yearlings and foals now, as well as the stallion. I spent part of every day with Cloud, and valued her as I would a child of my own body, but I spent little time with the other animals. We needed Sam.

Cornu had given the children instruction in knife and stick fighting when I went to him for advanced lessons, but he decided we needed an escort to bring us safely to Merricks-hold, the clan center. He sent word to my mother's gillies that I had need of them. Gillies took an oath of service for life, and before the spring was sped the six men my mother had released came to us. Some of them had begun families themselves and perhaps could ill be spared from their duties, yet they came. Service was tied to honor among my people.

Cornu had been to Merricks-hold; I had not. "It's about three hundred Roman miles from here to Carlisle," he said, "and another eighty from there to Merricks-hold. We'll follow the old Roman military road that runs north from Caerleon to Chester to Carlisle. Carlisle is at the edge of the Solway estuary. It anchors the western end of Hadrian's Wall. When we turn north and then west from there we'll still be using Roman roads, for Merricks-hold is built on the site of an old Roman fort."

It took us the better part of the first month of spring to bring our herd to Merricks-hold. The weather was often squally, with sudden showers, but the road Cornu had chosen was well drained, and we were not delayed. I was happy to think I would be in time for Beltane. I was still a virgin, for postulants were not permitted to participate in the fertility rites at New Avalon. Perhaps Gawaine would be at Merricks-hold, and I could celebrate the Great Mother's feast day with him. Perhaps.

When we reached Carlisle, some twenty days after our departure, we skirted around it, crossing another Roman road Cornu said was called the Staneway, an ancient road built before Hadrian's Wall was erected. We found a place to cross the wall where Pictish brigands had broken it down and thrown the turves and stones that composed it into the facing ditch. We found the north road leading out of Carlisle and traveled along it without hindrance. As far as I could tell no one had discovered our presence.

At the end of the second day past Carlisle we halted at an abandoned Roman fort Cornu called Birrens. He said the Roman name was Blatobulgium. I liked Birrens better. It seemed to be in excellent condition for being hundreds of years old. The defending walls of faced stone and red Roman brick were still in place, and the roofs of the baths within the walls were sound and unbroken. We had seen other forts from which farmers had taken stone and brick to build houses and pasture walls. There were no farmers around here.

Two more days saw us to Merricks-hold, and I could understand why both the Romans and the Scoti chose the site to build on. It was located on a bend of the Nith River. Far in the distance to the west rose a range of mountains, the tallest of which Cornu told me was Merrick's Peak. The town was walled and contained perhaps six acres, with the round huts of Scoti families scattered in the surrounding fields as far as one could see. They called the settlement Dalswinton.

The Merricks were Scoti from Ireland only three generations back who had gained this land from the Picts through alliance, war and intermarriage, depending on the times. Women might marry out of the clan, as my mother did, but their children were acknowledged as belonging to it. I knew I would be welcome at Merricks-hold. I was as much a Merrick clanswoman as my mother, Igraine the Gold, or her sister Morgause, present queen of the clan. And if Morgause had no daughter yet, I was heir-apparent, as I had been told by my mother.

When Cornu and I rode up we had passed dozens of little crofters' holdings, and doubtless word of our coming had preceded us, for Morgause was waiting for us. Morgause looked like my mother, but warmer, livelier and not as breathtakingly beautiful. I was sure men would love her on sight, but perhaps not kill to possess her as Uther had done for Igraine.

"Sister's daughter!" she called, holding out her arms to embrace me. I dismounted and hugged her, aware that I stood a hand taller now. I remembered she and my mother had been much the same height. Maybe Igraine was an inch taller and ten pounds

74

lighter, but it was not remarked upon. In any case, it was obvious I would tower over my mother now!

Morgause was all dressed up for me, wearing a red gown that would grace a bedroom as well as a great hall. A pity it was wasted on me.

"You are a positive giantess!" she exclaimed, pushing me back to gaze up at me.

"I think I have stopped growing," I said, "at least, I hope so." I'd dressed up also, wearing a new gown of my favorite hunter green, with my mother's gift, the corbie crow caught in a fowler's net, hung from my neck by its golden chain. Cornu had said I looked suitable, and Susan had claimed indignantly, "Is that all you can say? She's the most beautiful person in the world!" I'd laughed, for I believed Susan equated size with beauty. She had a small opinion of herself, calling herself little and scrawny, but at fourteen she was beginning to fill out. She might surprise herself yet. I'd noticed Sam looking at her speculatively.

"You look as a queen should look," Morgause said, "not fat and dumpy like me."

Oh, yes. Fat and dumpy. For sure.

Gawaine was living at Merricks hold and joined us at the feast of welcome. He talked incessantly of the horses we had brought along. Oh, it was good to see him! He was so tall, a true Gael with a fine red mustache starting, of which he was inordinately proud. All he could talk of was our horses.

"They must be Roman," he insisted for the tenth time. "Horses like that were never bred here."

Cornu shook his head. "Their bloodline is Roman, truly enough, but they were all born in Britain. Duke Gorlais selected breeding stock that was lighter in bone and rangier in structure than you find among hill ponies and draft horses. He called them hunters, because they have great stamina and courage and will follow a stag all day if necessary to make the kill."

I smiled. Cornu had selected the stock, having convinced my father of the value of such animals, but gave the credit to my father as a good liege man should.

As Gawaine talked, he kept glancing at me, seeming to find me puzzling in some way. Later he told me why. We were sitting on the hillside, looking out over Merricks-hold, and something told me Gawaine had been here before with other girls.

"I never thought of you as grown up," he said. "You were just a child when I saw you last."

"You weren't much more," I countered. He was not yet nineteen, I thought, but he looked older, more like a man in his twenties. Perhaps it was just that I had been seeing only women, if you don't count Cornu or the guards, who were all older than my father had been when he died. Perhaps, but I thought not. Yes, Gawaine was definitely good-looking. He knew it, too.

"Do you remember, you are pledged to me for your first Beltane?" he asked in a voice laden with special meaning.

"Never!" I said in mock dismay.

"You promised," he insisted, gazing into my eyes soulfully. Lud, he was something!

"We are cousins," I said. "Your church does not allow first cousins to marry, although the druids make contracts for princes and princesses of the royal clans to marry. Would you enter into a brehon contract with me?"

He backed away hurriedly. "Marry?" he questioned, his voice almost squeaking. "Who's talking about marriage?" He was horrified, as I thought he might be. Good.

"What else did you have in mind?" I asked in a shocked voice, teasing him.

"We're too young to think of marriage," he responded earnestly. "Beltane is for unmarried people."

"Lud, I thought it was a pagan ceremony to insure fertility of the fields and flocks," I said demurely.

"Our priest says that is heresy," Gawaine responded.

"Then why would you participate?" I asked in as sincere a voice as I could manage, seeing how I felt. He thought I would be easy!

He blushed. "It is not heresy to participate, only to believe," he muttered.

I hooted. "Your priest never told you that!"

"No, but it's true, anyway," he said, looking away. "Everybody knows that!"

"Oh, I see. Well, I'll have to ask Morgause about it," I said. "Perhaps royal princesses have some special responsibilities to the clan at Beltane."

"Ask my mother? Don't do that! What's wrong with you?"

"I'm just thinking of the clan," I said, widening my eyes in a way I'd practiced in Hilda's polished mirror, coached by Julia to Susan's shocked protests.

"Damn the clan!" he said, flushing. "The clan is sending me to Rome as a hostage!"

"What?" I asked, astonished.

"Uther Pendragon died in London early this year, and Rome ordered the leading families in Britain to send hostages to Rome, insuring good behavior while a successor to the High King's throne is chosen."

"I knew Uther was dead, but what does that have to do with you?" I demanded.

"I'm my father's oldest son," he said. "Why else would Uther have taken me for a page? I know you don't think much of Lot, but the Romans recognize his worth. His grandfather was Ambrosius, and Ambrosius was once High King of the Britons. That's why!"

With that he rose and stamped away, offended in his male dignity somehow, leaving me to think over what he had said. Even if I had no intention of speaking to Morgause about Beltane, I'd have to ask her about the hostages. It sounded odd. Mostly, however, I thought about Uther's death. I had dreamed of avenging my father by killing Uther, and had realized it was too late when Hilda told me he had died. Who could I wreak my vengeance on now to still my father's ghost? And why should there be doubt about Uther's successor if he'd already named his son by Igraine as his heir?

Gawaine apologized that evening. It took time. "Look," he said, "when I . . . well, when I . . . I mean, I meant no . . ."

77

"What is it, then?" I asked as helpfully as I could, batting my eyelashes at him. The mirror practice had not been time lost.

"It's just that I have to go away, and there is nothing to draw me back," he blurted. "If I knew you were waiting . . ."

Oh, dear! I thought. "You are the nearest thing to a brother I have," I told him when he was through stammering. "I would like for us to be friends as we have always been," I said. "Won't that be enough?" I hoped not!

"Friends? You can be friends with Aggravain and Gaheris," he said.

"Your brothers? No, I could not. I confess I don't even like Aggravain much. I've only been here a short time, but it seems to me he's always spying on me. Gaheris is too little and too much his mother's child for anyone else to get close to, except you. He seems to follow you around like a pet dog. I'm surprised he's not here with us."

He nodded, and it began the start of a new relationship for us. No more teasing for a while, until we became more comfortable with one another. I was almost sure he'd seek me out at Beltane, though.

Aggravain became a pest. I ignored him except to hit him in the belly with my closed fist a time or two when he came too close, whispering his vile suggestions. At thirteen he was as tall as I and wildly curious about sex. I couldn't even attempt to talk to him as I did to Gawaine. Hitting him was the only way to engage his attention, but it wasn't he who worried me. It was Lot, Morgause's husband.

Lot never touched me or said anything he shouldn't, but his eyes were on me when there was no reason. He was a big man, a head taller than me, and looked strong. I remembered my mother called him a strutting warrior, and the description fitted. His hair and beard were still a fiery red and he moved like a person confident in his mastery of others. He was fussy about his clothes, wearing a fresh tunic every day, unlike Gawaine, who had to be reminded by his mother still. I couldn't speak to anyone about it without making trouble, so I kept my peace, but it was an uneasy one.

When Beltane came, I stayed near the twin fires and watched the folk drive their cattle between them to insure the fertility of the herd. The priest, who might have been a cousin of Father John-Martin from his sour look, cast a baleful eye on the proceedings, mindful of who participated and who did not. His long face condemned everyone, and did little to recommend celibacy. I wondered if priests are trained to frown all the time.

Youths leaped over the flames to exhibit their courage, and girls fled shrieking from them into the woods, making enough noise to guide their pursuers. Gawaine pretended to be in the hunt, avoiding my eye studiously, but he never seemed to settle on any one girl. My rank protected me from being dragged away by strangers, and Gawaine seemed afraid to approach me as long as I sat where Morgause could see me.

There was much to eat and drink, as at all good parties. I found need to relieve myself, if only to make room for more food, but didn't want to stand in line to go to the outhouse that had been set up. I slipped away and set off for the stables where it was dark and should be deserted. Coupling was supposed to take place in the woods, under the stars, on this occasion. I had finished doing what I had come for and wished to sluice my hands with water from the horses' drinking trough, but as soon as my hand sought the door that led from the stables I was grabbed roughly and pulled backward. I caught my heel on a rough board and fell heavily on my butt.

Gawaine would never treat me so! "By the gods, Aggravain," I swore, "this is too much!" In my anger I did not immediately realize it wasn't just my cousin persecuting me again, hoping to get lucky. A knee was thrust between mine as I tried to rise, and my cloak was raised, pinning my arms. Both of my hands were held above my head in the grasp of someone much stronger than me, and certainly stronger than Aggravain, while another hand groped me.

"What in the Mother's name is this?" I cried in confusion, struggling to free myself. My irritation and confusion turned to gut-wrenching fear as my attacker penetrated me. I knew considerably less about rape than my attacker, and it must have seemed ridiculously easy to him, though I continued to struggle. Belatedly I gave voice to my emotion. "Help!" I screamed. "Rape!"

The man whispered curses, attempting to muffle my cries with my cloak, but I turned my head and screamed anew. Freeing one hand, I raked it across where his face must be. It was bearded. The cloak was pulled down, and the man struck me repeatedly in the face with the back of his hand, filling my mouth with blood and stunning me into silence.

The door to the stable burst open suddenly, and someone was standing there with a rush torch. I could not make out who it was in the glare of the torch, but I spat out blood and cried, "Oh, help me!"

My attacker released me and rose. Oh, Lud! It was Lot! How could he? I scrambled backward until my back came against the wall.

Lot was furious. "Leave; this is none of your affair!" he shouted.

In response, my rescuer struck at him with the torch, and threw himself on Lot, driving him away from me. The torch fell into a pile of loose hay, and the hay flamed up all around us.

"Fool!" Lot grated, knocking the man to the floor and running with a bucket to the trough for water to kill the flames.

Gawaine, for it was he, crawled over and knelt beside me, asking anxiously, "Are you all right? I was looking for you!"

"No, Gawaine," I said, pushing myself away from him along the wall and rising to my feet. "I am not all right." I seized a pitchfork hanging from a peg and, holding it like I would a boar spear, ran at Lot as he returned with water for the fire. He dodged away from me, spilling the water, but I put one tine into his shoulder. He grasped the neck of the fork with his other hand and pulled it loose, tearing the handle away from me and throwing the fork against the wall. I scrambled after it.

"You bitch! Are you trying to kill me?" he snarled.

"Oh, yes," I grated through my bruised throat, "I am trying to kill you. I will, too." For the first time since I could remember, I let my anger run free on purpose, and as it washed over him like a corrosive bath, he reeled away, stumbling backward to keep away from me. He fell on his knees and covered his face with his arms, screaming with fear.

Gawaine grabbed me from behind and said the only thing that could have stopped me from killing his father, for Lot was at my mercy. "The horses!" Gawaine yelled. "They'll burn. We have to get them out!"

"Oh, Cloud, no!" I dropped the pitchfork and rushed through the flames to the box stalls in the rear of the barn, opening the doors and driving the frightened beasts through the smoke and rapidly growing fire. There was too much smoke for me to tell one horse from another, and when I reached the doors myself I kept on running until I came up against the barn fence, and was violently sick. Cloud found me there and nuzzled the back of my neck frantically, seeking reassurance. I was too sick to hug her.

Morgause found me there, retching. "What has happened to you?" she said, pulling me erect and gazing intently at me. She was stronger than she looked. "Why is your face bleeding?"

I touched my mouth. It was nearly numb from the beating Lot had given me. An exploring finger found several loose teeth.

"Lot wanted me to join in Beltane," I muttered. "I thought it was only Aggravain, and didn't fight hard enough early enough."

"Lot did this to you?" she asked, eyes flashing. "He beat you and forced you?"

"He raped me," I said flatly, pushing her hands away. "Your husband raped me."

The look of anger on her face was replaced with one of grim resolve. "How dare he?" she said between her teeth. "I promise you, daughter, he will regret it the rest of his life. Where is he?"

"I stuck a pitchfork into him, and he ran out into the night," I said. "I don't know where he is."

"We will find him then, but he is not important right now. Come, you must be examined," she said, and she tugged at me impatiently until I followed her, all the while calling for her women to attend her.

Cloud followed me like a great dog, butting me with her nose, wanting me to ride her. She attempted to enter the great hall behind me, and I could hear her whinnying and kicking the door in protest when they barred it against her.

An hour later, after I had been looked at, prodded, smelled and declared truly raped, I was bathed and had my various wounds dressed with unguents. People came to look intently at me, both men and women, all through the process, disregarding Susan's bitter objections. "Get her a shift, someone! What's wrong with you? Have you no sense of decency?" she exclaimed, all in little understood Welsh, for which, at least, I was grateful.

When Morgause and I were once again alone except for Susan, who refused to leave when ordered to, my aunt said, "This is a thing that must be addressed formally. Many of the clan mothers are here for Beltane, and they must be informed of what has happened this night. Forcing a virgin carries the death penalty among our people."

"He is your husband," I said, appalled at the necessity of telling a group of strangers about what had happened to me. It was bad enough being poked and questioned by Morgause's women, whom I knew at least slightly.

"He is not of our clan," Morgause said. "He has only contractual rights here, and he has abrogated them with this action. He is no longer my husband, but an outsider who has injured a woman of the clan." Her usually mobile face was set and uncharacteristically stern.

"What will they do to him?"

"What you tried to do," she answered, "but first they must find him. He seems to have disappeared, and Beltane night is the worst night in the world to try to organize anything serious. If he makes his way back to his own clan lands in Lothian, he will be out of our reach. If we catch him and the men bring him in alive, which is in no way sure, he will be tried by the priestesses of the Mother. It is a great offense to the Mother to profane her holy feast day."

"The priestesses will not harm him," I said. "Their vows prohibit them from taking life of any kind."

"They will hoist him to the top of a tall pine tree and bind him there with his sword in his hands, fixed so he cannot drop it. They will ask the gods to judge him, and leave him there until lightning claims him. There is time for reflection and regret, and for fear, if one is fearful."

"Does the lightning always come?" I asked.

"Always," she responded. "The Mother has a pact with the Father. When one of hers has been injured by one of his in this way, the Father must claim him as his own." I reflected on her words and decided I would be satisfied with that.

Gawaine came and said, "The fire is out but for Lud's sake come and calm your horse! She's already hurt two men who attempted to take her to pasture!"

I went out to Cloud with Susan, and took the both of them to the woods, sick of human attention. They watched over my sleep, joined by Cornu once he'd gathered up the horses, all saved from the flames by Gawaine's timely action. Beltane went on around us, but we were not disturbed.

Lot got away. He had seized one of the horses loosed by the fire and made his way west toward his own clan lands. When morning came, clansmen were sent in pursuit, but they turned back when they reached the Lothian Hills, for these hills are on the border that separates our lands.

"We will send clan mothers to the women of Lothian, explaining what has happened," Morgause told me.

"Will they return him to us?" I asked.

"No, they will send gifts in reparation. Though they are also of old Scoti stock, Lot and his men have become Christian. The women would respond to our appeals, if they could, but they will not be allowed to. He will be punished, however, for he has broken the treaty between us. At the very least, they will not make another marriage for him. He will have no sons with his name, and that is a matter of great importance to Christians."

I remembered how my mother was not able to give my father the son he wanted. He was a Christian. I asked, "What will happen to me?"

"You will be pregnant from this," she said. "Beltane liaisons, whether voluntary or forced, always result in pregnancy. How old are you?"

"Seventeen," I said, with a sinking feeling in my belly.

"That old? We should be thinking of a match in any case, then. If we can arrange it quickly enough, no one will suspect there is any problem. Even you would not know for sure, and that is better than hating the child because of the way it was engendered."

I looked down, considering her words. "I am supposed to be the High King's ward," I said.

"There is no High King," Morgause replied grimly, adding, "Anyway, a king of the Briton's writ does not run among the Scoti."

Marriage? I'd rather just have the child! Desperately I asked, "Who would have me?"

"My dear, I don't know what the priestesses may have told you, but in the eyes of men, you are beautiful. All Merrick women are." She smiled a bit smugly. "You may even surpass your mother, who makes me look like a hag in comparison, though there are some who speak well of me."

I laughed for the first time since yesterday morning. Morgause was gorgeous. "We look nothing the same, the three of us," I said. "My mother was called Igraine the Gold as much for the rarity of her beauty as for the color of her hair. I have heard you named 'Red Morgause.' Men roll their eyes when they call you that, as you well know. Look at me. My father's name for me was 'Corbie Crow,' because of my darkness."

"You have your grandfather's coloring, which was darker than mine or your mother's. I always wondered if he didn't have some Pict blood way back. Anyway, trust me when I say you have only to show a willingness, and any number of men would offer to contract with you. There have been some who spoke to me here at our feast, and one who came solely for that purpose, hearing you would be here."

"Truly?" I asked.

"Truly. I never lie to other women. Has anyone here taken your eye?"

"The only men I have known well enough to like have been

my father, Myrddin, Cornu and your son Gawaine," I said. "I have very little experience to guide me. Look, this is too soon! The idea of being married is the one thing I don't want to think about right now. I can still feel his hands on me!"

She eyed me speculatively for a moment and said, "If you were just any girl, no one would ask this of you. You are of the royal clan, and that changes everything! Do you think I wanted to marry Lot? I had a sweetheart, a boy I was desperately in love with when I was your age, and it made no difference at all. Marriage for us is a matter of clan policy, and we are not free to choose who or when."

I looked down rebelliously, but I kept my mouth shut. I guessed she didn't wish to do this, but that would not stop her. If she thought I would climb into bed with whomever she chose for me, she would learn differently soon enough.

Morgause sighed and said, "Since none of the men you like are eligible, obviously we must find someone else, though if Gawaine were free to contract it would solve many problems." She shook her head ruefully. "Damn Uther He's caused as much havoc with this family dead as he did alive!"

"Does Gawaine really have to go to Rome? Can't you send Aggravain instead?" I blushed as I said this. It revealed what I thought of Aggravain as much as what I thought of Gawaine. To stop her questions about either of these subjects, I cut off her response by asking, "Who was it who came to see me specifically?"

"It was a Pictish king named Urien from Gore. His lands comprise all the territory between the Orkneys and Lothian, both of which belong to Lot's people. It would be good for the Merricks to have a connection with Gore. Do you know much about Picts?"

"My father said they were good cooks, but were known to poison people they disliked," I said. "Gawaine says they're sneaky."

Morgause laughed. "There is more to them than that," she said. "They are the people who owned all the land in Britain when our people, the Gaels, first came here and drove the Picts into the cold north. Then when the Britons came after us and drove us into Ireland, a few of our people were trapped up against the Picts and made common cause with them against the Britons, and later the Romans. Lot's people are also Gaels, though he claims to be a Briton himself, when he isn't claiming to be Roman. There were many marriages between noble Romans, Picts and Gaels over the last four hundred years, though the common folk only marry among themselves. Our clan, the Merricks, were originally driven into Ireland with most of the Gaels, and only recently have come back into this land."

"What does this Pictish king look like?" I asked.

"He's small, wiry and dark, like most Picts," she said. "His first wife died, and he seeks another to raise his sons, someone who is not a Pict so there will be no question of inheritance."

"He wants a nursemaid, not a wife," I remarked.

"If that's all he wanted, he could buy one," Morgause said.

"He must be as old as my father," I said, trying to find objections.

"Not really. He's even younger than Lot, though I admit he's no boy. Although you wouldn't inherit anything, since the Picts are like us and reckon descent through the mother, your children by him would belong to our clan. They would also have special visiting and courtesy rights among the Picts. The contract would keep Lot from attempting any move against you directly or against our clan. He would not attack Urien's wife when Urien could retaliate against either the Orkneys or Lothian."

I understood. When I was teasing Gawaine about clan responsibility I knew in my heart it was true. It meant that my marriage to this Pictish king was necessary to protect my clan from the threat my rape had brought upon it. Though I would marry a man as old as Myrddin to bring that about, I was happy to learn that Urien wasn't that old, and I was more than merely curious about him.

When Gawaine heard of it, he was furious with me. "How can you think of marrying a dirty old Pict?" he asked.

"What makes you think he's dirty?" I asked him in as calm a voice as I could manage.

"They're all dirty! They never wash!" I didn't laugh at him, for

Gawaine bathes daily like most Gaels, when he's reminded, and he judges other folk as uncivilized when they do not.

"I have no choice," I said coldly. "The clan mothers have chosen him for me as they chose you to go to Rome. What would you have me do?"

"You're doing this because you blame me for my father's raping you, I know you are," Gawaine said in an agony of frustration.

"How can you say that?" I asked in surprise. "Lot might have killed me if you had not come to my rescue! If I haven't thanked you properly, it's because it's so painful for me to talk about."

He shook his head, unconvinced, and I suddenly thought of how he must have felt when I unleashed my anger on Lot. "I was not aiming at you when I struck at Lot with my rage," I said.

He looked up puzzled, "All I saw was how you tried to kill him with a pitchfork. You would have if I hadn't dragged you away."

Oh, Lud! I had so centered my anger that none of it spilled out. Only Lot had felt it. I could have held him helpless and killed him with it. Maybe I truly was a witch! Oh, no! I would not do witchy tricks! I was a shield-maiden. I swore it as a silent oath to Boudicca.

Gawaine saw my silence as indecision and spoke, grasping my shoulders to turn me so I faced him. "Come with me," he urged. "Come to Rome with me!"

Ah, Gawaine, if I but could! I thought, but I said, "And be a hostage?"

CHAPTER V

Urien came to see us the next day at the request of Morgause. As she had said, he was small, wiry and dark like my father, graying at the temples. He was not unhandsome, however, and, in particular, had a charming smile. He was dressed in a blue tunic, carried a blue cloak, and stout leather boots protected his feet and lower legs.

I could see he liked the look of me. Morgause had bullied me into letting my hair hang loose. It had grown long enough to hang past my shoulder blades and was a great nuisance! Gawaine glared at me, objecting to my making any effort to attract Urien. He had insisted on being present, as a kinsman's right, and was the only other male in the room.

"We have spoken together and agree to hear your proposal," Morgause said. A number of the women whom I had met last night when I had to relate my account of the attack were with us, smiling and silent.

"Among the Picts," he said, "each woman decides for herself whether or not she will take a husband. Please do not take offense if I ask the Lady Morgan what her wishes are in this matter." He spoke good though slightly accented Gaelic. Morgause told me Urien had spent several years as a fosterling at Merricks-hold, which was why he had been invited to the Beltane feast.

"It is my duty to behave as my clan mothers wish, and what I may wish is not of importance," I said. I didn't believe that! I'd leave Merricks-hold and live on the shore eating shellfish before I'd let someone force me into a marriage I didn't want.

"Ah, but it is to me!" Urien said, and smiled around at the women present, inviting them to agree with him.

I looked up in surprise. "I would really like not to have to say how I feel today," I told him honestly. If pressed, I would say no, no matter what the clan mothers wanted of me.

"You need not, then. I must be frank, too. You understand the contract we would enter into would not allow our children to inherit rights to lands controlled by the clan I lead," he said formally. "As a matter of fact, the lands I mention belong to my late wife's people. I, myself, have no rights separate from those my relationship to her and to my sons have given me."

"It is the same with us," Morgause said for me. "What we wish is an alliance with the clan you lead. Our daughter would be surety for us. Her continued presence in your house would be dependent on both your treatment of her and your allegiance to your word should we request your aid against our enemies."

"Who might those enemies be?" he asked cautiously.

"For one, my recent husband, Lot of Lothian and the Orkneys, who broke contract with us and has fled. He may think to turn his warriors against our borders like the oath-breaker he is. In such a case, we would expect you to help dissuade him," Morgause replied.

"I see," he said, though I was sure he didn't. "My people come and go through his lands at will, using his streams to trap furs, or catch fish, and his islands to shelter our boats. We have no trouble with him. He is well aware if he attempted to hinder us, we would drive him out completely, though possibly at great cost to us. We would tell him of our alliance, and I think he would not lift his hand against you."

Morgause and the others went apart to discuss his words, and I was left alone with him. Gawaine sat scowling in the corner of the room, and Urien glanced at him, guessing the reason. "We need not wait here," he said. "Let us go walking in the woods together and get to know each other better. Would you join us to provide us with a witness that nothing is done amiss?" he asked Gawaine.

Gawaine was so surprised he forgot to be petulant. He would have said no if he'd time to consider it, but the offer was so courteously made he accepted.

Urien put us at ease with his quiet voice and his astounding knowledge of the woods. "Picts are trained as hunters starting as young boys," he said. "They can follow a trail in the faintest of light and construct snares so cunning that they never fail to catch their prey. They fish with their hands."

"No!" Gawaine said in disbelief. "You could never catch the fish in our streams with your hands."

"You think not? Where do you like best to fish?" he asked, and Gawaine led us to his favorite place, a spot where a small brook made a turn around a huge old oak tree. There were shadows on the surface of the water, and the water danced and sang as if oblivious of our interest.

"Stay here and watch," Urien said, and removing his boots, he disappeared into the wood, appearing downstream bent over and wading up to the dark overhanging bank. His face was almost touching the water, and he moved very slowly, making no sound at all. He slowly put his bare arms into the water and moved closer and closer until he suddenly scooped a fine young salmon out of the water and onto the bank at our feet. He grinned at Gawaine. Before the day came to a close he had taught both of us how it was done. His careful instruction was patient and thoughtful, gauged to our experience. I thought fleetingly of how different Lot had been with me.

For the next few days we were much together, the three of us. I was a better archer than either Gawaine or Urien, and he praised me with a sincerity that made me glow. He could use a shepherd's sling with such accuracy, though, that he could knock acorns from the oak trees, fifty feet in the air. He taught us that, too, and we both became at least moderately proficient with practice.

"I was wrong to call him a dirty Pict," Gawaine confided in me one evening when we were together by ourselves.

"Yes, you were," I agreed.

Gawaine frowned at me momentarily, then said, "If I can't marry you, I'd rather have Urien do it than anyone I know."

It was an admission that surprised me, but I thought much the same. I wasn't sure Urien wanted to, now. He didn't seem to be interested in me sexually at all.

"Tell me of your sons," I requested one evening as we were sitting in the dining hall with the clan mothers in attendance. I hoped to get the discussion around to the possibility of marriage again. "How old are they?"

"There are four of them, counting the twins, ranging in age from the oldest at eight to the youngest at four. They are badly in need of discipline, and they are aware that servants lack the authority to make them do anything. I don't wish to spend all my time correcting them for faults it would be better they had not developed in the first place. They miss their mother and are resentful of the notion that anyone could take her place."

"That is what you want me for?" I asked boldly, disappointment edging my voice. I wondered what had happened to the boys' mother, but could not bring myself to ask. I sensed a deep reserve in the man, and feared he would consider that an invasion of his privacy.

"A friend of yours, a druid named Myrddin, suggested you might be the person who could bring order to my family. He mentioned you have a gift for healing young animals, and that is what is needed, I fear," he said, smiling.

"You reassure me," I said. "Myrddin would not put me in the way of harm." I meant it, and allowed the emotion of gratitude and relief to escape the barrier I had learned to erect against others. He was confused, not knowing what to think as the feeling washed over him, and the women looked up from their discussion as the emotion touched them as well. I had not learned to center other emotions on a single person as I could anger.

"I sense Morgan is happy with the arrangement we have discussed," Morgause said, coming to join us. "We have a druid who makes his home not far from here, a high-ranking brehon, in fact, who can give judgments and make contracts. We could take care of the whole thing while you are here, and Morgan could go back with you if you are willing."

"Nothing would please me more," Urien said, smiling at me. He did like me. "Many of your people are Christian," he said directly to me. "Would you need a priest to make the sacraments binding for you, Lady?"

"My father was a Christian, and a devout one, but his religion brought me no comfort," I replied. "I want no Christian sacraments."

Morgause sent for the brehon, an old man who long ago had escaped the persecutions set in motion by Paul the Chain, the Christian scourge of Britain, who came under orders from the Roman Emperor Constantine to rid Britain of pagan practices. I was surprised to learn that part of the ceremony was a close questioning to determine whether I understood the nature of the contract I was being bound by. I appreciated it.

"The priestesses explained what a marriage contract would be when I was in training," I said, smiling.

"Of course," the brehon said, "but you must realize this is the time for you to insist on any special clauses. Are there any conditions that might arise that would serve to cause you to declare the contract broken?"

"Some husbands beat their wives, I understand," I said. "Were anything like that to happen, I would break the contract with a knife." Urien laughed, but I was thinking hard. "I have a blood debt that I have not paid," I continued, "one that will not let me rest quietly. My father was murdered by Uther Pendragon, and no one has died for it. I have two lesser grievances, one against a priest in my father's old household who tricked me into leading my father to his death, and one against my aunt's husband, Lot of Lothian, who abused my trust in a way that demands blood. I would expect my husband to be sensitive to my feelings about these persons in any dealings he might have with them. I do not expect to shift my responsibilities in righting these wrongs, but I would expect support when I act on them."

Urien looked sober and considered my words for a moment, finally saying slowly, "I see no problem, Lady. Uther Pendragon is dead and beyond the reach of either of us. I have no contact with Christian priests by choice. As for Lot, he is my neighbor, but I have little to do with him in any case. I accept the conditions."

"Do you have any special terms?" the brehon asked him.

"No," he sighed. "The lady understands I have four young sons, none of whom has reached manhood yet. It is enough that she has to become the mistress of a household such as mine. No Pictish lady of my acquaintance would accept such a burden not her own. It would be most unfair to add restrictions to her," he added, and he smiled ruefully. I thought we would deal together very well.

We agreed I should take Cornu, along with Susan and Sam. Urien would have the use of my horses during the period of the contract, but Cornu would have responsibility for them, and ownership would remain with me. I could take them with me if I left after fulfillment of the contract. My people would serve only me.

The clan mothers gave us a small feast, quiet in that it followed Beltane, and everyone was tired. Some formal acknowledgment of the new relationship between Clan Merrick and the southern Picts was necessary, however. We left for Urien's homeland before the morning was over, on a clear day in early summer.

The trip to his home took some weeks, and I realized he must have been desperate to find a suitable wife, to have come so far in the hope I might be the one. First we rode north on the Roman road that ran past Merricks-hold, until we reached the headwaters of the Clyde. The horses liked to travel on an open track, and farmers had kept the road open with wagon teams, delivering grain to the market of Merricks-hold. Its metaled surface was still intact.

The Clyde flowed north and west, away from our destination, but it ran between mountains and was the easiest route. When Urien led us north and east again we encountered the Antonine Wall. A Roman emperor had built it to contain the Picts, but Cornu said it was so ineffective that it was abandoned as soon as a new emperor came into power. The horses liked it, though, and were reluctant to leave it when we swung north again to skirt the Firth of Forth, an estuary of the sea with violent tides.

Urien's retainers, men whom the Gaels would call gillies, set out a tent for us each night and retreated beyond earshot so we could have privacy. Cornu joined them, and I could hear the sound of his flute. As always, Cornu's music had an almost magical effect on me. His erotic songs kept me glowing and smiling for Urien, something I would not have believed possible so soon after suffering rape at the hands of Lot. Oh, but this was different! It wasn't the scenery that made the trip seem timeless, though we were fortunate in the continued clement weather that usually follows Beltane. I spent the days riding Cloud in a state of near dream. It was the nights when I was alive.

Urien thought it was his lovemaking alone that was responsible for my ardor, and I saw no reason to explain the effect Cornu's music had on me. At least he was as gentle and experienced a teacher as he had been when he showed me how to catch fish with my bare hands. I was grateful, and surprised to find that I was capable of feeling such passion. I was ashamed to realize I was thinking of Gawaine as we made love, but since I kept it to myself it did not mar the relationship I was building with Urien. Mostly, however, I didn't think at all, just felt. So this was what my mother had meant when she refused to apologize for enjoying her liaison with Uther. Now I understood!

Daytimes, Urien told me about his children. Urien rode one of my geldings, and I rode Cloud, moving slowly in the cool air. We saw snow on the mountains near us, but did not worry about it. Urien's gillies walked, ranging the woods beside us out of sight, often as not, and Cornu, Sam and Susan followed us at a distance discreetly, herding the horses. Cornu wanted Urien and me to become friends, to have time alone for us to discover each other. We did and we were.

"Pictish mothers give their babies ridiculous names to fool the Spirits of the Woods so they will leave their children alone," Urien told me. "Names that are descriptive of beauty or goodness would make the children targets, particularly of the dread Oak King."

"I know something of this," I said, "but I am under the protection of the Great Mother. I do not fear the Oak King."

"I wanted you to know that it was not because their mother didn't love them that she gave them such names as Sausage and Bacon."

"Sausage and Bacon?" I asked incredulously.

"They all have pig names," he told me, smiling faintly.

"What are the others?" I asked.

"Ribs and Gravy," he replied.

I laughed. I couldn't help it. "What do the boys think of them?"

"They think they are funny, just as you do, except for the youngest. He insists his name is Accolon, and will not answer to Gravy, so he is much teased. Boys take real names after the Samhain feast in autumn in the year they turn eight."

"Do they name themselves?"

"Yes," he said. "They take responsibilities in the family following their initiation at Samhain, and along with the name comes some independence and accountability for their actions. Gravy is merely insisting on being taken seriously earlier than most children."

"How will I ever communicate with them?" I asked in sudden consternation. "I don't speak Pictish!"

"They all speak Latin, of a sort," he responded. "Their mother insisted, saying that the sons of kings would have need of court language. I am afraid it's sadly mixed with Pictish, for they use Pictish words when they don't know the Latin. Perhaps you can teach them correct speech," he added in a doubtful tone.

I laughed. "If I can't Cornu will," I said.

Where I was curious about Urien's children, he was curious about Cornu. "Is he a slave?" he asked. "I have never seen so strong a man."

"No, he is a free man," I replied. "He joined my father's household when I was a child and was my father's shield-bearer until my father was killed. Then he gave his allegiance to me. I do not think he would leave if I asked him to, and I do not wish to do that. He is more friend than follower."

"I have no desire to request his leaving," Urien said. "It is well that you have so devoted and competent a man to look after your stock."

We rode along the edges of the high hills through oak woods on the trip northeast and saw little game. Urien had never seen hawk hunting before, so I borrowed Cornu's hawk, let Urien carry the bird, and taught him how to release it when we occasionally found a rabbit or fowl worth the chase. There was barely enough game to feed the hawk and none for us. Urien told me there was no game to be found on the hills themselves. The dense pine forests of the slopes cut off sunlight so there was little brush, hence scant food for even the smallest birds or animals; squirrels and a few lean foxes were the only denizens of that part of the woods.

He said the strong winds had deforested the Orkney Islands as well as Caithness, the northern tip of Caledonia, and that we would find good sport there. Many Picts live on those bare lands, herding their hardy sheep and short-horned cattle and quarreling over the few pieces of arable land. He also said Lot laid claim to the Orkneys, demanding and receiving tribute from the Pict chieftains, but payments were meager and more ceremonial than useful. Lot's own folk were in Lothian. They were Britons.

We found Urien's village built on oak pilings and crossbeams a few hundred feet into a small, pretty lake. He told me this sort of construction was called a crannog. Its guarding broch, a double-walled round tower, was some forty feet high and thirty feet across, made of undressed stone set into a stone foundation next to the causeway to the crannog. Between the outer and inner walls of the broch were set oak braces that served as stairs leading to a platform on top. From there men could shoot arrows and throw spears at invaders, without exposing themselves. The causeway from the shore to the village had several sections that could be detached and floated away, leaving open water.

"Who would attack you here?" I asked.

"In the past, our enemies were the Gaels," he answered. "Also the Romans, when we lived near their Hadrian's Wall. However, we have never been attacked here by anyone. If such a thing were to happen, it would probably be a rival Pict chief, rather than Lot's Britons."

The village looked difficult to capture, particularly if the broch were defended. There was no one on the high platform that I could see, and we had to hail the village to get someone to bring the floating bridge after the gillies led our horses away. Cornu went with them to make sure they were properly taken care of. So, this is Gore, I thought. I wondered which of the miserably small huts I could see would be my home. Even the deliberate austerity of New Avalon was more commodious than this!

Before we could enter the town, cries from the edge of the wood drew our attention, and a swarm of small boys came running to us.

"Ah, it seems the gillies have told my sons we have arrived," Urien remarked.

"Come quickly, Geen has been hurt!" one of them shouted, and jumped up and down in the same place, urging us to join him and the others. Urien set off at a trot, and I ran easily beside him.

"Who is Geen?" I asked.

"Their dog," he replied. The children scampered ahead of us through the trees when they saw we were coming to join them. We found them clustered in a tight circle where a dog was yelping in pain. They parted to let us come up to the animal. He was magnificent, a deer hound that might have weighed twenty pounds more than I did, all bone and muscle. Just now he was on his side licking frantically at a hip that was sticking out in an odd way, and whimpering deep in his throat. Urien freed his belt knife.

"Geen is suffering," he said. "There is nothing to be done for a dog with a broken hip. You must let me ease him."

"No!" the smallest boy said, agony in his voice. "Mama gave him to me!"

"What happened?" I asked, kneeling by the animal, allowing comfort to flood from my mind and wash over it. The wave of emotion touched the children as well, of course, and even Urien sounded less stern when he spoke. He was still concerned, however.

"Be careful," he warned as I extended my hand for the dog to smell. "He might bite. Wounded animals are unpredictable, even as gentle a beast as Geen."

I smiled up at him. "He will not hurt me," I said. "Now, one of you, tell me what happened," I said again, looking at the boys.

"The stallion kicked him," one said. "Geen was afraid the stallion would hurt Gravy, and came between them, growling. The stallion just kicked him for no reason!" This was said indignantly, and accompanied by an accusing look at Urien.

"You know you have been warned to stay away from the horses," Urien said. "You are fortunate it isn't Gravy lying here."

"I only let my Mama call me Gravy," the small boy objected, glaring in turn at his father. "My name is Accolon!"

I put my hand on the hurt dog, concentrating on keeping him quiet with my mind while I examined the injury. "It appears his hip is merely displaced, not broken," I announced. "With your permission, I will try to put it back where it belongs," I said, and I sought the smallest boy's eyes. He stared back at me suspiciously.

"You know how?" he asked.

"I have done such a thing before," I said. "I spend much of my time caring for sick and hurt animals."

"Do it," he urged.

"I will, then," I said, gripping the animal's lower leg in one hand while placing my flat hand against the outthrust, misplaced thighbone. I rotated the leg gently to learn where the articulation was, then pulled down, lifted and pushed all at once. As I snapped the bone back into the socket the dog gave an agonized yelp and scrambled to its feet, trembling. An instant later, he was licking my face, a reaction I am used to, but never really have come to like. He turned to the children, greeting them all, but I intervened firmly and made him lie down again.

"He must be kept quiet for a few days, to give himself a chance to mend," I said. "That hip could slip out again if the tendons have been damaged." The boys nodded in agreement, crowding me away, so they could pet the animal into submission.

"We'll watch him," one of them assured me.

THE CAPTIVE BIRD

I glanced at the smallest boy to see if he approved, and found him looking at me with his whole soul in his eyes. He stretched up his arms, and I lifted him to hug him. With his arms around my neck he whispered to me, "You can call me Gravy."

Urien's house turned out to be a walled compound with one large, thatch-roofed rectangular hut together with a number of small round ones. A long communal table dominated the central room of the large hut. Everyone who lived in the compound took their meals there. An attached smaller square hut served as a kitchen. A curtained alcove at the back of the large room served as our bedroom and clothing wardrobe. The bed itself was built of stout posts sprung with tightly tied leather straps that supported a down-filled mattress. I found it surprisingly comfortable, but I'd found the pine-needle-covered forest floor surprisingly comfortable but a few days earlier.

The other huts contained stored food and provided private quarters to the several families that served Urien's household. Susan decided she wanted a pallet in the large communal room, to be in easy call, and Cornu and Sam made themselves quarters out near the horses.

Susan seemed shocked by her first glance at the poor and primitive quarters. Urien was supposed to be king of the southern Picts! Susan had expected a castle. So had I, come to think of it, but there was a wealth of furs strewn around, used casually as rugs or wraps, that would grace any king's house. And the cleanliness of the house was an improvement over any castle I'd ever seen. There were no vermin. Rats were controlled by the tamed forest cats that had the run of the place, beasts weighing up to twenty pounds and only slightly sociable. They didn't bite or scratch if unmolested, and only the youngest and most inexperienced children tried to pet them. I vowed I'd raise some kittens by hand to make better friends of them, but Urien laughed at me. He'd see.

Over the next few weeks I came to know the boys better and found them less in need of discipline than affection. The oldest, Sausage, continued to be wary of me, fearing to have his influence over his brothers diminished, I thought. I treated him as much as possible as an equal, and he came to confide in me about little worries when no one else was around. Even so, I didn't hug him as I wanted to, thinking it would offend him beyond hope of forgiveness. The twins took care of each other in many ways, easily adapting to my presence. They were the easiest to reach, for they had each other and were the least needy emotionally. Accolon, for so I thought of the youngest and called him unless we were alone, was the child most bereft by his mother's death. He had bad dreams that he whispered to me.

"The Oak King will come and eat me," he told me. "My brothers say the shamans have already decided."

"Peace, Gravy. I will let no harm near you," I would say, and he would relax when I hugged him. However, unless he was near me, or with Geen, he was fearful. I spoke to Urien about it.

"It is true, I am afraid," he said. "The king's house must furnish a sacrifice to the Oak King every eight years. Once it was the king himself who was stretched out on the stone for the druids to carve, but now one of his sons is usually taken. I have been king for that long, following my marriage at Samhain."

"I will not permit it," I said, "I will not permit that child, or any other of the boys, to suffer such a fate under a shaman's knife," I said.

"The shamans only choose a sacrifice," Urien told me. "They do not cut the victim open, for they cannot read the fates in the way the guts spill. Only the druids can do that. One will be here at harvest for that purpose."

"It will not serve," I said. "Let them cut a bull or a ram if they must have blood. My contract with you gives me the responsibility for looking after these children. I will not let any one of them go." I was serious. They had all become dear to me, but most particularly Accolon, whose need was greatest.

"You cannot defy the shamans," Urien said uneasily.

"Can I not?" I asked, staring at him haughtily.

"You aren't even Christian," he said, trying to make me see reason. "Why do you object?"

"No, I am not Christian," I retorted. "I am something stronger, something that was here before the shamans made their bargain with the druids. I am under the protection of the Great Mother, and I will bring all my children under her arm," I said.

"Take care," he said. "The shamans have a bad reputation for poisoning as well as curing."

"They will not poison this household," I said grimly, "nor will they bring cures here. If I can cure animals, I ought to be able to cure little boys."

He shook his head, but I put my plan into effect immediately. I instructed the household that no shaman was to be allowed within our compound for any purpose. I said that if I learned my orders had been disobeyed, it would go much the worse for whoever was at fault. Among the servants I found the women with me, but the men inclined to grumble about it. They were not around much except to eat, so their objections were of less importance than they might have been. Women were held in subjugation among the Picts during ceremonies honoring the Oak King every harvest, the feast of Samhain. The Great Mother's spring ceremony, the feast of Beltane, was not marred with blood sacrifices.

"Urien," I said, "I am willing to answer for what occurs here in the compound, but you must tell the men to obey me. They think they can ignore my orders because I am a woman."

He was troubled, but he loved his sons and saw my interest was in saving them, so he stood with me, and the open grumbling stopped.

I continued my campaign to win the children over. "I am as strong as the shamans," I told them, "and I will protect you from them, but you have to do as I say. Will you accept me?"

"You are our father's wife, not our mother," Sausage muttered, but he was uncomfortable opposing me for he wanted to be friends. He was already eight, and too old to be subject to the shamans' choice. The victim must have been born within the eight-year cycle to be acceptable to the Oak King as a substitute for his father.

"Morgan is a royal princess!" Susan retorted scornfully. "In her country someone like you wouldn't dare to disagree with her."

I wondered when she had decided that. I had held myself aloof at New Avalon to gain privacy and had justified it on the grounds that I was royal, but that had been a bluff. I thought she had known. Sausage looked alarmed and challenged, so I ignored Susan and said, "As oldest, you are the leader of your brothers. Remember, the shamans cannot touch you. You are too old for the Samhain sacrifice, but your brothers are not."

"What can I do?" Sausage asked, in a doubting tone. The others watched and listened.

I thought for a moment and decided to open the campaign I had planned. "Water is the Great Mother's element," I said. "I am at home there. I can teach you to swim."

"Why? What good would that do? The shamans say only animals and birds swim. Men are not supposed to," Sausage objected.

"Well, they would say that, wouldn't they, since the Oak King of the Woods does not control water? I will put you under the protection of the Mother so that the shamans will fear to touch you, or your brothers. You must agree first, however, for they will not move without you."

"Teach me," Accolon said gravely, holding out his hand for me to take. He, for one, wouldn't wait for his brother's permission! With a deep breath Sausage nodded as well, and I had won my first battle.

"It is well for you to know," I said, "that the King of the Woods does not control all of the animals. Wolves belong to the Mother. We will become a wolf pack with Sausage as the leader." I nodded to the oldest boy, who accepted the nomination with another nod.

"What about you?" Susan asked. "You should be leader."

"Wolf packs are led by males," I replied, "although there is a lead female as well who shares the responsibility, or so my old friend Myrddin told me. He is a man who knows much about wolves," I explained. I was thankful that Myrddin had shared his knowledge with me on the trip north from Dimilioc, when he saw how interested I was.

"I can give you advice, but I am not a Pict, and have no authority that does not stem from your father," I explained to them. "Sausage will take a name after Samhain and become the heir to his mother. He even has an advantage over your father in that he is also a member of the clan your father married into, while your father is not. Sausage can protect us all if we stand behind him."

It was true, and Sausage knew it after I pointed it out. I could see that for the first time he was willing to consider taking the responsibility I had outlined for him.

"I will be with the hunters after Samhain," the boy said, "but I will spend as much time with you as I can." It was a start.

We had our first swimming lesson that afternoon, retreating to a point of land that protruded into the lake and was hidden from the crannog. We planned that I would teach the boys while Cornu paddled among us in a coracle, one of those light, unstable boats the Picts used for fishing, to keep them from drowning while they learned. With Susan's help the first lesson went very well, except that Geen hindered us. Seeing the boys in the water concerned him. He kept dashing in and trying to pull them to shore, until Cornu left the water to quiet him down.

"Just like a Geen," Sausage muttered, as he tried to evade the dog.

"What is a Geen?" I asked, laughing. "I never thought to ask before."

"Geens are giants that look after the Picts," Sausage told me seriously. "The High Kings of the Picts are always Geens."

I decided I'd have to put the question to Urien to get more information, for that seemed to explain it as far as Sausage was concerned.

We were wet when we returned and found trouble awaiting us. A shaman sat with Urien and pointed his finger at us as we entered the compound.

"It is her doing," he accused. "She is a creature of the Mother. I warned you! She has given the Oak King such an affront that it will take two sacrifices to recover his good graces, not the one we had planned."

I felt fury rise in me, but checked it when I heard a voice saying quietly in my head, "Steady, girl." Girl? It was Cornu, speaking to me as he did to the young mares to gentle them down. Did Cornu think of me as a young mare? I realized he did, and it amused me, giving me control of myself again. The shock that crossed the shaman's face faded as I stopped throwing my anger at him.

"If you are speaking of my charges," I said coldly, "there will be no sacrifice drawn from their number."

"The dead mother of the littlest one calls him, as we have all seen. He is already marked," the shaman said.

"If that were ever true, it is true no longer," I said and drew my mother's gift from around my neck, the enameled corbie crow caught in the fowler's net, held by a golden hand. I placed it over Accolon's head, letting the pendant come to rest against his breast.

"This is an amulet of such power that any man attempting injury to the boy will have his testicles shrivel up as if they were caught in this fowler's net," I said, pointing to the pendant. "The boy is under the protection of the Great Mother, I swear it!" I continued the warning in a portentous voice, "Touch him at your peril!"

The shaman gasped. "This is blasphemy!" he said, in a scandalized voice.

"Only to persons like you," I responded with contempt. "What kind of god do you serve, who must feed on the blood of little children?"

Hissing, he backed out of the house, with averted eyes.

"Is this true?" Urien asked.

"Of course," I replied, realizing any other response would assure the failure of my plan. I didn't want to discuss it, so I gave him something else to think about. "What is more to the point, what was he doing in my house?" I asked. "Are my rights less than any other Pict's wife, that my husband brings guests to my house without my permission? Persons whom, in the past, I have refused to admit?"

"My apologies," Urien said. "I was in the wrong. The man was here before I realized it, and he was speaking of your teaching the boys to swim. He seems to be against it."

"And you?"

"Not at all. I am not from here, remember? My people were

fisher folk, and all of us learned to swim. I know it scandalized my wife when first she learned of it, for it is not done here."

"Your wife? And what am I?"

"I am not doing this well, am I?" he asked in a mild voice.

I decided I had gone far enough. "It is my turn to apologize," I said. "I find I am quick to anger now that I am carrying a child."

"My dear!" he said, for I had not told him before.

My status changed from the day of that revelation. Cornu and Susan were protective to the point that I threatened to commit several kinds of self-destructive acts if I were not allowed room to move in. And Urien and the boys fussed over me as if I were doing something special. I wondered why until Sausage told me quietly that his mother had died in childbirth, along with her child.

Aided by Susan, I was able to keep the children near me in the compound through the Samhain festival by pleading my belly, and the shamans found someone other than Accolon for their sacrifice. I did not attend, nor would Urien discuss it with me later, saying merely that I was right, and that it would not happen again under his rule.

I expected the Pictish women to befriend me when they saw I was pregnant. The women at home would have done so to a stranger married in, I thought, though I wasn't sure. In any case, I was wrong. I couldn't complain to Urien, for he could not control the women in this thing. Besides, he left my bed when I was seven months pregnant and moved into the bachelor quarters with the hunters and other unmarried men. He told me that Pictish customs would not allow him under my roof even to eat until three months after I had delivered. We sat and talked under the portico when he came to see me. I thought we did it better among the Scoti.

About the women, I realized friendship should be offered freely if it was offered at all. I knew there was resentment at my marrying the chief man among them; an alien woman had come among them and stolen the chance they had sought for their daughters.

With Cornu as midwife and Susan as nurse, I birthed a big, healthy boy in the winter, a scant nine months after my marriage to Urien. I had told the Great Mother's priestesses Cornu didn't practice midwifery, but he seemed very knowledgeable, nonetheless. As for the baby, I was unable to tell, at least at first, if Lot or Urien was his father, but Urien was very quiet around him. Only later I realized this baby must be bigger and blonder than Pict newborns. His blue eyes and red hair looked like most of the babies I had seen in my short life, however, and I saw no reason to apologize for the way he looked. At the time he looked fine to me.

The boys loved him. He became the new baby in the family, much to Accolon's satisfaction, and Sausage, who had taken the name Drake at Samhain, bestowed his old baby name on the newcomer. I saw no need in hiding the baby from the Oak King, but the boys were so insistent, I acquiesced reluctantly. Sausage, indeed!

Susan quite deserted me in her consuming interest in the child, even neglecting her visits to the horses. Cornu told me Sam was quite put out by her absence. She appointed herself the baby's nurse, and except for feeding it on a schedule worked out between Susan and the baby, I had less responsibility in caring for it than I had expected. That was all right, for certainly the baby didn't suffer from neglect, and Urien's boys needed me.

When Drake left the house it became apparent how much of my time had been spent in his company, and how important he was to his brothers. The twins were almost disconsolate in his absence. They had tagged him like shadows, one on either side, ready to join in anything Drake suggested. Their acceptance of me was not a substitute for the absence of their brother. They needed a father, and where Drake had really been too young, Urien was too distant, perhaps too old, to have the patience they needed to teach them to be independent.

Cornu was the most patient man alive. I decided the boys would do well spending time with him, so I suggested they all learn to ride. Susan was happy to see us out of the house so she could have the baby to herself, and Cornu welcomed the boys. Even Sam, nearer their age than Cornu, soon became nearly as important to them as Drake had been.

"All I ever hear is, 'Sam says this, Sam says that,'" Susan grumbled after supper one evening when Sam and Cornu had left and we were clearing up the dishes. I looked at the twins and winked, and over their faces came a look of sudden and delighted understanding. They realized how it was between Sam and Susan. I'm not sure they didn't see it before Susan did.

Cornu purported not to be able to tell the twins apart, except when they were together. "One of you is darker than the other. Bacon and Ribs are no fit names for the two of you. I'll call you Kenyon and Duncan, light and dark." They immediately called themselves Ken and Dunc, shortening the names to sound more Pictish. They even agreed together to take those names at Samhain, and became Ken and Dunc to everyone.

Drake, my renamed old Sausage, developed a special need. Cornu told me the shamans had sought him out for special attention while the boy was purportedly in the hunters' care. He had taken to hiding at night to escape the disciplinary punishment being meted out to him.

"When you hear this tune, go to the compound gate. Cloud will be waiting there with Sam to lead you to a pool fed by a waterfall. Behind the curtain of water Drake will be waiting. He needs your help." Cornu whistled a few notes softly. They were unfamiliar, but I would recognize them if I heard them again.

I waited that night for the notes to sound before venturing out. Susan had moved into the bedroom to be nearer the baby, and in Urien's absence, I saw no objection. I hoped it would not be too long. It was now three months since I delivered the baby. I felt Urien should have come back by now. Anyway, Susan would take care of the baby if he awoke while I was gone.

Cornu played his flute most nights for the horses, and the Picts were used to it. This night was no different except that I was listening for a signal. It came, much embellished, but I knew it.

I rose, put on a cloak against the chill, for it was still winter in cold Gore, and found Cloud and Sam waiting for me. There was no snow, despite the cold, so we could pass in the cloudy night without notice, a gray-cloaked figure mounted on a gray horse led by another gray-cloaked figure. When we reached the appointed spot, Sam melted away, and I stripped off my cloak and boots to leave in Cloud's care before slipping into the water. Oh, I'd forgotten how cold unwarmed water could be! I swam under the curtain of falling water and found a miserable child waiting. He was dry, so I knew there was another entrance to the cave. I wished I had been entrusted with the secret of that, I thought, as I tried not to shiver.

"Morgan, the shamans are going to make me fail the training," he told me, after I'd hugged and rocked him in my arms until we both stopped shaking. He seemed so thin!

"Don't they feed you?"

"They withhold food as a punishment," he said in a matter-of-fact voice. "Cornu found out, and when I can escape at night he feeds me. I'm always hungry!" This was not what was bothering him.

"Why would they do such a thing?" I asked.

"They say I am not worthy of being trained to be a hunter!" he said with agony in his voice.

Ah, now that bothered! "Does your father know?" I asked.

"They do it because of him. He brought a woman who worships the Great Mother into the community and will not send her away. He cannot help me. If he shows it hurts him, they make it worse."

"I see. Well, since I'm not a Pict I need not be bound by customs that allow children to be abused. If your father can't stop them, perhaps I can!"

"Oh, no! The hunters won't pay any attention to a woman! They'd laugh! I just wanted to tell you I may not be able to help my brothers like I promised."

"I see. Well, after I put arrows through a few of them, perhaps they'll take me seriously," I said. "Tell me, is the shaman the same one who wanted to sacrifice Accolon?"

"Yes," Drake said.

"Perhaps we can show him how wrong he is," I mused. I remembered him as an old, frail man. There might be a way. . . .

Drake was much cheered by the plan we developed, but aghast

at the possibility of what could go wrong with it. Still, he was so desperate he was ready for anything.

At daybreak next morning when the hunters were eating in the men's house, with the boys behind their circle feeding on scraps tossed them like so many dogs, I entered the men's hut boldly. There were a number of unmarried women serving the men, women Cornu had told me slept with the hunters indiscriminately.

Urien was among the first to see me, but Drake rose from his place at the outer ring of the boys where the least amount of food fell. He walked toward me, carrying two headless practice spears.

On seeing me, one of the hunters said, "Your foreign wife has decided to be a men's house whore, Urien. What's wrong? Can't you satisfy such a giantess?"

Briefly it crossed my mind that perhaps Urien had stayed in the men's house to try to look after Drake. If that were true, I'd forgive him if he told me. Even as I thought this, however, I drew an arrow from my quiver and shot it so it pegged the speaker's breech-clout to the ground as he squatted, a bowl in one hand and a horn spoon in another. Shock stilled his mouth a moment as he considered what the arrow might have done, and before he recovered I nocked another arrow and drew the bow so that it pointed at his head.

"Open your mouth again, Dung-face, and I'll stick your tongue to the back of your throat." I'd practiced the words with Drake until I'd memorized them. My accent may have sounded funny, but no one laughed.

"Speak, boy," I told Drake.

He stepped up beside me and pointed at the scrawny shaman. "This man says I am not worthy to be a hunter. I challenge him to test me, here and now." With that he cast one of his headless spears at the shaman, striking him solidly in the ribs. The shaman howled and seized the shaft. Several of the other men started to rise to punish such effrontery.

"No! Sit!" I ordered, thrusting them back with a controlled release of the fury I felt, pointing the arrow at one after another.

"Are the Picts cowards to let a challenge go unanswered?" It was the other sentence in Pictish I'd memorized.

The other men sat back down as the shaman slowly rose, the headless spear shaft in his hand. He advanced on Drake, who held his remaining stick in two hands as Cornu and I had taught him. I stepped away, giving them space, watching the hunters to make sure there was no interference. Drake would take care of himself. The Picts did not train in stick-fighting. We had worked with Drake before he joined the hunters until he was reasonably proficient, good enough to handle an unskilled man without a man's full strength. The shaman was old and out of shape.

Suddenly the shaman charged, swinging his stick in an overhand smash with the intent of striking the boy to the earth. Drake met the charge almost contemptuously, with a thrust to the belly, a parry for the now nearly powerless blow the shaman had launched, followed by jabs and smashes that laid the man bleeding and senseless at his feet.

"This boy is going with me, now," I said in Gaelic. Let them ask Urien what I had said after I left. "If he is not welcome here, I will send him for fosterage to Merricks-hold, where his courage and skill will be honored. I am under contract to see this boy is raised to be a true man. If that cannot be done here, it will be done there."

One man started to jeer, and I shot the horn spoon from his hand. No one else offered to speak again, but I noticed Urien wore a slight smile which he hid with his hand. Good. Maybe he'd pay some attention to me now.

Drake and I walked out, back to the compound, where between mouthfuls of food he related to Susan and his brother all that had transpired. He stopped from time to time to smile at me, no longer the suspicious child I had once known.

The chief hunter came to see me that very afternoon to claim Drake. "The shaman's guild has assigned a new priest to serve us while the other recovers. We have given the guild to understand that the old one will not be welcome back." He handed me my two arrows. "We hope you will not have need of these again," he added, smiling. "Drake will be given the training he deserves, I promise you," and he beckoned to the boy to come with him

With a sigh and a wink Drake picked up in one hand the remains of the roast fowl he'd been eating, and a fresh loaf of bread in the other, before following the man out.

Though Urien had told me that he would not be allowed to sleep under my roof until three months after I had delivered, in truth, I saw little of him after the three months passed. My life was filled with boys, however, and I pretended I barely missed the companionship of adults. I had Cornu to talk to when I got lonely, and he seemed always to know when that was. Mostly, I was too busy to brood about my lack of friends, but Urien's continued absence bothered me more and more the longer it continued. Why was he not with me? Had he found another woman he liked better, one of the whores? In truth, I burned with frustration. I had been sexually awakened by Urien, and I was now no longer content to sleep alone.

I found some enlightenment from a bold-eyed slut who went out of her way to accost me. "Do you not wonder, woman of the Gaels, why your husband has not returned to sleep under your roof-tree?" She was insolent as she looked me up and down.

"And if I did, would I likely confide in an underbred bitch like you?" I responded in kind.

"He said you had more heat in your tongue than in your crotch," she spat at me.

Her words stung me. Could Urien have said that of me? I missed his company. Indeed, I had begun to love him. I thought we had become friends, at least. The beast peered out of my mind-cave and glared through my eyes. The slut clutched her throat and gasped as the edge of my anger hit her.

"I think perhaps you did not take his meaning correctly," I said, rage thickening my voice. "I have heat enough!" There was no Cornu present to stop me, but I shut my mind of my own accord and let her go. She fled, making the sign of Lud with her fingers as she glanced back in terror over her shoulder, lest I should follow her.

111

After that I ceased to make overtures of friendship to the other women, knowing gossip about me would keep the best disposed of them from responding. On the rare occasions I saw Urien, I treated him with a chilly indifference, which after a time or two he reciprocated. The estrangement was complete, and I had no idea what had brought it about. I thought often of Merricks-hold and of Gawaine, and wondered if he were happier in Rome than I was in cold Gore. I almost hoped so.

In growing anger I considered returning to Merricks-hold, for it was no part of my contract that I was to suffer such disrespect. In the end I didn't go only because of the boys. They had become too dependent on me, something I had worked hard to achieve, for me to leave them for such a reason. If they lost a second mother, it would scar their lives. They would never learn to trust again. I also knew that if I were not here to guard them, the shamans would claim one or more for sacrifice. No, I could not leave.

The boys learned things from me, and from Cornu, they could learn from no one else, not even the hunters. Together we taught them to train and care for their horses, and they learned to ride as well as any Gael. I could not teach them arms, but Cornu could and did: how to handle a sword, how to dress a shield and how to launch a spear. I could teach them to stick-fight, and as they became skilled with the staff they became more proficient in the other military arts. Stick-fighting demanded balance and judgment, and the consequence of error was immediate. There was nothing like a rap on the side of the head to make the demand for attention seem real.

The result of this concentrated attention was that the boys became my boys as much as their father's. More, really, for among the Picts, hunters trained boys to become men, and boys were not assigned as pupils to their own fathers. My boys came into adulthood as much Gael as they were Pict! I swore I would fulfill my part of the contract out of pride, if nothing else, and I did.

When each of the boys came of age and joined the hunters, they learned about the cave behind the waterfall; and when Cornu's flute called me, I went to them with Cloud, carrying food. I judged this was what they chiefly needed, some token of what the world had been and would be again. Even the twins, so dependent on one another, came to me. Indeed, often I had them and one or more of the others as well. It seemed to me impossible that this remained a secret for so many years, but at least no one put a stop to it.

The boys stayed in training until they reached puberty, then after an initiation ceremony they became hunters, free to move about the community at will, honored by all. Often as not, they came to the compound, all but Urien. I never asked them about him, and they never volunteered information about their father. I often wondered what they thought.

My son chose the name Uwayne when he reached his eighth Samhain, and I had no more boys to look after named for pig parts. The hunters took him as they had his brothers.

Uwayne was as different from the other boys as I was from the other women in Gore. At eight, he was red of hair, like the red of burnished copper. The shamans believed him to be marked by Lud, the sun god. I feared they would claim him, and indeed, they had spoken to Urien when the boy was a baby; but Urien had said the boy belonged to my clan, and I would have to agree to give him up. Such had been my reputation that they never asked it of me.

Uwayne's coloring was not even like mine, which had inspired my father to call me Corbie Crow. It wasn't like Urien's or, indeed, any of the other Picts, for they are all olive-skinned. It wasn't like my black-haired father, nor my golden-haired mother. It was like Lot's. This was apparent very early to me and, I fear, to Urien, though he never spoke to me about it. I had no more children, nor opportunity to do so. I was not surprised, therefore, when he came to see me following the Samhain festival marking Uwayne's eighth birthday.

"Our contract has run, Lady," he said, a distant tone in his voice. He was dressed formally in his best blue tunic as he had been when I first met him in Merricks-hold. It could have been the same one, for all I knew. He'd caught me in an everyday, rough, brown woolen gown and with my hair wound in coils under a woolen cap. I'd been cleaning house. Damn the man, I thought.

"My sons are grown and have been praised everywhere for their modesty and decency. You have fulfilled your part of what you promised, as I have mine. Now that Uwayne has taken his name and left this house, as is fitting for a Pictish boy, I no longer have an excuse to resist the considerable pressure from Lot and other kings here in the north when they request I join them. They wish to go against Brastius, Warden of the North, and the Bishop of London, who together have found a claimant for the throne of Britain."

He's going to turn me away! I thought. I would make him say so. "I am not surprised to hear that Uther's throne is still open," I said coolly. "My father was contemptuous of the many petty kings that vied for power. But who is the claimant that Brastius Red-beard has raised, and what is this title, Warden of the North?"

"The claimant is Arthur, supposedly the son of Uther and Igraine, hidden away these many years."

"My brother, then," I said proudly. "He is the rightful heir." From the look on Urien's face I saw he neither believed my statement nor accepted the claimant as king. "But what of Brastius?" I repeated, not to be insulted by his scorn.

"Soon after you came to me we heard that Brastius had in some way displeased Uther," Urien said. "He sent him to fight Picts and never recalled him."

"I had not known this," I said.

"Who would think it would interest you?" Urien asked in a cold, indifferent tone.

I flushed and bit my lip to hold back the retort that I might have uttered. Gossip about high personages had been table talk when I was a girl. I wondered if Boudicca had better control of her emotions than I did. "Oh, but it does!" I managed to say lightly. "I had warned Red-beard that my mother would not be pleased to learn his camp followers had been allowed to despoil

114

her things at Dimilioc. I had even threatened him with banishment to a post on the frontier for the rest of his career, fighting Picts. Warden of the North, indeed! Perhaps I am responsible for that. Do you think so? Your people believe me to be a witch, do they not?"

"No one who knows you believes you are capable of evil," he said stoutly. That surprised me.

"I knew, of course, that Uther Pendragon had escaped my blood curse, but I wonder, what did he die of?" I asked.

"It was a lingering death, men say, perhaps poison," Urien answered, looking uncomfortable. This was not the conversation he had intended to have with me.

"My father would have supposed it was a Pictish cook," I remarked, and it was Urien's turn to color up.

"As a matter of fact, that was claimed," he responded in a frigid tone.

I did not care. I was thinking of what he meant by saying the contract had run. What was he getting at?

Since I did not respond to his invitation to continue the quarrel, he resumed his planned speech, saying, "My people have chafed under my restrictions. They have wished to join their neighbors in the battle that is imminent, but I have held back as I promised you I would, refusing to take Lot's hand in friendship, though I know not what he did to earn your enmity."

I wondered if that were still true, but could read no clue in his face.

"I will now rethink my position," he went on, "for I now consider myself free to do so. I tell you this so that you may make what plans you will. Lot is coming here to urge me to join with him before the moon changes."

"You surprise me," I said. "Moreover, you speak as one with a grievance. Have I wronged you in some way?"

"Bastardy is not considered a disgrace for a child among the Picts," Urien replied, "but the man who has been fooled is considered a joke. I could have been trusted with the information that you were already with child when we entered into contract. I could have passed it off by saying I'd purchased a cow with a calf, or some such pleasantry. Now I hear people speak of Urien's Redhead, never directly to my face, you understand, but I hear it, and I cannot respond."

"A cow with a calf?" I asked in icy tones. "You believe I was pregnant? Can't you count, man? It was nine full months after we entered into contract that I delivered Uwayne. I promise you, I knew nothing of any pregnancy." That was almost true. I had not known for sure.

"Perhaps not," he said, "but you are as dark as a Pict, and people look at the two of us and talk."

"Not to me," I said, "but I now understand better why you never came back to our bed after Uwayne's birth. Truly, you do surprise me! I had never thought you merely timid, afraid of talk! I had thought the fault lay in me, that my looks had somehow been ruined by childbirth, and you no longer found me attractive. What a fool I was! Had I but known how you felt, I might have explained why my mother was called Igraine the Gold. Dark as I am, I am considered some sort of rarity in my family, as you say Uwayne is, and yet I do not believe anyone ever taxed me with the charge of bastardy."

"I would not quarrel with you at parting," Urien said. I had the satisfaction of seeing a look of doubt replace the mask of cold certainty which he had worn at the beginning of the conversation. But he had thought through what he intended to say and continued formally. "What's done is done. You have the love and respect of all my sons and my gratitude for what you have accomplished with them."

"Parting? Are you speaking about leaving with Lot or am I going somewhere, then?" I asked, ignoring the compliment and fastening on the meat of his utterance.

"You will not wish to greet Lot as mistress of this house and be forced to offer him the hospitality required to be shown guests," he said.

116

It was not a question, and furthermore, he was right. "You did not ask it of me in the past," I observed.

"I would not, for I had contracted not to do so," he responded.

"I see, and now that the contract has been completed, as you say, you are free to do as you please."

He did not reply, but he did not look away.

"Oh, very well," I said, weary of the conversation. "I would wish to go back to Merricks-hold. I will take Uwayne with me, for he belongs to my clan, not yours. It's in the contract," I added bitterly.

He looked embarrassed. "Uwayne does not wish to go," Urien said.

I gaped at him in outrage. "You discussed this with him before you spoke to me? How could you do such a thing?"

"Because I feared this might happen," he said ruefully, "and I guessed how Uwayne felt. He has been accepted for training by the hunters. He has looked forward to this day for years, having seen his brothers go through it, one by one, as they came of age. I know the contract states he belongs to your clan, but if he were allowed to choose, he would not go with you now." Urien looked at me, really looked for the first time since we began the discussion, and finally said, "Accolon would go in his place, if you would allow it."

I was shaking inside, and clenched my hands to keep from wiping them on my gown. The palms of my hands were as wet as my mouth was dry. I wondered if I were going to be able to keep my temper through the rest of this extraordinary conversation. I finally said, "Let them tell me themselves, both Uwayne and Accolon, and I will consider it, but let it be later. For now, it would be a courtesy if you would leave. I have to think about this by myself." He nodded, and got up and walked out without speaking again.

Accolon and I had always had a special relationship, one I did not have even with the child of my body, Uwayne, who was as much Susan's child as mine. I wondered if Accolon really were willing to go with me, to leave his people for my sake. I wondered if I could allow it.

No one came to my house for the evening meal, nor for breakfast the next day. I finally sent a servant to Urien, saying I wished to see Uwayne and Accolon, together; and they came for the evening meal, uncharacteristically quiet, even shy. I had cooked things I knew they liked: oat cakes, sausage, dried roots in butter and fresh meat in a hearty stew with fresh bread and cider to drink. It was a feast, and I enjoyed it with them before I talked to them seriously.

"I am returning to Merricks-hold in a few days," I said. "Urien and I are agreed that my responsibilities here have been met. I am still young enough to find another husband, and my clan mothers will arrange for one if I ask, although I may not. I have been spoiled having so many boys to play with. What if I birth girls?" and I smiled at them. They were united in their scorn of girls, Uwayne at eight and Accolon at thirteen.

"We don't want you to go," Accolon said seriously, and Uwayne's eyes teared.

"I know," I said. "But it's not as if we'll never see each other again. When Uwayne is finished with his training he will have to come and meet his cousins. Your father even thought you, Accolon, might come along on the trip to keep me company for a time, and the other boys, too, of course, if they wished."

Discussing it in a commonplace way, I was able to disguise the hurt I felt at being torn from my children. I had thought my parents had deserted me when I was a child, and I did not want the boys to think of me in that way. On the other hand, I could not stay, for I was no longer welcome. And I could not take the children away without Urien's approval. Mostly, I did not wish the children to be as upset as I was myself. Urien's name went on the list of persons with whom I had unsettled accounts, just below the names of Uther Pendragon, Father John-Martin, fat Brother James and Lot. I seemed to have more enemies than friends.

Oh, how I cried over Uwayne's decision to stay with his father! Before we left, I rode by myself into the mountains where I could weep apart without exposing my grief to the whole village, "spewing emotion," was the way Hilda had put it.

"Is this all?" I raged, walking among the boulders and waving my hands wildly, followed by Cloud, who could make no sense out of my behavior. "I'm only twenty-six; is my life supposed to be over so soon?" After more pacing and waving, and nearly tripping once when Cloud nudged me too forcefully, I screamed, "What have I done wrong?" I counted on my fingers. "I have been a dutiful daughter, a loyal clanswoman, a faithful wife and a caring mother, and for what? For this? To be cast aside like a worn-out shoe?"

The Great Mother made no response, nor did I expect it. I think I was spied on, however, or at least guarded; for in the end all of the boys, with the exception of Uwayne, decided to escort me back to Merricks-hold. I had thought Drake might come, and Accolon had already promised, but the twins, who had taken the names Ken and Dunc at their Samhain feast, did surprise me, for they were thoroughgoing Picts.

"Sam cannot manage the horses without us, and Cornu said we would be welcome," Ken said hopefully.

Dunc was more direct, as always. "We would not have you leave without us, Lady."

"What will your father say?" I asked faintly, on the verge of being overcome by emotion. Had Boudicca ever heard such a thing?

"He has Uwayne," Ken said, shrugging.

I hugged them both, embarrassing them, but pleasing them all the same. Though they were not demonstrative, I knew they cared for me.

We were fortunate in the boys' decision, for our horse herd had grown so large we needed help to herd them back to Merricks-hold. On parting I gave Urien one of them, a purebred stallion now five years old, out of my own Cloud. He could train it as a battle horse and use it as a stud to throw good foals from the tough hill pony mares. I also left the other Roman horse/hill pony crosses Cornu had bred.

I toyed with the notion of joining Arthur, the claimant son of

Uther, to fight against Lot, but I could not lead Urien's sons against their father.

Urien gave me a basket of forest cat kittens, just weaned. I had once asked for some, and I was touched that he remembered. It was with mixed feelings that I bade him farewell and turned my face south once again.

Part II
The
Dark Queen
468 - 486

The seat of empire has passed from Rome to Constantinople, and in Britain, Mordred, the bastard son of King Arthur, is born and hidden away.

CHAPTER VI

I was concerned about Susan, wondering if she could fill the hole in her life. She had fussed over Uwayne for years. The fact that he left her willingly, gladly even, looking forward to his life as a hunter in training, could hardly add to her self-esteem. I found I had wasted my time worrying. Susan appropriated the kittens, fighting off teasing efforts to claim one or another of them by the boys. She even helped Cornu set snares for rabbits each night and fed her charges with tender morsels from the entrails, picking them over gingerly for appropriate pieces. Each night she deposited a kitten in someone's lap with instructions to pet it into gentleness, even me, but she reclaimed them at bedtime. Sam was amused into silliness, and courted her good opinion with unneeded questions about the care of kittens while the rest of us watched a relationship build between them. Sam had waited a long time; Susan was perhaps twenty-three by now, and blooming with youth and vigor. Well!

The roads were still frozen for the most part, but the heavy snows had blown away in the warm winds of early spring, and we trudged through mud occasionally. It didn't slow us much, for there was still relatively little of it.

I had not journeyed on Cloud in years, not since I'd left New Avalon. Most mornings in Gore we had gone riding, mostly just the two of us, and she was in condition, but she was no longer a filly. I'd had six foals out of her, the superb horse I'd given Urien on parting, two other stallions we'd gelded, and three fillies still too young to breed. Cloud must be fourteen at least, by now. We were closer than sisters, for she knew my thoughts without the necessity of my uttering them. I used no reins on her.

Morgause, my dear aunt, was delighted to see us and had the boys sitting at her feet like so many swains within an hour of our arrival. It was a potent magic she had. For me the big surprise was finding Julia.

"Oh, how I've missed you," Julia said, hugging me and Susan. "You weren't gone a week when I knew I'd made a mistake not to go with you!"

"Why didn't you, then?" Susan asked, pert as always.

"Hilda had convinced me I was needed at New Avalon," she answered.

"How long did you stay?" I asked, looking at her with interest. She wore the white robes of a priestess of the Great Mother.

"I stayed seven years, long enough to be ordained. Morgause sent word to Hilda that the Scoti needed more trained women, and I asked to be included. From what I can see, however, I might as well have stayed at New Avalon. We're stumbling over one another here."

"Morgan, you must send these splendid young men to Brastius Red-beard," Morgause told me, after the boys excused themselves to help look after the horses. She sat on a Roman couch, looking as queenly as Boudicca, dressed in one of her flowing robes that seemed to reveal as much as they covered. She hadn't changed much. Susan left with the boys, leaving only me, Julia and Morgause in the salon.

"Red-beard? Whatever for?" I asked in surprise. "Surely as Warden of the North he is not looking for Pictish soldiers!"

"You haven't heard? Brastius is regent for Igraine's son, the one who has been chosen as Uther's successor. The boy is sponsored by Myrddin," she added, seeing the frown start to form on my face. "Brastius is gathering men to Uther's old red dragon standard. Lot and some of the other kings refuse to honor Brastius' claim and will fight to deny it. They call the claimant 'Uther's bastard.' "

"Uther's bastard?" I repeated like a person of diminished intelligence.

"He is a boy of fifteen, they say," Morgause told me.

"I know who he is," I said impatiently. "Cornu told me on the trip from Dimilioc to New Avalon that my mother was pregnant by Uther. It was for that reason I was sent to New Avalon, rather than to Merricks-hold, to be out of the way for a few years until Igraine could coax Uther to allow me to return to Tintagel. And then Hilda told me, just before I left New Avalon, that on his deathbed Uther had named this child his heir. Whatever else the claimant is, he is no bastard! And why are you so concerned about who rules Britain, anyway, that you should peddle such tales?" I asked. She should know better than to traduce Igraine's son before me!

"If Lot and the others are successful, Lot will claim the throne himself," Morgause replied, ignoring my outburst. "I have had many lovers, but I never had one who broke off a relationship until Lot did. He has bragged of it in places where I have friends. I am determined he will not establish himself in a position where men will honor him."

I observed her closely, and she was serious. "My own quarrel with Lot is as old as yours," I told her coldly, "and I am also willing to see him dead. However, I would not risk my boys in such a venture. Besides, their father, Urien, sides with Lot. My boys are too young to choose between Arthur and their father."

"Your boys are young, but so is Arthur, as I told you, or Brastius would not sit as regent," she said. "They would all be trained before any conflict occurred, and would gain fame and honor enough to last a lifetime. Brastius will generously reward those who flock to him now, when he needs them."

"Cornu taught the boys to fight with sword, shield and spear," I said. "They do not need further training."

"All the better. As you said, your quarrel with Lot is as old as mine," Morgause urged.

"My quarrel with Uther is even older," I observed. "Uther owes me a blood debt for my father. I have sworn to collect it, but I have a new problem now, it seems. I have found a brother and find he is the son of my enemy; and my enemy is dead. Uther followed the Roman practice of the father claiming the children. He was a Christian, not an adherent of the Great Mother. If Arthur chooses his father's people rather than his mother's, is he still my brother? How should I decide what to do?"

"You are as bad as Igraine," Morgause said. "My sister won't declare for Arthur, either, though her support would go far in establishing the boy's right to claim the throne. She knows the boy is no bastard!"

"Why should she speak up?" I asked. "Has Arthur acknowledged her?"

Morgause shrugged as if to say, "Who could know?" and was quiet for a while, toying with a tasseled fan made of the feathers from some exotic bird. When she spoke again her choice of topic caught me by surprise. "I never heard for sure," she said. "Were you pregnant from Lot's rape?"

"We were talking of bastards, weren't we?" I responded with deceptive lightness, and glanced at Julia. She had learned to sit without moving while others talked, following the discussion only with her eyes. "Well," I pondered, as Morgause's face took on a guarded look at my hesitancy, "I don't know if Lot had burnished copper hair and gray-blue eyes staring out of a milk white face in his youth, but my son does. Urien is small and dark, as you will recall. He dismissed me from our contract when our son came of age to join the hunters. Urien said I had finished the work he had set out for me, as if I had been a privy digger! With that lack of subtlety that marks the speech of Picts, he spoke of having purchased a cow with a calf, referring to his belief that I was pregnant when I married him. He held my pregnancy against me all the years I was with him, though that phrase 'with him' is somewhat misleading."

Morgause lost her calculating look about halfway through my response and, rising, came to throw her arms around me. "Oh, I am so sorry," she said. "I had no idea things were that bad for you. Why didn't you come home?"

"Because Urien did nothing to break the contract with me," I replied calmly. "Being a husband was not spelled out, you remember. It was just something we all took for granted, and for the first nine months everything was fine. It was only after red haired Uwayne was born that we became estranged."

"Lot has much to answer for," Morgause said grimly. "Why did Uwayne not come with you? He belongs to us by contract."

"He chose to stay and go through the training given by the Pictish hunters for all boys who reach their eighth Samhain. It is good discipline and quite unlike anything available among our people. It is more like the training the Mother's priestesses give our girls."

"And later?"

"He may come to us later. Urien will not let anything happen to the lad, for he loves him as much as any of the rest of his sons, perhaps more." It cost me much to say it, but it was the bitter truth.

"Well, there is much for you to do here," Morgause declared. "You must learn what it takes to be a queen, for I am getting old. You may be needed before you know it."

Julia laughed, a joyous sound that brought Morgause and me to look at her in surprise. I joined in the laughter, and even Morgause grinned, self-consciously.

"You will never be old, Morgause," Julia said, "maybe ancient in a hundred years or so, but not old!"

I nodded agreement, and Morgause smiled complaisantly.

"What of Gawaine?" I asked, after Julia left chuckling to herself. She had stayed long enough to bridge the strain that existed between Morgause and me. She knew how I had been sent away to Urien, following Lot's rape. Too soon, it was! Julia had been well trained.

"Gawaine married into Rhegid, the kingdom that borders us on the south, and has two young sons."

"Married into Rhegid?" I asked. "Was he not a hostage in

127

Rome?" I felt my being shrink within me. Married? Oh, why had he not waited for me?

"He was sent back. The clan mothers married him to a local heiress, a priestess of the Great Mother. Gawaine was to sire daughters, and his wife had a name picked out for the first girl, Lovey, if you can believe it. When the baby turned out to be a boy, she settled on Lovel. The second she had named Flora until it was born. His name became Florence."

I didn't laugh. Damn the clan mothers! "How did that serve the clan?" I asked.

"We have Scoti pressuring our shores, wanting to leave Ireland and settle among us. Gawaine's responsibility is to keep them north of the Solway so that we can direct their affairs."

"I see," I said. "One further question, why did Rome send Gawaine back?" I asked.

"They recognized any possible claim to the throne was Lot's, not Gawaine's. Gawaine belongs to Merrick Clan; he is a Gael, not a Briton under our custom. Lot's father was a Briton. Under Roman law, Lot is a Briton."

"What possible claim would he have, even so?" I asked.

"Oh, his grandfather was supposed to be Aurelius Ambrosius, the old High King, or maybe it was his great-grandfather. I never quite believed it."

I grinned. Morgause was a true Gael. Paternity was a thing of little consequence to her. One thing I was sure of, I would not stay in Merricks-hold and be given to some other local landholder to serve clan interests. The clan mothers had used me for the last time.

I brought the matter up to Cornu. "Remember that fort we passed on our way here from New Avalon?" I asked. "Why can't we settle there?"

"Birrens? I remember," he said, nodding. "The fort is as big as Merricks-hold. How would you defend it?"

"I will take wild Scoti, newly arrived on our shores and hungry for land. The clan mothers here will be happy to have someplace to send them."

I spoke of this to the clan mothers at the feast of welcome given us. Before they could respond, however, Drake, my old Sausage, spoke for his brothers, saying, "You are our second mother. Our father has asked us to join him, but we will not, knowing how you feel. We will go with you instead." I was so proud of him, standing tall and speaking seriously as a man should, but the decision came as a surprise. I was sure Urien would think I had in some way constrained the boys.

I must have looked troubled, for the twins came up to stand beside Drake and Accolon. Ken said, "We will not leave you, Mother."

"Your father will be most unhappy," I replied.

"He knows," Drake said. "I think he was even pleased to find an excuse not to take us to war." That sounded true.

I turned to face the clan mothers, and found them nodding and smiling in agreement. We left within a fortnight, much faster than Morgause had predicted it would be possible to move. Our light wagons could be picked up and physically carried across bad sections of road, if necessary. Furthermore, our horses were easier to move harnessed than running free. Cornu led us, riding the old stallion, and the boys were also mounted, riding guard.

It took us seven days, moving steadily, but without particular hurry, progressing between eight and twelve miles a day, depending on the terrain. Everyone was in high good humor, for the travelers were young and saw the trip as an adventure. We had selected only men and women who were beginning families and wished to become independent of their parents. There were fewer than a hundred couples in all, but enough for our purposes.

I was amused to see Sam and Susan join them as naturally as if they had all grown up together. Susan made no announcement of the new status of her relationship with Sam. Cornu and the boys carefully did not tease them, but Susan spoke to me privately. "You have to get married again, Morgan," Susan confided in me. "It's wonderful!" Funny, I had not found it so.

The buds of spring were visible on the trees, and I was aware that the first responsibility we would face would be to plant fields.

We had ample supplies from Merricks-hold to last until harvest, but from then on we would be dependent on our own efforts.

The fort had not deteriorated since Cornu and I had last visited it; there were no other folk living in the area when we took possession. The walls were still unbroached. The Romans had leveled fields for raising grain to feed troops once stationed at the fort, and we cleared and sowed some two hundred acres with barley and oats even before constructing housing, enough land to provide fifteen bushels of grain for every member of the settlement.

First we built a bridge to cross the dry moat that circled the fort at some twenty feet deep and twenty feet across. Then we brought our wagons within the fort and were sure casual outlaws would not pilfer our stores at night.

Within the fort, only the bathhouses were still sound. The wooden barracks had rotted, and their tile roofs had cracked and blown off in the winds of a hundred years. Those tiles that were still sound we stacked to one side for later use. The broken ones were piled to be ground up as an ingredient for pozzolana, the mortar used by the Romans to cement stones together. We threw all the trash out of the fort, burying it far enough away not to be a nuisance. Working together, we made round wattle and daub grass-thatched huts for each new family, crowding them all within the walls.

The baths became our communal hall where we stored our grain, prepared our food and ate. Grain had to be stored so it stayed dry, and the air tunnels under the bathhouse would ensure that. When we built new granaries, we would have to construct them so.

We met with all the people each evening to discuss plans as they became necessary. I lived there in what Cornu said had been the bath's dry room. He said before winter came we would clean out the space under the floors and rebuild the furnaces and flues that warmed the structure with hot air. I looked forward to it. I was by myself, for Susan and Sam were with the horses, and the boys stayed out in the woods with Cornu, acting as scouts, watching for strangers. I wondered if Boudicca had ever been lonely.

"We must clear out the moat that guards this fort, and make a new gate," Cornu warned us one evening after the crops were planted.

"Who would come against us here?" I asked.

"Men are marching to war," Cornu said in reply. "Men traveling from one place to another have no friends. They will take food where they find it. Let us be sure they do not take ours."

I nodded. It was a serious matter, for we could not replace our stores. The deep ditch that circled the wall held a thicket of mixed second growth, chiefly alder, hazel, birch and laurel, all laced with nettles. I thought it might serve as a natural barrier, but Cornu thought otherwise.

"In fall when this dries out it would be the easiest thing in the world to set it afire and roast everyone in the fort." He was right. I hadn't thought of that.

Working in almost constant rain, we cleaned the ditch and established open country from it to the old woods some three hundred feet in every direction, establishing the same boundaries used by the Romans. I had been concerned that fire arrows might be shot into the fort from the protection of the trees, destroying our thatched huts. Now it would be a powerful archer, indeed, who could menace us.

We had been in occupation three months when Drake rode in one day warning us of approaching mounted men. My people were called to the fort by a Roman bronze war trumpet Cornu had found in the armory at Merricks-hold. I was standing on the wall parapet overlooking our new stout wooden gate when they rode up.

"Who is this who builds on Rhegid lands?" an angry voice demanded, speaking heavily accented British speech.

"Rhegid lands run to the Solway," I said. "These lands are mine!"

"Who speaks?" the man insisted.

"Morgan, daughter of Igraine of Merrick clan," I retorted.

The rider had been wearing a formal masked helmet, but on hearing my words he pulled it off and shouted with joy, "Morgan!"

It was Gawaine! My heart did its foolish thing, leaping about in my breast like a dog off leash. He must have learned to speak British to deal with his wife's people, I thought, for he knew none when we were young.

"Cousin," I called. "Well met!"

"But of course, what else?" he replied, and riding his horse to the gate, he stood in the saddle and leaped, scrambling up the wall to stand beside me.

We'd have to do something about that bridge, I thought, as he caught me up in a bear-hug and kissed me soundly on the mouth. "Have you come to Rhegid to be near me at last?" he asked, teasing.

"Near Rhegid," I responded. "Your mother thought you needed watching. I have had much experience with boys." I nodded to Drake and his brothers ranged below us, looking up, all still on horseback. They had strung their bows and held nocked arrows pointing at Gawaine.

"Is there not some danger they will hit you as well as me?" he asked in mock alarm.

"But little," I said. "I trained them. You had best explain yourself, either in Pictish or in Latin, for they know but little Gaelic and no British. First, let me introduce you."

"Latin? Picts speaking Latin?"

"Cornu taught them," I said. "He said it was a necessity for a gentleman." I was teasing, but Gawaine nodded soberly. It was condescending of him, and I decided not to speak to him in Latin, though it was my father, not Cornu, who held views on Latin being the language of gentlemen. Cornu spoke soldier's Latin, and any polish in the boys' speech had come from me. I decided not to use Latin in front of Gawaine, for we had spoken Gaelic together as children. I said to the boys in Pictish, "This is my close kinsman, son to Morgause. You need have no fear for my safety, though my cousin is a hasty man, as you have seen."

"You are welcome on my land," Gawaine said in Latin, after I had finished.

The boys grinned. This was our land!

"As kinsmen of my cousin you are kinsmen of mine. I will serve you in any way I can, for her sake," and he bowed to them. His Latin was excellent, I decided, but no better than mine.

The boys slacked their bows and moved to one side to watch the gate. At Cornu's bidding it was unbarred to allow Gawaine's riders to enter the fort. Men emerged from the huts to take the horses and lead the men to the hall, but the majority of our people stayed out of sight, by Cornu's orders. Gawaine might be friendly enough, but that was no reason to allow him to count our warriors.

At table I asked Gawaine, "How do you look upon Uther's son, for whom, men say, Brastius Red-beard and Myrddin have claimed the throne?"

"Let my father contest it if he will, in Roman style," Gawaine answered. "It is his grandfather through whom the claim runs. As for me, I am my mother's son, a member of clan Merrick, as much as you are, and holder of lands in Rhegid by marriage, which brings me to the question, what are you doing here?"

"Do your claims run this far, in truth?" I asked, busy eating tender rabbit. This was a change from our usual evening meal of porridge, cheese and bread.

"I claim for the clan all the lands from Carlisle to Merrickshold," he answered.

"So," I reasoned, "as a clan Merrick female I have the right to settle in any part of it I care to, wouldn't you say?"

He was silent for only a moment, watching me closely before grinning and replying, "Aye, I would. I don't know how my wife's father, chief magistrate at Carlisle, will view the matter, but I will stand by you. He claims everything within a day's ride of his town. You may be just beyond his reach."

"Then he's slow indeed, unless he travels with oxen," I said.

Cornu came into the hall and joined us. "I have not seen you since you were King Uther's page, off to visit family for the summer. How do you fare, my lord?" Cornu asked.

"And I remember you best when you lived in a bear cage," Gawaine responded, rising to grasp Cornu's forearms in greeting. "There was something about stealing a horse shortly after you escaped, wasn't there? And now you are shield-bearer to my fierce shield-maiden cousin as you were to her father?"

"I try," Cornu replied. "She is less biddable than her father was."

"You know her well," Gawaine agreed.

I could study Gawaine without having his eyes on me as he stood and talked to Cornu. He had become a tall man, bearing himself without a stoop. Only in standing beside Cornu did he look as slender as he once had.

That night Gawaine slept with his men in the hall, and when he returned to Carlisle I went with him to call on the magistrate there, Gawaine's father-in-law. Of my own people, only Accolon accompanied us. We had skirted Carlisle when we came this way years ago, and I was impressed by its size. It was as big as Exeter, the only other real city I knew. You could see the Roman fort wall which surrounded the inner city, but houses spilled out beyond in random fashion, a burgeoning wealth of people.

The palace had been built around the old Roman baths. I recognized the long arched roof, like a loaf of barley bread. It was comfortably warm, and I realized they must have rebuilt the hypocaust, the underground heating system Cornu had promised to repair for me. I would insist on it! There were paintings on the walls, realistic hunting scenes, in fresh colors, if badly proportioned. I mentioned them.

"My daughter paints," the magistrate said, nodding to the plump, pleasant woman who stood next to Gawaine possessively. Gawaine's father-in-law seemed a bumbling, well-meaning man with a conscious pride in his family. His wife was a simple soul, very like a faded copy of her daughter, Gawaine's wife. On the trip down Gawaine had told me his sons were away, fostering.

"My cousin is the heir to clan Merrick, after my mother," Gawaine said of me in introduction. This seemed confusing to his father-in-law, for power ran down the male line among the Britons.

"My father was Duke Gorlais," I said. "After his death my mother married Uther Pendragon."

This the man could understand, and he insisted on addressing me as princess thereafter.

"My father was a duke, not a king," I objected.

"The daughters of dukes are princesses," he insisted.

We stayed overnight and left in the morning, bidding Gawaine good-bye at the city gate. He looked wistful, and I wondered how happy he was with his plump wife. He had flirted with me politely, something he could no more refrain from with any female not his own than a dog could resist smelling over new acquaintances, and for much the same reason, I would judge. One never knew when an opportunity might present itself for something extra in a new relationship. If I had been his wife, I'd have brought him to an understanding about this type of behavior, but his wife ignored it. Perhaps she was wise.

Pictish men tended to make but indifferent farmers, being more at home in the woods, or at sea in their frail leather boats, than behind the plow. My foster sons and a few of their friends spent much time away from home seeking fish and game, as much for sport, I believed, as for any economic benefit. One good result, however, besides a varied diet, was that strangers seldom entered my country without being detected. The hunters often encountered travelers and brought them to me when they could, knowing how I relished company. Though it happened rarely enough, we eventually heard of most things that occurred in the larger world south of Hadrian's Wall.

It was Gawaine who brought the bard to us to sing of Britain's new High King. Uther's son, Arthur, had been crowned in the city of London at Pentecost. The details of the boy's discovery, as the bard related them, sounded like the kind of thing made up to give legitimacy to an otherwise sketchy claim, I thought. I was amused to hear the bard singing of Arthur's pulling a sword from an anvil mounted on a stone after all other claimants had failed to do so.

I wondered what really had happened, and what Igraine thought of it. She had no other children by Uther, so far as I was aware. I still wondered if the boy had been sired before or after she became Uther's wife. Was he truly Uther's son or perhaps a child sired by my father, Gorlais? I was not the only one who wondered. Gawaine told me his own father, Lot, still referred to Arthur as "Uther's bastard."

I was not surprised to learn that Lot had not accepted Arthur as his sovereign, and subsequently that Lot was collecting followers to march against him. If Lot could depose the usurper, he could realize his ambition and crown himself. Urien allied himself with Lot in the effort, as he had told me he would, but his sons did not, except for Uwayne. It wrenched me every time I thought of Uwayne with his father.

Just when I was hoping to learn of developments, hunters brought word visitors were being escorted to the castle. I waited for them, standing in my favorite place on the wall parapet beside the gate, and saw the expected riders approach from some distance off.

We had our harvest in, a good one, including extra grain to feed new settlers as they came to join us, family by family. We had run out of room inside the fort, and the new families began to build huts in the fields as they cleared them, extending the open land. We were ready for whatever might come.

"It is Father, I am sure of it," Accolon said. "See? He is riding with Cornu." Of the brothers, only Accolon made his home with me and spent as much time with me as he did in the woods.

"I recognize the horse," I replied dryly. I should. I had given it to him. I also noticed the horse was thin, with the look of too many miles ridden on too little food and rest. Urien saw me from a distance and turned to Cornu as if seeking confirmation. I was glad I had thought to wear a colored dress, a new one of hunter green. My only ornament was the crow captive in the fowler's net that hung around my neck, returned by Accolon after his escape from the threat of the Oak King. My hair hung loose today, well brushed and as gleaming as Susan could make it. She stood beside me, watching.

Urien's face was calm when he rode up and said, "Lot has been defeated." It was less than a year since I'd seen him, when I left Gore. Warrior's dress of padded leather became him well.

"By whose hand?" I asked in response to his announcement.

"Some men say the Pict King Pellinore's; others say Arthur's, the new High King of Britain," he answered. "Certain it is that he is defeated. I saw him turn and flee."

"And you did not stay to succor him?" I inquired, though more was implied by the question than the words alone expressed.

"And I fled with the rest," Urien agreed, enlarging on my suggestion. "It is true, then, what men say," Urien remarked, looking up at me still.

"What is that, my lord?" I asked.

"They say you have become the greatest beauty in Britain," he said.

"I own no looking glass," I told him, "and do not see what others see, but in any case I do not believe it. Men see what they will. I am no seductress."

"It is nevertheless true," Cornu said, grinning at me.

"I would sooner believe it if I did not know the speaker," I replied tartly, glaring at him, but failed to quell him, as usual.

"What went wrong between us, Lady?" Urien asked ruefully.

"I do not know," I replied. "I have never known, except that you withdrew your friendship from one who was little more than a girl, and who needed the support of someone strong enough to insist that others accept her."

"I would make it up to you, Lady," he said.

"How?" I asked, glaring at him. "You would erase the memories of lying alone in my bed those years in Gore, aware some slut would smirk at me the next morning knowing where you had spent your night?"

"I have treated you ill, Lady," he said, nodding slowly.

"And for no reason," I agreed. "You may have suspected Lot was my lover. If you had asked, I would have told you I was like a daughter in his house until he got drunk at Beltane and raped me."

"You could have told me," he said.

"Told you what? That I was a violated virgin? What would you have liked to hear?"

"The truth, Lady."

137

"The truth, my lord, is that I liked you well enough once. I might even have come to love you, in time, but that time is long past. However, you and your followers are welcome here for the sake of your sons, and they will see to your comfort. You must remember, though, you are only a guest here and will never be anything else, comparable to my situation in your home in cold Gore. Furthermore, I will not receive you. For now I will go to live with my kin at Carlisle and stay among them while you are here, that I may have nothing more to do with you. Please wait outside until I am able to gather my things to leave." I stepped down from the parapet, leaving him staring at the wall.

Those things I wished to take were packed so quickly that the horses Cornu hitched to the light wagon were not left standing long enough to get cold. Aside from Cornu, only Accolon and a few gillies accompanied me out the gate and through Urien's men. Cornu insisted on taking some of his precious horses with him, herding them from the back of my father's old stallion, so I drove the wagon. Accolon no more knew how to drive a wagon than any other king's son would.

"That was high-handed," Cornu grumbled, when he came up to pace beside me.

"Was it not?" I agreed, glancing at him and grinning. "Many snubs and sleepless nights I suffered in cold Gore were erased by that high-handedness."

"How do you think he feels?" Cornu asked in a low voice, nodding his head toward Accolon, who had ridden ahead.

"He is not happy," I said. "He admires his father, as do all of his sons, but he loves me and well understands I spoke only the truth. For my part, I am not happy, either. Urien is not a bad man, as men go. He is only timid about what others might say."

I found Morgause and Julia waiting for me at Carlisle.

After greeting me, Morgause said, "We learned of Arthur's victory days ago. I would go to see him and offer him allegiance at the request of the clan mothers, but I am unwell. When I recover, I shall go anyway, for I have private things to discuss with him," she said.

"Private things?"

"I met him after the first battle with Lot's forces," she said. "Arthur and I have unfinished business, but it can wait. This cannot."

"If you are suggesting that I go instead, put the thought out of your mind," I warned her. "I am not content merely to hear he is Uther's legitimate son. I must see Igraine before I declare myself either his friend or his enemy. At the least, I will not acknowledge Arthur as my brother until Igraine publicly claims him as her son. So far, Arthur has not sought her out to give her the honor due her." I looked at her more closely. "What is wrong with you?" I asked.

"If I didn't know better, I would say it was morning sickness," she said in a grumpy voice.

"It is," Julia confirmed, her mouth a thin line of disapproval.

"Are you sure?" I asked.

"No, she's not," Morgause said crossly, glaring at Julia, and went back to her argument. "Myrddin told me Arthur was Igraine's child, hidden at Uther's request to keep him from the Oak King," Morgause said. "He acknowledged Arthur as his heir only after his health began to fail."

"Failing health?" I asked, frowning. He had seemed vigorous enough to me when he threw his boot into my face.

"Uther suspected he was being poisoned," she replied, "and feared his heir would not long survive him."

While I was thinking about this Morgause was quiet, but when I looked up she spoke again. "The clan mothers want you to go," she pleaded. "Your old friend Julia will speak for the Mother. You do not have to acknowledge Arthur as king. We just want you to judge what kind of king he is likely to become."

I shook my head. "First I must go to my mother," I replied.

"Well, at least bear Julia company until she reaches Arthur and go on to Tintagel from there, if you must," she urged.

At this, Julia, who had been listening to our dialogue, smiled entreatingly. She was a little plumper than when we were girls, but still dear to me and as pretty and sunny as ever. "Do travel with me," Julia urged. "Gawaine and his brothers will escort us, so we need have no fear from robbers. You will be safer than if you travel alone, and we can talk all the way. I so long to know what you have been doing."

"Tell me first why you are going to Arthur," I demanded, troubled to see her interest so fixed when I didn't know how I felt myself.

"It is said Arthur may not be a Christian," she said. "When Paul the Chain scourged Britain just before the Roman legions were pulled out, he made no distinction between devotees of the Great Mother and the druids who worshiped the Oak King. They say Arthur does not like druids, for some reason or other. Perhaps we can win him to the Mother."

"Where do you expect to find him?" I asked.

"They say he is at Caerleon, near where the Roman legions were stationed. There are barracks there that he is making habitable for his warriors, and the people of the area are used to feeding soldiers. Some clan Merrick warriors joined Arthur when the clan mothers would not make up their minds which side to support. Some of them have returned, strutting and bragging about the victory. We have a few of them with us who will lead us to meet Arthur, and earn us a polite reception."

"I know where this place is," I said. "Myrddin told us about it when we fled from Dimilioc. I will go with you, but I shall not meet Arthur until I have seen my mother, Igraine. I know who Arthur is supposed to be, but only she can tell me if Arthur is Uther's son or my father's. Arthur is either my brother, whom I would love dearly, or he is the son of my father's slayer."

"It may not be that easy for you," Julia sighed. "Either way, he would still be Igraine's son." I knew that was true.

Ah, it was good to be with Gawaine again! The trip was an unfolding of our flight from Dimilioc half a lifetime ago, it seemed. I recognized landmarks, remembering what Myrddin had said about them, and Julia, Gawaine and I made a game of who could recall the most. In this, we appealed to Cornu for judgment, for he had made the trip more than once before. Accolon listened mostly, laughing often. He, of all the boys, was most at ease with Cornu, though Accolon believed, as they all did, that the horns on Cornu's helmet were real, and that he was one of the satyrs who followed the Romans to Britain. The boys claimed his leggings were his own fur, and the sandal straps that appeared to bind them to his legs were there for show. I told him this once, and he laughed with genuine enjoyment, but he never refuted the tale. I believe it pleased him to be thought of in this way.

Whoever or whatever he may have been, Cornu was my friend, and held my trust completely. My only complaint about him was his seemingly unquenchable appetite for nubile girls. He left more progeny in Gore than our stallion did. He drew them to him with his music, for I had never heard his equal on the flute. There were times when I was so lonely I nearly went to him myself; but someone with more need or less fear always reached him first, I think, for his playing always stopped before I could resolve my doubts. I was apprehensive, therefore, when he began to play as we traveled south, but this music was different. He knew all the songs Julia did, and his flute and her voice brought us joy each day.

"You should serve the Mother, as I do," she told him once.

"I do," he replied, and smiled. I knew what he meant, and I gathered Julia did, too, for she cast her eyes down and laughed gently. The Mother was the goddess of fertility, after all.

CHAPTER

VII

When we reached the place where the great Roman roads met, Fosse Way and Watling Street, we camped for a bit to get information about Arthur's whereabouts. I feared we would hear from travelers that Arthur and his court were in London, but folk said that Arthur was building a great castle on the Usk River, not far from Caerleon. I did not wish Julia to seek Arthur until we knew for sure where he was to be found.

Perhaps the Great Mother did take an interest in her priestesses, for someone granted Julia's wish to have me beside her when she met Arthur. A procession came to the crossroads from the west, armed men escorting someone in a sedan chair. They stopped to exchange tidings, and a woman left the chair to join us. She was thin, dressed all in black, and wore a nun's habit. I did not know her until she spoke. Ah, Lud! Her glorious hair was gone, but it was Igraine.

"Mother?" I asked, feeling ridiculously young again.

"Oh, Morgan, my child!" she cried and ran up to hug me fiercely. "Oh, I have missed you so!" She released me to look up at me. I was the taller by a hand.

"What happened to your hair?" I asked stupidly. I had a clear recollection of it tumbling down her back as she whirled on Uther in her bedroom the night he threw the shoe at me.

"It's gone like my other vanities, I hope," she said gently.

"But it was beautiful!" I exclaimed.

"It were better had I been bald," she replied, shaking her head. "I have thought so often of your last words to me. 'You'll be sorry!' you said. Do you remember?"

"I didn't mean to curse you!" I said.

"Oh, I know, child. It's just that you said it with such conviction I came to believe it. So, I think, did Uther."

Igraine's greeting to Julia was no less affectionate than to me. Julia was the daughter of Igraine's younger sister and had been Igraine's favorite lady-in-waiting when she lived with my father. She was too pretty as a girl to expose to Uther's roving eye, so my mother had sent her to New Avalon with me.

I drew them into the pavilion that had been erected for me, and sat Igraine down on the couch-bed, taking a stool at her feet beside Julia. Susan brought us wine and little cakes, looking at Igraine with frank curiosity. My mother smiled at her, but did not speak. Her treatment of persons she saw as servants had not changed, at least.

"You are so thin! Have you been sick, Mother?" I asked, and the depth of my concern surprised me. My feelings for my mother had deeper roots than I had supposed.

"Sick? At heart, perhaps, for many years. Too late I regretted what I had done to your father. Yes. I was sorry, but it was not your doing. You must not think that."

I didn't know what to say. There was a priest with her, riding a mule, a thin man, like almost all priests I had ever seen. I wondered if they were required to fast. "That is not Father John-Martin," I said doubtfully.

"Oh, no! You will not have heard this, and I know it will grieve you," she said, "but soon after he returned from escorting you to Dimilioc, Brother James was found hanging from the rope that rings the great bell in the chapel tower. It was odd, for the clapper had been removed, perhaps so no one would be alarmed by the noise and discover him earlier. His hands had been bound, so he was quite deliberately killed. Nothing but the bell clapper was

143

missing; there had been no robbery. Father John-Martin was with Mark at Dimilioc, serving him as the new King of Cornwall as he had served your father. He was so shocked when he heard of Brother James' death that he went back to his people in Ireland." She shook her head sadly. "We buried Brother James in the church-yard in Tintagel. We will say a prayer for his soul together, if you like."

"I think not," I said gently. "I haven't had the habit of Christian prayer for many years." She looked distressed, so I added lamely, "If you would say prayers for anyone, you might remember your daughter."

"You are always in my prayers," she said. "I will now pray you will return to the Faith, although I do not believe in your heart you have truly left."

"I was never truly a communicant," I said, and bit my lip, remembering it was my mother's resistance to Christianity that kept me out of the church when I was a child. Left to myself, I would have joined quickly enough, if only to please my father.

My mother read my face again. "Do you remember your father calling out to you to pray for him as he rode off to Dimilioc?" she asked.

I nodded grimly. "I did, while he was alive," I said.

"He will need your prayers all the more now," she urged gently, but I shook my head and changed the subject as Accolon entered.

"This is my son, Accolon," I told her.

She rose and embraced him, then held him at arm's length to see him better. "A son as old as this? However did you manage it? You, yourself, are not yet thirty!"

Julia laughed, watching the two of us together.

"Accolon is fourteen and the son of my heart, not my body," I said gravely as the boy flushed with pleasure. "I am not nearly thirty, as you suggest, but merely twenty-seven," I added, with mock severity. "The son my husband, Urien, and I had together is nine and still with his father. He is in the training all boys among the Picts undergo, after which he will join me," I said, though I feared that wasn't true.

"Forgive me," my mother said. "I do remember how vast the distance between twenty-seven and thirty seems when you're only twenty-seven. I confess, they both appear impossibly young to me now!"

"All of my father's sons, of which I am the youngest, have followed my mother to settle lands in Rhegid," Accolon said. "Our lands in Gore are cold and barren, and other Picts may take them up if they wish."

"Lot's sons have done the same," I said. "They are expanding the clan lands south from Merricks-hold. Gawaine is married into the leading family in Carlisle, and has children of his own. My sons may marry there or into clan Merrick so Rhegid will be united."

"You have been fortunate," she said, carefully not asking about Urien.

"Yes," I said, "but I am not the only one with sons, I hear. Morgause tells me this new High King, Arthur, is the son of Uther, and hardly older than Accolon. How can this be?"

"You must know I had a son by Uther after you left. Uther sent the child away, and things were never the same between us after that. I believe Arthur is the child stolen from my side, though I have never seen him," Igraine said. "He was conceived the night Uther came to Tintagel and you walked in on us. My marriage to Uther made him legitimate." She was blushing and looked embarrassed. I thought it odd that such an old scandal would still move her.

"How can you know it was not my father?" I asked bluntly.

"You may remember, I tried to tell you at the time that your father and I were becoming as comfortable together as brother and sister. That, though it suited him, did not suit me. My affair with Uther was an attempt to interest Gorlais in me again. It didn't work. I had not slept with your father in months before Beltane. Father John-Martin had convinced your father to follow the way of Christ and to be celibate. He kept referring to Brother James, who was even younger than your father, as an example to follow. I confess, I never liked that Brother James, and I promise you, I

145

shed no tears on hearing of his death. I know it was sinful of me," she mused. "That's why I pray for him now. It's a penance."

"So, Arthur is Uther's, then!" I said. "Does Arthur know about me?"

"I don't know that he knows about me," Igraine said. "It was only as Uther lay dying that he called his advisors together and swore them to secrecy, making them pledge to crown Arthur, his only legitimate son, as soon as it was feasible."

"Of what did Uther die?" I asked, for I was still curious.

"Who knows? The druids say it was because he owed them a life. After ruling eight years, a British king has two choices: to lie on the stone and be sacrificed so the seers can foretell the fate of the people in the writhings of his death agony, or to provide a son to go in his place. Something went awry, I know not what, but neither happened for Uther. The druids said the Oak King took his health and then his life in punishment."

"What do you think?" I asked.

"I think he was poisoned."

"And whose hand held the flask?" I asked. If it were a kinsman, my responsibility for seeking a payment for my father's death was over.

"I know not," she said, "but I assume it was those same druids. I spent my time among Christians, and no one spoke of it to me."

I considered this. It was not enough. I could not be content to know druids had discharged the blood debt I owed for my father. I would have to find some way to do it myself. It had not been on my mind for years, but seeing my mother had made it real again to me.

I spoke of the matter to Cornu after my mother had retired for the night. "My mother says Brother James was found hanging from the church bell at Tintagel after he returned from Dimilioc," I said sternly.

"Can that be?" Cornu responded mildly. He did not say it in wonder.

"Apparently so. Did you have anything to do with it?" I asked bluntly. Cornu and I tell each other the truth, always.

He sighed. "Yes, Lady," he admitted, not looking up from his task, braiding a rope from thongs of leather.

"Could you not have told me?" I asked, watching him.

"To what purpose?" he responded, as if surprised.

"I had marked him for my own," I said.

"I was in your father's service, Lady," he said gravely. "I heard the tale of his betrayal of your father, or enough to guess the rest, from the guards Brastius assigned me. The priest knew of your secret way of escaping the castle with Gawaine when you were children, and he told Brastius to expect you to lead us out that way. That's why there were so many armed men waiting for us, more than a mere sentry's guard. For that it seemed good to me that Brother James not wait for justice."

"It was him and not Father John-Martin?"

"Yes."

I considered the matter. "I do not fault the deed," I said somewhat crossly. "I only wish I had known."

"Knowing does not seem to make you happy," Cornu observed. "Perhaps you would have been less happy if you had known it earlier."

It does no good to argue with Cornu. "Why did you take the bell clapper?" I asked.

"I kept it to give it to you, should you ever seek proof," he said. He bent over one of his saddlebags and pulled out a long, rough bar of black iron, pierced at one end and knobbed on the other. He gave it to me, and I found it weighed less than two pounds and was about as long as my forearm. It would make a most useful weapon in a tavern brawl.

"It's not very big," I said, for want of anything else to say.

"It wasn't a very big bell. You may remember it was only a chapel, not a church."

I leaned over and hugged him. "Thank you, Cornu," I said, and left to think about it. Would Boudicca have done it that way?

We broke camp after my mother had rested a day or two and went straight for Caerleon, down the old Roman road that connected it to London. We could see it from miles away, rising from a low hill over the River Usk.

"He calls it Camelot," my mother told me as I rode sedately beside her sedan chair.

Camelot was even more imposing close up. The gatehouse and tower were of coursed stone, and a Roman arch had been built framing stout oak doors, studded with iron. A single tower, twenty feet high, loomed over the gate, and men watched us from the second floor as we rode up. A scaffold surrounded the tower, and workmen were adding to its height even as I watched. I saw Myrddin among them, standing beside a fair-haired, beardless youth, who looked for all the world like Uther. I guessed it was Arthur. I waved to Myrddin, and he leaned over to see me better.

"Greetings!" I called. "It is Morgan, come with Igraine to see Arthur!" Myrddin waved and spoke to the youth, who waved somewhat hesitantly as we passed under the portal.

People swarmed to help us alight. Igraine had barely arranged her shawl so that it fell over her shoulders instead of her short-cropped but still glorious hair, when Myrddin led the youth up to us. Arthur stopped a few paces away and looked at Igraine intensely, glancing once at me with a half-smile, but turning back to Igraine.

"I remember you," he said. "I know I was supposed to be too young, but I know you. You look just as I remembered!" and he smiled a blinding smile and held out his arms to Igraine, rushing to embrace her. Igraine, nearly as tall as he, hugged him back with desperate strength, crooning words but half audible to me. He nodded his head again and again as if he heard and understood her. Finally he stood back, still smiling, and told her, "Welcome, Mother. Welcome to Camelot!"

Igraine was weeping, but so happy she could only nod in reply, reaching for him to hug again. Finally she turned him to me and said, "This is my daughter, Morgan, your sister, whom I love dearly and wish you to love in turn."

Arthur released Igraine and came to embrace me courteously. "I have heard the name of Morgan on the lips of men who speak of fair maids since I can first remember anything," he said. "You must stay to grace our court."

"I am better at patching up small boys or birthing foals than making curtsies, brother," I said. "If you need help of that sort I would be happy to be of use to you. And I would have you welcome my son Accolon, who would fight at your side, if you let him."

"A sister's son! I didn't know! Myrddin, you didn't tell me," he complained, glancing at the tall man who had joined us. Arthur clasped forearms with Accolon. "It is an unlooked-for happiness to meet a new kinsman, Accolon. I bid you welcome!" Arthur was little older than Accolon, but his assurance was such that Accolon could only smile back and nod foolishly.

"Greetings again, Myrddin," I said, to remove Accolon from the embarrassment of attention. "Most happy am I to see you here," I said.

"And I you," Myrddin answered. "I hear you have become a healer. I am not surprised. We must find time to talk of this, and other things." He then turned to Igraine. "I must ask your forgiveness, Lady, for a wrong I was constrained to do you when you were too weak to understand the necessity. I hope meeting your son to some extent mitigates the deed."

"Weak?" Igraine started softly enough, though her face was set in stern lines. "I was not even awake! Had I not been in drugged sleep I would have fought you to keep the child! What you did was wrong! I will never forget it was you who took my baby from my side." She was almost panting with agitation and took a moment to contain herself, putting a hand over her eyes and bowing her head. "But I must forgive you," she continued in a calmer voice. "My spiritual teacher has impressed upon me that my hope of salvation lies in that, but I do not forget!" and she looked at him sadly for a moment. Myrddin hung his head, acknowledging his guilt, and I felt shame and grief flow from him as if the act were but newly done. It was hard to be the guardian of a king.

"Kay, this is my mother and my sister, Morgan," Arthur said

149

to the tall, thin, sour-faced man who had come up silently to join us. "Kay is my foster-brother, and seneschal of all my lands," Arthur said in introduction. "Please have rooms set aside for them, as close to mine as possible," he instructed the man.

Kay bowed, but I got the impression he strongly disapproved. Arthur colored up and glared at him until Kay almost smirked, altering his face only slightly, but enough to see. He bowed again and left, without speaking.

"Do not mind him," Arthur said to us, visibly annoyed as he led us into the courtyard and then to a reception hall, where he seated us. Pages scurried around unbidden to serve us refreshments. "He always called me Arthur the Bastard when we were boys. He knew I was Uther's son, but did not know who my mother was. If he shows you any discourtesy, tell me, and I'll have it stopped."

"Why do you keep him near you?" I asked, looking around and comparing Camelot to my own holding. I would have to add painted walls, I decided, for these were much like Gawaine's, only more magnificent.

"I can watch him better," Arthur said grimly, "and besides," he added shamefacedly, "I promised his father."

After we had eaten, Igraine went to rest, with women from Arthur's retinue leading her away, making much of her. Arthur showed me around, after I told him of my interest.

"I am rebuilding an old Roman fort," I told him.

"I thought of that," he said, "but decided to use stone from Caerleon, and rebuild in a different spot. This is a better site than they chose, more easily defended. I don't understand why they wanted to build on low ground."

From the tower we could see over the valley, including where the Romans had their fort. Wagons were coming from the site, hauling stone to Camelot to continue the replacement of the wooden palisade with masonry. "Perhaps the Romans had no fear of enemies," I said. "Their wharves were next to the fort for easy access. They must have felt their numbers and discipline were enough to protect them."

Arthur nodded gloomily. I imagined he found disciplining Gaels and Britons a thankless task.

"Look," he said, pointing to a drawing spread out on the table. "I want to build a great feasting hall for my knights. It will be round, and open to the sky except where people sit. Do you see?"

I did indeed. It looked like a Roman colonnade over a circular walk. "How many men do you want to sit at table at one time?" I asked.

"It will be big enough for a hundred and fifty, if I allow two feet for each man," he replied. "It will have to be some thirty Roman paces wide to allow room for wenches to bring food and drink around."

"I don't like to sit that close to people when I'm eating," I said.

"Perhaps you're right," he said, "but I don't expect to have that many at every meal. Most of them will be out questing."

"Questing?"

"Looking for adventure," he explained.

"Lud's balls!" I muttered to myself.

Over the next few days, Arthur spent time with Igraine and me. Nithe, Myrddin's ward, whom I had met on the flight from Dimilioc so many years ago, was here, still with Myrddin. She often joined Igraine and me when Arthur was with us. She told us she had been with Myrddin when Arthur was taken from Tintagel and had known him all his childhood. Igraine held Arthur's hand as she questioned Nithe closely about his boyhood days. Arthur laughed to hear tales of his youth, particularly of how naughty a boy he had been. I could see Nithe loved him, and had taken the place of his mother, young as she must have been. I thought it eased Igraine's mind to learn Arthur had been loved as a baby.

I sought out Nithe while Igraine rested each afternoon. Igraine seemed uncommonly frail to me, but would not complain of any physical problems when I asked her.

"I thought to see you married and bossing children, by now," I told Nithe.

"I thought so, too," she confided. "I am managing my love life but poorly." She told me of Pelleas, one of Uther's bastard sons who had been as much a father to Arthur as Myrddin had been, particularly when Myrddin was absent on long, mysterious journeys. Pelleas had been apprenticed to Myrddin and had become a smith, as Arthur had become a king. Myrddin was a master smith, the best in Britain, she said, as well as a kingmaker. Of the two, he was rather prouder of his work at the forge, she thought. Pelleas was now smith to Arthur, and she promised to take us to meet him.

"You must not call me by name, Nithe," I said, "for I will ask him to change the nature of an object that would cause me grief should it be traced to me. If he knows not who I am, he will not make the connection."

"A mystery?" Nithe exclaimed, "Will you tell me? I have claimed you for kin, and you can trust me!"

"It is not my secret alone, but I will say that this is the clapper from a bell that once hung in my father's chapel. At the time it was taken from its place, a wicked man was hanged from the bell pull-rope, a man who had betrayed my father. I can say no more without endangering others, as well as myself." She nodded, looking thoughtful, and I wondered if she might have heard something of the matter. I did not fear discovery at her hands, however. She was, as she said, kin.

The next morning early I stole away with Nithe to meet her friend Pelleas. It was chill. The leaves had begun to turn from green to the reds and yellows of autumn. Nithe looked uncommonly pretty, for the weather had brought color to her cheeks, and she seemed happy. We found Pelleas at his forge outside of the castle walls, on the bank of the Usk, wearing only trousers and boots, despite the frosty morning. I was astounded at my first sight of him, for I had never seen so large a man, not only tall, but muscled. Sweat ran down his bare chest from the effort of hammering red iron on his anvil. He stopped when he saw us, thrust the cooling bar back into the coals of the forge, and wiped his hands on a linen rag before coming out to us.

"It is good to see you, Nithe," he said, and I could tell from the feeling that flowed from him that, indeed, Nithe held his heart. She knew it, too, of course, for she was one like me, who could judge feelings.

"You work too hard," she told him. "You should spend more time of an evening with us in Arthur's quarters."

"With the exception of you and Arthur and Myrddin, I do not like the company," he said. "Arthur's cousins from Armorica are rude and overbearing."

"They will not hurt you," she said.

He snorted and said, "No, that they will not!" This seemed to be a disagreement of long standing between them, for some of the joy went out of her.

"I asked Nithe to bring me to you for a boon," I said to him.

"Forgive me," Nithe said. "This is my friend, Lady Corbie." I smiled to hear my father's old pet name, amazed that she should have remembered my telling her that so many years ago.

"I give you welcome, Lady," he said civilly, and smiled, a smile of singular sweetness.

I could feel Nithe catch her breath to see it. I wondered what manner of relationship it was between these two people.

"You have only to name the service, Lady," he continued.

I gave him the bell clapper. "Could you make two knives of this piece of metal? I would change it from its present shape, for it could be used to incriminate a good man who practiced rough justice on one who wronged me once. I would have a knife of my own, to remind me that the gods will not be mocked, and one for him in thanks."

Pelleas looked at it, and nodded. "Come by tomorrow about this time, and they will be ready for you. Bring Nithe," he added in a teasing voice. "The only time I see her is when she is doing errands for someone else."

Nithe was busy the next day, so I went at the appointed time bringing Cornu instead, and the knives were ready as Pelleas had promised.

"I am sorry that Arthur would not let Nithe come," I said. "Is there some barrier that prevents your speaking plainly to her of your feelings?" I have found that much time is saved when people come to the point.

"I am a Pict, Lady, and she is foster-sister to the High King."

"And you are his blood brother, I am told," I retorted.

"You do not understand, perhaps. It would not do for the king's sister to marry a Pict."

"My sons are Picts," I said. "I was contracted in marriage to King Urien."

"I apologize," Pelleas said. "I know Urien. He fought well, saving Lot's soldiers from total annihilation in the last battle against Arthur."

"You were there? You saw Lot flee?"

"No, I was in a different part of the battle, but the man who defeated Lot was also a Pict, King Pellinore. He has sworn to kill Lot next time."

"I would be in his debt," I said. "Lot is my enemy."

"I will tell Pellinore so," Pelleas said. "He would do much to serve a lady of such beauty as yours." And he smiled again.

I understood something of what attracted Nithe to him so strongly.

After we left, Cornu said, "I have never seen a Geen before." He was inspecting his knife. Mine was more delicately shaped than Cornu's, but both had a clean, simple look that gave them beauty beyond mere utility. Wavy lines shimmered down the blades, and Cornu said some of the iron had been smelted with charcoal and turned to steel, and some left as mild iron. The two had been beaten together while white hot, and the result was a layered metal that allowed a thinness, flexibility and strength beyond what other smiths could make. Pelleas was as good as Myrddin, Cornu told me.

I remembered the dog the boys called Geen because of its size and understood the name better. I also wondered, if things did not work out between Nithe and Pelleas, perhaps they could work out between Pelleas and me. I was more attracted to him than to any other man in a long time!

Cornu was smirking. He always smirked when he thought he knew something I didn't, but long since I learned not to ask what it was, for he always pretends there is nothing to know. Nevertheless, I wondered what it was this time.

CHAPTER

VIII

Morgan, the most frightful thing has happened," Igraine said to me, shaking me awake from a deep, delicious sleep.

"Could it not wait another half hour?" I complained like a child, but I was already rising as I spoke. I smiled to think I had responded so. It must have been the sound of her voice, like a summons from the past, that did it. I had little time to rest in my life at any time, and had been up with a foaling mare most of the last night.

My mother was sitting on the chair by my bed, already dressed. "I have just learned that Arthur and Morgause had an affair," she confided in a near whisper. Susan slept on a pallet in my room, and Igraine did not wish to wake her. The kittens, hearing voices, came bounding out from their basket, rubbing up against Igraine's legs, and leaping on me and Susan in hopes of breakfast.

Igraine laughed briefly, apologized to Susan, and continued in a more normal voice, "They were inseparable for days, as well as nights, I fear. I must get back to my chapel where I can pray for them."

Even sleepy as I was, I understood that. "Morgause is his aunt," I said. "Surely he knew!" One of the kittens, a half-grown male, hindered me as I attempted to lace my sandals. He growled fiercely, biting the leather thongs.

"Apparently not," Igraine said, not distracted as I was by the small creature. "He does now. Whatever was Morgause thinking of?"

"She is not a Christian like Arthur," I said, trying to pay attention. "She wouldn't think anything of it. You know sexual relations are casual among the Scoti," I added, and immediately regretted it, remembering Igraine's affair with Uther.

"I know that! I am as much Scoti as you are," she said in an exasperated voice. "Don't you know? Morgause is pregnant by Arthur! Incest is the gravest kind of sin, and my son's soul is at risk. I have to pray for forgiveness for him, for he is merely embarrassed; he does not see the need. I fear he is but an indifferent Christian at best, but that will not excuse him in the eyes of God. I can't pray here! There is no proper place for it. I need quiet for concentration. I must go home right now."

I might have pointed out I was no more Christian than Morgause, but forbore to bring up the matter. Igraine knew it. She needed support now, not resistance. "I will go with you," I told her.

"No, no. I have spoken to Myrddin. He will escort me. He needs to be of service to ease his own conscience. And Julia has asked to travel with me. It will be like old times," she said, smiling. "It is better so," she added gently. "You go to Morgause. She is at New Avalon and will need your skill with delivery of this new baby. Imagine, at her age!"

I spoke to Myrddin before they departed. "It should be my place at her side," I objected to him.

"I cannot stay here just now," Myrddin said. "Arthur is angry with me because I object to his plans for marriage. He is much too young, but Kay has convinced him he will not be acknowledged as rightful king until he has a tie with one of the lines of royalty recognized by Rome."

"Is it true?" I asked.

"Who can say? It has driven a wedge between us for now, however."

Igraine, Myrddin, Julia and their guards left within the hour, and it was with mixed emotions that I watched the little party ride away from Camelot. My mother was in her sedan chair and looked even more frail than when we had arrived, despite resting for several weeks in Camelot. She and I had become closer in the short time we had been together. I regretted not being able to be with her longer, but she was very clear about not needing me.

I sought out Arthur, finding him in the tower room studying his construction drawings.

"Why were you not there to say good-bye to our mother?" I asked him bluntly.

"We'd said good-bye," he replied sadly. "I watched her leave from the window. She never even glanced back."

"She seems driven," I admitted. "Is it true about Morgause?"

Arthur looked embarrassed. "Nothing happened between us that needs praying over," he muttered, but did not meet my eye.

I left it so. In truth, I hoped Arthur's lack of concern might mean his commitment to Christianity was not as devout as it might have been. With Julia gone, it was up to me to win him to the Mother's cause, if I could.

Nithe had ridden out with Myrddin and Igraine but was back within ten days, tight-lipped. Myrddin had ordered her to return, bearing tidings he himself felt unable to carry: Igraine was dead. "The journey was a trial to her from the start," Nithe told me. "By the time we reached Fosse Way, where the going was easier, she was seriously ill but refused to rest, insisting on spending hours on her knees in prayer each night. She died three days ago, and Myrddin determined to escort her body to Tintagel for burial."

I did not weep. Igraine had not wept for me.

Together Nithe and I sought out Arthur, and Nithe gave him the message Myrddin had charged her with. Arthur took my hand and led me to a bench against the wall, under a narrow window where he sometimes watched the boats come up the river from the sea. "This has been hard on you, has it not?" he said.

"I do not know how to take her death," I admitted. "I am not sure about how I felt about her alive."

Arthur nodded. "Myrddin told me she had chosen the maiden

158

aspect of the Great Mother at her initiation into the mysteries. He said such women are more attached to the men in their lives than to their children."

"That may have been why she was as she was," I agreed, "but it doesn't account for me. I chose the mother aspect."

It was from Nithe, later, that I learned Arthur was a Christian out of policy rather than conviction. "Druids in training cannot be required to serve as warriors," she said. "The same is true of Christians studying to be priests, but few Britons are attracted to the priesthood. It is less of a threat to Arthur's need for an army of fighting men than druidry."

"I have not seen Arthur show personal interest in any religion," I said.

"He says he is a Pelagian Christian," Nithe replied. "Pelagius was a Briton who claimed men could win to God without priestly help, through good works. Priests from Rome still insist that salvation can be found only through God's grace, but Myrddin encouraged Arthur to adhere to the teachings of Pelagius."

"What good works does Arthur intend?" I asked.

"He is creating a brotherhood of warriors who pledge themselves to do good. When hostages have come to Camelot from kings Arthur has defeated in battle, as custom dictates, they are allowed to join the brotherhood, becoming peers instead of prisoners."

"He spoke of building a feasting hall," I said.

"Yes, a round one. His brotherhood is called the Fellowship of the Round Table," Nithe said.

"The hostages do not try to escape?" I asked.

"They pledge their words not to do so, and it binds them as effectively as iron fetters," Nithe said. "They are grateful, of course, for this treatment is not expected."

"I see. He may be wiser than he seems."

"I was surprised," Nithe responded. "I watched him grow up and saw no indication that he was as long-headed as this. Perhaps Myrddin put the idea in his mind."

Among the young men who attached themselves to Arthur, either as hostages or kinsmen, were two young sons of a noble from the south who became friends with Accolon. They were but boys, barely older than Accolon, but tall and fair and handsome. Where the older brother, Guy, was amusing, singing all the time and playing a lute to accompany himself, the younger, Jerome, was quiet almost to shyness. I was surprised, therefore, when Accolon informed me that Jerome wanted to make me his lady.

"I'm old enough to be his mother," I said, amused. "I would not have a liaison with a child!"

"It's not that!" Accolon said, blushing. "True knights need a lady to whom they can dedicate their deeds, bringing her honor."

"It's a new notion that Arthur's cousin, Lancelot, brought to us from Armorica," Nithe explained when I looked perplexed. "The relationship is supposed to be chaste and ceremonial."

"Do you have such a devotee?" I asked Nithe, arching an eyebrow.

"Didn't you know? Your son Accolon swore to be my true love only yesterday. He said he couldn't pledge himself to his mother without looking odd, so I received the honor. He thinks Jerome can be trusted to observe the proprieties, so he is allowing him to serve you, if you will accept his devotion. Better him than someone about whom there would be gossip."

Susan giggled, earning a scowl from Accolon.

"Gossip? Has there been gossip about me?" I asked.

"Well, Gawaine is more openly friendly than is seemly," Nithe said in a deceptively cheerful voice. She could be wicked sometimes.

It was my turn to blush. "We are kinsmen," I said, "nothing more."

"Of course," Nithe responded in an airy way that earned another giggle from Susan.

I ignored her. "You think there is no harm in allowing young swains to make ballads about us, or whatever it is they wish to do?"

Accolon looked from me to Nithe, as interested in her reply as I was.

"No harm at all. These are romantic boys. Perhaps it is better if they fix their affections on ladies of advanced age, like us, who cannot possibly reciprocate their feelings, than for them to chase tavern maids."

She had a point, though I winced at the words "advanced age"! Accolon left us to seek out Jerome, and together they went to Cornu for help. Cornu slyly taught them some of his more salacious ballads. He changed the words so they were acceptable, but still recognizable to Nithe and me, who had heard them many times. Nithe could barely keep countenance as the boys' young voices serenaded us at night. All in all, I was happy when I was summoned to New Avalon to attend Morgause, and could leave this silliness behind.

Morgause looked wonderful. She was over forty, though how much over I did not know. Gawaine, her oldest son, was twenty-nine. Morgause once said she had married soon after puberty, and was pregnant almost immediately following marriage. There was no mystery there. The clan mothers were not fools. If Morgause had not married as soon as she was able to bear children, she'd have had bastards one after another. In royal houses that was not good. Intrigue gathers around royal bastards like dogs around a bitch in heat. This one would be no exception.

The birth was not easy, and Morgause showed little interest in her baby, another boy. Perhaps if it had been a girl this time it would have been different. Morgause named him Mordred, an ugly name I thought, and a colicky, fretful thing he was. He whimpered for what seemed to be most of the time he was awake, and slept but little for a newborn. I didn't take to him myself, and I like boys, generally.

Morgause caught childbed fever the second day after delivery, and we found a wet-nurse for Mordred, a woman who had recently lost a baby of her own. She took Mordred home with her so Morgause would not be made restless by his constant fussing.

By the fifth day, Morgause was delirious. The Great Mother's priestesses nursed her carefully and compassionately, but would have lost her had I not taken over and driven them out of the sickroom. I opened the windows to air the place out, took the covers off her bed and bathed her with cool water to bring the fever down. I dosed her with an infusion of willow bark, a specific for this condition in dogs, at least, and it worked, as I was not surprised to find. I packed her vagina with moldy bread, both to stop the bleeding and to fight the infection, and that, too, worked. The sisters were scandalized, for they had pronounced her beyond any hope but prayer.

When Morgause was well enough to receive visitors, I returned her to the care of the priestesses and retired to my own room to rest. I had not seen much of it in a fortnight. Morgause told me later that the women had accused me of practicing witchcraft in curing her. She then asked me what in the world I had done, and why. She was satisfied with my answers to the point that she made me promise to come to her if ever she was so foolish as to become pregnant again.

Hilda was pretty short with the priestesses, all young women with little experience and consequently prone to depend too much on rules rather than judgment. On learning what had transpired, Hilda questioned me closely on the methods I had used. She then made them standard practice, thanking me publicly both for saving Morgause and for teaching how to save other women in like distress. The young priestesses tended to be sullen around me thereafter, but not insolent. I had hoped to make friends here of women my own age, but in this it seemed I was not to be successful.

Most of the time during the next months I spent with the animals, for I preferred to work with them rather than people anyway. I had found animals were grateful for anything you could do to ease their pain, and did not question motive. Occasionally one would try to snap or scratch from panic, but I filled their minds with calm feelings and avoided injury.

One of our young stallions was docile to the point of timidity, and proved to be just the sire for the hill pony mares owned in the community. Peasants lived with their animals, and a bad-tempered bull or stallion was too dangerous to keep. This one covered every mare within a ten-mile radius, except for my own breeding stock under Cornu's care. He threw large, placid foals in the spring that were welcomed, loved, worked like members of the family and fed considerably better than family during lean times.

Maybe the long nights beginning in early fall were responsible, but there were also a number of newborn children among the peasant folk who lived around New Avalon. I was kept busy between foaling colts and midwifing, with help from Cornu on difficult cases. Perhaps it was the large crop of babies that attracted the druids, who came one night, stole a number of them and disappeared into the woods before an alarm was raised.

Accolon, who had accompanied me and Cornu to New Avalon, brought me the tidings while it was still dark. "Mordred has been taken, along with the other babies," he said. "I will lead a group to track the raiders to find where they have taken them. They were seen. They were druids!"

I knew what that meant. Druids would cut open living children to read the fates in their writhing agony upon the altar stone. They even burned children to appease their gods. Being celibate themselves, druids had to steal children, buy them from their parents, or intimidate whole communities into furnishing them for the dread rituals. Those who followed the Mother deplored the practice of child sacrifice and resisted it whenever possible. It was the most serious breach between the Mother's people and the druids, and one seemingly impossible to mend.

I worried about Morgause, who had already been feeling guilty about the little time she had given to her child anyway. She was sure to see the raid as a punishment from the gods. When I went to visit her she was crying fitfully.

"It's my fault, a judgment on me," she said, looking very pretty wrapped in a green plaid with dark blue stripes. She had lost flesh when she had the fever, but appeared willing to gain much of it back, judging from the remains of the meal I found in her room.

"The Mother does not make children suffer to punish their parents," I said. "Surely, you know that!"

"It's the druids," she wailed.

"Since when have you been answerable to druids?" I asked. "Be sensible!"

"What can we do?"

"Accolon was trained by the Pictish hunters. He can see at night as other Picts do. He will follow the trail they leave until he finds where they have gone. Then we will go after them." I promised grimly. I looked at the folk assembled. There were a large number of young women, all of the mothers who had lost children, I thought, along with their sisters and friends. I saw a few men, older and bearing the marks of service in the wars of one or another petty king. A number of these old veterans without families had come to serve the Great Mother in the few capacities allowed men. They carried shields, spears and swords and appeared determined to accompany us.

There was no virtue in making preparations before it was time for them to be carried out, so I thought to wait until dawn to assemble a group for battle. I suggested that the women and old men go home to rest and return at dawn, but they refused, lying down outside the gate wrapped in their plaids. A cold drizzle made the situation even more miserable.

Cornu and I chose geldings for our party, for mares were too valuable to risk in battle and stallions too temperamental. The exception was the old stallion Cornu insisted on riding, my father's old war-horse.

When I could think of nothing else to do, I went to my post over the gate and watched for Accolon. When I saw him coming from a distance, I woke our people and drew them up for review. Everyone had a packet of food tied behind the folded plaid he sat on to spare his horse's back. The plaids were handy in other ways. Not only did we commonly sleep rolled up in them at night, but we would bury our dead in them at need.

Our veterans were ready, and the women, some two dozen who had elected to go with us, were armed with fighting sticks and knives. Cornu had banded their staves with iron and inserted short iron spikes in the ends to give them a formidable appearance, like little spears. I wasn't sure how useful that would be, and feared it might slow the stick work, but Cornu told me it was as much for looks as anything, and the women liked them. I said nothing of my doubts. Indeed, I carried one myself.

When Accolon rode in, he came straight to me, and the folk gathered around to listen. "The druids have taken the children to Caerleon, the town that is springing up on the site of the old Roman camp near Camelot," he said. "We have left watchers to track them if they leave, but I do not believe they will. There seems to be some feast in preparation at Camelot itself, and we think perhaps the children will be sacrificed then."

"Not if we arrive in time," I vowed. "Eat, rest and follow us, please, as soon as you can. Bring Morgause with you. We may have to use her to appeal to Arthur."

He nodded and rode off.

"We ride to Camelot to see the king," I told my people so everyone could hear, then raised my staff in signal before setting my horse to a quick trot. We would be in the saddle all day, and I wished neither to ruin the horses by forcing them to strain, nor to spend much time resting. These horses could trot forever, I thought.

We raised Camelot at first dusk. I left the others under Cornu's command some two hundred yards from the gate, while I rode in by myself. I was challenged as I came up, but announced myself as the High King's sister to gain quick admission. Indeed, Arthur had seen us arrive and came down to greet me, along with Nithe.

"You have come to my wedding," Arthur said joyfully, reaching out his arms to help me dismount and giving me a big hug on my way to the ground.

I laughed despite myself and pushed free only to be hugged by Nithe in turn. "Desist!" I pleaded. "I have a problem that can't wait. The druids have stolen babies from New Avalon and taken them to Caerleon. We fear they may be killed. Would the druids seek to do that as a sacrament at the wedding you spoke of?"

"Hardly," Arthur said, "I have small use for druids, and Guenevere, my wife-to-be, has even less. She even brought her own pet bishop with her to marry us."

"The druids may not be content with that arrangement," Nithe warned.

"It matters not," Arthur said. "However, I will send some knights into Caerleon to question the druids, and we will have answers to these questions before daybreak. Meanwhile, bring your people in. We will feed them and find them camping space within the walls."

"They will not come," I said. "Myrddin once told me a good commander does not give orders he knows will be disobeyed. Where is he, anyway?"

Arthur frowned, but Nithe answered, saying, "Myrddin likes not this marriage. He and Arthur have quarreled over it. Myrddin has not returned to Camelot from Tintagel, where he escorted Igraine."

I was sorry to hear it. Since Arthur and Nithe were busy with their other guests, I rejoined my own people. Watchers reported soon after that two knights were riding at a smart pace from Camelot into Caerleon. I was happy to see Arthur had not been too busy to redeem his word.

We camped at the edge of the woods and awaited developments. If all else failed, we would seek our children in Caerleon, come what may. With time to think, I asked Cornu if he knew who this Guenevere was.

"She's the ward of the Lion of Grance," Cornu said. "Your devoted follower, Jerome, is the son of Grance. Guenevere's mother was Rowena, daughter of the Jute chief, Hengist. Her father was Vortigern, once High King of the Britons, but deposed by Uther. It's not a happy story."

"How did Grance become her guardian?" I asked, ignoring the reference to Jerome.

"Grance's wife was sister to Vortigern. Their father was a Roman centurion, so Guenevere is both Roman and royal Briton. She will make a worthy queen."

I hoped so. At midmorning next day, Accolon rode up and told us Hilda, Morgause and some of the ladies of New Avalon had sailed down the Usk. We watched them dismount, wave and go into the castle. They were dressed to call on royalty, as I had not been, and I thought they would probably join the wedding party. In midafternoon we saw druids and their followers, both men and women, coming from Caerleon, carrying our babies. They were conducted by the two knights sent to fetch them, and it appeared as though they were going to surrender the children to Arthur. Be that as it may, we mounted and fell in behind them, riding up to the gate. We paused, for guards barred our way, but we could hear voices raised in anger.

The wait seemed interminable, and I had just decided to force our way past the guards when a moment later Pelleas walked out, pushing the scarlet-robed head druid before him. I could not see the druid's face, but Pelleas' was a mask of anger. Pelleas threw the druid into the dust before the gate and stood there until the druid's followers streamed out around him, picked up their leader and scurried off, cursing over their shoulders. They did not have the babies with them.

I dismounted, gave the reins of my gelding to Cornu to hold and walked up to Pelleas. "Greetings, knife maker," I said. "I have come seeking the children the druids stole from my people. Will you bring me inside?"

He looked at me blankly for a moment, then recognized me. "You look like a warrior's bride, Lady Corbie," he said.

"I am no man's bride," I replied, "but a leader of these people who have been wronged by the druids."

"Come with me," he said. And with the women who had lost babies behind me, I followed him, not to the hall but to the women's quarters, where he pointed and said, "They have taken the children there."

I thanked him and entered, and found Morgause clutching Mordred. The other mothers claimed their babies, clucking and cooing over them anxiously. I was distracted by the sound of people shouting and smelled the metallic stink of blood in the air.

"Why are you crying? What is going on?" I asked Morgause. I noticed the children seemed to be all right as I looked around quickly, for the mothers were not protesting.

"The druids killed Hilda," she replied.

Anger came upon me. That gentle woman killed? "Why?" I demanded, but Morgause shook her head, unable to tell me.

Julia was standing near Morgause, wringing her hands. She heard my question and turned to me to respond. "Hilda protested when the arch-druid insisted on his right to sacrifice the babies to seal the marriage of the High King." As she pointed at the door open to the hall, I could see Arthur and others were kneeling over someone on the floor. I had never seen Julia so upset, not even when she was forced to flee from Tintagel so many years ago. "Then one of the arch-druid's attendants, a knight named Balin, beheaded Hilda with his great sword," she gasped between sobs, completing her story.

"And Arthur permitted that?" I couldn't believe it.

"It happened so quickly, he was caught by surprise. We all were," Morgause said. "Arthur cursed the killer and declared him exiled. If the man had not been one of Lancelot's chief knights, he might have done more."

"Might have done? Who is this Lancelot that Arthur permits his followers to commit such crimes?" I asked, astounded, consumed with outrage. Trying to keep this anger bottled up in my head's cave was almost too much for me.

"He is the son of King Ban of Armorica, the kingdom of the Britons from overseas. Ban is Arthur's chief ally, a fellow king."

"It seems this Lancelot has too much power, or Arthur too little," I said grimly, "but that can wait. I will not be bound by him."

I led my people outside and, leaving a few of them to watch the babies, followed after the druids' party. Their group was about our size though perhaps better armed, with only a few women among them. When we came within hailing distance of them I called out, "Halt!" They turned and huddled together protectively.

"You have come into my land and stolen children from families under my protection," I cried, speaking what I believed, though perhaps I had no right to claim it. "You have also killed one dear to me, a lady known for her gentleness and much loved for her kindness. My brother, the High King, has exiled the dastard who did the bloody deed. I now declare the arch-druid, who ordered it done, outlaw to my people. His life shall be forfeit if ever he comes on lands under my protection again!"

"Who is this female?" the arch-druid shouted. "Disperse this rabble and bring me her head!" He was on horseback, but his followers were afoot, and we dismounted to meet their charge. I engaged a man with a sword and buckler, deflecting his blow and jabbing at his face with my stave. There were four basic strokes in stick-fighting: slash left, slash right, jab and smash. Warding off blows from iron weapons consisted of catching the flat of the blade and turning it away when possible, and ducking or jumping out of range when it was not.

I was not fighting in anger, but in a cold determination to prevail over this haughty man. Hurting people gave me no pleasure. Did Boudicca like hurting people?

The targets for stick-fighting were the elbow, the knee, the crotch, the belly, the head and the neck. All might be slashed at, except the belly, which required a jab or smash to reach. The face and crotch were also vulnerable to jabs and smashes. My opponent was slow. When I feinted a jab to his crotch, he lowered his shield, and I thrust over it to catch him with a smash to the mouth with the butt end of the staff, breaking his teeth and taking him out of the fight. It is more effective to wound than to kill, for a wounded man requires a comrade or two to bear him from the field, while a dead man is just dead.

I stepped back to see where I was needed, and saw I wasn't needed anywhere. Druids were not hardy fighters. Nithe had said that men took training for the priesthood among the druids to escape the military levies. If Arthur were wise, he might encourage it among his enemies. Every extra priest was one less warrior.

"Mercy!" the women among the druids cried. "Mercy!"

"Throw down your weapons!" I shouted, and they did. Several of our veterans were for slaughtering them as they knelt before us, but I walked between them and the druids, pushing the soldiers back.

"Let them be," I ordered, and aside from insults hurled at them by our women, no further harm was done them. I quieted my people and addressed the enemy. "Hear me, Arch-druid! You and your followers, go to your homes in Caerleon, gather your belongings and leave this land! Go to Mona, from where the Mother's people were driven, if you would be safe. You are not safe in Britain. I will come looking for you when the moon changes, and if you are where I can find you, I will kill you, women as well as men. Now, leave your weapons on the ground, rise and go!" They were too terrified to defy me, and fled, abandoning their injured. I had to borrow wagons from Camelot to gather them up, bind their wounds, and dispatch them to join the others.

I reported to Arthur what I had done. "I acted in this matter to lay some responsibility on those who murdered Hilda, who is honored among my people," I told him. "I understand her killer left here under your protection."

"Hardly," Arthur retorted. "I sent him back to Armorica to keep myself from following my heart in this matter instead of my head. I wanted to kill him with my own hands! The Lady Hilda brought my sword Excalibur to me and deserved my deepest thanks."

"What is the killer's life to you, then?"

"Nothing. However, he was one of the best of the knights Lancelot brought to help me in the fight against Lot and his friends."

"Were they useful?" I asked slightingly.

"Not yet," Arthur replied, coloring at the tone of my voice, "but I expect they will be. Lancelot brought them too late to join in the fighting for the first battle with Lot, but another is shaping up."

"Then I will leave him to you for now," I said reluctantly, "but the clan mothers will have to decide what punishment is appropriate for Hilda's murderer. I warn you, in council with them I will urge some action stronger than the one you have taken. Personally, I will remember a man named Balin." He nodded gravely, and I left.

Pelleas joined me at our encampment in the woods. He told me that Arthur's betrothed had decided to accompany Hilda's body to New Avalon for the funeral rites rather than continue with the ceremony which had been so inauspiciously interrupted. He looked unusually grim, and I wondered why.

"Was the Lady Hilda someone special to you?" I asked.

"She was Nithe's mother. I looked to comfort Nithe and found her weeping in Lancelot's arms," he said morosely. He went off shaking his head.

Since Hilda had come down with Morgause by boat, her people decided to take her body back to New Avalon for burial the same way. We caught up with the funeral party and rode beside them on the bank. Morgause sat in the boat next to a tall, fair-haired girl, who, I decided, must be Guenevere, Arthur's bride-to-be. She was beautiful and obviously upset. She also seemed nervous to find us escorting her, and though Morgause clearly was in a position to reassure her, she continued to eye us suspiciously. Small wonder, covered with blood and bandages the way we were. Poor girl, I thought, what a wedding day!

The men in the boat rowed half the night, making slower time against the current than they had coming down. There were no tents for the passengers, had they wished to stop and camp. It appeared as though the trip had little planning in it. Small wonder, I thought, considering the circumstances. When the oarsmen finally became too tired to continue, they tied the boat to a tree leaning out over the water. We made camp on shore beside them and sent over hot food and cloaks we had taken from the druids, which alleviated most of the discomfort they might have had otherwise. After breakfast early the next morning they set out again, gaining New Avalon by noon.

Julia and her maidens had sung for much of the journey, songs of praise for Hilda and grief at her passing. I wondered how the New Avalon community could function without her. I thought Morgause was too indolent to lead, and Julia perhaps too religious. I was aware I might be asked, and wondered how I might respond. I then did what I often do when I have to make a difficult decision. Pretending to myself it had already happened, I considered how I felt about it. I found I did not want to become responsible for people as Hilda had been. If I had liked that sort of thing I would still be in Rhegid. I didn't mind taking care of animals, for they couldn't argue about things. People did. Even under Hilda's guidance there had been quarrels at New Avalon. If the members of

171

her community had been small boys instead of young women, I might have felt differently.

I don't know what Arthur's bride expected to find at New Avalon, but she was relieved to meet the women who had served Christ with Igraine. We had two funeral ceremonies, side by side: A Christian lay reader, one of Guenevere's attendants, chanted prayers, while Julia sang hymns from the Mother's funeral rituals as Hilda's grave was dug and covered over. There was no priest, and consequently there were no confrontations over ceremony.

I met Guenevere, the woman who would be Arthur's bride, and I liked her well enough. She had spirit. Morgause told me that when they left Camelot, Guenevere made no promise to return to Arthur, and perhaps had not yet made up her mind to do so. Not every woman as young and inexperienced as Guenevere would keep the High King waiting, I thought, and I admired her for it.

After several days elapsed, Guenevere's guardian, the one who styled himself the Lion of Grance, rode up from Camelot to fetch her, convincing her that she must go through with the marriage. Accolon, Cornu, Morgause and I escorted her back to Camelot when she decided he was right. We also took Mordred and his wet-nurse, an amiable but homely young woman who had no other family.

Arthur greeted us with what appeared to be mixed feelings. He was happy to see Guenevere back, of course, and was most solicitous of her. We waited until she had been sent off with Kay to the quarters prepared for her before Arthur turned to us.

"What do you want done with your son?" Morgause asked him bluntly.

Arthur had been told that Mordred was among the babies rescued from the druids. Whatever Morgause had been to Arthur once, they were not lovers now, I could see.

"This baby can't stay here, Morgause," Arthur declared flatly. "It has to be sent somewhere safe. King's bastards always are the locus of trouble. Why do you think Uther sent me away to hide?"

"His name is Mordred, Arthur, not 'it,'" Morgause snapped, "and I can't keep him either, for much the same reason. He's as

172

much an embarrassment to me as he is to you. More, probably," she added bitterly.

No, they truly didn't seem like lovers. They stood eye to eye, nearly equal in height and with much the same coloring. The family resemblance between the two was remarkable.

I missed Myrddin, whose solution to this problem would have been quick, sensible and humane. Nithe took his place, saying, "Send the baby to Samana. She can raise him with her own son."

"Do you think she'd take him?" Arthur asked wistfully, but with an air of hope. "Maybe I could send along some of Guenevere's dowry to cover the cost of raising a child," Arthur suggested.

"Wait," I said. "I'm not following this at all. Who is this Samana person?"

"Samana is the daughter of the Duke of Lyoness, and was Arthur's first wife," Nithe replied, looking away from Arthur for a moment.

"First wife?" I asked, astounded. Arthur was little more than a boy! First wife? Arthur looked flustered. "You're not married to this new woman as yet," I continued, "and from what I've seen of her, if she learns you've sent her dowry along with your bastard son as a present to your first wife, you won't be having a second wife soon. If you manage men the way you seem to manage women, you're in for a short reign." The man was an idiot!

"Samana was Arthur's childhood sweetheart," Nithe answered for him, when Arthur looked troubled and seemed unable to find words. "Her father, Cador, Duke of Lyoness, contracted Samana to Arthur for one child, who was to be Cador's heir. Samana had to return to her father's house to raise the child. I guess Arthur feels the need to establish an heir himself."

"At his age?" I asked, in disbelief. "What's his hurry?"

Arthur flushed, beginning to look mulish. Morgause found a pillow and sat down on it with the air of one to whom entertainment had been promised. She was beginning to enjoy this, even if Arthur wasn't.

"It's more complicated than it seems," Arthur said. "I have to make an alliance with an established royal family to gain acceptance as High King. I have to do it soon, or the country will become so weakened by fighting off other claimants, there will be nothing of value left for the winner."

"What kind of royal house are you speaking of?" Morgause asked, when it looked as if the discussion was over.

"One with Roman connections," Arthur replied, looking earnest again.

"What do the Romans have to do with anything?" I asked. "They left Britain in my grandfather's time."

"They have not given up their claim here, and regardless of whether they return, the great families of Britain all trace their ascendancy to Roman times. I must do that as well."

"But you do," I argued. "With Uther as your father and Igraine as your mother, who would question it?"

"I thought you were aware that Lot questions whether Uther was my father. As for Igraine, she was a Scoti, and the Scoti rulers never had Roman acknowledgement. Your father, Gorlais, was only a duke, though I understand the house goes back before Roman times. However, if I'm his son, and not Uther's, I am not royal. It's as simple as that. Guenevere is the daughter of Vortigern, a High King acknowledged by the Romans. I need the connection."

"Myrddin didn't think so," Nithe observed.

"Don't take up Myrddin's quarrel!" Arthur warned, angry at last. "He left Camelot when I wouldn't change my mind. I won't change it for you, either. Kay has told me what people are saying. Kay hears everything. I must make this marriage!"

Kay again, I thought. Kay had much to answer for.

"Do you intend to tell Kay about Mordred?" Morgause asked, suddenly serious.

"What difference does it make?" Arthur snarled, turning to her. He was like a bull being baited by dogs, with the three of us snapping at him.

"Mordred is my child," Morgause said, lounging back against the wall indolently. "I don't like Kay."

"Why, nobody likes Kay," Arthur said, dismissing this argument

174

with a wave of his hand. "And, no, I don't confide in him. I just listen to him. Sometimes."

In the end, at Arthur's request Gawaine agreed to take Mordred to Samana, along with the baby's wet-nurse. The way the nurse simpered when Gawaine helped her climb into the cart showed what her expectations were, but the way Gawaine rolled his eyes in mock appeal when she wasn't looking said much of what Gawaine thought of her. I wished I could have gone with them just to watch.

I needed to get away from Jerome, who was becoming a pest. Nithe thought it was funny, but Nithe laughed at almost everything. She sang snatches from the songs Jerome recited under my window at night. Nithe had not grieved long for Hilda. I knew her mother better than she did, and felt worse about her murder. Nithe said Hilda had given her away to Myrddin as a child, and she owed her mother nothing but formal respect. I wondered if that was also the reason why Arthur had not immediately acknowledged Igraine.

On my orders, Susan brought a rushlight in my room at sundown to deceive the boy into believing me there while I was happily in the stable with the horses. It did Jerome no harm and gave me peaceful nights.

CHAPTER
IX

I decided not to go back to New Avalon, but stayed on at Camelot, drifting, not able to make up my mind what to do. I missed Gawaine. I had kept Gawaine at arm's length after being teased by Nithe, but I now wished I had gone with him to Lyoness to bring Morgause's son to Samana. Arthur asked me to attend his wedding to Guenevere, which was held in the small chapel he had set up for her private devotions. It had been hastily rigged out with rail and altar, but rich tapestries hung on the wall, and a jeweled crucifix glowed against the blue altar cloth.

The priest was a man who had come with Guenevere from Grance's land in the summer country. He was a dark man, much worn by life, I thought. He had the air of hiding some great sorrow that twisted his heart.

Pelleas and Lancelot stood for Arthur. Pelleas was bristling, giving Lancelot suspicious sidelong glances, but Lancelot ignored him, completely self-possessed. Nithe and Ettarde, Grance's daughter, were more intent on the ceremony, conducted in a Latin that sounded stilted to my ears.

The reception in the great hall was subdued, for it had recently been the scene of Hilda's murder. Not until evening turned into night and a sufficient quantity of ale and wine had been drunk did voices rise in drunken song. I left as soon as I saw the bride and groom slip away. I had a mare I expected to deliver that night, and felt myself more needed there.

I found places to hide, or work to do, like birthing foals, that Jerome did not wish to participate in: it was the best way to escape his attentions. Nithe sometimes joined me, and demonstrated a remarkable skill in it. She soon knew where I could be found most of the time. It was but a month after Arthur's wedding to Guenevere that she sought me out where I was napping in a hayloft, having been up most of the night with a mare in labor. Why did animals like to deliver their young at night? I wondered.

"I am sorry, Morgan, but you must attend," she said, shaking me gently. "Something frightful has occurred."

"The mare's hemorrhaging?" I asked, my mind still fixed on the night before, but with a feeling of foreboding on hearing the words, so like the ones Igraine had used to tell me of Arthur's committing incest with Morgause.

"No, oh, no! It's Accolon! He's been killed!"

"Accolon?" I asked, barely understanding her words. "My Accolon?"

"Yes. We were out with the falcons, Arthur, Kay, Guenevere and I. Arthur had dismounted to coax a young bird off her kill, when Accolon came to us, riding like a fury, and skidded to a stop before Arthur, kicking dirt all over him. Arthur tripped and fell, backing away, and Accolon was on him, beating him with a sword. I rode to them shouting Accolon's name, and he stopped for a moment. 'My lady?' he said, 'You here?'

" 'What are you doing?' I demanded, and he said, 'Ask Kay,' turning back to Arthur. But as I distracted Accolon, Arthur rose to his feet and attacked. Accolon was no match for him. Arthur has wrestled since boyhood and is immensely strong. He broke Accolon's neck between one breath and another and threw him on the ground. He then picked up the sword Accolon had carried, and found it to be his own Excalibur. I've never seen him so angry, and I risked being seriously hurt coming between him and Accolon. Arthur wanted Accolon's head, and I barely prevailed on him not to cut it off. In his hurry to get back to find the cause of Accolon's behavior, Arthur made us leave his body where it lay in the woods. He has men looking for you now."

"Has he? Then he shall find me," I said, pushing past Nithe. I jumped to the barn floor and ran through the light rain toward the castle with hay still clinging to my tunic. My hair was in wild disarray. Nithe followed close behind me, calling for me to wait. I did not.

I found Arthur sitting on his throne in the great hall with his naked sword across his knees. He did not speak as I ran up and stopped before him, pushing one of his pages roughly to one side. "What have you done to my son?" I demanded.

"Be careful whom you claim, sister," he said, anger tightening his voice to something little better than a rasp. "I have killed a traitor."

"Accolon? A traitor? It is a lie!"

"Lie? He came to kill me with my own sword. Ask Kay or Guenevere or Nithe. They were there."

"To kill you? If my son came to kill you, you would be dead. You are not even bleeding," I said in disdain. I couldn't seem to stop myself from shaking.

"He struck Arthur three times," Guenevere said from her seat beside Arthur. "If the Holy Father had not protected him, he would be dead. God turned the blow so Arthur was struck only with the flat of the blade and not the edge."

"I see," I said, and I did, though dimly. "Among the Picts, a man is beaten with his own sword for cowardice. What did you do to merit such a punishment?" I asked him.

"Me, a coward? Me? Never have I been accused of cowardice," Arthur retorted angrily.

"You have been now, by the hand of my dead son," I said. "I will find out what it was and have an accounting for it, brother," I continued. "If ever there was doubt in my mind that you are Uther's son, at least that is settled. His was ever the coward's way."

"Stop!" Guenevere said. "Accolon was angry because I had sent his friend away. If anyone is to blame it is me."

"Away?" I sputtered. I wondered how I had been so successful in avoiding Jerome, but Arthur spoke over me.

"My lady?" Arthur asked, frowning and looking at Guenevere.

"Jerome has been pledged to the church. I thought it not fitting that he should be forming an attachment for your sister and sent him away to be free of her influence."

"My influence? Do you suggest I encouraged his devotion?" I asked, outraged. I could feel my hold over my temper slipping away, and fought to curb it.

"You at least permitted it," she said primly.

"In that sense I permit it to rain, my lady," I said, still choking with rage. "I like rain as little as I like calf love. Look at me, Lady," I said, though conscious that I was not at my best with hay sticking out of my hair. "Some of the folk say I closely resemble my mother, Igraine the Gold, though to be accurate, her hair was the color of ripe corn, and mine shines like a raven's wing, to quote ballads I have heard. Do you really think I would toy with a child like Jerome?"

"I encouraged Morgan not to hurt the boy's feelings," Nithe said, standing at my side. She cast her cloak over my shoulders. I was shivering.

"I assure you," Nithe continued, while I fought to control my anger, glaring first at Guenevere and then at Arthur, "I promise you, it was as innocent as Lancelot's devotion to Your Majesty."

Both Guenevere and Arthur looked uneasy as wisps of my rage escaped me, and Guenevere flushed at Nithe's reference to Lancelot.

"Accolon had declared his love for me in the same manner," Nithe said. "If I had not stopped him, Arthur, by invoking my power over him, you would know now if he meant to kill you or not. I know that he did not."

Arthur paled at this, but did not respond directly to her. He merely turned to Kay, allowing him to speak in his place.

"Whatever the queen may have done, it was not grounds for an attack upon the king," Kay said.

"Indeed, not," Nithe said. "Accolon said to ask you about it, and I am doing so now. You have never been my friend, Kay, but you are too proud to lie. What was the cause?"

"The boy overheard talk that the queen had found it necessary to send Jerome away because of Morgan's loose behavior with the boy. It was said the king agreed with the need, and planned to warn his sister about her conduct."

"Conduct?" I asked, my head spinning. "I was accused of debauching Arthur's page? Who are these gossipers?" I turned to Arthur and asked him directly, "Is it true? Was there such infamous prattle?" The beast in my mind-cave was growling.

"I know not," Arthur said, and I could sense, angry though I was, that he spoke the truth. "I never listen to gossip, and forbid it in my presence. I didn't even know Jerome had been sent away, and I am not pleased to learn it now."

"If there has been talk, I didn't encourage it," Guenevere said defensively. She was flustered. "Never did I accuse you of wanton behavior. It is unfortunate that such a construction was put on my sending Jerome away. I sent the boy away at the suggestion of Bishop Ninian, who was promised Jerome for the church."

"Unfortunate? It's infamous!" I raged. "When you have children, my lady, I trust nothing so unfortunate comes to them. In the meantime, you would do well to be more cautious in choosing your advisors. You cannot claim responsibility for many more disasters like this one and live!" and I glared at her with all the menace I felt. I was not able to contain my emotions completely within myself; enough leaked out to cause her to flinch and shrink away.

"What is this?" Arthur gasped, for he, too, felt it.

"This is a mother who goes to find her son, and mourn him as a mother should. It was not kind to allow him to lie unattended in the forest, for the crows to eat," I said bitterly, staring at Arthur.

"Perhaps I was wrong in that," Arthur said. "I will make amends, if you will allow it."

"That I will not. Nithe will take me to where he lies and will weep with me. I could not bear to see you near me," I said, and I turned away.

"Let us not part in anger," Guenevere said. "There is no fault in this."

"No fault?" I gasped. Didn't the woman understand?

"We forgive you," Arthur added, nodding.

"You forgive me? Me? Lud! I will never forgive you! May you never have a son to lose!" I grated, and my anger struck the two of them as if I had used a mace. I left them sitting stunned and shaken. No one tried to stop me.

On the way to where Accolon's body lay, Nithe said, "You asked where Accolon could hear such talk, and received no answer."

"Do you know?" I asked.

"I can guess. Kay keeps beer available for the young knights and squires, at least those without families, in the cellar below the kitchen. Cornu has told me the gossip is so venomous there it borders on the treasonable."

"And Kay permits it?"

"He never says anything himself, but somehow extra flagons of beer find themselves on the table of those who speak the worst about Arthur's friends and relatives."

Cornu was waiting for us when we reached the spot where Accolon lay. "When his horse came to the stable without him, I followed the tracks back to his body. I wrapped him in my cloak and waited for you, my lady," he said.

"It was well done," I muttered. I understood Cornu grieved as deeply as I, for Accolon was as much his son as mine.

We decided not to bury him, but burn him where he lay on the mossy earth. We laid wood over him, and as the fire raged I unbound my hair and drew my knife, cutting the long strands close to my head and throwing them into the flames. Nithe started to do the same, and I stopped her.

"It is not necessary," I said, gently.

"Allow me," she replied, her voice choked with sobs, "Was I not his lady?"

At that, the tears came, and she and I and Cornu clung together and wept bitterly. He had been so fair and so young!

Before we returned to Camelot, I knotted my golden chain and placed the crow amulet around my brow to bind my shorn hair, the pendant against my forehead. I would remove it when the blood debt to my fallen dead was paid. The fire burned out, yet I did not go back to the castle with Nithe, but to the stables; I had made my living quarters there, to be near the animals. In the room Arthur had allotted to me in the castle I kept my few fine gowns, and little else. I had no interest in any company I would find at Arthur's table this night, and ate a bowl of oat gruel Cornu cooked for me over a small fire only because he insisted. Susan and Sam found us sitting in the near dark. Susan's kittens crowded near her feet. The young tom that most often sought me out came to jump into my lap and purred, pushing his head under my hand. I put my face into his fur and hugged him.

"Whatever have you done to yourself?" Susan asked, shocked at my unkempt appearance. There was enough light for that, I thought wryly.

"What it looks like," I said, ungraciously. "I cut my hair."

"Nithe came to supper looking much as you do. Arthur was angry about it, and got tongue-lashed for his pains."

"Good for Nithe," I said.

"I know!" Susan whispered. "Accolon dead! Arthur said that you had cursed him; Guenevere has taken to her room and will see no one."

"Cursed? Susan, Arthur killed my son. He is lucky to be alive! What do you want from me?"

"I am your friend, always," Susan said firmly. "I want nothing more. Accolon told me of overheard gossip concerning you and Jerome, and I laughed; it was ridiculous. I am sorry he did not understand, but all the same, there is something magnificent in a boy beating a king for slandering his mother, if you think about it."

"I have thought about it," I said. "I would know who set the gossip in motion. Was it Kay?"

"Oh, who could tell? Gossip breeds in this court like maggots in dead meat. If Accolon had not reacted as he did, the gossip would have sunk below the surface when some other lie invented to savage another reputation boiled up." Susan was looked on as a servant, and Arthur's people spoke in front of her as if she were not there.

"If he had not acted as he did, he would not be Accolon," I retorted bleakly. "I still hold Arthur responsible."

"Arthur has made it an exiling offense to gossip, but his orders are disobeyed when he is not present," Cornu observed. "Arthur spends no time in the kitchen and little enough in the queen's chambers, where there is ever more talk than work."

"The kitchen?" I asked. "Isn't the kitchen Kay's domain? I asked you before, is Kay the source of this?"

"Kay has never been friend to Arthur, for all that they were raised together," he answered. "I know little more of what transpires in the kitchen or the cellar than Arthur does, but I know that much. Kay and Guenevere are friends, however, spending more time together and sharing more common interests than Arthur and Guenevere do. I think both Kay and Guenevere were involved, but I cannot believe either of them wanted things to go this far, at least not the queen. There is no malice in her. She was merely bored."

"It is not enough," I said, after considering Cornu's statement. "Some active ill will is at work here. It is even possible that Arthur is the true target and Accolon was merely used to damage him."

"That has occurred to me, too," Susan said. "I wish Myrddin were here. He would get to the bottom of this fast enough."

"So will I, in time. I am in no condition to think about it now, and I cannot become clear-headed enough in this place to reach any conclusions. I have to leave Camelot!"

The next day I found Nithe and confided my intention.

"I thought you might think that way, and I have spoken to Arthur about it," Nithe said. "Arthur is more upset for his part in Accolon's death than he allows to be seen. He is very fond of you, and it tears at him that it was his hand that brought you such grief. I think he is afraid of even approaching you, but would make amends if he could."

"That may be, but it is not possible unless he brings punishment on those truly responsible. Since he doesn't know who they are and, from my reading, is not clever enough to find out, he will not be able to make amends, will he?"

"Where will you go?" Nithe asked to change the subject.

"Perhaps back to New Avalon, at least for now," I said uncertainly.

"Let me suggest you consider going back to your own village in Rhegid," Nithe urged. "Urien's other sons need your guidance. I hear your true son, Uwayne, has joined them there," she added.

"My true son? I think Urien's true son," I said. "Is Urien with him? Does he seek to stay eight years as my guest to pay for the years he sheltered me in Gore?"

"He is said to be lord in Rhegid now," Nithe said.

"Is he, though?" I asked. "I think I will do as you suggest. At the least I owe him an accounting of Accolon's death, and in addition might need to remind him of who I am." Next morning I found her determined to accompany me, at least as far as New Avalon.

"I have a duty I owe there," she said, "and I am sick of this place."

"And what is that?" I asked.

Nithe seemed not to have heard me, for she did not reply.

Cornu was approached by a dozen Cornish knights, who asked to accompany us. We talked about it.

"They remember your father, Morgan. Gawaine recruited them and sent them to Arthur, but they have not been well received in Camelot. Cornish knights have a reputation for cowardice, and have been taunted, forcing them to fight every day. They don't wish to go back for they are all younger sons, and must attach themselves to some noble house."

I had them come to me, and asked if they had sworn fealty to Arthur. "He wouldn't accept us, Lady," one said.

"Then I will," I said, and held my hands out for them to kiss. They greeted me as Princess of Cornwall, and swore to serve me wherever I took them. Cornu had horses for them and I thought seemed happy to have an escort for us. Cornu took our breeding stock with us on every trip, with the fear they would be neglected or stolen without him to watch over them. Arthur had hoped we would leave them with him, for our horses were better than his. He would not ask, though.

Nithe joined us with her own horse and pack animal, ready to go. "You spoke of a duty you owe in New Avalon," I said to her again as we set off side by side up the Usk. I clutched my favorite kitten so tightly he growled in protest, gently biting my hand to remind me of my manners. Cloud flicked her ears back in attention, and I relaxed my grip on the little creature. He settled down on the saddle pad, leaning back against me. The soft rain of yesterday had cleared the air, and everything sparkled in the morning light.

"You are one of the very few," Nithe began, sighing in response to my question, "who knew Hilda was my mother."

"Yes," I said. "I've known it for years, for Hilda once told me. In fact, I've sometimes wondered if maybe Myrddin was your father."

"Oh, no. My father is Bishop Ninian, the same priest who saved Jerome from your clutches," she said. "You saw him at Guenevere's wedding. He officiated. You can believe that he and Hilda would not have agreement on how I was to be brought up. He wouldn't even speak to me, pagan that I am."

"Yes, that I can believe," I agreed. I remembered seeing a priest kneeling over Hilda's body, next to Arthur.

"My father wanted me committed to a convent where I was to spend my life on my knees praying for his soul," Nithe said. "I was to make amends for his sin with my mother."

"I can see my own father doing that, had the occasion arisen," I said. "He was also God-ridden."

"Well, my mother wouldn't have it and, to save me, gave me into Myrddin's keeping. My mother was the daughter of Myrddin's sister, I believe, and the relationship that ran between them must have been a strong one for him to have taken on such a burden. Before Myrddin left Camelot he made me promise to take care of New Avalon should anything happen to Hilda, for it meant much to her. I am doing it for him, not her. My mother barely acknowledged me."

"You wept at her death," I said.

"You saw that?"

"No, Pelleas did. He thought you went to Lancelot instead of him," I said.

"Oh, Lud," she moaned. "I did it again, didn't I?"

"Tell me about you and Pelleas," I urged. "You never say much about him, but I sense he is much on your mind."

"He is that," she admitted. "I have resisted surrendering to my feelings for him as long as I can remember. I will not be free if I go to him, not ever again."

"Is he so possessive?"

"No, it's not him, it's me. Oh, he's so bloody noble I could kill him! I'd been trying to get him to commit himself for ages, though even then I wasn't ever sure whether I would accept him or not. When he finally spoke I turned him down. Can you believe it? And he let me go to follow after Lancelot without a word. But what a fool I was for going!"

"And Lancelot?" I still had half-formed plans to make Lancelot pay for Uther's betrayal and death of my father. Lancelot's father and Uther had been cousins, which accounted for the close tie between Lancelot and Arthur. If Nithe and Lancelot were lovers, I might have to find another surrogate.

"It's hard to explain about Lancelot," she said. "He seems to have no more interest in sex than a boy of eight."

"Maybe he follows the Roman soldiers' practice in that regard. Does he like boys, perhaps?"

"Not boys. I have seen him hug his comrades, and kiss them affectionately, and maybe he is so in love with the idea of being a knight that nothing else matters. Myrddin once told me he should have been a priest."

"Does Pelleas know this?"

"Of course not. Do you think I'd do something intelligent like telling him?"

I laughed ruefully. "You are not about to release Pelleas to me then, are you?"

"Not while I live," she said, smiling at me with closed teeth.

I laughed again, but I knew not what at.

When we reached New Avalon, we sorted out the various responsibilities we had individually taken on. I would go to Khegid and claim my lands, taking as many of the Cornishmen as wished to go with me. I also found that a number of the young women I had trained in stick-fighting wanted to come along as well. I wondered if the young women were not more interested in the unattached men in my party than in serving me, but why not?

When I spoke of it to Nithe, who had been welcomed at New Avalon as Hilda's successor, she said, "New Avalon has more mouths than it can conveniently feed. Frankly, it would be a service to me to take some of them with you."

She came to bid us farewell when we set out for Morgan's hold, promising a visit when she could free herself of the duties she had taken over. We had horses enough for all, and set out east to Fosse Way, with twice as many young women as we had men. Winter had not yet set in, and the crisp fall days were a joy. The Cornish knights were delighted as the women vied for their attention. Once on the old Roman road, we followed it north until we reached Hadrian's Wall, and rode west along the Staneway until we reached Carlisle and could cut north to our fort. I was impatient to put my life back together again. I needed work, long, hard days of it. I had missed the harvest, unfortunately, but I could cut wood for winter fires and work out my grief over Accolon's death in exhausting labor.

I had hoped to find Urien at Carlisle, but Gawaine's people told me he was living with his sons north of the wall. I knew what that meant. When we came to my village, I found it much changed. A palisade of oak logs had been erected along the top of the fort's stone enclosure wall, adding height and giving protection to patrolling soldiers. We were not noticed at first in the bustle. Tents were everywhere.

"It is a staging ground for the next battle with Arthur," Cornu said, and I nodded, observing carefully, counting the numbers as best I could. I thought perhaps a thousand men were camped in the great commons that fronted my village.

A lone horseman rode toward us. I recognized the horse before the rider. It was Drake, Urien's oldest son, my old Sausage.

"Oh, well met!" he cried, jumping from his horse and running to me so he could drag me, protesting, from mine to hug me. Some of my men were scandalized, but the young women who had not yet made commitments looked him over critically.

"Have done, you impetuous child!" I said, pushing him away. "What is the meaning of this mess?"

"This mess, as you call it, is a feast for my wedding," he said. He was joined by a tall, red-haired Scoti woman who hugged me enthusiastically, giving me the kiss of greeting. I liked her immediately.

"Men!" she said scornfully. "As if I'd let the likes of these in any wedding of mine."

"What is your name, child?" I asked, disentangling myself and laughing.

"I am called Moira by my people," she replied, "but Drake and his brothers call me Big Red because I tower over them. Did you not feed them, Lady, when they were small?"

"It is my recollection that they ate all the time," I mused. She was as tall as I. "I think it all went to mouth," I added.

"Ah, that would be it," she agreed. "Terrible talkers they are. Drake said true for once, though. We are feasting. Would you join us as our honored guest?"

"Of course," I agreed, and walked arm in arm with her through the gate. Men called to her, salacious remarks for the most part, which she answered in kind but more cleverly and less coarsely.

"How long have you and Drake been together?" I asked.

"Barely a month. Too short a time to have my husband off playing war," she answered grimly. "Why, I'm not even pregnant yet!"

In the great hall I found the wedding party assembled. Ken and Dunc came to greet me joyfully. They had been drinking mead.

I saw Urien stand as I entered, watching me warily. My heart contracted as I recognized Uwayne standing with his father, hesitating, not sure of what to do. His boyish air was at contrast with his new height. He was taller than his father.

"Have you come to join us against the usurper?" Ken asked hopefully, causing me to turn back to see him, grinning in delight.

"Probably not," I replied. "I thought rather to reclaim my home. Who are all these folk, anyway?"

"Warriors," he said. "We march against Arthur before the moon changes. This is to be the decisive battle. Say you'll come. We could use men like these," and he glanced at my Cornish troopers, who had followed us into the hall and preened self-consciously at the praise. They had not been so valued by Arthur. "But where is Accolon?" he asked.

I shook my head, saying, "I bring sad news that I must give to your father. Accolon is dead, killed in a fight with Arthur because of a stupid misunderstanding."

All animation left his face, and tears began flowing down his cheeks. Both of the twins put their arms around me in comfort. Picts were taught as young boys not to cry like women, so they wept silently. I was once told the reason for it: a wounded man, hidden from an enemy, would be discovered if he wept aloud. Ken tried to speak and failed. He tried again through gritted teeth, "That's all that was needed to give purpose to me and my brothers. We were committed only to helping our father before. This will make it personal."

"I feared it would, but before you tell the others, hear this. Arthur was as much the victim as Accolon. Accolon was told lies about Arthur, that Arthur was traducing my name. Accolon attacked Arthur and Arthur killed him in self-defense."

"And yet it was his hand," Ken said grimly.

"His hand, but not his fault," I amended.

"So I will take my vengeance as a duty, and without joy in it," Ken said.

"At least keep it from Drake and the others until tomorrow. It would be a shame to spoil Drake's wedding feast."

"Our battle cry will be 'For Accolon,'" Ken promised, and led me to a seat beside Drake.

Uwayne was trembling like a roe deer as we came near, until I held my arms out to him and said his name. He came to me and hugged me fiercely. "I have missed you," he whispered.

"And I you," I told him, patting his back as I had soothed him when he was a child. He was as tall as me, thin, but with good bone that promised to carry a man's weight in time.

When he released me, I put my hand out to Urien. "Welcome to my house," I said to him. I could do no less at his son's wedding feast.

"I have enjoyed your hospitality for some time, Lady," he said. "I have tried to be useful here."

I nodded. "It is evident," I said. "I thank you." I did not use the formal phrases that would make my house his house, and he understood the omission.

The feast spread to the men camped out in the commons, with food and drink that Drake told me had been brought up from Carlisle. As with all feasts among the Gaels, there was music and dancing along with the drinking until men collapsed and snored in drunken exhaustion. Drake and Big Red were well and truly married.

Urien came to bid me good-bye two days later. He had slept with his men in the fields, turning the house over to me and my people as a matter of course. "I grieve for Accolon," he said, "and for you, Lady. We will think of him in battle with his killer. I would welcome your support and the aid of those you have brought with you in this venture."

"Lot is your general?" I asked.

"Yes. However, the Picts will not serve under one who is not a Pict, and have chosen me as their leader."

"I will release my people to you if they wish to go," I said. "I could not hold them against their will, in any case. I will not urge them, however, for if I must choose between Lot and Arthur, I would still choose Arthur, even after Accolon's death. He wept for Accolon. Lot did not weep for me."

I had thought the Cornishmen would join him, but they did not. "We wished to fight for Arthur," one of them told Cornu. "We would not feel right about going against him so soon." So we kept the Cornishmen within the walls, establishing them in barracks that had been built for Urien's men.

Within three days Drake, Urien and the many hundreds in the tents were gone. I do not know whether news of Accolon's death was responsible, or if Urien feared I would relay word to Arthur that a force was moving against him, but they left late one night. The commons was a shambles, and it took the better part of a week to clean up after Urien's men. There had been no farewells, but that didn't surprise me. Picts believed there was something of prophecy in saying good-bye.

I was not a Pict. I would have liked to wish Urien's sons a safe journey. There was something of prophecy in that, as well.

CHAPTER

X

ornu was worried about something. He told me he was uncomfortable when he thought about the bands of armed men that drifted through the village area, and I instructed him to institute some defensive measures for the security of our people. First, he called a general muster to learn what number of folk we were. I was surprised at the turnout. Upward of a thousand folk came to the welcome-home feast we gave ourselves as a pretext to gather everyone together. I was both honored guest and hostess.

Of that number who assembled to eat and drink with us Cornu reckoned there were perhaps two hundred young men and women of fighting age, that is, old enough to have the strength necessary for fighting, and young enough to run away when fighting was senseless. He thought of people in much the same way he thought of horses. These were the breeding stock to be saved at all costs; so if the village were overwhelmed, only nonproductive children and older people would remain to be put to the sword by an enemy. I was relieved to learn he thought of me as still of fighting age.

We held games to learn who could run the fastest, ride the best, wrestle and stick-fight the most skillfully and knife-fight the dirtiest. Cornu offered useful prizes to the winners so the contestants would truly strive. They used light rods for staves and short, blunt sticks for knives to keep injuries down, but there were still welts and bruises at the end of the day. We knew though, afterward, how to plan for our defense.

Cornu selected twenty of the lightest and best riders, most of them women, and formed a mobile cavalry. Their weapon was the flail, and when they could swing it without hitting their horses, he had them dashing around the commons striking at posts that were erected to simulate enemy on foot. Another group practiced the sling; both men and women who had served as shepherds had used that weapon to drive wolves away. Their battle station would be the roof of the bathhouse; the children spent time fetching and piling round stones there for their future use.

I would have liked to have a contingent of archers, but there was no one skilled enough to serve except Cornu and me. It took years to develop an archer. He had taught me when I was young, and later Urien's sons when they were boys. I fletched arrows at night, tipping them with iron points Cornu forged along with tools for the village. I made over a hundred arrows, and there wasn't a fowl in the courtyard with an easy butt. When I asked the children to bring me feathers, they ran down every chicken they could catch and yanked out their tail feathers. I hadn't quite meant that, for chicken feathers were not as good as goose feathers for fletching arrows. Still, they would do.

We were joined by Julia and Morgause several days after Urien left. They were driving a light wagon drawn by two horses that should have been out to pasture years earlier. It turned out these animals had been considered too old to be useful in war and were left behind by Lot's men.

I had not seen Julia since she left with Myrddin to escort my mother, Igraine, back to Tintagel. It would be good to have her company again.

"Lot came to Merricks-hold and requisitioned all the sound horses, most of the stored grain and every man old enough to fight," Morgause said.

"He even took the Mother's stores," Julia said breathlessly. "Imagine!"

"He stole our cattle, saying they were needed to feed the men for the war with Arthur, but in truth it was little more than a raid, and most of the beasts were sent back to Lothian," Morgause finished grimly.

"Gawaine will be furious," I said.

"Gawaine is with Arthur and has become Lot's enemy," Morgause replied.

Morgause took over management of our manor house with Julia as her assistant. I was grateful for her help, for I had work to do with Cornu to ready our defense.

Morgause instructed some of the older men to dig a well in case of siege, and worked with the women to turn grain into bread that could be wrapped, stored and hidden against the future, if Lot came here and broke our defenses. Morgause looked very well, having recovered her figure, and showed more energy and address than I could remember, ever. She heard of Accolon's death dry-eyed, but hugged me fiercely and went back to her women to work them longer hours.

Julia also surprised me, for sometimes she took a hand in the training of stick fighters, mostly to get away from Morgause, I thought. I had forgotten how able Julia was, thinking of her mostly as a priestess. Together we could demonstrate blows and wards more quickly and convincingly than working alone against one of the other women. We had thirty women stick-fighting with journeyman proficiency within a week, most of them my old pupils from New Avalon.

Big Red was a natural, with her long arms. She became a teacher within a few days, having mastered the rudiments, and appointed herself my personal guard in the process.

"Sure, what would I tell Drake if he came back and found you dead, then?" was the way she expressed it.

The Cornish knights formed our men into teams, two Picts with shield and knife and one tall Gael in the middle with an ax. They were all familiar with knife and ax as everyday tools, and the shield work was not difficult. The older men carved new shields to replace those broken in practice, and the fighters learned to think of the shield as a weapon of offense as well as defense. Striking an opponent under the chin or on the foot with the edge of a shield was a disabling blow.

These men had been serfs, for the most part, before coming to our village as runaways. Here, land had been assigned them for their own use. Lot would take them all as burden bearers if we let him, if he came to us as he had to Merricks-hold. It was the possibility that we might successfully resist that kept these young men and women working well past the time I was ready to drop from exhaustion.

Cornu took his light cavalry out as scouts, guarding the road to our village, watching for Lot's men, and we were fortunate in taking that precaution. Lot came sooner than we expected; I feared before we were ready. At least we had enough notice to bring our cows and horses into the palisaded fort, and all of our people were brought in by relays of Cornu's warriors.

Cornu had grim words for us all. "Aim at the horses," he ordered. "If we kill enough of them, Lot will back off. He cannot replace them, and without horses he cannot hope to win against Arthur." Privately he told me how much he resented the necessity of giving such advice.

"I hope you're right," I told him. "I know you value horses as highly as men. If Lot is the leader he should be, so will he, but he may overlook it in the heat of battle."

"Maybe," Cornu said. "Remember, my lady, Lot is the only person the others will follow. You must take care not to kill him, for only he can order the fighting to cease without losing honor."

I was thinking of his words when Lot's host came into sight. I was dismayed by their numbers. Urien had only a thousand. Lot had three times that, counting wagon men and camp followers, all of whom could fight if pressed. As Lot rode up, I took my accustomed place over the gate, where I stored the bow and the arrows I had made. When he was fifty paces off, I sent an arrow into the ground at his horse's feet, bringing him to a sudden stop.

"What is this?" he yelled.

"You can come forward, if you dare, but I'll put an arrow through the man who follows you," I yelled back. Big Red stood beside me, holding a shield large enough to shelter us both if the need arose.

He said a few brief words to those who rode with him, then advanced alone to within twenty paces. "Is it you, Morgan?" he asked in surprise. "Men have spoken to me of your beauty, and I have regretted not finishing what we commenced so many years ago. I see I am not too late."

"If you would have a corpse, perhaps those words have meaning, for I would die rather than have them come true while I live," I said. I was surprised to find how bitterly I hated this man.

"Come, let us be friends," he said, extending his hand. "I would take nothing that is not mine. You were a female under my roof, eating my food, and owed me obedience. I did no wrong."

Morgause joined us on the parapet. "Then you were stupid to run away. Perhaps you should have remained and demanded your rights," she said ironically.

"Perhaps I should have," he responded insolently.

"Your balls would be resting on the Mother's altar if you had," she said in a matter-of-fact tone. "We are not through with you yet, trust-breaker." Softly in the background Julia began to sing, and I felt my hair raise on end. It was a sacrifice song.

Lot paled, for he felt the power in Julia's words, but he spoke blusteringly enough. "We need your horses, cattle, stored grain and serfs, both men and women. We go to join Urien and the other kings against Arthur."

"They are not mine to give," I said. "These are free men and women, and the herds and crops are their own. I do not take from them without payment, nor will you."

"But I will," he said. "Do you think this puny fort can hold back my warriors?"

"No, I do not," I said, "but I spoke of payment. We can make the taking of it so costly an enterprise that you, who thought only to augment your strength here, will go to Arthur much weakened."

"It would delay us but a day," he said coldly. "We would lose more time raping your women than we would fighting your men."

"And will you lead them in both activities, then? I've never seen you kill," Morgause replied in a tone to match his own.

"You will, my lady!" he replied boldly.

"Then know this, Lot," I said. "I have a hundred arrows for my bow, and each one will I aim at you. If you lead your men, you will die. If you fear to do so, you will be called a coward by your own men. The tale will follow you, I promise it. Everything considered, you would be best advised to go on south, for you can gain no advantage here."

Lot glared at the two of us, and turned his horse away, trotting back to confer with his men. He had courage, I gave him that. It would have been the easiest thing in the world to put an arrow between his shoulder blades, and well he knew it. I wondered why I did not. Except for Cornu's warning, I might have.

Lot raised his spear and called a double handful of his men around him, giving them instructions, and then led them screaming, directly toward our gate. I waited until they were fifty yards away, gritted my teeth and, remembering Cornu's words, put an arrow through the chest of his horse, bringing it to earth. I hated this! With arrows Morgause handed to me, one by one, I shot three more horses in the time it takes to draw a breath. The sling maidens had hidden below the raised wall along the roof edge of the bathhouse. They rose and sent a hail of fist-sized rocks into the charging men and horses. Several horses went down, and men reeled and fell, bringing the charge to a milling halt.

There was no leader to form around, and suddenly they started to flee. At that moment the manor house gates were thrown open by men stationed there for that purpose, and our light cavalry poured forth with their flails singing. The rocks that rained on the heads of the enemy horsemen had so distracted them they were not aware of the pursuit until they were overcome. Our warriors ran through them, wheeled, and drove the riderless horses before them, back into our compound. We shut the gates once more. The sling women disappeared, and only Morgause, Big Red and I were visible to the foe. We watched with interest while Lot's troops ran to where he lay, picked him up without regard to any pain he might be suffering, and carried him away, out of reach of our arrows and stones, along with others of their fallen comrades who still lived.

"Nothing will happen now until Lot is able to take command again," I said. "Let's get some food to the fighters while we have a chance." We had been too busy to think of eating once we learned Lot and his people were coming, and I was hungry, if no one else was. Morgause left to see my orders were filled.

I smiled grimly when I remembered my father had commanded the defense of a fort in a siege. The odds against him were nowhere near as severe as those I faced. He had died. I wondered how I would fare. Boudicca, watch over me, I prayed silently.

An hour later, as we stood watching, a herald approached under a flag. "Hear me, Lady," he called. "I would come and parley."

"Come safely, if no treachery is meant," I responded. It was not inconceivable that a herald would seek to get close enough to kill me, hoping to end the resistance.

"I mean no treachery, Lady. I am not armed," he assured me, dismounting and showing his open hands. It wasn't quite true, for his belt held a knife; but I held a nocked arrow, and I deemed I could kill him before he could draw his knife and throw.

"Come, then," I said.

"Don't trust him, Lady," Big Red said to me, drawing protectively close.

"Why should I fear him with you here?" I replied lightly, but I smiled at her, and she colored up like the girl she still was.

The herald walked up to where we could talk without shouting, a device to worry my followers. Serfs were not consulted when disposition of their lives was made, and these folk had been serfs too short a time ago to be sure of me. The herald said, "King Lot sends his greetings to the Lady Morgan and says his original offer is still open. Give us your horses, cattle, grain and serfs, both men and women, and we will not molest you or the other ladies."

I replied so that many of those near me could hear, and the herald winced at the loudness of my voice; but I wanted no question in the minds of my people to gnaw at their resolve. "You say Lot wants our horses, cattle, grain and folk, both men and women. What use would you find for our women?"

I repeated the herald's words loudly, so he raised his voice in reply, realizing I had not been tricked. "Your serfs?" he asked. "We have too few camp followers for all the men who have joined King Lot. They would become camp women, of course, cooking, washing clothes and servicing the men at night. Think well, it is better than being dead," he said, and I knew he was appealing to them directly, playing on their fears.

"And after the battle?" I asked.

"I am sure they would be allowed to return to you, if you wished. Nay, I would pledge myself for it!"

"And the male serfs?"

"Even those, the ones still able to walk. You know there is a terrible toll on serfs in this kind of battle, Lady," he said, dropping his voice.

Yes, I knew. "Hear me, then, herald. I told your king we have no serfs among us. All the men and women who serve this community do so as free people. I own no cattle, no grain, no horses except for the breeding stock that we have not trained to ride to war. Everything Lot demands belongs to others, not to me. I cannot respond to his request, for I have nothing to offer."

"He will not believe that, Lady," the herald said.

"No more than you do, I take it. Very well, though I speak the truth, let it be said that if I did own these men and women, horses and cows and stored grain, still would I refuse. If all these folk and goods were mine, Lot would still have to take it all from me by force, for I would give him nothing. If he tries to force us, it will be as ashes in his mouth, for we will kill every animal, burn the grain and fight to the death, taking as many of his folk with him as we are able. Tell him that!"

The herald saluted, turned, took up his horse's reins, mounted and rode off, shaking his head. He did not relish bringing my words to Lot and his chieftains. I wondered if Lot would wait for morning to attack. There were only a few hours left before dark.

I need not have wondered. Lot was so furious he charged without waiting for his men, and they swarmed behind him in their thousands. I shot his horse down again at fifty paces, throwing Lot under the hooves of his warriors' horses, and hoped he would be trampled. His warriors stopped again, bereft of a leader, and he rose as from the grave, pulled a man out of the saddle, remounted and came on. This time I killed his horse within a dozen strides of the gate, and started shooting others as fast as I could nock the arrows. There were horses kicking as they lay dying, and I hoped one of them would finish Lot for me.

I hated shooting the horses, but Cornu was right. There were no options. Besides, I could not miss a horse, but a man would attempt to dodge the arrow shaft. I had no time for misses. I repeated Cornu's words like a litany, over and over, "Horses are more valuable than men in battle. Men can be replaced . . ." It did not comfort me.

There were a hundred mounted men, and they were restricted to attacking the gate, for the horses could not cross the ditch. The foot soldiers could, though, and they swarmed down and hoisted one another up the steep edge. They were easy targets, for they could not protect themselves and climb at the same time.

The sling maidens rained rocks on the heads of horsemen and footmen alike, stunning man or beast on every throw, but still they came on. They split at the gate, running along the walls to avoid my arrows. The walls were over twice the height of a tall man and made the fort impregnable without ladders. When the warriors attempted to scale them by standing on each other's shoulders they were met by ax-men and knife-men fighting beside women with staves. A few who won their way up and jumped into the forted area were met by Cornu and his light cavalry with their flails whirring, ranging inside the wall, going wherever they were needed to beat the invaders down. It was magnificent, but it would not be enough. There were too many of them, and too few of us.

I had stopped shooting horses, and was shooting men, cursing the necessity of doing either. Some of the raiders had cut small trees from the edge of the forest and were using them like ladders, leaning them against our walls and attempting to scramble up before they were thrust down by our ax-men. One tree became ten, and ten a hundred. I dropped my bow after sending my last arrow into the face of a man who, having gained the roof, was grinning triumphantly, and I picked up my stave, to slash and thrust at those who joined him. Big Red fought by my side, weeping in rage and shouting curses at the men she faced. I heard the sound of the great Roman battle horns captured years ago, but was not sure where they came from until they sounded just below the gate.

I glanced over and saw Drake waving a horn and arguing furiously with Lot. Urien rode up and joined them with his other sons. Lot was surrounded by them, and in a fair way to becoming their prisoner if he refused to do their bidding, so he sent a herald out to call his men away from the battle. Lot's men retreated to the edge of the forest, and Urien's took over the old camp space we had just recently cleaned, space between the manor house and Lot's forces. Drake came looking for me, and I gazed down at him as he reached the gate.

"Hail, Mother," he said smiling up at me. "Are you all right?"

"The better for seeing you," I responded, smiling back.

His smile was replaced by a frown as he said, "There is blood all over you!"

I looked myself over and said, "Little of it is mine, a few small cuts, perhaps."

"Is my wife with you?"

"Big Red?" I asked, laughing for the first time in many hours. "She has fought by my side like a shield-maiden of old," I told him. Big Red was sitting at my feet leaning against the parapet, exhausted. She grinned up at me, then rose to look down on her husband.

"Lud's balls," Drake said softly, looking up at her. He stood in the saddle and leaped up to catch the edge of the parapet. She hauled him on up as if he had been a sack of meal. They embraced, and I was happy to learn he truly cared for her, for I had come to like her more and more.

I descended from the wall, stepping over dead men with arrows in their throats, men I had killed, and slid back the great iron bolt that barred the small sentry door, a portal set into the front gate. Drake's men burst in and set off to find their families. I locked the door again and went back on gate duty, looking over the field, shaking with emotion. I opened my mind and allowed the compassion I felt to flow out and saw looks of surprise come over some of the wounded who were still conscious as my feelings touched them.

There were dead and dying men and horses everywhere, but few of ours among them. I was tired, but not too tired to look after our wounded. I left one of the Cornish knights on watch and set the others to collecting those who had been hurt and needed help. Morgause was already at work with Julia, their training among the priestesses of the Mother in evidence as they moved from person to person, stanching the flow of blood where necessary, and encouraging those not badly hurt to bear the pain until they could be attended to.

I had stored quantities of healing supplies, moldy bread, goose grease and clean linen bandages chiefly, and had them fetched to the atrium of the manor house, which had been turned into a healing floor. There were not above twenty persons in need of help, until one of the women asked if we should treat the enemy or just kill them.

"Ask them which they prefer," Morgause said in a practical voice. I know not how many chose the knife, but we worked on twice as many of them as we did of our own.

"We lost nine persons, no more," Drake said to me when I sat back on my heels to rest. "Three were young women. I am told they fought valiantly."

"Then we shall give them all heroes' funerals," I said. "Prepare a pyre outside the gate, and we will send their spirits onward."

"What about Lot's men?" he asked.

"Have them carried into the field, and let his people do with them what they will, both dead and wounded. They are no longer a concern of ours," I answered him, and so it was done. It was dark when we finished, and the voices of the women chanted a lament to fallen heroes led by the clear, sweet voice of Julia. The glow from the funeral pyre still stained the night sky when I fell asleep.

I did not see Lot before he left, but Drake told me he was in a horse litter, so bruised from having fallen each time I shot a horse out from under him that he could not walk, much less ride. Drake stood beside me in my place above the gate, and I watched the litter go past. I saw a curtain move as Lot peered out, and heard him curse. It was funny. I laughed and laughed, the healing sound washing away the anger I had held close these many years against the man and his brutality. The curtain closed with a swish, and I laughed louder. The sound was carried throughout the fort and into the field. Some of the women joined me on the roof and laughed with me. It must have been bitter to hear, and I doubt not the sound echoed in Lot's dreams. Oh, but it was good for me! Boudicca would have been proud.

Drake told me Cornu had sent a messenger to him where he and his brothers had camped with Urien outside of Carlisle, when Lot came down upon us. Drake's return saved us, and I made him my heir, promising to care for his family until he returned. He still planned to go with his father to fight against Arthur. As the oldest of Urien's sons, he was the logical person to take over the lands I had claimed, now that Accolon was dead. Uwayne never even entered into my thoughts. He was his father's son, not mine, at least not any more than Urien's other sons.

The folk were so elated over their success in holding Lot's men at bay, they insisted on a victory celebration. Whole pigs and cows were slowly roasted in pits dug into the sod, lined with stones and covered with live coals. Folk left to tend to affairs at their homes, finding them destroyed, often as not. Still, many a secret store of mead and barley beer was dug up and brought to the fort to share. Promises were made to rebuild where help was requested, and the experience served to bring the people together. I heard the fort named "Morgan's hold" by person after person and decided at long last I had found the place I belonged, above all others.

Folk who had not fought, but merely cowered in the shelter of the palisade, turned to and swept the field of the remnants of Lot's passing. Lot had buried his men under a long, low mound, and I had sod cut to cover it, holding the men deserving of respect I would not have given their master. Some of those men were from Merricks-hold, pressed into service by Lot.

There was food to eat, drink that would grace a Beltane feast, and couples in the grass making love as if it were a feast in honor of the Mother. There was sanction for it. Julia declared a holiday and blessed the feasting.

Folk from Merricks-hold drifted down to join us, men and women who had avoided the gangs Lot sent out to capture workers for his war. There was little food left at Merricks-hold, for there had been no warning for them of Lot's coming. We shared, however, and they helped us to celebrate. I found myself paired with a tall, towheaded youngster who had come to Merricks-hold from Ireland with his parents but a few years past. His name was Hemiston, and his eye was for me. I took him to the woods and lay with him as an affirmation of life, more open than I could remember, before laughter had freed me from the dark shadow Lot had cast over my spirit. I mourned Accolon in my inner being, swearing to myself that I would bring his ghost to rest, as with my father so many years ago. I had not forgotten.

CHAPTER XI

rake came to see me after the victory feast. "Our father is determined to redeem his word to Lot," he said. "He says Lot did not understand that Morgan's hold was the home of his sons when he attacked it."

"That may even be true," I replied. "It would be enough for him to know that it was my home."

"What lies between you, then?" Drake asked.

"It is a personal matter and nothing that would affect your honor," I told him. I saw no reason to acquaint my sons with the truth of Uwayne's parentage. Reassured, Drake led his brothers to follow Urien.

Big Red joined me on the parapet over the gate. I was looking south to where my sons had gone. An uncharacteristic frown creased her forehead.

"I cannot rest, Lady," she said to me.

"Nor I," I replied.

"When do you think the battle will take place?"

"Not for some weeks, I would guess. Cornu tells me that a muster of this size is always slow, for there has to be agreement on where to meet, how many men to furnish, how much in provision is necessary and a hundred other details. The longer it takes, the more complicated it becomes. Sometimes people just get tired of waiting and drift away."

"I never thought much about warfare until Lot came down on us, planning to rape and steal. I don't like to think about Drake out there with men like Lot."

"He is in bad company," I agreed.

"I know, and he is on our side! Can this Arthur be any better?"

"I know little of Arthur," I said, "but I would think the men around him will be as fierce as Lot and his warriors. I remember one, Brastius Red-beard. I liked him, because he treated me well, but his men ambushed and killed my father. Brastius was one of Uther Pendragon's generals."

"Why would you not help Lot against him then?" she asked me frankly.

"When I was about your age Lot raped me," I said. "I will never take his side, not against hell itself."

"Ah," she said. "That explains much. Had you no kinsman to take him to account?"

"Men of my clan tried to get him, but he fled. This is the first time any of us has seen him since."

"If Drake knew that, he would not have gone with Lot," she said flatly.

"No, he would not, but I could not tell him. My son Uwayne is Lot's, not Urien's. It is not something any of my sons need to know."

"No, I see that. Does Lot himself know?"

"He does not. That's another reason to maintain silence. I don't want him to have any claim on Uwayne. My son is enormously proud of Urien, thinking him his father. Urien is no friend to me, but I would not take this away from my son."

"Life has not treated you fairly, Lady," she told me.

"Hasn't it? Perhaps not. I know no remedy, however."

The girl brooded beside me, both of us resting our elbows on the skirting wall. "What if he gets hurt?" she asked suddenly.

I thought maybe that had been uppermost in her mind. "Battle wounds are always serious," I said. "Unless someone who knows how cares for them, they tend to fester, even quite minor cuts. It's the worst thing about war, the way men suffer."

"I feared it, Lady. I can't let Drake die from some scratch for want of someone to soak it and keep it clean. I know him. He makes light of hurts. I have to go to him, somehow."

"He won't like it," I told her. "He wants you safe here. If you were with him you would be a prize of war, and the thought would make him cautious, and more vulnerable."

"I'll hide," she said. "I won't let him know I'm there. If I don't go, and something happens to him, I'll kill myself!"

The girl was overly dramatic, but her desperation was real enough. I doubted if she would carry through her threat, but I understood what lay behind her words.

"Can you ride a horse?" I asked.

"Of course," she replied, surprise flaring her nostrils slightly.

I smiled inwardly. Most women cannot ride. "Well, we might contrive to travel as a knight and squire. It would hardly be safe to go as females without attendants in these times."

"Knight and squire? You would go with me?" she asked, delight radiating from her.

"Why, yes, I think I would. I confess, I would be easier in my mind also if I could keep my eye on the boys. Besides, if Drake learned I had let you go by yourself, he would never forgive me." That was true.

"Oh, grand! When can we start?"

"Let me talk to Cornu first. He'll have suggestions that will be helpful. The hardest part will be in convincing him to stay behind."

"Why can't he come with us?"

"We might disguise ourselves to pass as a man and youth, but no one else in the world looks like Cornu. If he were with us, do you think Drake or Gawaine would be fooled?"

"I hadn't thought of that," she admitted.

Cornu was as difficult as I thought he would be. "You have mares in foal and couldn't leave them without losing some," I reminded him. That was true, too; I never lie unless I must.

He hesitated, squared his shoulders and said, "I have trained Sam and Susan to handle stock. They will be all right."

"They will not, and you know it," I said. "Nine out of ten mares need no help in delivering, but the tenth one will need you, not some stable lad."

He nodded, defeated. "I am needed here," he admitted. "Are you sure you must go?"

"I think, perhaps, yes," I replied. "I still have my old boar spear. It will make as good a lance as most knights carry. With my hair short I can cram it under a helmet. I can pass all right, for I am as big as most men. I'll wear a chain-mail face guard to hide my features."

"What about the girl?" he asked.

"She is more fierce than me by far," I told him. "She can carry an extra spear for me, and use it as a quarterstaff at need. Did you see her fight?"

"No, was she good?"

"I'm glad she was taking care of me and not striving to do me injury," I told him.

We found armor taken from Lot's men that could be made to work for us, chain-mail shirts and simple casque helmets. Big Red cut her hair like mine, to my dismay, but she said it would be too difficult to keep clean otherwise.

"Drake will never forgive me for allowing you to do this," I said, "particularly since you sacrificed your hair. It was so beautiful! How could you?" But I laughed, for she looked so defiant.

"Who gave you permission to cut your hair, Lady?" she asked me, for mine was still short.

"We look a pair of fools, in truth," I admitted.

Cornu gave us geldings to ride, big calm horses with little imagination. They were faster than most large mounts, however, and trained to respond to the lightest pressure from the knee. I bade good-bye to Cloud, trying to explain to her why I was leaving her behind. How could I tell her she was too dear to risk in battle, and perhaps too old? I also told Susan to keep the cats in, for the male cat that had adopted me would try to follow. I'd named him

Tag, for that was what he did. Tag was very cross when I went anywhere without him, and generally managed to track me, only to ignore me elaborately when he was sure I had noticed him.

I loved traveling. I had done much of it, mostly in the service of others, and this time was no exception, but there was no pressure to reach a destination. Armies moved more slowly than small parties. We caught up with Lot's forces, skirted them and were ahead of them within two weeks. We took oat and barley cakes for trail fare and begged bread and cheese from local peasant farmers, warning them soldiers were coming. They were thankful, and drove their stock into the woods as soon as we left.

The weather continued fine. Fall could be wet and cold, but this season the bad weather held off as if the gods wished no impediment to the coming battle with Arthur. I wondered whom they favored.

Big Red was not a quiet companion. She constantly talked or sang or whistled, the latter an art at which she was adept. She never expected answers to her questions, which was restful, for I paid but scant attention to her. It was entertaining, all the same. If she needed a response it was her habit to touch my arm, and she did so now.

"Lady, what does yonder man want?"

I followed her gaze and saw a man on horseback come out of the trees at the bend of the road. He was armed with a long slim-bladed spear and carried a large, iron rimmed, painted wooden shield for defense. As we watched he started his horse in motion and rode toward us, lowering his spear to point directly at me.

I unstrapped my small, round, leather target shield and held it by the handle fixed across the inside of the iron center boss. I let the man run his horse most of the distance between us before nudging mine in motion, swerving it to the right in front of him just before his spear touched my shield.

I reversed my boar spear and jabbed him on the side of the neck with the spiked butt end as I passed him on the wrong side. His horse nearly crashed into us, and shied to avoid us, pulling the man off-balance. When I turned my gelding in a tight arc, the man was fighting to stay in his saddle. I came up behind him and hit him with an overhead smash where his head and neck met, knocking him out of the saddle. We trampled him as he rolled on the ground. I brought my horse to a stand in front of him, nudging him with the point of my spear, not gently. He groaned and opened his eyes.

"That was a palpable foul," he accused.

"You attacked me without provocation," I told him coldly. "Tell me something that will keep me from skewering you where you lie, bandit."

"I am a knight in service to King Arthur," he said. "I will be avenged."

"By whom?" I asked grimly. "Have you watchers?"

"My squire has gone for my brother," he said.

"I hope he fights better than you do. I'd hate to wipe out an entire family," I told him.

"Tell me your name so that I may know I have not fallen to one of lowly birth."

"I choose not to tell my name, but if it's any consolation to you, I come from a royal house," I told him. "Can you rise?"

"No," he said after essaying an attempt. "You have broken my shoulder."

I dismounted and rummaged through the pack on our spare horse to find medicines. "Watch him, Squire," I told Big Red. "If he is dissembling, rap him one with your quarterstave." I usually called her by name, but I thought of her as Big Red. It fitted her.

"Aye, my lord," she responded, grinning. Both of us wore the chain-mail masks attached to our helmets, hanging so as to leave our eyes free to see, but covering our lower faces. Big Red had a deep voice, like mine, and neither of us had to disguise our speech when we donned male attire.

I unfastened the man's helmet, and examined his wounds. The tip of the boar spear had luckily missed his jugular vein, but a great bruise was spreading from the point of impact. I pulled his chain-mail shirt over his head, to his cursing, which ceased as he fainted. After that it was easy.

"I broke his collarbone," I said, setting it and binding his arm to his chest so he would not disturb it. "It is not serious, but will be painful and disabling for some weeks."

"Serves him right," Big Red said, heartlessly. "You'd better mount, Lady, for here comes his brother, if I'm not mistaken."

I looked up. This one had only a spear in his hand, held at the balance point, and was riding as if he were interested only in the man on the ground. His shield hung from a saddle thong. Glancing briefly at me, he stuck the spear into the turf and dismounted to kneel by the prostrate man.

"How came he so?" he asked.

"He attacked me, and I knocked him out of the saddle," I said. "His shoulder is broken."

"Did you bind him up?"

"Yes," I said. "He fainted. He will be all right with a few weeks' rest to mend."

"What is your name?" he asked, standing to look at me. He was as tall as me, and stronger, a twin to the man on the ground.

"Why is that important?" I countered.

"There are only three knights in Britain who could unhorse my brother: Lancelot, Pelleas and Tristram," he said. "They are all bigger than you."

"There are now four knights," I said, nettled. "Would you like me to prove it on you?"

"Nay, I am not armed for combat."

"Then it were best you guard your mouth," I said. "Only a coward talks so if he does not intend to back his words."

"Some other time we may discuss this," he said. "For now, I am concerned for my brother. He is pledged to stand with Arthur against Lot within a fortnight. Will you stay and watch him so I can go in his place? His gillies will need supervision. I won't be long. The great battle plain is less than two hours' ride south from here."

"That I will not. I might carry his shield so that men will think he has come, though," I said.

He considered this a moment, looked down at his brother, back

211

at me and came to a decision. He retrieved his brother's shield and brought it to me along with his own. The one he gave to me had crossed swords crudely painted on it.

"My brother is Sir Balin, the Knight with Two Swords," he said. "Men will recognize his device. I always ride as squire to my brother. Let your squire take my shield." Its device was twins, holding hands.

"I know your brother for something else," I said. "He was the murderer of Hilda, Lady of the Lake. I will stop by here on my way home from battle. If your brother waits for me, I will try a passage of arms with him again. Next time I will try to kill him."

Big Red took both shields as a proper squire would, and we left the man standing open-mouthed, gazing after us.

"If I were a bard I would make a song out of this, Lady," she said. "I may try it, anyway," she decided, and an unfocused look came over her face as she started mouthing words silently.

"Well, sing it to yourself," I told her. "Now we have a way to join Arthur's band when they take to the field, and no one will question us. I will be Balin. We can move through the battle and find Drake as we planned. Don't give us away."

She nodded and from time to time sang little snatches of the ballad she was composing. "What rhymes with skewered, Lady?" she might ask. I thought she was teasing, but I feared I would be hearing more of it some time later before my own fire at Morgan's hold.

When we reached Camelot there were so many folk around that we were ignored as I had hoped. Indeed, the only way to get attention was to grab someone physically and shout in his face. We were happy not to do so. I covered Balin's shield with a bit of linen sacking so the device would not show, and Big Red did the same with hers. We avoided Lancelot's men, for Balin was supposed to be one of them.

No one questioned us, and we took our places at the end of the line of battle when Lot's men came in sight, and uncovered our shields as I had promised Balin's brother. "We can ride around and get behind Lot's men from here," I told Big Red. "It ought to be easy to find the boys and keep an eye on their progress."

212

Lot's men charged, some of them from light wagons, others on horseback with footmen following, waving the great two-handed swords they used and screaming battle cries. Even on the edge of the line we found ourself flanked because of Lot's greater numbers. I used my spear like a club and knocked men from our path, hoping I would not hurt them overmuch. Big Red rode behind me through the gap I created, and from the corner of my eye I could see her laying about with gusto. She was enjoying this!

We broke through the wall of men and horses and found ourselves behind the main fight. Before us were a motley band of squires, supply-wagon drivers and women Lot had stolen along the road. We rode parallel to the line of advancing men, looking for Drake, and found him with Urien's horsemen. Insofar as there was any organization to the charge, Urien's troops represented the right wing of Lot's army.

"There he is, there's Drake," Big Red said, pulling her horse up beside me and pointing.

"All the brothers are there," I responded, and we watched as they slammed into Arthur's line of pike men stationed in front of the cavalry. They pushed through, with terrible losses, only to be engaged one-on-one by Arthur's knights before they had a chance to regroup. The pike-men had closed their ranks and met the foot soldiers, creating such a jam of struggling men that Lot's people could not retreat.

The wagons were swept clear by mounted men. Holding long chains between pairs of riders, they dashed by the wagons and pulled the warriors to the ground, where they were set upon by ax-men.

Lot's horsemen had to fight their way back through the foot soldiers to win free, and they fled in panic up the hill, straight for us, chased by Arthur's warriors. I unfastened the chain-mail face veil for better sight.

"There he is," Big Red said, and started past me. I grabbed the reins of her horse and stopped her.

"Wait!" I commanded. I saw him, too, riding one of Cornu's black geldings and holding another man halfway across his saddle in front of him. Another rider coming from behind him crashed into him, and knocked both Drake and his wounded comrade to the ground. The impact tore his assailant's helmet off, and I recognized Lot's flaming red hair. Lot did not hesitate, but rode directly over Drake.

Big Red tore the reins loose from my hand and urged her mount forward to aid Drake, screaming, "No! No!"

I was cursing, "Lot, damn you! Damn you! Damn you!" over and over as I set my spear and rode straight toward Lot himself, who was now first in flight as he had been first in fight.

He saw me at the last minute, and knew me, for he grimaced as I called him by name. "Die, Lot, bastard!" I yelled. My boar spear caught him in the chest, and the shock of it nearly knocked me backward. If I had not braced myself with my stirrups, I would have fallen. Before I could pull the spear from his chest, a mounted knight swung an overhand stroke with his sword and cut Lot's head off cleanly, splattering blood all over my horse's legs.

I wrenched my spear free and looked into the face of a giant of a man. "Your trophy, I think," he said as he glanced at my shield. "Young Balin, isn't it?" He casually speared Lot's head with the point of his sword and held it up to me. Lot's eyes were open, and I could swear they gazed at me accusingly.

"It would not serve my needs," I said faintly.

"Oh, well, very generous, I'm sure," he said, and attached Lot's head to his saddle by tying his hair to a saddle thong. It bounced against his knee as he rode off ponderously on a huge, fat horse, saluting me with his free hand.

I shook my head and pushed past him to gain Big Red's side. Her horse was kicking at the oncoming riders, and I dismounted, turned my horse to stand beside hers, shielding Big Red and the fallen men. The battle swirled around and past us, as if we had been a rock in the road. I marveled at it.

"Oh, help him, Lady," Big Red implored, and I stooped and felt the pulse in Drake's neck. It beat strongly. The other man was dead, however.

"We'll make a horse litter out of spears and cloaks and carry him out of here," I said.

The geldings shielded us from the oncoming rout, screaming and kicking out so that men veered away, leaving us free to attend to Drake. Big Red and I rigged the litter and attached it to my horse by tying the ends across its butt, allowing the iron spear blades to drag on the ground. Big Red walked beside Drake, holding him on, and I mounted Big Red's horse, riding in front to clear a way with my leveled boar spear.

We could hear men and horses screaming in pain as we went north, even after we could no longer see them.

"Will he be all right, Lady?" Big Red asked me for the tenth time.

"I won't know until I have examined him properly," I said. I had visions of a horse's hoof striking his head, and feared for the worst.

"Then do it!" she screamed, and I resignedly turned the horse off the path into the bordering trees.

"We are still too close for safety," I told her, "but perhaps we can conceal ourselves."

She only grunted and had lifted Drake from the litter before I could come to help her. She held him cradled in her arms like a sleeping child. Big Red was strong!

"Careful, careful." I muttered, spreading a cloak from the litter on level ground. I helped ease him down gently, and together we stripped him so I could examine him. He was well-muscled and fine-boned, like most Picts. He seemed to be fit and healthy, and except for a few scratches, unwounded. Still, he was unconscious. I examined his skull, pressing against it with my fingertips to see if it moved. Blood caked his hair from a deep cut in the scalp. The bone was sound, however.

"I judge he has a bruised brain," I said. "His eye pupils are not dilated, and there is no blood coming from his ears, so it may well be not more than that. We'll just have to wait until he recovers consciousness to tell truly."

"How long?" she asked.

"I don't know," I replied. "In general, the longer he is unconscious, the worse the prognosis. Bathe his face and wash his hair. We'll have to cut it away from the scalp wound to bind it properly."

This was something she could do, and she set about it with a grim efficiency. I probed the cut to be sure there was no fragment of metal broken off in the bone, but it was clean. Drake came to as we were winding the bandage around his head.

"What is this?" he muttered, and tried to sit up.

"You bumped your head," I told him sternly, and recognition came into his eyes when he heard my voice.

Then he saw Big Red. "Ah, Moira, what do you here?" he asked.

"We pulled you from the battle, the lady and I," she told him. "Some great red-haired lout was trampling you under his horse's hooves," she added in a tone which implied disapproval.

"I never saw him," Drake said defensively.

"Well, I should hope not!" In spite of her teasing words, she was close to tears. I thought I might leave them alone.

"I am going back to the battlefield," I said. "I may be able to help others."

"Don't go back to that terrible place!" Big Red objected. "You could get killed there!"

"That's unlikely, and there may be some of Drake's brothers in need of help," I said. "I'll be back by nightfall. Don't build a fire until I return. Stay quiet. I don't think you'll be seen, but take precautions."

"We could move farther back under the trees," Drake said.

"No," Big Red and I said together.

"You are not to rise," I said. "You have had a shock and must remain quiet for a few days, or there could be bad consequences."

He looked stubborn, the way he had as a child when he was considering disobeying me. "Keep him down," I told Big Red, and she nodded with a determined air. She turned her gaze on Drake, and he grinned. I thought he was in good hands.

I rode back to the battle, carrying my own small, round target

216

shield instead of Balin's large battle shield. I wasn't worried about being recognized anymore.

There were others looking over the battle scene, stripping the dead and trying to help the wounded. I encountered the twins, Ken and Dunc, doing what I was doing. They rode over to me.

"Well met, Mother!" they said in unison.

I rode up between them and hugged them both.

"Have you seen Drake?" Ken asked. "We have his horse, but we can't find him."

"We fear Arthur's camp followers have already despoiled his body," Dunc added.

"Moira and I have him," I told them, untangling myself from their noisy embrace.

"We might have known!" Ken said. "You always looked out for any of us when we got into trouble! Is Drake all right?"

"He was knocked off his horse and got stepped on," I told them. "If he hadn't had a rocklike Pictish head, he might have been hurt. Are you both all right?"

"Not a scratch," Ken said.

Dunc laughed in relief. "He'll never live it down. Knocked off his horse!"

"King Lot ran into him from behind and went right over him, not even swerving," I told them. "I think Lot's horse kicked Drake."

"Lot, hey? He got his, they say," and two pairs of eyes looked at me keenly.

"Do they?"

"King Pellinore said he gave a finishing stroke to Lot after Lot was felled by as neat a spear thrust as ever he saw," Ken said.

Dunc added, "He said it was Balin of the Two Swords riding a new blaze-faced horse." They both glanced at my animal. My horse was a blaze-face, a son of my father's old stallion. All his offspring were marked so.

"Sorry to hear it," I said. "I just got here, myself." The twins nodded gravely at this information, as if I had not just told them I had already taken Drake from the field. I wondered if they knew

I had taken Balin's shield into battle. It was hard to tell with these two.

Then Ken said, "Take Drake's horse. You'll need it to get him home." And he handed me the reins.

"We may be some time returning," I said. "Drake may have to lay up for a few weeks until he can travel comfortably. Don't worry about us." Taking the horse, I waved them good-bye. As I rode back to Drake and Big Red, I mused that I might have aided some of the other wounded, if I had come earlier. It was too late now. The ones that would live were up and limping around; the others were dead or fast dying, their wounds already festering.

"How did the battle go?" Drake asked me when I returned.

"I never asked," I told him, and he laughed. His color was better, and he said he was hungry. I caught fish for him, enough for Big Red and me too. With the passage of so many men, there was no game around. It had either been killed or was hiding deeper in the woods. With the oat and barley cakes, fish was as much as an invalid should eat, anyway.

Within a week Drake absolutely refused to stay on his back another minute. Though standing made him dizzy at first, he was soon fit enough to travel, at least if we went slowly, walking our horses and stopping early.

We found the small hermitage where Balin and his brother had been staying. It was filthy.

"They left here two days ago, Lady," the hermit said.

I looked at him and wondered if he had ever bathed. "You're welcome to stay, if you wish," he said, eyeing us and calculating how big a donation he might ask for.

"Thank you, no," I said. "I have unfinished business with Balin, but if he is not here it must wait, I fear. He didn't say he was returning, by any chance?"

"No," the man said reluctantly.

We got away and continued our journey. I felt like a chaperone with two young people to supervise, rather than a mother or a queen or even a witch, as some name me, on the rest of the trip. Big Red flirted with Drake all the way, and he played up to her in a most satisfactory way. It almost made me feel young again. As it was, I was delighted when Hemiston found us a day out of Morgan's hold and swept me up in a rough embrace.

"Why did you go without me, Lady?" he asked me when I got my breath back. Drake and Big Red were laughing.

"Well," I said. "If I had known how badly you were going to miss me, I am sure I would have asked you to come along."

"Don't treat me like a child, Lady," he admonished. "I care for you and do not rest easy out of your sight."

"Ah, Hemiston, lad!" I exclaimed. "Truly, I had no idea!"

"What did you think, then?"

It simply had not occurred to me. Perhaps I needed to think about it. "You two go on," I told Big Red and Drake. "It seems Hemiston and I have some talking to do." I tried to be cool about it, but since Hemiston had not released me, the effect was not all I could have wished. I did not see them go.

When we finally reached Morgan's hold the next day, I rode through the gates by myself. From the way people smiled without saying anything, I knew Drake and Big Red had told everyone why I was late. It didn't matter.

What did matter was that I found Urien sitting and giving judgment from my chair in the great hall.

"Welcome home, Lady," he told me, rising but not moving from in front of the seat.

"What are you about?" I asked him, ignoring his words of greeting. "I thought you had gone to battle." Hearing my voice, the few petitioners left scurried away, not wishing to be present in what looked like a confrontation between great ones.

"The battle is over, Lady, and what I am doing is what I have been doing all my adult life," he said, "playing a king's part."

"If that is your wish, go back to cold Gore where you might be welcome," I told him. "Here you have been tolerated as a guest of my sons, nothing more."

"Nothing more? Gawaine left these folk in my care."

"He did not, then," I snapped, careful to keep my temper within my head. "Gawaine has no say north of Hadrian's Wall, Urien. Surely, he told you that."

"He did not. If you object to my being here I will go back to Caerleon, but wherever I am, I shall rule this land."

"Would you like to contest it, knife to knife, like our fathers once might have?" I asked him. I took from my belt the knife Pelleas had made and tested the blade edge with my thumb, glancing over at him.

"Fight with a woman?" He laughed in scorn.

He moved barely in time to save himself from being emasculated. Cornu and Uwayne appeared from behind me, and while Cornu held Urien off, Uwayne whirled me around to face him.

"What are you doing, Mother?" he asked in horror.

"I'm trying to convince your father that he is not welcome longer in Morgan's hold!" I stormed at him.

"You could not chain me tightly enough to keep me here," Urien snarled, holding up his severed belt with one hand. "You might have unmanned me!"

"For all I would know of the matter, that was done a decade ago," I said in reply.

His face went white at the taunt. He brushed Cornu's hands off, pushed by without glancing at me and left my hall.

"Do not come back, Urien, neither you nor your people!" I shouted. "Stay away from my lands!"

Uwayne left my side to follow his father.

"Son," I called, running after him. He turned to me, misery in his face. "You do not have to go," I told him in a pleading voice, extending a hand in entreaty. "My words were not for you!"

"But they were, Mother," he said, and turned away.

"Uwayne!" I called again. He did not respond this time, and I watched him walk away. I had no way to hold him.

Urien left the stallion I had given him tethered to my gate. It was lean and scarred from battle, but young and strong. My father's war-horse was ancient, and even Cornu realized we needed a new sire for our mares. Cornu said he'd breed Cloud one more time in hopes of getting a mare to replace her, though she had not caught the last two times she was in season. Perhaps a new stallion would bring her into foal. Even so, I hardly thought it a fair exchange for a son.

Wintertime was upon us when Gawaine came to visit. "It is over," he assured me. "Arthur is the High King of the Britons, without challenge." His face was grim.

"Why are you not more happy, then?" I asked, after hugging him impulsively. "Isn't it what you wished?"

"Many died. Saxon mercenaries in Arthur's services were offered shelter in Pelleas' Pictish hill fort. Saxon mercenaries are treacherous. These betrayed Arthur, having sold their services to Lot secretly. When they entered the fort, they killed all they found there, mostly women and children, for Pelleas and his men were away fighting with Arthur. There is great bitterness."

"Who would open his door to Saxons?" I asked in wonder.

"It was asked in Arthur's name," Gawaine said.

"Even so." I shook my head. "Does Pelleas hold Arthur responsible?"

"More than that. He thinks I conspired with my father, Lot, to deceive Arthur, and that Arthur trusted the Saxons on my assurances. You know that I would give no pledge for Saxons!" he said, looking at me hopefully for reassurance.

I nodded.

Morgause came to join us. "What of my other sons?" she asked him, after embracing him in welcome.

"Your sons fought well, and Arthur praised them at the feast of victory that we began before Pelleas brought us word of the Saxon treachery." He frowned in recollection, and I could see that the matter held him deeply. I wondered if his honor was involved, somehow, despite his assurances.

"Is your family well?" I asked, to change the subject. His wife and sons were still at Carlisle with her people.

"They are well enough, but not happy, for they must leave their home. I will move them to Camelot to join Arthur. I have been made a Knight of the Round Table, the brotherhood Arthur formed to keep his laws. Until Guenevere gives him an heir, I am Arthur's successor and must stand near the throne in truth as well as in men's minds." He looked keenly at me, and I wondered if he had heard I had cursed Guenevere with barrenness for her part in the death of Accolon.

"What will happen to Lothian?" Morgause asked.

"Arthur has judged it to be mine, if I want it. He would have friends on his northern border to hold the Picts from his own lands in Britain, for he has fewer friends among them than you do," Gawaine said, smiling at me. "He sees the Saxons as his chief enemies, since their treachery in battle has become evident."

"How can you hold Lothian if Arthur expects you to live in Camelot?" Morgause asked. "Will you appoint your brother Aggravain to be your regent?"

"Would you?" Gawaine asked bluntly. "I, myself, would not trust him with anything I valued, not for fear he would steal it, but that he would destroy it."

"Lot sent beasts and grain he stole from Merricks-hold back to Lothian for his own use when he raided the clan house," Morgause said. "My people will face a hungry winter unless they recover their goods. If you wish, I will bring my people there to keep your lands for you. It would be the saving of them as well."

"I feared to ask it of you, but it is what I would wish," Gawaine said. He adored his mother. I was slightly jealous of her as I had never been of Gawaine's wife, a nice, plump, simple girl who was interested only in babies. Her children must be pretty big now, I mused.

"The only problem I would see is your leaving Merricks-hold," Gawaine said to Morgause. "The wild Scoti will flow in and threaten us all, if we do not control their access and bring their folk in with promises of fealty to our clan."

"Morgan will see to it," Morgause said unexpectedly. "Her Scoti lineage is as good as any. Remember, she is the only daughter of Igraine, who was the next eldest daughter of the royal clan. If I am not there, she will be."

And I was. All the lands between Merricks-hold and Morgan's hold became known as Galloway, the land of the foreign Gaels, the Scoti of Ireland. I was acknowledged as the local head of the clan Merrick by the priestesses of the Mother when Morgause moved to Lothian. Morgause was still clan chief. Julia stayed with me as priestess of the Mother, the only condition I required to take over the added responsibility. I would not subject myself to pressure from the clan mothers through some old priestess who would do their bidding without question.

If I was jealous of Morgause, Hemiston was jealous of Gawaine. He saw Gawaine as a rival with whom he could not compete. Knowing that, I should have foreseen what would happen when Lancelot came through, questing.

"Welcome, Lord," I told him. "I am starved for word of Camelot."

"You should come to Arthur's court, Lady. You would find no one there to rival your beauty."

"Oh, dear, what has happened to Guenevere?" I asked in mock alarm.

"Arthur's knights always except the queen," he said lightly, "Guenevere is flawless."

"Indeed! Has she given Arthur an heir as yet?"

"No, God has closed her womb," he said, a shade of sorrow fleeting over his face. I studied him as he brooded on my words. He was handsome, but not as Lot had been, all color and fire. Lancelot's hair was black and his skin very white where the sun had not burned it. He was big, but moved with grace rather than power, more like Urien than Arthur.

"Some say she was cursed, Lady," he said, raising a troubled gaze to me. I noticed his eyes were gray rather than blue; at the same moment his words sent a chill through me. I wondered if the color changed with his mood.

Was he accusing me? I knew what I was! What concerned me more was the possibility that what he said was true. I knew my anger could hurt people. I did not know how far-reaching my rage could be. "Would her God permit that?" I asked, as much to reassure myself as to respond to him.

"No," he answered with conviction. "Guenevere is very devout."

223

"Ah! Then it is between her and her God," I stated, closing the subject. I hoped it was true.

We had been talking in Latin, and Hemiston, who had joined us at table, must have thought we were quarreling, for he asked bluntly, "Is aught amiss?"

"Why, no," Lancelot said, arching a perfect eyebrow. "I have been trying to induce Queen Morgan to visit Camelot. Her beauty should grace a Christian court, not be hidden in this wilderness." He looked around our hall as if the rustic look of the place offended him. I was amused, but Hemiston was not.

"I do not see myself as an ornament, Lancelot," I told him, and turned to Hemiston. "I am a person, Hemiston, not a thing to be moved around and gazed upon for some man's pleasure. Do not be concerned."

"Would our queen have to become a Christian in Camelot?" Drake asked with seeming innocence. Big Red nudged him under the table, but Drake merely shifted his foot from under hers before saying, "Would she then come back and baptize the lot of us, do you think, Hemiston?"

"Nay, she would not do that, would you, Lady?" Hemiston asked anxiously.

"Lancelot says Queen Guenevere is more beautiful than our own queen," one of the twins stated.

"Did he now? Then he lied," Hemiston blurted.

"Every man thinks his lady is the most beautiful," Lancelot said. "I will defend my choice against any man who denies it." Lancelot spoke in Gaelic for Hemiston's benefit; a Gaelic heavily accented, but understandable.

Before Hemiston could respond, I interceded. "Enough of this!" I commanded. "Lancelot is a guest here. Were he not so, I would still have no man of mine challenge him, for I would have a dead man on my hands. Lancelot has no match in single combat." I glared around the table, and the boys looked abashed, but Hemiston left, wounded by the comparison.

"See what you have done?" I scolded Drake in Pictish. I still had enough of that tongue to correct unruly boys. "One of you had better keep an eye on Hemiston so he doesn't do something foolish." The twins helped themselves to a joint of beef and went after the angry man.

At the end of the meal they approached me and said, "We could not find him. He has taken one of the horses and ridden off."

"Just as well, perhaps," I said, "though in the unlikely event he intends to ambush Lancelot, it were best you track him. I don't want to send word to Arthur that his best knight came to grief at the hands of one of my followers." They were sober enough now and took me seriously, for they collected companions and began looking for Hemiston in earnest.

Lancelot set out the next morning, and I was giving judgment in my hall between a couple of farmers who claimed the same pig when the boys escorted Lancelot back into my presence. They also carried the body of Hemiston, and laid it at my feet.

"What is this?" I cried.

"We were too late, Lady," Drake said. "When we found Hemiston, he had already challenged Lancelot. He was pledged to fight. We could not in honor stop him."

My cat Tag sat on the right arm of the throne chair Cornu had built for me. He sat and glared at Lancelot standing before me. Tag was impressive, weighing forty pounds. The pet crow Cornu had taught to speak a few words flew into the room and perched on the other arm out of Tag's reach. Cocking his head at Lancelot, he shrieked, "Kill!" It was Cornu's idea of a joke to train a crow to speak as Morigan, the crow goddess of war, might speak.

Lancelot's face was always pale, so I could not tell if he was afraid, but he crossed himself and said, "You are said to be a witch, Lady."

I ignored it. "Could you not turn him away?" I asked Lancelot bitterly. "You saw him for what he was, a lovesick country boy. You knew he had no chance against you."

"I knew no such thing, Lady," Lancelot maintained arrogantly. "He looked a proper man to me."

"In all important ways, he was," I said. "His only failing was a belief that I was something to be loved."

"Love? Him?" Lancelot asked in an amused tone of voice.

"Aye, love! You think we yokels have no feelings of that sort, but breed like pigs in season?" I asked, anger beginning to build in me. I struggled with it, and to keep it down I gave my voice a colder edge than I intended.

"Not at all," he said loftily. "I'm sure he loved you, in his way."

"It was the way of a man for a woman," I said. "You would not speak so if you had ever experienced it. May it never be so with you."

A look of concern crossed his face.

"Furthermore, tell my brother I will permit no Knight of the Round Table to cross my border because of your cowardly behavior!" Then I lost the battle with my temper, for my words were accompanied with such a burst of anger that Lancelot stood as a man struck a heavy blow, stunned.

"Oh, get him from my sight," I ordered. "Take his horse, strip him of his armor and let him walk back to Camelot. If he ever returns to these lands, kill him." And I hid my face to weep. I vowed to have no more to do with Camelot and, true to my word, sealed my borders against Arthur's knights. I had known nothing but pain from association with Uther's line. I wanted no more of it.

Part III
The
King's Sister
486~488

Clovis, King of the Franks and the first of the Merovingian line, begins consolidating his empire by invoking the God of his Christian wife, Clotilda. In Britain the quarrels that center around Queen Guenevere threaten the reign of King Arthur.

CHAPTER

XII

I set about making a kingdom, centered at Morgan's hold; men named it Galloway, the land of foreign Gaels. The name was fitting in that Scoti came to us from Ireland, but there were non-Gaels as well: Picts from the north seeking free land, and Cornishmen disgusted with the rule of King Mark, who had succeeded my father. These latter spoke of a pledge I had given as a child when I left Dimilioc, a promise that in time I would welcome them to a new kingdom. All we needed were women, and these came in little groups, widows from Arthur's wars. Only Arthur's knights were stopped at the borders and turned away.

For the folk that were coming we needed housing and safe storage for harvests. The housing was easy. There were trees enough to build houses for every family in Britain in our forests, and need enough to cut the trees to provide fields for planting. The two went together. Harvests were chancy in this climate, for unseasonable weather could ruin a promising crop with a late frost, or an early one, for that matter. I wanted enough food stored to feed everyone for a year in case of disaster. That year's stored grain had to be eaten before it went bad, so the plan was to collect all grain harvested and to place it in a central granary within the fort's walls to be issued as foodstuff at need. To avoid shifting sacks of grain about we built two huge storage granaries.

229

We set aside all the tile we could find within the walls of the fort, separating broken ones from those whole enough to serve as roof covering. With Cornu supervising the construction, the granaries were made of stone with adzed wooden floors. The whole tiles we had saved were used for roofing, and were waterproof as well as fireproof. The broken tile we ground up and mixed with burned limestone and water for mortar, which, when hard, cemented the stones of the walls together and sealed the tile roofs. The Romans called it pozzalana, and Cornu had learned to work with it from them.

While we were building, I bespoke a tower. I wished to see farther than it was possible to do from the wall by the gate. Cornu built one for me, round like a Pictish broch, outside the gate, but connected to the wall. It rose two stories higher than the wall, and from the roof, which I could reach through a trapdoor, I could stand and watch the seasons pass.

The ground floor became my throne room. I gave judgment from there when the clan mothers brought matters to me, but it was a common room at other times, used by anyone who requested it. There were weddings held there and namings for children with much feasting. I was always invited, and found much pleasure in it. The level that opened into the tower from the top of the wall was my private quarters. Above that was the treasury and armory, though, in truth, we had more iron than gold, and little of either in this room. Our iron was at work in the fields, or leaning up against the walls of farmers' houses, as swords and spears, for we kept a trained militia, not standing troops. The gold was in Cornu's care and was used to trade for things we needed in daily use. We had no stores of precious metal.

As our population grew, only those persons who served me or the Great Mother continued to make their homes within the fort, though all were welcome in times of crisis. Julia was my priestess, and Susan kept the larder, dispensing grain when families came to ask for it, keeping tallies of amounts in and out. Drake was my leader of scouts and hunters, Picts for the most part, and young Gaels for whom farming held little joy. Sam was in charge of the stock, taking advice from Cornu, but in most cases following his own decisions. Cornu was my bard, my chief advisor, and my closest friend, as always. I had no consort, taking one or another lover at Beltane to honor the Great Mother, but I ruled alone.

The Gaels followed the Rule of Three. There were three levels from the folk to the priestesses to the Great Mother, and three from the folk to the clan mothers to the ruler. The Gaels believed that where there were more levels, communication broke down, and accountability for actions was hard to assign. Disputes within families were settled by the clan mothers, and between families by the ruler, with advice as needed from the clan mothers. So it had always been with us, and in this I followed where others had gone before. Indeed, I could do no other. The choice was not mine.

Gawaine stayed at Arthur's side, fighting his battles against the Saxons and living at his court. I missed him, but because I did not speak of it, no one knew, except, perhaps, Cornu. The burden of rule chafed me, and I thought myself unfitted for it.

Big Red, now a clan mother, spoke to me, seeing my unhappiness and saying, "The reason your sons all adore you is because you have always treated them as if they were worthy of respect, even when they were small. You listened to them seriously. You were always scrupulously fair, and took the time to explain why certain things had to be. What is different in that from what a queen must do, if she is to rule justly?"

It would not have been enough if it weren't for my grandchildren. Susan and Big Red had their first babies the same month. I delivered them, both girls, and from the first they were as different as children could be. Big Red's child was called Little Red, of course, and finally Pinky as her hair lightened in color. She was self-opinionated from birth, refusing to cry when I gave her the spank of life on delivery. She just opened her eyes wide and glared at me. I never spanked her again, nor wished to, for she was as temperamental as our weather, sunny, but given to sudden squalls.

Susan's child was serene and stubborn. She did not declare positions, as Pinky did; she just went her way. She named herself Mimi, and would answer to no other name, though several were given her. By the time she and Pinky were two, their mothers were well into their second pregnancies, and the children spent most of their daylight hours with me in the throne room, or up on the tower roof watching the sky and the fields or out walking about the fort; in short, wherever I was. They followed me about as faithfully as Tag, my cat, did, and for much the same reason. Somehow they had reached some sort of agreement about me, namely that it was I who needed looking after, not them.

"Where you going, Morga?" I would be asked sternly if I sought to leave the throne room, even for a moment. They never actually forbade me to leave, but they eyed me suspiciously if I merely said I'd be back in a moment and gave no other explanation of my destination or intentions. It might have been irksome had they not been so serious about it, watching each other to see if they reached agreement that I should be allowed to go about my business this one time.

On court days they sat on the lowest step of the throne platform, nodding and whispering to each other as cases were presented. While they didn't participate directly in the questioning, on more than one occasion I saw the arguments being presented to them rather than to me. They were not aware that I thought it amusing, but Cornu could hardly keep countenance.

The children enlisted Cornu in discharging the responsibilities they had taken on regarding me, and the demand for his acceptance of their most outrageous requests concerning my welfare must have taxed him sorely. What was never in question was their commitment to me. I shuddered to think what harm they could do if they plotted against me rather than for me!

In time they were joined by other children. Drake's twin brothers, Ken and Dunc, married a pair of sisters: hearty, strapping girls not unlike Big Red. Their children, when they were big enough to walk without stumbling continually and after they had been housebroken, were welcome in the throne room while their mothers worked in the fields. Drake and his brothers cut trees, built houses and broke fields for their wives, but after that they spent their time in the woods, leaving whatever crops were to be raised to the women.

The hunters supplied meat to all who wanted it, and were welcome to stored grain like everyone else. Their wives did not need to till the fields, but they wanted growing things about them. As long as they could leave the toddlers with me, they were free to work.

Pinky and Mimi took charge of the newcomers, standing as my surrogate on all routine matters, but bringing to my attention anything out of the ordinary. I comforted anyone who needed it, cleaned scrapes and bruises and found honey cakes for those special occasions when nothing else would do, all under the approving eyes of the little clan mothers. Pinky and Mimi understood the Rule of Three.

I trained the children to speak and read Latin, using little stories that held their interest enough to pay attention. Cornu widened their understanding by telling of his adventures in far lands he had visited, explaining the strange customs of the folk among whom he had lived. Julia taught them to sing, and strangely enough it was in singing they discovered how to work as a group. In time the children, both boys and girls, learned to swim, to ride and to practice the rudiments of stick- and knife-fighting. In the process of mastering these accomplishments, they decided they all wanted to become warriors and emulate the Knights of the Round Table, of whom the bards sang.

Bards were as welcome in the hall in Morgan's hold as elsewhere. More welcome, perhaps, for we had but little contact with Camelot after Hemiston was killed by Lancelot. I had not lifted the restrictions I placed on Arthur's knights, refusing them entrance to my lands.

Nevertheless, at midmorning one sunny day in early spring things changed. I had disposed of all the complaints that came before me early and had sent Cornu and the children out into the commons to play hurley, a game requiring much running and shouting and bashing at a ball with sticks. Even the toddlers took part, under Cornu's watchful eye. The children had passed through the recent winter healthy enough, but needed sunshine. I needed quiet time for reflection.

The door was open to permit folk easy access to the court, and

I saw two men ride up, stop their horses and speak to the door guards. One dismounted and entered the doorway against the light. It was Gawaine, finally come to see me, and at first my heart did not know him. He was bareheaded, with a dirty bandage around his forehead; he wore his hair no longer or better kempt than his short beard. His eyes were fevered.

"No greeting, cousin?" he asked ruefully, coming to a stop before me.

"Gawaine, oh, Gawaine!" I cried in sudden recognition; at least I knew the voice! I stepped down and embraced him, and saw his face in a shaft of sunlight which entered one of the high, narrow windows. "My dear, whatever has happened? You look so ill!"

"Oh, I have been questing. Has no report of the quest for the Holy Grail yet reached this happy realm?" His tone was bitter.

"We've had wandering knights come to our borders claiming a right to anything up to and including penned horses that might enable them to reach that goal. I fear they were not treated with as much courtesy by my people as, perhaps, they deserved," I answered. "All we know of it is what the minstrels have sung about it in our great hall. Some say the Grail was the bowl Christ drank from at the Last Supper. Others say it was the cup in which the blood of Christ was caught when the Redeemer bled from a wound given him by a Roman soldier. Do you know for sure?" I heard myself babbling, in my confusion.

"I have no idea," Gawaine said sadly. "I have never seen it."

"Has the search gone badly for you, then?" I asked.

"It has ruined me," he replied bitterly. "If I could sit, cousin, it would be a boon. I am nearly too weak to stand."

I hastened to seat him on the throne step, and called for pages to bring a pallet, a basin to bathe him in, hot water, food, drink and my medicines. At my cry for help, the second horseman dismounted and came running in. It was Gawaine's brother Gaheris. He had no word for me; his attention was fixed on his brother. I turned away from him to speak again to Gawaine, who sat beside me on the step, leaning against me.

"Perhaps you have heard of the dark Queen of Galloway in

234

your travels, the witch with the healing touch," I said lightly, testing his blood heat with the back of my hand on his face. I didn't like this. He was burning up!

He caught my hand and said, "There is something I must tell you before you expend care on me. You may not want to help me after you hear it. Indeed, it was for that purpose, to tell you of my transgression against you, that I came so far when it might have been wiser not to have attempted to journey at all."

"Whatever it was, I hold you blameless," I said. "You would not knowingly hurt me, any more than I would hurt you."

"But I must speak," he said, and might have, if he had not fainted dead away. I broke his fall easily enough and laid him stretched out on the broad throne step.

"Several of you move that throne to one side," I said to the pages. "Place the pallet on the platform, out of the draft. This is my cousin, whom I love well, and he is direly ill."

Gaheris brushed them aside and picked up his brother without help. There were other strong hands to move the throne from the dais and lay out a pallet for him there. Shortly afterward I brought Gawaine out of his swoon to inquire about the wound. As I began to bathe his forehead and gently pull on the filthy bandage to loosen it, however, he fainted again, and I moved with more dispatch, worrying less about the pain I might cause than what I might find. The cut was long, shallow and ragged at the edges, as much a bruise as a gash, around which the hair had been clipped away some weeks past. A stubble was growing back in, matted with blood and pus. It was infected.

Julia herself brought the medicines, hearing of my need for them, and together we cleaned the wound, shaving his hair from one side of his head, and packing the area with a poultice of moldy bread. I questioned Gaheris about his brother's condition.

"I was not with him when he took the blow," Gaheris said shortly. "I'd followed him, knowing he'd end up in some kind of scrape, though he bade me not to, saying no one could come to harm on such a holy mission." Gaheris snorted with disdain. "I found him like this," he finished. And getting no more out of him,

I soon ceased the interrogation. Gaheris obviously disapproved of Gawaine's being here. Perhaps my reputation as a witch had traveled all the way to Camelot.

Julia and I stripped and bathed Gawaine, with the help of several men at arms who ordinarily guarded the throne during court days. At other times they were on the gate, charged with inquiring of strangers what business they might have inside the fort. Guard duty was a responsibility of our militia, and the schedule was made out by Drake. I understood it was considered an honor and was much vied for among the local farmers. Gaheris retired to the bench along the wall and watched.

"He is so thin, Morgan," Julia said, looking at his emaciated frame. "Surely he has not been eating enough to keep him alive."

"There is good bone and muscle there, all the same," I said. "He will mend if we can control the infection. My greater fear is that the blow that caused the wound may have bruised the brain, or cracked open the skull so that the infection will kill him." I pressed gently on the wound, both to stanch the bleeding and to see if I could detect movement in the bone. It seemed sound enough, but I still worried.

"He looks worn and frail," Julia said, as if speaking to herself. "I would never guess he is only your age to look at him."

"He made much of the point that he was almost two years older once," I said, smiling thinly. "Do you think I look less worn by my forty years than he?"

"No one looking at you would take you for older than thirty, as you well know," Julia replied tartly. Julia had gained weight. I had not, and, indeed, I believed I did look younger than my years. She knew I was but teasing her, however, for it little mattered what a queen looked like. What mattered was what forces she controlled, though perhaps if I looked less "regal," in Drake's words, my power would also be less. Fortunately, perhaps again, I did not need to find out.

Gawaine's fever did not break the first night nor the second. Julia was worn out from lack of sleep, and I sent her to bed lest she become ill herself. So, except for the silent presence of Gaheris,

I was alone with Gawaine when he awakened on the night of the third day, clear-eyed at last. Dawn was coming, and in the dim light I thought maybe his fever had broken, but forbore touching him to find out. I was afraid I might waken him completely, and I wanted him to sleep as much as possible. It so happened his eyes lit on Gaheris before he saw me. I was sitting on the throne which was placed behind him. I had not wanted the rushlight attached to it that burned through the dark of the night to shine on his face.

"Get me on my feet," Gawaine ordered Gaheris, who had come to his side on seeing him wake.

I do not believe Gaheris had slept any more than me.

"I have to piss and would not shame myself by wetting myself like a bairn," Gawaine growled.

Gaheris helped him to rise. In the process he saw me, and I placed my hand under his elbow to aid him. "Let me get you a chamber pot," I said.

"Ah, my lady, you do not see me at my best, I fear," Gawaine said ruefully, acknowledging my presence with a pat on my hand. "Gaheris can manage this I feel the need of pissing against a wall. I cannot explain it, but I need only this to be on the mend again. I am through with such Roman affectations as chamber pots!"

I released him, and Gaheris conducted him effortlessly to the door, nearly carrying him. I thought about Gaheris while they were outside, not having done so in some days. My attention had been all for Gawaine, which was probably the usual lot of Gaheris, I mused.

Gaheris was as tall as Gawaine, but with heavier bone and coarser musculature. He had been knighted many years past, but insisted on tending Gawaine as if Gaheris were the rawest squire. Gawaine told me once that when he was taken to Rome as one of the possible heirs to Britain's crown, joining the sons of other chieftains given as hostage for the good behavior of their fathers, Gaheris had grieved as for one dead.

Once Gawaine was restored to Britain, Gaheris was like a dog whose master had returned after a long absence, and nothing Gawaine did had managed to discourage Gaheris' attendance upon his person since. I wondered how Gawaine had escaped him to be hurt alone.

Gawaine didn't even much like Gaheris, and I could well understand it, for Gaheris was a sullen, jealous, uncommunicative sort of person, even with Gawaine. He was given to unexpected sour remarks which served to surprise a company which had forgotten he was present, as much from their apparent bitterness as from their rarity.

When they returned from their errand, Gawaine proclaimed himself hungry, and I could see he was, indeed, on the way to mending. There was bread and cheese and beer close at hand, along with apples, ever his favorite fruit. He ate hugely, insisting we join him, which Gaheris did, matching him bite for bite. I watched, amused at the gluttony of the brothers, and was happy to see Gawaine so well disposed toward eating. I fancied I could see him filling out before my eyes.

When, finally, Gawaine declared himself full on learning there was nothing more to eat, I suggested he nap until breakfast time, when there would be hot bread and honey, and butter from our creamery, along with fresh country milk. I even promised him a chicken, if he could wait for one to be killed, plucked, drawn and roasted, and eggs and salt pork at the least, if he could not.

"I have slept enough to last until spring," he demurred. "Like any bear who has hibernated the winter away, I want to do nothing but eat and perhaps talk a bit. I have been aware of you, my lady, and little else, in my delirium. What have I told you?"

"Little enough," I said. "My son Uwayne seemed much on your mind, but I know not why."

"Ah, my lady," he said with a stricken look on his face, "the matter of Uwayne. You do not know, then?"

"What should I know?" I asked, with sudden dread.

"Alas," he sighed, "I am not ready for this, nor will I ever be. It was my misfortune to meet Uwayne on the cursed quest I spoke of, both of us with our faces covered. I was pulled into a fight by one of Lancelot's many cousins, with whom I had been traveling. He challenged three knights, and I had to rescue him, for he was no match for them. I hit one an unlucky blow that brought his death, Morgan. When I took off his helmet, I found it was Uwayne. I mourned for him as a kinsman must, but I know not how to make amends. What would you have of me, my lady? It is yours, up to and including my life as blood price."

I looked away, feeling the blood drain from my own heart. My two youngest sons, Uwayne and Accolon, accidentally killed by the two men I held as brothers, Gawaine and Arthur. What curse was this? Did my father reach from beyond the grave, taking what I had not given him, blood price for his own death?

"Uwayne was his father's son," I told Gawaine when I could speak again. "Urien once attempted to keep me from entering my office as Queen of Galloway, implying it was better that a man should rule, and I drew a knife on him to drive him away. Uwayne took his father's part. I lost my son then, Gawaine. My grief now is muted. I cried more tears when he chose his father over me than for anything except the deaths of Gorlais, my father, and Accolon, my true son."

Gawaine took my hand and said, "Do not weep, or I shall be unmanned, my lady, though, I promise you, I wept when Uwayne died in my arms, smiling as he ever did when we were together. He spoke of little things, like remembering you and Cornu teaching him to swim. He laughed, Lady, speaking of how Cornu disliked water, and I wept so hard to hear the sound of joy in such circumstances that he died without my seeing him go."

The old, hard knot that was in my breast dissolved, and my own tears followed in truth. "You do not know what comfort you give me, even with these tidings," I said. "I had thought my son hated me."

"Ah, no, Lady," Gawaine said, holding me and rocking me like a baby in his arms, my head against his shoulder as we sat on the throne step. "He ever spoke of you with love. His last words were of you."

In some ways this was harder to bear than word of his death.

I thought about the boy he had been, proud and independent, but attached to his father and his brothers rather than to me, from the very start. I realized my tears were doing Gawaine no good, so I fought for control, and pushed myself away, wiping my eyes.

"So, how did you get hurt?" I asked, not wishing to speak further of Uwayne, at least not yet.

"It was some time later," Gawaine said, seemingly relieved to change the subject. "I was by myself and came upon a band of knights trying to force entry into a stockaded farmhouse. I rode down to relieve the farmer, defending the weak and lowly as a true knight must, and was in a fair way to accomplish it when someone rode out of the forest and hammered on everyone. I didn't see him and was knocked out of the saddle with a terrible blow that split my helmet and laid my head open."

"Oh Lud! What happened next?"

"I was carried into the farmhouse, and most of the other knights rode off. It seems they were only seeking lodging for the night, and were tired of begging for it. The farmer had daughters and didn't want them exposed to lusty men."

"They let you in," Gaheris said suddenly, smirking.

"As you will recall, when you found me I was in no condition to be lusty," Gawaine retorted sourly.

Gaheris laughed in his singular way, and Gawaine lost patience.

"This is my story, Gaheris. If you don't want to hear it, go outside. If you must stay, shut up!"

Gaheris subsided into the shadows, but did not leave, as I knew he would not.

"I didn't recover consciousness right away," Gawaine continued, watching Gaheris to see if he'd dare interrupt again, but turning to me as he got back into his story. "When I did, I was told Galahad, Lancelot's son, had come out of the woods and hit me from behind."

"But why?"

"I would guess his idea was to stop the fighting by hitting everyone who was doing it," Gawaine said with disgust.

"It worked, too," Gaharis observed.

"Oh, aye, it worked."

"That's all?" I asked, after I was sure Gawaine had ended his tale. He was looking at me expectantly, and I had to say something.

"Gaheris had found me by that time," Gawaine responded, "and the quest was over for me. I was in no condition to pursue it farther."

"So you came to me?"

"Not right away. After two weeks of lying on my back, eating almost nothing because I couldn't raise my head to swallow even liquids without getting dizzy, and couldn't chew without the most excruciating pain, I went back to Camelot in a horse litter."

"Was the food that bad or was it the wound?" I asked.

"What there was of it I couldn't keep down. Head wounds make you throw up everything you eat. I was like a newly pregnant bride."

I nodded. I knew about both morning sickness and head injuries.

"Only when I could ride without fainting did I come here to see you to speak of Uwayne. I also wanted to get away from Camelot, so I asked Arthur to let me replace Brastius Red-beard, who has been Warden of the North since Uther's time."

Brastius Red-beard! I wondered if he held me responsible for his long exile. I had foretold it. He would remember that. "Won't you miss your family and your friends at Camelot?" I asked.

"My wife is happier when I'm not about the house, and the boys are pages now. As for my friends, there weren't any there! I was the first to return from the Grail quest. I didn't want to have to explain to every strutting braggart who wandered in why I had come home early after vowing to be out for a year and a day." When I didn't respond, he burst out, "I am sick of Camelot, sick of Gaels pretending to be Romans! I'm sick of trying to be civil to the man who killed my father. I can't hold him as my enemy because he's a brother Knight of the Round Table!"

"Pellinore?" I asked, knowing it to be but a half-truth, at best. I was never sure if my blow served to end Lot's life or if Pellinore's was the final stroke. Between us, I thought, we had killed him. I could not tell Gawaine this, for he would hold me or my sons responsible and take blood debt. I was not worried about myself, but enough of my sons had died for bad reasons. Gawaine would not put it off, as I had for Gorlais, my father. His honor would be involved in it. For me it was something else; I was not sure what anymore.

"Aye, Pellinore. It has come to me that my father, Lot, will shadow my life until I put his ghost to rest. Christians don't know everything! Lot was not a Christian, anyway, and his ghost would not be bound by Christian rules."

It was as I had feared. "It would seem as if Lot's ghost was using Lancelot's family to remind you of your duty," I agreed reluctantly. "Do what you must to quiet your ghost. I have my own. My own father's rest is also tied up with Lancelot, one way or another. His father was kin to Uther Pendragon, who had my father murdered."

"Do you forgive me for Uwayne's death then, Lady?" Gawaine asked.

"Oh, yes! I thank you for your tale. It helps me to resolve a problem of my own. Never fear! I will bring the death of Uwayne to Lancelot's door, not yours. I would advise you to make your peace with Urien and his sons, however, for they may not see it the way I do."

He nodded soberly, and I left to rest. It had been a long vigil.

CHAPTER
XIII

awaine's convalescence lasted through the spring. We fell into our old camaraderie, teasing, flirting and laughing like the children we had been. All of my people liked Gawaine. I remembered suddenly the one exception: Hemiston had eyed him with the suspicion a careful housewife gives to rat droppings. I missed Hemiston.

As summer approached I sensed there could be difficulty about Gawaine if I had to make a choice for a Beltane partner this year. The prohibition that prevented Gawaine and me from marriage did not prevent us from coupling during a holy feast day I was afraid if I opened that door I would never get it closed again

Gawaine saved the situation by announcing he was pledged to report to the post to which Arthur had appointed him as Warden of the North. I reminded Gawaine of how I had warned Brastius Red-beard that Uther would send him to fight the Picts in the north for allowing his camp followers to make free with my mother's clothes at Dimilioc. Gawaine's going there seemed ill-omened.

Gawaine saw my frown and said, "I, too, recall your words to Brastius. I was there, remember? It was that recollection which caused me to seek the post, relieving Brastius after these many years. I need the solitude, and folk hearing of it might think me doing penance, at last, for my sins."

"I wonder if Brastius welcomed it like that," I replied.

"If he wanted to leave he would have done so," Gawaine said. "He never spent more than three months a year on the border. The Picts raid only in the fall, after harvest and before winter sets in. Brastius is at Hadrian's Wall now only to avoid joining in the quest for the Grail."

"He may be less angry than I had supposed," I said.

"No one is angry with you, Morgan. I have Arthur's word he hopes to see you in Camelot once again. Except for Pelleas, he has no other kin as close as you."

Once Gawaine decided to leave, he was all in a hurry to do so, saying his work was waiting for him. Soon after, he departed, with Gaheris dogging his steps as always.

I missed him. I was lonesome. It wasn't just that Gawaine had left, but that I had had company for a time—someone I could talk to and laugh with. I had spent far too much of my time with children over the years. It grew worse during the following long winter, and by spring I was near distraction. I could hide my unhappiness from all but Cornu, and as soon as the roads had dried enough in the spring, he came to me with a suggestion.

"Lady, what think you of bringing some horses down to Camelot to sell?" he said. "We could take a place near Caerleon and set up a horse fair. It would save people from traveling all the way to Exeter for Roman-bred horses, and ours are superior to anything there, anyway. The market ought to be good, with knights coming home after the Grail quest and all."

I was reluctant. Camelot had not been lucky for me, but Cornu enlisted Drake in his cause. "I would like my sons to see Camelot," Drake cajoled me. "Perhaps you could convince Arthur that he should take them in service as pages." Drake told me he thought the period he and his brothers had spent with the hunters had been most valuable in learning independence, and sending his sons to Arthur would serve much the same purpose.

The upshot of all this was that within two weeks Cornu and I set out with fifty horses, six grooms and a troop of my grandchildren who had passed their eighth birthday, under the leadership of Pinky and Mimi, now ten and very bossy. The boys would be lucky to escape their attention as Arthur's pages.

The children rode horses they had helped Cornu to train. These were theirs, and they were expected to put the care of their animals before their own needs. I rode a gelding foaled by Cloud's daughter, and sired by the stallion Urien once tied to my gate. Cloud was at pasture, content to stay at home; I'd said good-bye to her wishing it were not so, for she was dear to me.

Tag came with me, riding on a pad strapped to the gelding's rump. He'd gotten too big to ride in front of me on the saddle as he had once, but would stand and rest his paws on my shoulders to peer over my back when he thought he needed to see what was ahead. He weighed forty pounds now, and was all the guard I needed to protect me from anything short of a dragon.

What to wear in Camelot was of much concern to Big Red and Susan. They were coming with us, leaving their toddlers with the twins' wives. I was surprised at how much reassurance that gave me. The children were all dressed smartly in wool tunics, fur leggings, cloaks and caps. They sported sturdy leather boots and bore knives and iron-tipped fighting sticks. They looked like an army of dwarfs.

We all had fur cloaks and hats of our own as fine as anything we'd find in Camelot, and our wool and linen gowns were sturdy and warm. They just weren't very dressed up. Cornu came to us with a bolt of shimmering dark green cloth that he said he had of a trader out of Egypt on one of his horse-trading trips. I had never seen it before. The cloth was a finely woven cotton, very soft to the touch. Julia took it from us firmly and fitted the three of us with gowns that fell to the ankle, and hung from one shoulder, leaving the other bare. She furnished belts of gold rope for each of us, part of the Mother's hoard entrusted to her by Morgause. There were jewels, too, warm amber for Susan, jet for Big Red, and a necklace of sapphires set in gold for me, which was finer than anything else she had in her treasure trove. She said we must not be shamed in Arthur's court as country folk of little worth.

The trip was pleasant, for the weather stayed dry though cold, not unexpected in early spring. We stayed first in Carlisle, then in pavilions we put up each night to sleep out of the frost which still formed each night. Cornu drilled the children in cavalry tactics as we rode.

I was familiar with the smell of Britain's villages, that uneasy mixture of old fish slime, drying hides and dung piles against the north side of every house. British farmers measured their wealth partly in the size of their manure piles, which served the double purpose of warming the house during the long winters and augmenting the meager soil in the fields each spring. There was a new stink in the air as we rode south, something worse than manure, something alien to the countryside. It seemed to be emanating from the yellow cloud that hung across the horizon as we neared Camelot, riding south along the Usk Valley. It became more foul as we came in sight of Arthur's stronghold.

"Whatever is it?" I asked Cornu finally. I did not need to elaborate. Cornu managed to hear things people never thought to tell me.

"I wondered when you would ask," Cornu replied. "What you are experiencing is known locally as 'Guenevere's Bane.' "

"She is responsible for this?" I asked, astonished.

"Not at all. It is the consuming passion of her life to do away with it. The Abbot of Usk is responsible. He has established a copper smelter and bronze foundry at the mouth of the river, where barges of ore from Cornwall and coal from Wales can be brought together."

"But this is appalling! Why does Arthur permit it?"

"The abbot provides Arthur with refined metal that can be used for all sorts of things, including war. He is willing to overlook a little inconvenience to get it."

"A little inconvenience! Is that what he calls it?"

"Yes, as a matter of fact. Everyone, seemingly, has told him what they think of the notion, and he's become stubborn. Kings are pretty inflexible when they choose to be. Who can overrule him?"

"You know, I would never be permitted such an indulgence at Morgan's hold," I said.

"You are not Arthur," was his response.

It had been years since I'd seen Camelot, and I was amazed at the changes in it. Arthur had done wonders. With the pacification of the Saxon shore, he had been faced with the need to keep his warriors busy.

I remembered the gate and the round keep, so like a Pictish broch, that guarded it. Both gate and tower had been built of cut and coursed stone, taken, Cornu said, from the ruins of the Roman barracks at Cuerleon. Cornu knew everything. I recalled that the gate's tall wooden doors were hinged with iron and studded with iron bolts forged by Pelleas. I had not expected to see the wooden palisade replaced with the same Roman-cut stone, but so it was. A second keep had been constructed, round and impregnable as the first. The two flanked the gate, and gave a most impressive appearance.

There was something else new. Arthur had built a moat around the entire hill, and flooded it with water from the Usk. A bridge with chains to lift it upright against the gate had been laid across the ditch, and persons and wagons moved in and out in a steady stream. It was a good idea. We should do that at Morgan's hold. Lot would not have been able to charge our gate if we had had a moveable bridge.

We rode over the bridge without hindrance, too small a party to be dangerous, though our passage was noted by sentries on top of the two keeps. When we came under the gate we were stopped by a porter in livery, who asked our business in a civil voice. A second wall stretched between the two keeps, enclosing a space easily defended from above. It was another good notion, and I resolved to incorporate it in Morgan's hold as well.

"I am Morgan, Queen of Galloway, here to see my brother, Arthur the King," I told the porter. He bowed very low, and asked us to wait for a moment while he informed his master of our arrival. Arthur himself came running to meet us, followed by the porter, somewhat out of breath.

"Morgan!" he called. "Well met!" He hugged me as I dismounted to greet him, then pushed me out to arm's length to look me over. He was becoming a trifle far-sighted, I thought. "But, you do not change, any more than Guenevere! What is it with women that they look forever youthful?"

Dear man! I did look well, then. It seemed as if the shadow of Accolon's death had never fallen between us. "What is it with men that they become more honey-tongued as they grow older?" I responded.

"Ah, yes," he replied, grinning. "And these troopers, who are they?" he inquired, looking over the children lined up for review, sitting their horses at attention with Cornu and our half a dozen gillies grouped loosely behind them.

"These are my grandchildren, my own guard of honor," I said. "Children, this is my brother, Arthur, High King of the Britons." They did not move a muscle, sitting their horses at attention, eyes staring straight ahead.

"Grandchildren?" he asked. "I can't believe it." He looked shrewdly at me again, and shook his head. "Have you brought the boys to me as pages?"

It was that easy. We had not told the children what we were planning, but the boys lighted up and I realized it was something they had dreamed about. "I will consider it," I said. "It is possible." I felt I should talk to Pinky and Mimi before committing the boys. The girls could not stay even if they wished to. Camelot would not understand female pages, and girls were too valuable to give away in any case. I could not leave them here. I hoped they would understand.

"Good. Think about it. That's all I ask. Maybe they'll help persuade you," he added. I realized he had seen and correctly interpreted the look the boys gave me. Kings and queens learn how to read men's faces, and these were but boys.

We were shown rooms, and the boys, to their immense delight, went with Cornu to the soldiers' barracks. Susan, Big Red and I were given three rooms in the women's quarters and became guests in Arthur's court. The differences between Morgan's hold and

Camelot were mostly of scale. Camelot was vast! The individual rooms were no more comfortable, nor the food better prepared or superior in taste. There was more variety, perhaps, but nothing that set it apart. There was a feeling of majesty about the place, with its huge great hall that made you realize it was a High King's palace.

Guenevere met me at the welcoming feast with civility which masked a cold reserve. I was here as Arthur's sister, and as the head of a friendly state. She and I were not to be friends, I perceived. She had not forgiven me for cursing her. I was not offended; I still remembered Accolon.

Big Red, Susan and I wore our green gowns, and they were as fine as anything we saw. We all wore our hair down, bound at the brow with the simple golden bands. Mine had a red stone set in it, marking me as a queen. Tag escorted us, walking before us grandly, and jumping up on a high stool Cornu had placed behind my chair, to guard my back. Arthur's dogs growled, but Tag ignored them, more than their equal in a fight.

As my shield-bearer, Cornu was armed with a leaf spear and stood at my back. It was a place of honor. Only visiting royalty could have weapons in the presence of the High King.

Together we made a sensation in Arthur's court, used to royalty from abroad though it was. Big Red was striking, her color was so vivid, and Susan had such delicate features and glowing skin that she looked like the embodiment of the Great Mother as maiden. I looked like myself. Cornu told me bluntly I was the most beautiful woman in Britain, Guenevere included, before we entered the great hall, perhaps to give me confidence.

Big Red laughed, and Susan said scornfully, "Lud, she knows that!"

Guenevere had arrayed herself in white and gold, and looked more like a plaster saint from a Christian church than a real person. By the way Arthur looked at her I judged the gown was new and expensive, a gown he had not seen before. Guenevere had dressed for me! A minstrel sang praise songs in my honor, which Guenevere was too civil to protest. Bards were free to sing what they will. I would wager she did not often hear other women praised in her hall.

Morgause, my gorgeous aunt, came late, in a low-cut red gown that would have been scandalous on anyone else. I hadn't known she was at Camelot. She greeted us with every mark of distinction, in contrast to Guenevere's coldness, and took us to her suite after the feast to talk of home.

"How long have you been here?" I asked.

"For years! Pelleas came with his dreadful Picts and drove all the Britons out of Lothian, did you not know?"

"I can't imagine his being brutal," I said.

"Actually, he wasn't," she said, looking coy.

"You didn't!" I exclaimed.

"I did," she said grimly, "and got another son, would you believe it?"

"Oh, Morgause!"

"It was almost worth it," she said, smirking.

"Are you behaving yourself now?" I asked, shaking my head. I couldn't see Guenevere allowing unseemly conduct in her court. "Something agrees with you, you look so young!"

"Oh, Morgan, I'm in love again!" she admitted in a whisper.

"Who is it?" I asked in amazement.

"One of Arthur's knights," she said. "I must not reveal his name, for you will laugh. He is not as old as Gawaine!" and she fanned herself in mock distress.

Gawaine came seeking me next day. "Ah, cousin," he said. "I hear everywhere of how your beauty outshone even the queen's at her feast of welcome for you."

"Only Cornu thought so," I commented dryly. "He sees me still as a young woman. What are you doing in Camelot?"

"Arthur sent for me. Rumors have reached him of Pellinore's death."

"What have you to do with that?" I asked.

"More than I should," he replied moodily. He took his leave, saying his wife was in Caerleon and would be upset if he did not have his evening meal with her. I gathered she was jealous. It seemed odd that anyone would fear my influence in such a way.

All in all we had a triumph, but one I knew we could not repeat until we had more clothes, so I asked Cornu to find us other quarters as soon as possible. He asked around and found a vacant manor house a half hour's ride from Camelot. It had once belonged to a knight who had fallen in the Grail quest. We paid his widow a fair sum, and she moved back to her people at Bath, well content. Arthur wanted to take all the horses himself for the royal stables, but Cornu convinced him it was better to let individual knights add them one at a time. It was better for us, too, for Arthur was a shrewd judge of horseflesh. We would make more money out of sales of individual horses, brushed and fattened up.

We moved to the manor house, and I took my grandchildren with me, permitting them to attend classes at Camelot when Cornu had time to take them. I spent my days doctoring horses and small boys and girls and stayed away from court.

The children got sick. At first I thought it was the change of water, but when they started coughing I realized it was the appalling yellow cloud drifting up the Usk that was causing it. I went into Caerleon and found much the same situation there. When I was sure in my mind, I went to see Arthur at Camelot.

"We are being poisoned by that pall of smoke from downriver. Whatever is it?" I asked him.

"You, too? Guenevere has been after me to do something about it for months. It's a bronze smelter. Irishmen have built an abbey there and bring tin from Cornwall, copper from the north and coal from upriver to one place. I am fortunate to have them."

"Fortunate?"

"They give me good prices for their goods, and I need bronze for all sorts of war gear."

"You will not do anything to stop this fouling of the air?" I asked, feeling anger building up in me again.

"I will not," he said stubbornly.

"Then, I will!" I said.

"You have no authority here," Arthur warned me.

"Authority? What authority do I need to keep someone from

poisoning my grandchildren? They are ill from this pestilent stink, I tell you. So are your folk in Caerleon."

"We are not bothered here," he said, waving his hand to indicate Camelot itself.

"You think not? Why is Guenevere upset then?"

"She says the view is ruined from her window," Arthur replied. "The smoke hugs the low ground, and we are above it."

"That may be, but I can taste it here in the back of my throat," I said. "You have not escaped, even if you think so."

"I will not close the smelter down," Arthur said with finality. He had the air of a man goaded past any chance of willful compliance.

"Very well. You have made your stand. Now I will make mine." Without saying what it was to be, I left. Let him wonder. I went back to the manor house and fussed over the boys, watching them closely for several days. They got no better. Finally, I took Cornu and together we rode down the wagon road to the mouth of the Usk, half a day's ride from the manor house. I kept a wary eye on the sky, for it was threatening, and summer storms often carry lightning. I would not like to be out-of-doors with lightning striking close by.

We found a dock built parallel to the shore to allow ore barges to unload. A number of stone buildings adjoined, all with the look of new construction. More startling was an oared galley, a Saxon ship by the look of her, coming in to make landfall.

"It's Pelleas and Nithe!" Cornu said as he gazed at them, his voice showing rare surprise. Cornu's eyes were exceptionally keen. We rode down to the dock to greet them. A slim youth jumped to the dock with a line and was about to make it fast to a piling when an officious man, who had been watching with an impatient air, jerked it from the youth's hand and threw it back into the boat.

"What do you think you're doing?" the youth asked in a high voice. I looked again. I had passed for a man often enough to detect it in someone else. This was a girl! She was an exceptionally pretty one, too, with enormous eyes and a mass of curls tight to her head, looking like a pile of glossy buckeye chestnuts.

"What do you think you're doing?" the man repeated in an insolent, mocking way. "This dock is for ore boats. If you want to land, go upstream, pull in and wait until someone comes to tell you where you can tie down. Get along now, or I'll have the watch out."

The man was an idiot! There were shields hanging over the rail of each oar-seat. I could see spears laid along the seats between the rowers.

"We're an oared boat," the girl said, misunderstanding. "Can't you see?" And she pointed at the oars the rowers had shipped on the port side to keep from being broken.

"Don't get smart with me, boy," the man said. He was evidently less observant than I. How anyone could mistake this child for a boy was beyond me. "I mean scows with copper ore or tin or coal. You look like persons with no respectable business to me, and we won't be putting up with thieving tricks around here, I tell you." Following that speech, he cuffed the girl over the ear, knocking her sideways into the boat.

Pelleas leaped to the dock, reached the man in two strides as he started to turn away, picked him up by the neck and the crotch and hurled him over the boat into the water. He came up sputtering under an oar, banged his head and went down again. This happened several times, for the rowers were hitting him on purpose until Pelleas stopped it.

"Pull him in," he said.

Two of the oarsmen jerked him from the water, and he was passed overhand to the dock, where he wheezed and coughed at Pelleas' feet for a few moments as Pelleas glared down at him. Then Pelleas grasped him by his tunic, hauled him to his feet, letting his toes just touch the dock, and shook him into full consciousness.

"Hear me, little man," he said through his teeth. "Run to whoever is in charge of this place and tell him Pelleas, a king of the Picts, wants an explanation of the evil stench that pervades this place and the sea for miles around. Tell him if I do not have an accounting before the sun stands straight overhead, I will discover the reason myself and likely put an end to it. Tell him it is an abomination if he is not aware of it." Pelleas dropped the wretch to his feet, where he staggered for a moment before he took off running.

I dismounted and walked over to Pelleas. "You may remember me, my lord," I said. "You once made me a knife from a bell clanger. I am Morgan, Queen of Galloway."

"Of course I remember you, my lady," he responded, taking my hand and smiling down at me. "I don't recall that you used that name, though."

I blushed like a girl, a habit that infuriated me, but which I had never been able to control. I remembered telling Nithe I did not wish him to know my identity, for it was best that the clanger not be connected with me. What had I called myself? Was it my childhood name, Corbie Crow? Oh, please, no!

Pelleas turned to Nithe, "Our Lady Corbie is now the Queen of Galloway, my dear."

Nithe swarmed over the boat side from where she had been looking at a lump on the girl's head, suffered when the girl fell against an oar, and rushed over to hug me.

"Morgan, my heart's sister! How good to see you! What are you doing in this foul place?"

"I've come to close it down," I said. "The smoke is making all my grandchildren sick."

"Wonderful. We'll help you, won't we, Pelleas?" and she turned to him, knowing his agreement from long association. I was happy to see them together. I had feared she might have delayed too long, sending him away in bitterness.

"We'll soon see," he responded. He stayed on the dock, forbidding anyone else from the boat to join him, but I saw them free their swords from their waterproof wrappings in readiness. Cornu dismounted and came to stand by me, his long heavy flute in his hand. I had a fighting stick that I leaned on to watch.

A mob descended on us, led by a tall man with a tonsured head and red face. He blustered up to Pelleas and asked, "What is this outrage? Who are you?"

Pelleas grasped him by the throat and pushed him backward toward the crowd, saying, "Tell your people to give way and back off or I'll snap your neck! Do it now!"

The poor man couldn't breathe enough to comply, but the crowd needed no special urging. They faded away at the sight of Pelleas up close. He was still by far the biggest man I had ever seen. My head came to his shoulder height, and I was taller than any but the biggest Gaels.

Pelleas released him enough so the man could gasp, "This is sacrilege!" His voice was almost a whistle, with the air pinched off by Pelleas' grip.

"Don't kill the fool," Nithe admonished, so Pelleas let the fellow go. He tried to rearrange his clothing and stand up to Pelleas, but he looked like a child before his parent. Still he persevered, saying, "I am the Abbot of Usk, under the protection of the Holy Church! You will roast in hell for this!"

"You seem to have brought your hell closer to men than needful," Pelleas replied. "As for me and my people, we do not live under the rules that bind Christians, nor do we have a hell assigned to us. Therefore, I will not suffer yours now or later. This is a copper smelter, is it not?"

"Copper and tin," he said haughtily. "We make bronze here for King Arthur and the uses of the Church."

"I see." Pelleas said. He was not impressed by the abbot's invoking either Arthur's name or the Church. "Tell your people to shut it down immediately."

The man turned and fled, toward the stone building from which the smoke was billowing.

"Shall we inspect the place to assure ourselves he will follow our command?" he asked us.

"I am curious to see whatever it is that creates this yellow stink," I said. "Besides, I am not sure he will comply."

One of the oarsmen took our horses' reins while Cornu and I strolled over to the smelter with Pelleas and Nithe. The door had

255

been shut and barred, as I had thought it would be. The abbot intended to defy us.

Pelleas looked at the smelter and with a swift, flowing movement leaped up to catch the edge of the roof and swung himself up. I glanced at Cornu, and even he opened his eyes a trifle wider at the sight. Pelleas climbed the steep roof to the smelter chimney that was in its center and wrapped his arms around it. He pulled the stones in upon themselves, and they fell into the chimney stack as neatly as putting eggs in a basket. The smoke was blocked!

Pelleas joined us back on the ground, leaping from the roof as lightly as a boy. This time I glanced at Nithe, and she was watching me, smiling her closed-teeth smile that said, "This man is mine." I remembered she had done it once before when I inquired if Pelleas were free. I laughed and patted her and this time was rewarded with a real smile. She was teasing!

"They'll be out like bees from a smoked hive," Pelleas said, and even as he spoke the door burst open and men tumbled out choking and rubbing their eyes. I stopped the abbot by poking him rudely in the belly and pinning him against the wall.

"We are under King Arthur's protection," the man bleated.

"I am the king's sister, Morgan, Queen of Galloway," I told him. He crossed himself. "You have heard of me, I gather," I said coldly. "I allow no one to foul my air. I promise you, Arthur's protection does not run so far."

"But we are chartered! This is done under the king's allowance! We've paid for it!"

"And I say there can be no allowance for what you do here. Why, man, this offends heaven and earth!"

Pelleas came to stand beside me and said, "We are Picts. We are not under Arthur's laws, and from this time on, neither are you. You are under my rule for as long as I am in this country. If I smell this smell again I will round up your people, make them tear this abbey down stone by stone, and throw the stones into the sea."

"And I will curse the stones," I added, thrusting my anger at the man. He quailed, and I turned him loose to flee, skirts flapping like an old crone.

"Well, I thank you," I said. "That might have been difficult to do alone."

"I wonder," Pelleas said, and he smiled. Why had not such a man come into my life? I did not look at Nithe again for fear she could read my mind.

Pelleas and Nithe decided to stay at the abbey for a few days to intimidate the abbot. I approved, but I was still worried about the boys, and Cornu and I rode back to our manor house.

We found an urgent message asking us to come to Camelot. Arthur's son by Morgause, Mordred, had been hurt, and his life was feared for. We paused only to change horses and collect my medicine bag before riding on to the castle. We found Mordred unconscious in the infirmary that served Arthur's soldiers. Arthur's doctor was a worthy enough man, but given overmuch to bleeding and purging.

"I have taken two pints of blood from his neck, to reduce the pressure on his brain, but he has not regained consciousness," I was told.

"When did this occur?" I asked.

"Just last night. Terrible it was!"

"But what happened?" I asked, allowing Cornu to examine Mordred uninhibited by the doctor. Cornu taught me much of what I know, but I was the one with the reputation. The doctor might object to Cornu's touching his patient. Cornu had more experience than me in treating the kinds of wound that men take in battle.

"He was hit on the head," the doctor said. "I gather he came upon his brother, Gaheris, holding a bloody sword and standing over Queen Morgause. It is said Mordred was about to kill Gaheris when Gawaine struck Mordred down. It was bad enough to have a man kill his mother without having one brother kill another for blood debt!"

"Morgause? Dead? And by Gaheris' hand? How can that be?"

257

"She is dead, Lady," he said stiffly, as if I had doubted his medical judgment.

Before I could question him further Gawaine entered, wild-eyed. "Thank Lud you're here, Morgan," he blurted. "Can you save him?"

"His skull is not broken," Cornu announced.

"Then, thanks to the doctor here, we have a chance," I said.

I saw the man relax and preen. His help would be needed, and as long as I could keep the actual treatment out of his hands, Mordred might be all right. Young people were resilient, and Mordred didn't appear to be in worse straits than Drake had been with a similar injury.

"He must be on his feet for the funeral," Gawaine said.

"He may not even recover consciousness by then. In any case, it will not do. These head injuries are tricky. If he isn't kept quiet now, he'll have trouble later on."

"You're thinking of the boy. I'm thinking of the clan. He'll have to go to the rites, if Gareth and I have to hold him on his feet unconscious. Don't you understand? Gaheris has killed Morgause! The boy will be kin-wrecked along with Gaheris if he's not there!"

Men are such fools. With Morgause dead, I would become head of clan Merrick, but kin-wrecking was men's business. I would have nothing to say about it!

Someone entered the infirmary, blocking the light from the doorway. I looked up and saw an enormous man coming to the bed.

"Here he is now," Gawaine said. "Gareth, stay with Mordred and make sure he's ready to join us at the rites. Tear his clothes and cut his arms and face so he bleeds. He has to show mourning. Carry him out at dawn."

The big man nodded, and I looked at him more closely. He was little more than a boy in age, not bearded as yet, but he was huge like Pelleas! His eyes were as blue as Gawaine's, so there was no question, but I asked anyway, "You are Morgause's son?"

"Yes," Gareth said dully, his eyes now fixed on Mordred's face. He looked up. "I cannot cut him, Lady," he said.

"Nor can I. He has bled enough," I said, and proceeded to help Cornu tear Mordred's tunic and rub blood on his face and arms from the basin of it that the doctor had placed on a nearby table. Cornu made shallow ritual cuts on Gareth's face and arms and smeared him with Mordred's blood from the basin as well. It gave them both a most garish appearance.

"Now, we will let him rest," I said. "When Mordred recovers consciousness and begins to sleep naturally, I will wake him. If you stretch out on a pallet in the corner, I will call you when that happens." Gareth looked grateful and laid himself down. He seemed to be more stunned than grieved.

"Wherever did he come from?" I asked Cornu. "Is he truly Morgause's child?"

"Extraordinary, isn't he? Pelleas is his father, I believe. He was conceived before Pelleas and Nithe became betrothed. She sent Gareth away to grow up with Mordred when the boy was five."

So! I could believe it, seeing the boy. I grieved for Morgause, that lovely, bawdy creature. I wondered what sick fancy had moved Gaheris. And poor Guwaine! He looked twice his age with the shame and grief that had come to him.

Mordred recovered consciousness just before dawn.

"You have been hurt, Mordred," I said. Men with head injuries could often forget things immediately preceding the injury. It was true with Mordred.

"Gaheris killed our mother," Gareth told him.

"Samana? Gaheris killed Samana?" Mordred asked in confusion, struggling to regain his feet.

I raised an eyebrow at Cornu, and he said, "You remember. Samana was Arthur's first wife, and is still his friend. She raised Mordred and Gareth."

"No, not Samana," Gareth was saying, holding Mordred down with seeming ease. "Gaheris killed Morgause."

"Ah, Morgause." Mordred relaxed. "But why?"

"He found Lamerok in her bed," Gareth told him, glancing first at me.

I had not known that! Lamerok was indeed half her age. He

was the son of Pellinore, the man Gaheris and his brothers credited with killing their father, Lot. No wonder Gaheris was angry.

"Gawaine says you are to get up and go to her funeral," Gareth told Mordred.

Mordred did not respond, but when dawn broke, Gareth tenderly lifted the boy to his feet and all but dragged him to the meadow outside Camelot's walls to the fresh grave that had been dug.

I followed, for I was Morgause's clanswoman. It occurred to me when I was taken to a place beside the bier that I was now clan Merrick head as well. It was raining steadily, with puddles forming in the open grave; the gray sky gave the whole scene a dismal aspect in keeping with the occasion.

Julia was conducting the rites. "Make it go as fast as you can," I told her. "Mordred will die if we cannot get him back to where he can be quiet." Mordred was barely conscious, standing between Gawaine and Gareth at the head of the grave. With a little push all three of them might have joined Morgause on her bier, for none of them appeared hale. Gawaine looked as bad as either of the others. He had overdone it, as was his nature, and I wondered if he would not be my next patient, bleeding as profusely as he was from the ritual mourning cuts.

Arthur stood bareheaded in the chill morning air, also showing ritual bleeding scratches, and his face was set in grim lines, for Gawaine had brought druids to the rites. The rain washed the blood into his beard.

The druids stood on one side of the grave chanting, while Julia sang praises to the Mother on the other side. The effect was not as I might have feared. Possibly because of Arthur's presence, no effort was made by either the druids or the Mother's people to demand precedence in conducting the rites.

Guenevere and her ladies were not present. I knew trouble would come of it, by the black looks Gawaine directed toward Arthur.

I was right. After the funeral I found Arthur and Gawaine in the great hall standing nose to nose. Gawaine was yelling, "Your queen did not give my mother the respect she was due!"

"What would you?" Arthur replied in a reasonable voice. "You know how God-driven Guenevere is."

"You could have ordered her," Gawaine said more quietly, but in a sullen voice. He had seen me come in.

"To attend a pagan ceremony? I could not have done so in any conscience. You know I have outlawed druidry, and you know why."

"Oh, aye," Gawaine answered impatiently. "You thought to stem the flow of young men away from your army to the ranks of the priesthood, where they would be exempt from military duty. So you said, but, man, we're not talking about druidry!" He was shouting again. He was more than merely upset!

"I am," said Arthur. "A further objection I had was that I could not countenance the burning of children for the gods, which the bloody druids think must accompany every rite of passage."

"You defy the gods?" Gawaine asked in horror.

"I don't defy the gods, only the druids."

"Only the druids? You object to the sacrifice of children? And which would you choose for sacrifice, then," Gawaine asked with heavy scorn, "a valuable adult or a child not grown to use?"

"I would not choose either. My father, Uther, sacrificed a son every eight years to prolong his own life, at the insistence of the druids. My brother, Pelleas, has a long white scar across his belly where the druids laid him on the black stone and slit him open under a full moon. Myrddin sewed him back up and he lived, but no thanks it was to Uther. I also remember it was to have been my destiny before I reached the age of eight, had not Uther died first. I will not live under such a tyranny."

"Pelleas did not die, more's the pity," Gawaine acknowledged, addressing himself to the part of what Arthur had said that fit his argument.

"He did not die," Arthur agreed. "He lived to save my life a dozen times when I was too young to save myself. I see Pelleas in a different light than you do."

"The worse for you and for all Gaels," Gawaine said. "I myself can tarry no longer here with you. I must return to my lands in

Lothian to keep your brother's Picts from slaughtering your people and mine. Think on that."

"I do, and I wonder why," Arthur replied. "Why, after all these years, have the Picts become restive? Can they be mourning Pellinore?"

Gawaine glared at Arthur and took his leave with no more ceremony than if Arthur had been a tavern wench. I was surprised at Arthur's reference to the rumored death of Pellinore. I thought Arthur might have the right of it after all, on considering it deeply. Picts could well raid into Lothian to avenge Pellinore's murder if they believed it had happened at Gawaine's hands. Pellinore was the High King of the Picts; even Pelleas acknowledged him.

From the look on Arthur's face I knew he was considering calling Gawaine back to express his irritation at his lack of respect, while asking for more particulars of his dealings with Pellinore. I saw him think better of it, shaking his head. Arthur had not just lost a mother at the hands of a brother as Gawaine had.

"Morgause was not Christian," I told him. "You could not have ordered Christian rites for her."

"It's not me, it's Guenevere," he said impatiently. "Her priest damns all non-Christians with everlasting hellfire. Sometimes I think that the contemplation of her enemies' burning is all that resigns Guenevere to her lot." That could have been directed at me, for he gave me a bitter look as he left.

Gawaine took horse that night to go after Gaheris. Their brother Aggravain had not even waited for Morgause's funeral, so intent on vengeance was he. I wondered, though, whether Aggravain hunted Gaheris or Lamerok. I would judge neither man was safe. Gaheris was kin-wrecked and outlaw to the clan. Lamerok was as guilty as Morgause's killer from the point of view of blood debt, perhaps more so. He had never been kin.

I found Mordred had fallen back into a fever. Being dragged to the funeral had served him ill. His half-brothers, Gareth and Borre, raised with Mordred in Lyoness, had refused to accompany Gawaine and the others in their blood quest, preferring to stay and watch over Mordred with Cornu and me. I wondered if I would ever hear what happened that made the boys leave Lyoness and seek out Camelot. Cornu told me Borre was Arthur's son by Samana, Arthur's first wife. Both Gareth and Mordred were children of Morgause, of course, but where Mordred was the son of Arthur, Gareth was the son of Pelleas. It made no difference to the boys. They accounted themselves brothers.

CHAPTER
XIV

rthur sent for me next day. I found him standing with Guenevere in her weaving room. "Look out of the window," he said. "You and Guenevere have forgotten all about Pelleas and Nithe coming." I had not forgotten. I had expected Nithe and Pelleas would be arriving at Camelot on this day and wished to be there to greet them. The children were improving and I thought it safe to leave the manor house. I just didn't want to tell Arthur of my involvement with the closing of the smelter as yet.

"Nineve," Guenevere corrected him absently. "Her name is Nineve."

She moved over to let me look out of the long, narrow window. A dragon-boat was rowing up the Usk. I could make out the tall figure of Pelleas standing in the bow with Nithe beside him. They would be at the river quay in an hour.

"Will you come with us to greet them?" Arthur asked.

"I would be happy to greet Nithe and Pelleas," I replied to Arthur, and the three of us went together. Tag paced sedately beside me. It was a pleasant walk to the quay from the castle, particularly in the clement weather of early summer; we arrived at the quay only shortly before the boat did. Guenevere had thrown a light cloak over her gown, and my fur looked too heavy beside it. Halfway to the quay I took it off and draped it over my arm.

I'd have Cornu get me a woven cloak so I wouldn't feel so overdressed.

Arthur held out his hands to help Nithe alight and hugged her. She winked at me in conspiracy. I loved Nithe. She had changed very little in all the years I had known her. She was still naughty.

"As Arthur might say, you and Guenevere never age. It's a wonder that other women even talk to you," I said to Nithe, smiling. She had donned a cloak like Guenevere's. I had to have one!

"Few do," she replied, "but I have no claim to beauty, as you have. We entertain minstrels from time to time, and all they ever sing about is fighting, horses, hounds and hunting, and the beauty of either Arthur's fair queen, Guenevere, or his dark sister, Morgan. I am fair sick of it." She grinned to take the sting from her words and winked at Guenevere, but Guenevere merely shook her head without comment. She held out her arms to Nithe.

I released Nithe and turned to look at Pelleas. He had leaped lightly to the quay and towered more than a foot above Arthur. Arthur had him clasped by the forearms and was looking up to him as a younger brother might to an adored older one.

"You know my sister, Morgan, don't you?" he said by way of introduction when Pelleas looked away from him to me.

"I met her once or twice, perhaps. I often hear of her," he said, smiling in a teasing way.

"It seems to me as if it's only been a few days," I said, and he laughed. I gathered no one wanted to talk about shutting down the smelter. I know I didn't!

"Brother," Arthur asked, looking at the oarsmen, "where did you find all of these splendid young men?" They were splendid, now that I had the leisure to look at them, a score or more and all about sixteen, looking much alike, tall and well muscled.

"We are the sons of Pelleas," one of them said proudly.

"Truly?" I asked, raising an eyebrow as I looked at them, then back at Pelleas.

"So their mothers say," he replied, as Arthur kept grinning like a dog with a stolen roast of beef. He did everything but pant and slobber. Pelleas had raised him, Arthur had told me, and Pelleas was Arthur's hero.

"You're joking," I said.

"Not at all," Nithe said. Catching a suddenly vulnerable look on Guenevere's face, she added, "I am not so fortunate as to be their mother, but I love them as if I were."

"We are not all sons," one of them said. The tall young woman whom I had last seen upside down in the boat shipped her oar and joined us on the dock. She bore no resemblance to either Nithe or Pelleas.

"This is Viki, our daughter," Nithe said. "She adopted us twelve years ago and is our chief joy."

The boys grinned at this, evincing no jealousy. I decided I would have the right of this from Nithe in good time, so I merely accepted it without comment, curious though I was.

Next I examined the boat. It was Saxon-made, as I had judged when I first saw it at the abbey dock. There was a carved dragon's head at the prow. It appeared crowded with the young men and an inordinate number of huge dogs. Nithe saw me looking at them, for I loved dogs. I could not keep them, though, for Tag ran them off. Guenevere's two small bitches were whimpering and crowding up against her as they smelled the strangers. I looked for Tag and found he had discovered urgent business in the brush along the river. I knew he would hide there, watching. If I got into trouble with the dogs I could count on his coming to my rescue, but he wasn't going to socialize with them.

"We breed Roman bitch mastiffs to wolves," Nithe said, "and have two crossbred females with us, both with litters. The females stand between seven and eight hands at the shoulder and weigh as much as a small man. Between the two, they have eleven puppies. Lucy, the shorter, stocky one, has a litter of four about six months old, and Amber's litter of seven is but five months. While the dogs belong to Pelleas, the puppies are Viki's, all of them. She refused to leave them behind, for they are in the middle of training, and she could not trust the kennel master to finish them off properly. I should have insisted, probably," Nithe concluded, looking concerned.

"But where did they come from?"

"Oh, we had them trailing us in another row-galley. We couldn't well keep them in this boat for the whole trip, could we?"

"I wouldn't have thought so," I agreed.

"We had to wait for them, because some of them are presents for Arthur."

"Where is the other ship?"

"It's on its way back to Mona with a cargo of copper, bronze and tin," she said, winking again. "Pelleas thought if the abbot had no metal stocks he would have more difficulty setting up again."

Arthur caught the worried expression on Nithe's face and said, "You are welcome, all. Kay will find lodgings for everyone."

"I will not stay anywhere Kay is responsible for my hospitality," Pelleas said. I had forgotten how deep his voice was. Nor had I been aware of his animosity toward Kay and wondered about it, for I do not like the man myself.

"Kay would be honored to serve you," Guenevere protested.

"No, my lady, he would not," Pelleas replied. "We will continue upriver to Nithe's New Avalon. They are expecting us, but I could not go by without greeting you."

"Kay is not king here," Arthur said in an imperious tone. "He does my bidding. It is my hospitality that is offered, not his."

"Very well," Pelleas said. "We will stay with you, though when you see what the boys and the dogs can eat, you may regret it." He smiled before continuing in a serious voice, "I would not have you think we reject your kindness. You must be aware, however, that I am come to inquire into the fate of Pellinore. I have heard dire things."

"We will inquire together," Arthur replied.

The guarded look on Pelleas' face relaxed. Cornu had told me that Arthur never lied, and I would guess Pelleas knew that from old acquaintance.

Kay's duties as Arthur's seneschal included overseeing the

kitchen, and the feast he had prepared was a success. He must have been planning and supervising cooking for days. There was wild boar and venison and fowl of several types, including pigeons, herons and plover, served with rich soups and gravies. There were fish from the Usk and from the sea, freshly caught and baked in their skins, and other dishes I couldn't identify. Beer and wine and cider were available to drink, along with water for those who wished to dilute their wine in the Roman fashion, or preferred it to other beverages.

As usual, I ate and drank sparingly, as did Nithe, but Pelleas and the children had healthy appetites and more than did justice to Kay's offerings. Kay beamed at them, looking pleased as a doting grandparent, and Pelleas lost his stern appearance watching him. Arthur, Pelleas and Nithe kept up a running stream of reminiscences while I listened. Guenevere and Lancelot, sitting beside her, were silent throughout the meal, though Lancelot addressed remarks to the knight Lavayne sitting on the other side of him. I thought there seemed to be some tension between Lancelot and the queen.

There was but a small company at table, no more than forty, counting Pelleas' children among the guests, but Kay opened the great hall for us, for we were too large a company for the queen's hall. Its noble proportions gave the occasion a formal aspect that put everyone on their best behavior.

Of the other diners, I recognized only Lancelot and Lavayne. Another man who came in with them I took to be Tristram. I had heard they had but recently returned from the Grail quest together. They came to the table too late for introductions, though Lancelot saw me. He did not speak.

I had been done eating for some time when Tristram called for a harp, walked down to where Viki, Nithe's daughter, was sitting, and proceeded to serenade her with a fanciful love song.

Viki looked at her mother to see what was expected of her, and Nithe said, "If you have designs on my daughter, Sir Tristram, you had best think again."

"Not at all, my lady," he replied smoothly. "Her fresh beauty takes my breath away, and I could not help but express how touched I am by it."

"Her father is listening," Nithe said. "Perhaps he understands why some men speak so extravagantly to young girls. I do not."

I glanced at Pelleas, who contented himself with looking bored, but I read the emotion that flowed from him easily enough. He did not like Tristram.

Pelleas muttered something in Pictish which sounded like "Damned Romified bastard." He had no idea I understand any Pictish, and I did not enlighten him. Actually my Pictish was mostly limited to kitchen jargon and epithets, but it was good enough to understand Pelleas.

I don't think Tristram heard him, but he started another song of a less objectionable nature anyway, and a number of the young people clustered around to listen. "Come, Lancelot," he called, shrugging off the applause which followed the song, "I challenge you to a duel. You compose some impromptu verses in honor of our young guest, and I will do the same. If her mother sees she is the object of general admiration, she will not be so suspicious of me."

Not bloody likely, I thought.

Lancelot rose from his seat next to Guenevere and walked around the table to stand next to Tristram. They were much of a size, big men in any company but that of Pelleas. Lancelot took the harp and played, not as well as Tristram, but well enough. His song was clever, but I had heard the like of it before with the name of a different girl, sung by a different singer. Following him, Tristram took back the harp and essayed an original song. Both singers finished to much applause, and both claimed victory. There was no doubt in my mind about the matter. Tristram had a true feeling for music, and Lancelot was merely a competent performer. Viki kept her eyes downcast, but the smile playing around the edges of her lips signaled that she was enjoying herself hugely.

Guenevere, however, was not. She leaned across me to catch Arthur's attention and spoke softly. "Will you excuse me, my dear?

Our guests seem well entertained, and I have developed a headache. I think I'll just slip off."

Arthur glanced at her in concern, but she did not wait for a reply. When her ladies started to follow her, she urged them stay with a peremptory wave of her hand. Lancelot saw Guenevere depart and appeared distressed for a moment.

"Oh, my," Arthur said to me in mock dismay, "I'm afraid Lancelot is in trouble with Gwen."

"Do you mind?" I asked.

"Life is more pleasant for me when she is in sympathy with him," he responded. "They quarrel a lot."

We left the party when Arthur invited us to his rooms, Nithe, Pelleas and me. Viki would be safe enough under the watchful eye of Kay, who would brook no rowdiness in the great hall.

I enjoyed watching Arthur and Pelleas try to rediscover their old friendship over ale. Nithe obviously was doing much the same, watching and exchanging glances of amusement with me from time to time. I concentrated on knitting winter stockings. Riding horses was itchy enough in any weather, but in winter was unthinkable with bare legs. Besides, I liked to knit. It gave the impression of industry while freeing the mind.

"Nithe, hold with me in this," Arthur demanded. "I say Pelleas is a berserker and has no more right to fault my temper than a grouch such as Myrddin might."

"Be careful how you speak of Myrddin, please," she replied. "I have never see Pelleas in temper, though, Lud knows, I myself have given him sufficient reason to show one over the past twenty years."

"It would be nearer forty years, I should think," Arthur responded in an ungallant tone, "and while I will defend Myrddin in any company but this, with you and Pelleas and Morgan I will speak as I think. Now, have you never seen him cross?"

"Myrddin or Pelleas?" Nithe asked, glancing over at me.

"Don't be funny. Pelleas, of course," Arthur growled.

"Oh, yes," she said. "It puts him out of sorts whenever old boy-friends greet me with affection, which, Lud knows, a number do.

I have never seen him actually ungracious, however, except perhaps to Gawaine."

"We'll agree he's a boor around Gawaine, but I mean something more," Arthur insisted.

I thought of Gawaine's telling me Pelleas held him responsible for letting the Saxons into Pelleas' stronghold, and consequently for the subsequent murder of his people. Boorish is hardly the term I would have used, if what Gawaine told me was correct.

"I've heard tales," Nithe said slowly, "but I protest! Truly, I have never seen him really angry myself. Hasty, perhaps."

"Ah, but you've heard tales," Arthur said. "And hasty, was it? Come, speak up, what tales of haste are these?"

Nithe glanced at Pelleas, and so did I, but he seemed to have a sleepy smile on his face that I took to mean he was enjoying himself. "What is the point of the question?" Nithe asked. "Have you heard already about our recent call on the Abbot of Usk?"

"No, tell me," Arthur begged, eyes shining.

After glancing again at Pelleas, Nithe said, "We smelled the most appalling odor when we were still miles up the coast, so we put in to find what was causing it. We found a dock near the mouth of the Usk that seemed to service a smelter. When we pulled in, Viki jumped to the dock with a line. A lackey snatched it from her hand and threw it, then her, back into the boat. Pelleas jumped on the dock and pitched the man into the water." She stopped, looked demurely down, then raised her eyes and said, "But truly, I could not swear Pelleas was actually angry."

Arthur, who had been hanging on her words, almost squirming with glee, broke into loud laughter, pledging his brother with the ale. "You win, Pelleas," he said. "You are undoubtedly of such an even temper there is not a man in Britain to match you!" And he drank off his ale, while slapping his hand on the table where he and Pelleas sat.

"And then," Nithe said, leaning forward, "Pelleas jumped on the smelter roof and tumbled the chimney down into the furnace. I fear it may be some time before it is operative again," she said in mock sadness.

Arthur went off into whoops of laughter, to my relief. I gathered anything Pelleas did was all right with Arthur. Nithe caught my eye and winked again. She really was very naughty.

"Will this make trouble for you?" I asked Arthur, for I could now admit my part in it.

"Only with Guenevere," Arthur said ruefully, quieting down. "She's been after me to do just what Pelleas did for months, but the abbot paid me in good bronze, and I needed a stock of it for all sorts of uses. I have enough now."

"But why would Guenevere give you trouble?" Nithe asked.

"Because you did it and I wouldn't. If we don't mention it, perhaps she won't notice," he said hopefully.

I wondered how anyone could miss the absence of that yellow pall.

"Guenevere's religious," Arthur went on, "and was delighted to have an abbey so close to Camelot until this. She refused to donate alms to them once the smelting started, and even stopped going to mass when the priest defended the abbot. If she does find out, at least she'll be most happy with you."

"She won't find out about it from us," Pelleas promised,

Arthur gave him a grateful look, but was saved from responding by Guenevere, who flung open the door, entered and slammed it shut violently. Pelleas lost his sleepy look and sat up straight. Arthur rose to face the queen while Nithe and I watched quietly.

"What is it?" Arthur asked, alarmed.

"That damned Lancelot," she shrieked, tears of rage running down her cheeks.

"Whatever has he done?"

"After spending the evening sitting and giggling with Lavayne, he responds to a challenge from Tristram, and together they take turns singing love songs to Nineve's daughter. With me in the room! Me! And my ladies come back and are so sweet and consoling, I could scream!"

"She's a guest, my dear. Lancelot and Tristram were just trying to make her feel comfortable," Arthur said in a coaxing voice.

"Comfortable? Some of the songs they were singing to her made me uncomfortable, I can assure you. I wonder you permit her to mix so in company." This last remark was directed toward Nithe.

"Viki is used to it," she said mildly. "Many young men sing scandalous love songs to her. It's quite the thing among the Picts. I only object to men of Tristram's age doing so."

I glanced at Pelleas as she said this and watched his eyebrows disappear. He never disputed Nithe's word in public, and, I would guess, rarely in private, but I was sure he thought Nithe was sometimes light-minded. I moved my stool back from the fire. I always felt hot when this kind of trouble occurred.

Guenevere moved to stand between me and the men and turned to appeal to them. "You know what people are saying?" she demanded.

"I know very little of what people are saying, if you mean the court," Arthur replied. "What little I do know I consider beneath notice."

He did, too, I'd wager. He must have hated gossip as much as Cornu said. I wondered if it was part of being a knight.

"Of course you do," Guenevere said, "but there are others who do not, and that is my concern."

"Just what is your concern?" Arthur asked in a resigned tone of voice.

"Well, it should be your concern, too," Guenevere said. "It's your knight and your queen they are talking about."

Now, I felt even more uncomfortable. I had heard rumors that Lancelot and Guenevere had renewed their affair, and that Lancelot had appeared to tire of it. I didn't want to hear this discussed in front of Arthur.

"If you and Arthur need to talk, perhaps Pelleas, Nithe and I should retire," I said, "It's been a long day anyway, and they are probably tired from the trip." Nithe nodded with alacrity and started to rise, but Guenevere waved her down.

"No! Stay, Nithe," she pleaded. "I have no female kin at Camelot except you, and Pelleas is Arthur's brother. I feel we may discuss it with you here. I know Arthur will just put me off again if we wait until we're alone."

Oh, my! I thought. She didn't mention me, but I'd feel awkward calling attention to it by leaving by myself.

"I don't mind if they stay, my dear, and I've asked you what your problem is," Arthur said. Strain was starting to edge his voice.

"Lancelot slights me in order to squire other women," Guenevere blurted out. "People are feeling sorry for me."

"If Lancelot were to choose some nice young woman and settle down, I would be most pleased," Arthur said.

"He is supposed to be my lover!" Guenevere stormed.

"Truly?" Arthur said coldly. "I had thought him your champion, nothing more."

"You know what I mean," Guenevere replied impatiently.

"Evidently not," Arthur replied.

"You know that it is commonly said that Lancelot has not married because of his love of me!" Guenevere said indignantly.

"That is somewhat different from his being your lover," Arthur said.

"Oh, you know how people talk! It adds much to my stature to have the finest knight in Christendom at my feet." Guenevere looked at Arthur, somewhat puzzled. Arthur's face was set in stern lines, as if rejecting the entire conversation. "It reflects on your honor as well, to have such a queen," she added hopefully.

"If you think it inflates my reputation to be thought a cuckold, my dear, I am afraid you are mistaken," Arthur said in a deceptively mild voice. His face was stormy.

I didn't move, but I caught Pelleas' eye. He lifted an eyebrow and shrugged the tiniest bit. I thought he probably liked such scenes even less than I.

Guenevere blushed and looked confused. To my belief, Arthur had never spoken of the relationship between her and Lancelot in quite this way. She twisted her hands and bravely continued.

"It is not I that claim we are lovers," she said. "I am not responsible for what other folk say. Every true knight has a lady to whom he dedicates his feats of arms, as you know. I have always had Lancelot's devotion, or so I thought."

"What has changed?" Arthur asked. "If he chooses to honor other women from time to time, it is at least partly because such gossips as Aggravain have linked your names together in an unsavory way. Lancelot is still your champion," Arthur continued, trying to mollify her.

"Your beastly cousins hate me!" Guenevere stormed. "Gawaine, Aggravain and Mordred all wish me ill. But you ask what has changed? They are now saying Lancelot did not achieve the Grail quest because of his guilty love for me! What guilty love was that? I never knew any! They say further that people claim he was not worthy. Lancelot? Not worthy? But he believes it! He seems not to understand that if he ceases honoring me now, it will appear that there was truth in the rumor. How can he not be concerned? How can you not?"

"I would be concerned if I believed it," Arthur said bluntly. "As you point out, I am not responsible for what folk say, either. Besides, you wrong Gawaine. He is ever courteous to you, and young Mordred is quite smitten with you, I do believe."

"Gawaine is the worst! He could set a good example for his brothers, but he won't. You are just blind to his faults."

"Then I am fortunate I have you near to point them out to me, my dear," Arthur said with heavy irony.

She looked at him a moment and tried a new tack. "Well," she said, sitting down, "even you must have noticed that Lancelot is much in the company of Lavayne, the twin brother of that girl who drifted down the river in the flower barge last spring."

"Dead, she was," Arthur said, nodding, "and daft besides! Who would starve themselves to death for love? What purpose does it serve? And all Lancelot did was to borrow a token from her to wear on his helmet as a disguise since it is well known he never wears ladies' favors in tournaments! It worked, too. It damned near got him killed when someone, not knowing it was Lancelot, broke off a spear in him. He could never have done that if he had known who it was."

"His reputation is a fearsome thing," Guenevere agreed. "The lady, however, thought she had proof of Lancelot's love. Who am I to say she was wrong?"

"It was all in her head," Arthur said. "Lancelot never encouraged her to think otherwise."

"It was what her kinsmen claimed when they came for her body that people remember," Guenevere said. "They relate that she and her brother both declared their love for Lancelot, and Lancelot coldly turned away from her, saying he was unable to love her, and that many women had sought him in marriage against his will. He then permitted Lavayne to follow him without hindrance."

"Lavayne's father asked him to take the boy under his protection in his first tourney," Arthur said. "If you believe it was anything else, you wrong him."

"What is this 'else' you refer to?" Guenevere sneered. "Lavayne has established himself as one of the best of the young knights. He doesn't need protection anymore. Why is he still here?"

"What are you trying to say?" Arthur asked, angry at last.

"I'm trying to say that people are laughing at me. They are saying that Lancelot was never mine, that he has used me to hide his affairs with young men. That's worse than if he really did seek the company of other women," she added, glancing at Nithe.

Arthur hesitated in responding, seemingly embarrassed. "I am aware that Lancelot is not interested in women in a carnal sense," Arthur said at last. "I do not think he has any carnal interest in men, either. He's always been half a priest. I mean it. He's truly devout."

"You appointed this eunuch my champion, knowing that?" Guenevere asked in an outraged voice.

"Do you think I would have appointed him to be your champion if I thought anything else?" Arthur retorted. "Do you think me a fool?"

"If you take me for a wanton who cannot be trusted to conduct herself properly, I would say you were a fool," Guenevere replied. "This is insupportable! Everyone must be in on the joke! Were you aware of this?" she asked Nithe.

"I am not aware of it now," Nithe replied. "I knew Lancelot when we were both quite young. I believed him virile enough then. He got a son by Elaine, Pelleas' sister, did he not?"

"Oh, Galahad! He could be Lancelot's son, truly enough. He has no interest in females either! On the other hand, how would one know, with someone like Elaine, who the father of her child might be?" Guenevere paced back and forth, tearing at a kerchief in her hands. "They do say she dressed up as a boy and gulled him, though, do they not?" she asked archly.

"Elaine?" Nithe said. "Surely she could never pass as a boy, could she, Pelleas?"

"She is my half-sister," Pelleas replied. "I have never thought of her in those terms."

"You jest," Nithe said. "She's all over you whenever we visit your mother."

"She's merely affectionate," Pelleas explained, unconvincingly I thought.

Nithe snorted, and turned back to Guenevere, saying, "The one time she visited the court, I remember your remarking on how little clothing Pictish women wear. There was no doubt in your mind then as to whether she was male or female."

Guenevere hesitated, frowned and returned to the original discussion. "Well, can one of you tell me why Lavayne hangs around Lancelot's neck the way he does?"

"He doesn't hang around his neck!" Arthur said. "What you see is hero worship. I felt much the same way about Pelleas when I was young, I remember. Can you see us as lovers?"

I saw Pelleas' eyebrows rise in astonishment.

"Has Lancelot ever spoken of this to you?" Guenevere asked, ignoring the question.

"Damn it, Gwen, do you think it likely? Can you hear him saying, 'Oh, Arthur, I know you think I'm sporting with Guenevere, but actually I'm more interested in Lavayne?'"

"You don't have to be vulgar!"

"And you don't have to be disloyal, as you are, both to Lancelot and to me. For my part, I welcome his establishing a little distance

277

between you, for the sake of my reputation, if you don't care about your own."

"Of course I care about my reputation! That's what this discussion is all about! I would never do anything calculated to damage my reputation, or yours either. You must know that!"

"I know that if someone comes to me and accuses you of treason because you're sleeping with another man, I may not be able to ignore it," Arthur said bluntly.

Guenevere had risen again, and they were standing face to face now, well within spitting distance. It appeared as if they might just do that. Nithe was moving only her eyes, flicking back and forth from Arthur to Guenevere and occasionally to me or Pelleas. Pelleas had leaned back into the shadows, trying to efface himself. He looked ridiculous, like a horse trying to hide behind a rose bush.

I was seated so that I could reach out and touch either Arthur or Guenevere, and they both continually looked to me to enlist my aid in the quarrel. I was no longer amused.

"What makes it treason?" Guenevere asked defiantly. "Bed games are more common than not around here, as you would know if you paid any attention."

"You are the wife of the king. If there were any question about the succession, the throne would be weakened. That makes it treason," Arthur said in a level tone.

"It would seem there is not much chance of that, barren as I am," Guenevere responded bitterly.

"I have never reproached you for barrenness," Arthur protested.

"Nevertheless, I know what people say. They say I should be put aside and that you should take a new queen."

"A few may," Arthur admitted, "but if you have heard so much, you have also heard I have sworn never to do so."

Guenevere began to weep, retiring to a corner with her back to the room. She would take no comfort from Arthur, who came up behind her and talked to her in low tones. That made it possible for Nithe, Pelleas and me to withdraw quietly, which is probably what she intended.

Before sleep came to me I decided Guenevere had the right of it in her quarrel with Arthur. There was no credit to be gained for virtue when the possibility of failure was not present. In a sense, Arthur had cheated Guenevere by appointing Lancelot as her champion, knowing what he knew. If it had happened to me, I would have been furious!

CHAPTER

XV

Next morning we were up early. I had stayed over in Camelot to be with Nithe and Pelleas, as well as to keep an eye on Mordred, and was sharing a room with Viki. After looking in on Mordred and finding him asleep I joined Viki, who had taken her dogs out to scomber. They had nosed at us until we rose to tend to them. Kay had looked askance when Viki's two families of mothers and puppies joined us in our bedroom, and I knew he had visions of messes that would stain the floor coverings, which is why we had fresh rushes instead of carpets. The place did smell doggy, even though she said the puppies were all housebroken and the bitches would burst before committing an indecency. She said if they told her it was time to go out, it was truly time, however. She would hate to prove Kay right.

Tag refused to stay with me and had stalked off haughtily to the stables. The horses were company and liked having him around. He had the air of one who plans to catch his own supper.

Arthur had told me Kay had never liked the dogs that he, Pelleas and Nithe had surrounded themselves with when they were growing up, most notably with the great wolf-mastiff cross, Cavell, that Myrddin rescued from angry farmers. The mother and her litter had been killed, except the one puppy, when Myrddin drove the farmers off. They named the puppy Cavell, meaning "horse," from the size of her feet. When she matured, Pelleas had mated Cavell with a wolf, and when Arthur had inquired about Pelleas' hunters, I knew he was really thinking about Cavell.

We made our way to the kitchen by going downstairs, through the great hall and back to where the food had come from the night before. Soon we found ourselves outside and facing a separate building, tied to the great hall only by a common roof built so food could be rushed in to serve the diners without cooling in the wind or winter snow. I smelled the air and was happy to have my fur cloak. It was one of those clear, cold mornings you find in the early summer.

Viki talked to a good-looking scullery lad, charming him out of breakfast for us and the dogs. The boy was teasing her, while keeping a wary eye on me, but straightened up when he saw Pelleas and Nithe join us. The boy disappeared into the kitchen, to reappear with a huge basin of scraps left over from the feast. He carried it in both his hands along with a freshly baked loaf of bread under one arm for Viki. We bespoke two more loaves, along with cheese and apples and a skin of wine, country style, and were provided for with alacrity. I don't know if it was Pelleas' size, my reputation as a witch, or fear of being caught by Kay, but the boy looked apprehensive. I decided it was probably fear of Kay. The Mother's priestesses always taught us to fear the danger we are most familiar with, rather than a possibly greater, unknown one.

"You have no fresh apples?" I asked, looking at the dried fruit he had given us.

"No, ma'am," he replied. "We get them from time to time from the countryside, but the only ripe ones now are from Lyoness, and the sailors from there drop their stores at the abbey. Sir Kay went to see about picking up new supplies from the abbey early this morning."

He must have gone very early, indeed, I thought, for it was barely light out. I didn't want to be here when he returned, for it was likely that the abbot would not be in a cooperative mood when Kay told him he needed extra food for our party. I didn't think Arthur would permit Kay to be rude to us, though, regardless of how irritated he might be.

"Would you like to come with us?" Nithe asked Viki and me. "We plan to borrow a couple of horses, along with hawks, and go coursing in the hills near the river."

"No, I must stay close to Mordred for another day," I said. "I want to make sure his fever is gone before I go back to the manor house. When he wakes I will give him strict orders to stay down, and entrust Gareth to see that he does. I believe Mordred will recover, but his brain has been bruised, and he needs complete rest for a few days, at least. He would be all right now except for Gawaine's insistence on his attending Morgause's funeral."

First I stopped at the stable and gave Tag a juicy rib I had rescued from the scraps before it could be devoured by Viki's dogs. Tag forgave me and ate it daintily as I checked on the horses. Arthur's grooms had fed them, cleaned their stalls and put out tubs of water for them. They were in good hands.

I went back to the infirmary to be with Mordred, and had time to think about my aunt. I had been fond of her, for she was an amiable person, but I realized I had felt closer to her than she had to me. She was an experienced woman when she sent me off with Urien, knowing I was pregnant. She had known I would reap grief from the lie we had acted out for him, but she had not warned me. If I had told him, he would not have held me responsible and our life together would have been different. I brooded on the fact that the people I loved the most were the ones that brought me the most pain. My father had raised me as he would have raised a son. I felt responsible for taking vengeance for him as a son would have, but had found no opportunity to do so. Would Boudicca have dallied so?

My mother had betrayed my father and me as well, sending me away from my home before I had grown up enough to leave without tearing up tender roots. Gawaine, who swore eternal love, married a fat heiress without even thinking about waiting for me. Why should I grieve for Morgause? But I did.

Mordred awoke and smiled to see me.

"You are good to care for me," he said. I decided there was an underlying sweetness in this boy that he kept hidden from most people. I was touched that he let me see it.

"I do care for you, but you are well on the way to mending," I said. "Will you promise to stay in bed if I leave you this time?"

"I will obey you in all things, except where it touches my honor," he said formally, but his smile lightened the words.

On hearing Mordred's voice, Gareth came in from the adjacent room where he had been asleep. He had watched Mordred through the night.

"How is he, Lady?" he asked me as he looked intently at his brother, hoping to see his answer in Mordred's face. He looked drawn from worry and his long vigil.

"Ask me, brother," Mordred said. "I am well enough to ride."

"He is not, then," I admonished. "He needs days of not moving any more than he has to before he even stands on his feet. If you love your brother, see that he obeys my orders to stay quiet."

"But I'm hungry!" Mordred complained.

"Good! I'll have food sent to you." I was getting hungry myself since it was now nearly noon, and decided to risk walking in on Arthur and Guenevere by entering the queen's hall just off the kitchen, where it was usually possible to find at least bread, cheese, beer and dried fruit at midday.

I met Pelleas and Nithe at the hall door, bound on the same errand. Pelleas seemed to be always hungry, and responded with a smile when I asked him if he were ready to eat. We found Guenevere there collecting viands in a basket.

"Come with me," she called on seeing us. "I want you to help me talk Arthur into having a party."

"Is this the food for the party?" Pelleas asked hopefully.

"Don't be silly. This is to soften Arthur up. Bring a small keg, will you?" she asked him, smiling. He carried it under one arm, eating a fresh loaf of bread held in his free hand.

I was given a couple of flasks of wine to carry, and the four of us climbed the staircase to Arthur's room over the armory. He was busy with Kay, but broke off on seeing us.

"Come in, come in," he called.

"I have had the most unsettling day," Kay said on seeing us. "The Abbot of Usk is not happy with you," he added accusingly.

"Whyever not?" Nithe asked, as if surprised.

"You very well know," Kay said. "You were there when Pelleas pulled the smokestack down. So were you, Lady Morgan," he added spitefully.

"He did it to accommodate me," I said blandly, knowing Arthur might erupt in anger at any time. Perhaps I could deflect it to me.

"Was he accommodating you when he made them dump water on the fire in the smelter furnace? The slag cooled, and they'll have to dismantle the firebox and hopper to get it out," Kay said in a scolding tone.

"Why, yes, I believe he was," I said, raising an eyebrow at Pelleas. Oh, I liked this man! I thought.

"I was happy to oblige you, my lady," he drawled.

"Can this be true?" Guenevere asked, clapping her hands together. "I've not smelled that sickening odor for several days, but had no idea Pelleas was behind it. Oh, my dear," she said grasping his hand and kissing it, much to his alarm, "you have no idea how I've suffered from this plague, and no one would take my complaints seriously. I am most beholden to you."

"If they were stupid enough not to draw off the smelt, they deserve to have to dig it out," Pelleas said. "I promised them I would take it apart myself if I smelled it again on my visit, my lady. You have only to bid me do it, and I'll take care of it permanently on my way home."

"Oh, please," Guenevere begged. Pelleas gently withdrew his hand, smiling.

"That's all very well," Kay said, "but you don't have the responsibility of stocking this castle with war goods or food or anything else. Most of the produce and trade items that used to come directly here are unloaded now at the abbey, so the boats don't have to wait for high tide to make the run upriver to Camelot. If the abbot chooses not to trade with us, I don't know what we'll do!"

Arthur shook his head in an irritated fashion and said, "It won't come to that, for if it did, I'd be forced to take over the port and run it myself. The abbot knows that if you don't."

"But he's protected by the Holy Church," Kay said, aghast.

"And the Holy Church is protected by me!" Arthur said.

"The abbot says you haven't protected him from the wild Picts who have destroyed his smelter," Kay retorted, reddening and looking sidewise at Pelleas.

"The wild Picts are my brother and his family," Arthur said, "and they were offered an affront for which I would have done more than they. Imagine laying hands on a girl that way! I wonder at their restraint."

"You will not, then, restrain them if Pelleas makes good his promise to the queen?" Kay asked in a formal tone.

"Of course not," Arthur said. "And know this: I am not best pleased with the threat the abbot has seen fit to send through you."

Kay started to excuse himself, seeing Arthur's displeasure, but Guenevere bid him stay. "We're going to have a party, and I need you to help with it," she said to him. "We'll talk about the abbey later."

She was most winsome when she wished to be, and Kay unbent. Arthur looked wary, but Guenevere ignored him as she set up the food and indicated to us where we should place the keg and the flasks. Kay, professional at this kind of thing, took over, and within moments we had a very good facsimile of a party going in Arthur's study.

Pelleas smiled at everyone as he cut into a second loaf, stuffing it with cheese and dried apples. A flagon of beer was beside him on a short stool which he turned into a table, sitting on the floor with his back against the wall. When Pelleas was happy, no one could long be unhappy around him. Even Kay enjoyed himself.

I was content with a modest slice of cheese, a broken loaf and a glass of wine. I sat beside Nithe to watch and listen.

"I like parties," Arthur said, "but what is the occasion for this one?"

285

"This isn't the party, silly," Guenevere replied. "This is a lunch to hold us in one place while we discuss the party I want to have."

"Hmm," he replied, filling his mouth with food so no clearer response was possible.

"If you won't move to London where we can entertain in style, we'll have to do it here," Guenevere announced in an emphatic tone. She nodded several times to herself, with eyes slightly out of focus as if deep in thought. I knew her performance to be calculated, and I was sure Arthur did as well, but it was no less effective for that. It gave her the appearance of irresistible innocence. None of the rest of us said anything, awaiting developments.

"I think I'd like to hold a party for your cousins," she said. "Gawaine is newly back in town from that mysterious journey of his, and I'm sure he'd be pleased."

"Are you sure? I haven't see Gawaine around. Besides, I didn't think you liked him," Arthur said cautiously.

"See? Even you think that. It's high time I put a stop to that kind of talk. I know he's your favorite cousin, and perhaps I've not been as nice to him as I might have been in the past, but I want to start afresh with him."

"Lancelot is my favorite cousin," Arthur said mulishly.

"Lancelot has received far more attention than is good for him," Guenevere said lightly, but she was frowning. "It's time Gawaine got his share."

"He likes parties," Arthur said, "but he may be in a bad mood. I think Lamerok may have escaped Gawaine and his brothers. I do believe I would have heard if it had been otherwise."

Pelleas raised an eyebrow at this, but Arthur didn't explain the remark, and Guenevere ignored it.

"I thought I'd have some of Gawaine's kin, particularly the younger ones, along with their friends. My ladies will wait on them, acting as serving girls, to show them honor."

"Is that a good idea? If there's much to drink it may get difficult to keep the men in line," Arthur said.

"Oh, pooh! Any one of my ladies could stand off the best of them, given the inclination."

She bounced out to put her plans into action, followed by Kay, at her invitation. They left the food and drink behind, so we stayed.

"Will you be going?" I asked Arthur, seeing the quizzical expression on his face.

"None of us will be going. You heard her. She's interested in a younger crowd."

"Gawaine is older than you are," I said.

"I know, but he still plays. He doesn't like to be thought of as older than the others. When he calls me Sire, instead of Arthur, it's like calling me Father," Arthur said sourly.

I laughed. Arthur was so exactly right. Much as I loved Gawaine, his vanity and insistence on youthfulness was a little trying at times.

"What did you mean about Lamerok's escaping Gawaine?" Pelleas asked.

"I don't know how much you are aware of how it stands between them," Arthur said in a brooding tone.

"Assume I know nothing. Enlighten me."

"Part of it is old history. Gawaine believes Pellinore killed his father, Lot."

Oh, dear, I thought. That again. I wondered what they would say if I told them I had done it? That I had taken vengeance on Lot for raping me?

"Pellinore always claimed it was Balin who killed Lot," Pelleas objected. "He said he met the Knight with Two Swords on the field after he had unhorsed Lot with a spear, and Pellinore's blow was unneeded."

"How could he be sure it was Balin?" I asked.

"He said he recognized the shield. I had exiled Balin, so he could not come forward after the battle," Arthur said. "He wasn't supposed to be there."

"Anyone can paint a shield," I said, and I found Nithe looking at me oddly, so I shut my mouth.

"We'll probably never get the truth of it," Nithe said. "Balin and his brother killed each other while fighting without identifying shields."

I hadn't known that! Were these also deaths for which I was

responsible? I had taken Balin's shield, and I had cursed him, I recalled. Did my witching go as far as that?

"Gawaine thinks it was Pellinore, despite what Pellinore might say," Arthur said impatiently. "That's all that matters now. Both Pelleas and I fear Pellinore may be dead at the hands of Gawaine and his brothers, though I hope not. I must tell you, however, Lamerok believed Gawaine had murdered his father, and maybe he was right. Damn! If I knew for sure, I would do something, for I love the old man. He is my senior knight."

"Pellinore knighted me," Pelleas said. "He is my liege lord, and I also love the old man. If Gawaine has truly killed him, I will have to do something about it myself. I am less concerned for his son, Lamerok, but only a little less so. If Pellinore is dead, Lamerok may be chosen to be High King of the Picts."

"Pellinore told me Lamerok had stepped down in your favor," Arthur said.

"He is too kind," Pelleas said. "However, I have given allegiance to Pellinore as my liege lord. How can I accept an honor that diminishes his?"

Arthur nodded. In the formal world of chivalry, Pelleas had made an incontestable point. Discussion of the finer points of knightly rights and obligations always bored me. I excused myself for an afternoon nap. Besides, I didn't like to listen to people talk about incidents connected with Lot's death, knowing what I knew. I always wondered if I should not confess, but shrank away from the possible consequences. I considered it again. I decided on the nap.

Cornu came for me, waking me before I had properly fallen asleep. "Mordred's gone," he said.

"Gone?" I asked, tugging on my boots. I wanted more information. "He isn't strong enough to get out of bed by himself."

"He had help. He and that giant brother of his left this morning," Cornu said. "Their horses are gone, too."

"Damn!" I swore. "He'll kill himself! We'll have to go after him."

"I have horses waiting," he said.

I found a page on the way out and gave him a message for Big Red at the manor house, telling her I would be gone for a few days. I trusted the boys were well on their way to recovery, but I worried, nevertheless.

Cornu could track as well as any Pict. I brought Tag along, for he would follow me if I did not. Cornu and I could travel on dried apples, hard bread and cheese, with water to drink from the streams, but Tag needed meat. He hunted and ate at night, sleeping on his pad on the rump of my gelding during the day. It didn't delay us.

We went slowly, for the trail was cold, and I was never sure we were on it. Cornu claimed he saw hoofprints that he recognized. They all looked the same to me.

The search took days. "He'll be dead by the time we catch up to him," I grumbled.

Cornu grunted. As it was we found Gawaine, Gaheris and Aggravain fishing for salmon. "Well met, cousin," Gawaine said gleefully, hugging me in greeting. It was good to see him, but I could not tarry.

"I am looking for Mordred," I said. "He's wandering around with a cracked head, and I fear he is doing himself permanent damage."

"He was here yesterday, and he looked pale, but he could ride well enough. We asked him to stay with us, but he and Gareth rode off," Gawaine said.

Aggravain laughed in a nasty way, and Gaheris ignored us. He could only use one arm, and cursed steadily in a monotone at the effort it took him to fish that way. The other was in a sling. Mordred had told me he had broken his brother's arm when he came upon Gaheris standing over Morgause's body with a dripping sword in his hand.

"The bloody scuts ambushed Lamerok," Gawaine said bitterly, indicating his brothers. "We will have a full blood feud over this."

"We will not, then," I said. "I will arrange for paying the blood price."

"Pay? You will not!" Aggravain shouted, throwing his pole on the ground and coming over to us. Gaheris joined him, glaring.

"Will I not?" I said. "Who has a better right? With Morgause's death am I not clan Merrick head?"

"It is for men to say about blood price!" Aggravain insisted, spittle frothing his beard.

"But not until the clan mothers have heard cause. I will swear to them that it was my hand that struck Lot down, not Pellinore's!"

There was silence for a moment before Aggravain sneered, "You? A woman? Who would believe it?"

"You think I could not? Would you challenge me? Ask Gawaine how safe that would be!" I shifted my feet, wishing with all my heart he would move against me. Instead he snorted derisively and went back to the river, fishing pole in hand. He did not believe me!

I turned to Gaheris and said, "Gawaine called you bloody scuts. I say you murdered Lamerok for no cause. You will not carry this into blood feud with Pellinore's kin. I will not allow it."

"It is already done," Gaheris said. "Some may say it was Balin who murdered our father, rather than Pellinore. No one says it was you." Scorn dripped from every word. "Besides," he added, "Lamerok debauched our mother."

"And who in Arthur's court did not?" I asked coldly. "You would be laughed to scorn for making such a charge."

Gaheris drew his belt knife, but Cornu caught him by the wrist, twisting the knife from his hand. At that he was lucky: I was poised to cut his hand off. "You now have two sore arms," Cornu remarked dryly. "I hope you can get someone to help you when you wish to relieve yourself."

"Enough of this," I said, breathing deeply to relax. No one would fight with me. "Which way did Mordred go?"

"He went west," Gawaine told me, smiling grimly. "I hope you find him in time to be of help. I think I will return to Camelot. I would like to be there when Arthur learns who killed Lot."

"Do you plan to tell him?" I asked.

"No, but Aggravain will, if Gaheris doesn't."

We left them to their fishing. I was dissatisfied with Gawaine's behavior, but I realized I had no right to correct beyond what I had already said. If he had been my husband, he would have acted differently! I wondered how Boudicca had dealt with men!

We did find Mordred, in a Pictish village on the Strath River. We were directed to a rambling, palisaded, single-story structure that we were assured belonged to King Pelles. It was no more imposing than Urien's stronghold, and I recognized Urien's idea of elegant housing was shared by other Picts.

A round, stone watchtower stood some distance away, but was not manned. Ordinarily hunters would have brought advance warning of raiders in the vicinity, I realized.

An elderly, tiny, tattooed lady met us at the door and invited us in. I had enough Pictish to respond to her formal greeting, which delighted her. In response she spoke to me in passable Latin, and I was able to ask after Mordred. She led me to his side.

"Look, Cornu, how thin he is! He hasn't been eating." I glanced reproachfully at Gareth, who was huddled in a huge, miserable lump near Mordred's head.

"He tries but nothing stays down, Lady," he said. "Can you help him?"

"That is what I came to do," I assured him. "Go and rest. I will see to him." When he had gone we made a careful examination of the patient, and found nothing new.

"He would have mended by now if he hadn't been foolish," I said, and Cornu nodded. He changed the bandage on Mordred's head and found the wound clean.

I looked at the Pictish woman. She nodded, pointing to herself and breaking into a torrent of sound I could not interpret. I asked her to speak more slowly and found she was interested in his parentage.

I explained who Mordred was. When we got to the fact that his grandfather was Uther Pendragon, she put both hands over her mouth and giggled.

"What is it?" I asked, and received a new flood of talk.

This time Cornu took pity on me and translated. "She says when she was just a girl she ran away from her training as a priestess of the Mother. Her lover was Uther Pendragon. Pelleas is the son of that liaison."

So, Nithe's Pelleas came out of this tiny woman! It was almost unbelievable. From that time on nothing was too good for us, or for the sick man. "We will adopt him," she said. "He will take the place of someone who died young."

We stayed with her for another day, at the end of which Mordred awoke from his deep sleep, weak but rational.

"Now you see what happens when you do not obey your doctor, do you not?" I asked him.

"I was under a constraint I could not ignore," he said gravely.

"Will you stay down until your nurse says you can rise this time?" I asked. "I must go back to my home and check on my grandchildren. Otherwise I would not trust you in so important a matter."

"Right now I think I could sleep for a week or two," he responded. "In the end I will have to be dragged from my bed."

We left and made speed on the trip back. We had been gone ten days and I was worried. My grandchildren had not fully recovered from the smoke poisoning when I left them, though I thought them not in any danger. Some village women I had hired to take care of the manor house had promised to watch them. I hoped to find them well now that the smelter was no longer in operation, but I could not rest until I was sure.

CHAPTER

XVI

e rode directly to the manor house and were greeted by Big Red. She burst into tears, talking the whole time she clung to me, saying, "They're so sick, Morgan! All covered with red spots and burning with fever!"

Cornu had gone to see the horses, and I immediately sent for him. He joined me in the manor hall, which had been turned into an infirmary, and went with me from bed to bed as we looked over the children.

"I'm going for Myrddin," he said, and left at a run. I had never seen him frightened before, and it gave me a confirmation of my direst fears. Myrddin was at New Avalon, half a day upriver. I expected Cornu back by dawn. I hoped it would be in time.

"How long have they been like this?" I asked.

"Since three days after you sent word you were off seeking Mordred, though they were only beginning to get this sick then. But gradually they got worse and suddenly came down with high fevers and spots. Susan and I haven't slept a full night in a week!"

I looked over at Susan and nodded. She looked grim, but relieved to see me.

"Have we lost anyone?" I asked.

"No, but my youngest and another child no longer wake," she said. "Oh, Morgan, help us!"

"What has been done for them?" I asked.

"We've given them willow bark water for the fever, but we don't know what else to do," she said.

Well, neither did I.

"Have tubs brought in. We must bathe the children. We can cool them that way. Give them fresh, cold water in little sips. Force it on them if you have to."

"Won't they take a chill?" Big Red asked doubtfully.

"Not from this," I replied. Chills are not caused by chilling, but I couldn't say that and stay creditable with these women. I needed their cooperation.

The children complained that the light hurt their eyes when I examined them under the window, and I had the winter shutters installed to darken the room. That gave them some ease. Most of the children became more comfortable as they cooled down from the bath, and even the two sickest relaxed. I despaired for their living through the night, however.

I cursed myself. Why had I not been sure they were recovered from the smoke poisoning before I ran off after Mordred like a cow after a calf? These children were my first responsibility, not Mordred. He would have recovered without me, in any case, in the hands of Pelles' wife. Frustration brought me near tears, but I could not shed them with these frantic women reading my face for some sign. I resolutely smiled and told them all to get some rest. I said I would watch the children through the night, and the day would bring new tidings. I wished I could believe all that.

The women from Caerleon who had been hired as house-help must have been some time without sleep, for they all left except Big Red, who would not budge from the side of her sickest child. "He won't live, will he, Morgan?" she asked me in a flat voice, but hoping for reassurance.

"Cornu has gone for Myrddin," I said. "If the child lives until he comes, I believe all will be well. Myrddin has wondrous cures."

Together we watched the child breathe in ever shallower gasps, until I could barely see his chest move. He looked so wasted, and I remembered how sturdy he had been. His hair was red, like his mother's, plastered now against his skull and nearly black with sweat.

Upon hearing the sound of running horses I went to the door and peered out into the moonlight. Two riders swept up to the gate, dismounted and left their horses standing and steaming in the dim light. One was very tall and the other very short: Myrddin and Cornu without question. But, imagine Cornu leaving horses standing like that, sweating in the cold!

I took Myrddin straight to the kitchen, where he set out various vials and boxes on the table. Some potions he mixed in wine, which I furnished him, and others in water. It took almost no time.

"Cover the children's eyes and bring them in, one by one, the sickest first," he said. I went back into the infirmary and told Big Red to carry her child to the kitchen. I found the other dangerously ill child and picked him up, bearing him swiftly in after her.

We laid our little burdens on the table. Myrddin started spooning some potions into them, and rubbed them with others, delegating the latter task to us once he had well started it.

The third child was ready in Cornu's arms by the time Big Red was able to take her first into the manor hall. She returned with her second child, and I followed with another. The three of us kept a steady stream of children coming until they had all been doctored, the two girls last, for they were the oldest and strongest.

"So," Myrddin said when Cornu came back empty-handed, "is that all of them?"

"Yes," Cornu said. "Was it what you feared?"

"Not quite. We were in time, after all," Myrddin said. "In time for these, at least. There will be others in Caerleon for whom we may be too late. We must go find them."

"Was it the smoke?" I asked.

"That, complicated by a disease that children are subject to," he said. "It's running wild throughout this part of the country. Either, by itself, would have been serious enough." He was packing up his vials and boxes of powders as he spoke.

"Will they be all right?" Big Red asked him with the first hope in her voice I had heard since I arrived. Myrddin stopped for a moment, looked at her keenly and said, "The fever is already breaking. The problem now is to keep them quiet. Feed them every few hours when they wake, small amounts of nourishing soups and the like. Let them drink as much as they can. Make them drink, if you have to. They are dangerously dehydrated.

"They will want to get up and play by the day after tomorrow, but they must stay in bed at least a week. More rest would be better, but probably unrealistic to expect." Before he had quite finished his instructions, Big Red had hugged and kissed him soundly and run back into the infirmary to watch.

"She wants to see the fever break," I said. "She was so sure it would not. I feared only that you would not come in time."

Myrddin smiled. "It was a near thing. It will be even closer for the children in Caerleon. I will take Cornu with me, if I may. Together we might save at least some of them." And they were gone.

It was like prophecy. Morning came and the children woke up hungry, all of them. The two mothers were so relieved, they ran back and forth fetching the food and little toys for them to play with until I had to put a stop to it.

I spoke to the invalids. "You children need rest and quiet. I will tell you stories, and you must try to listen quietly and drift off to sleep. If you are going to be pages for the High King, you must learn to do as you are told. He does not permit spoiled children to serve him."

It was enough. The children had been waiting in anticipation for a chance to join Arthur, and were so obedient to my slightest order that it quite unnerved me. Big Red found me crying in the pantry.

"Well now, what is this?" she asked, hugging me and patting me on the back.

"I was afraid they would die, Moira," I said. "I left them when I should not have, and now they're going to be all right. Together it's just too much!"

"I know, I know, but they're calling for you. They want another story before their naps. Where do you get them all, anyway?"

"The stories? I make them up," I said. "I spent much time with my boys when they were younger than these, and they were always demanding stories from me."

"Well, these are demanding another one now, so get on in there," she said, and she gave me a little pat to start me to the door.

In time I found periods in which I could rest. I could not always sleep, but I had opportunities to think at length. Big Red, Drake and Susan all but ran Morgan's hold. I thought I might stay on at the manor house when it came time for Big Red and Susan to go home. I was not needed at Morgan's hold. Also, I admitted I craved more company than I could find there. Lancelot had been right. It was a rustic wilderness in some ways.

It was days before Cornu came back from Caerleon and days more before he went to Camelot to talk to prospective horse-buyers. I was absorbed in watching the children return to strength and vigor and had no time for him or the affairs of Arthur's court. That all changed when he arrived with a startling report.

"Guenevere gave a big party for Gawaine," he stated.

"Yes, I heard her start the planning of it," I said.

"Well, an Irish knight died at the party of eating an apple that had been set out for Gawaine. Gawaine accused the queen of trying to poison him!"

"Oh, he wouldn't! The fool," I exclaimed. Whatever was the matter with that man?

"Not everyone would agree with you," Cornu stated. "There was a trial by arms, and Lancelot showed up at the last moment to appear as queen's champion. He won, of course. Right after the trial, Guenevere persuaded Arthur to move the whole court to London for the winter. We'll have to follow if we want to sell any horses!"

"Just like that? You tell me Guenevere has been on trial for her life, and you want me to go to London with you to sell horses?"

"Yes, of course. They're not my horses."

"Are they not? Do you think that's an adequate response?"

"Yes," he said. "We'll take the three grooms and twenty horses. We'll leave the other grooms here with the mares and foals."

"We'll go nowhere until you tell me what occasioned this extraordinary event," I said firmly. Cornu had his own standards of what was important and what is not. We did not always agree.

"Very well," he sighed. "You know there has always been talk about Lancelot's devotion to Guenevere," he said.

"It's harmless," I responded, thinking back to the uncomfortable scene I had witnessed on my last visit to Camelot.

"It is not, then," Cornu disagreed. "It was talk about the queen that was responsible for the charges brought against her. No one would have dared if her reputation had not already been damaged."

"But why?" I asked.

"I do not know that," Cornu responded. "I know Gawaine's brothers are the source of most of the gossip. I think they are jealous of Lancelot for Gawaine's sake. They think Gawaine ought to be the one closest to Arthur."

"But surely you do not believe there is truly anything improper going on between Lancelot and Guenevere, do you?" I asked.

Cornu shrugged. He would say no more about the matter except that the gossip had poisoned Camelot. I trusted the trial had ended the vicious talk. Surely Gawaine's brothers would be more cautious about what they said now.

Resigning myself to Cornu's refusal to discuss the scandal further, I found other reasons not to go. "But who will take care of the house and the children?"

"Big Red," he answered. "I've already talked to her. If she can manage Morgan's hold, she can manage things here without us."

So, he had noticed, too. Very well. I packed for London.

Next morning we were to leave, and Cornu woke me early. He looked uncommonly serious. "The Abbot of Usk has refired his smelter," was all he said.

I went quickly to the hall and found a very grim Big Red dressing for war, with Susan's assistance. "Well met, Lady," Big Red said formally. "The poison smoke has started again. You can see it rising to the sky, where the first wind will have it down on us again. The children are just coming into full health, and I will not have them at risk again."

"Nor I," I said. "We will seek out this murderer of children together, alone if necessary, but I think we will have help." I turned to Susan. "Will you look after the children?"

She nodded. She was too small to be an effective stick fighter, though she had been skillful enough when young.

I had but donned my own chain mail and helmet when Cornu appeared saying, "We are waiting for you."

In the yard before the gate I found Big Red and our grooms, mounted and ready. A horse had been saddled for me. Farmers' wives from Caerleon stood at my gate urging us on, promising to watch over our children. Their own children had suffered under the pall of smoke.

"Lead us, Lady," Big Red said. I saw with approval that she had her fighting stick and belt knife, like mine. The grooms carried long knives and boar spears. Only Cornu and I had armor, but we only expected to face monks, so I was not unduly concerned. What opposition could they offer?

The ride from the manor house to the mouth of the Usk takes half a day usually. We made it in three hours, with the yellow pall before us rising like a menacing club into the sky.

We were seen and met by a mixture of soldiers and clerics, though not many of the former. They were led by the abbot. Suddenly I saw a gray face with a lantern jaw that I remembered from my childhood. It was Father John-Martin! I didn't think he recognized me, dressed as a fighting man, as he pushed forward to the abbot's shoulder to whisper in his ear.

The abbot's face showed a mixture of emotions when he looked from one to another of us. In the end, he addressed me. "My Lady," he said. "What means this hostile face?"

"You were told not to start up the smelter again without permission, and you have done so, haven't you?" I said.

"We heard King Arthur and the giant had left," the abbot said. "Sir Kay told us."

"Kay, again, is it? But, if you recall, I also objected to this abomination. Now you will have to go to the trouble of shutting down again, won't you?"

"But we are under King Arthur's protection. Sir Kay promised in his name!"

"He has no authority to do that," I said. "Only my brother can pass his word, and he has not done so."

Father John-Martin whispered again to the abbot.

"I am reminded that King Mark of Cornwall has offered us all the aid necessary to keep this venture going," the abbot said in a complacent voice. "When we feared King Arthur would not give us the protection promised, we applied to King Mark. Since he provides the ore needed for our foundry, it is much in his interest to do so."

"King Mark?" I asked in astonishment. "King Mark has offered you protection on Arthur's lands?"

"He sent some soldiers to us in token," the abbot said, barely containing his glee.

"Well, while there are others not here who have objections to this stinkpot," I said, "I am concerned only with mine. I have expressed them, and you have seen fit to ignore my warnings. What happens now is on your head."

I rode into the crowd, seized Father John-Martin by his cowl and dragged him through the half-circle of onlookers forming around us.

"This is the culprit that brought Mark into this," I said.

"Here, here, that is our priest!" the abbot protested.

"My father's priest, first," I said. "He tricked me into leading my father into ambush, giving him to Uther's soldiers, or so I believe. I would question him. Back off!" and I placed my knife against the priest's throat.

"You!" Father John-Martin cried. "I might have known! Dressed like a man in defiance of the scriptures!"

Cornu reached down and placed his hand over the priest's mouth, shutting off further complaints.

I dismounted and left him in Cornu's hands. Big Red followed my example and closed up beside me, taking a position on my left.

"Help him!" cried the abbot, and the soldiers with him rushed us. Cornu thoughtfully punched Father John-Martin on the back of his head and with his flute deflected a sword thrust before seizing his attacker's outstretched arm and throwing him into the river. He rode toward the crowd through the thin line of soldiers and, with the grooms, scattered the monks before turning to hem in the soldiers from behind.

Big Red and I stood and fought side by side. A shield-maiden with a fighting stick had the reach over a man with a sword, and in the hands of a skilled person a fighting stick was the better weapon. Big Red and I were the best stick fighters in Galloway.

Big Red and I thrust and slashed in unison, bewildering each man who challenged us. Our opponents were stunned, not killed, but between us we finished five of them while Cornu kept them from fleeing to the abbey. With retreat cut off, the remaining few soldiers jumped into the river to escape us and swam off. We let them go.

The abbot had tried to flee with the crowd of monks, but Cornu hauled him back to face me.

"As I told you, we have come to shut down this smelter permanently. Take care of it, Cornu," I ordered.

"Cornu is a smith," I told the abbot. "If he attends to it, it will be better done than if you did it. From you we require food and drink." And I herded the abbot toward the abbey itself and the few retainers that hovered just out of reach of the mounted grooms toward the abbey itself, as though they were a flock of sheep.

Big Red followed Cornu to the smelter. She wanted to assure herself it would no longer belch poison into the air. I stayed with Father John-Martin to question him.

"You hit him too hard," I yelled at Cornu when I examined the priest. "You broke his neck!"

Cornu looked so crestfallen as he continued to ride away, I knew immediately it was no accident.

I followed him. "All right," I said in disgust. "Why did you do it?"

For once he gave me a direct answer. "This one would not willingly tell you anything. Would you have tortured him?"

I stopped to consider his words. Indeed, what else was there to know? I shrugged, left Cornu and Big Red to set fire to the smelter and went on to the abbey. I ordered food to be prepared for us and served in the monks' dining hall. Cornu played his flute for us after we ate, and we took our ease for a while.

Finally I asked for the abbot to come to us. He had disappeared before I reached the abbey, and I wanted to make sure he understood what would happen if he rebuilt the smelter. The monks who served us said he was praying in the chapel.

"Fetch him to me," I ordered, and they hastened out to do my bidding. Even so, we waited the better part of an hour before the abbot appeared before us.

"I could not interrupt the mass and leave the host uncovered," he said to account for his tardiness, with no trace of an apology.

"When I summon you, I expect civil obedience, not sullen compliance," I told him, bending a stern eye on the man standing before me. "Too many unresolved problems flock around your head, like hungry crows. You are no longer welcome in this land. Take your people and sail back to Ireland, from whence you came. If you are here when I return from London in the spring, I will show you what it means to defy a queen."

"You cannot command me," the abbot said with a wild gleam in his eye. "God has cursed your rule for the heretic you are."

"Heretic?" I asked. "This to me? I am not even Christian!"

"Was it not your voice that gave permission to bury the bitch Morgause with druidic rites?" the abbot demanded.

"Druidic? Never! I serve the Mother!" I exclaimed, angered at his reference to Morgause.

"Ah, that one," he sneered. "Know we will never take heed of one who serves the Great Whore!"

"And?" I asked, rising and facing him eye to eye.

"And we will have a new smelter roasting ore before the moon changes."

Before he uttered the last word Big Red and I had seized him, one on each side, and shouting, "Out! Out!" threw him into the dust that lay before the abbey door. From there Big Red beat him to the dock and into one of the oar barges, using her fighting stick as a flail.

The rest of us rounded up the brothers from wherever we found them, the kitchen, the chapel, the fields, and herded them to the river dock to join the abbot, who lay as one stunned. We raised a sail for them and pushed the barge out into the stream to be drawn into the sea by the ebbing tide. No more resistance was offered than sheep give to wolves in the fold. We found no soldiers among them and assumed that they had all fled.

I looked around and missed Cornu, but as the bell of the church began to toll, I guessed what he had done. Cornu had acted in my stead, again, and Father John-Martin was surely hanging from the pull rope of his church bell. Cornu's bland expression dared me to question him when the bell stopped tolling and he soon appeared. I did not question him, nor did the others.

Cornu, Big Red and I began systematically to destroy the abbey. The smelter was already burning. We fired the rest of the buildings, all straw-thatched.

The abbot's men in the boats could see the smoke, and we could hear their curses, which served to drive us to greater efforts. With a great bar of iron in his hand, Cornu prised one stone from another until nothing was left standing of the church but the bell tower. He stood and surveyed the ruins of the abbey, and slowly a look of consternation came over his face.

"Guenevere will have my hide for this day's work," he said. "It's said she thought to win the abbot over by prayer."

"Tell her it was because the abbot started up the smelter again," I suggested.

"Ah, yes. That's the story. And we'll tell her Big Red did it!" Cornu said. We laughed away the tension, but privately I wondered at the abbot's connection with Kay. We waited for the incoming tide to float us back to Camelot in the abbot's own curragh, sustained by oat cakes and dried fruit Big Red had provided her with. Our grooms led our horses back. During the lull, Cornu found the wine stores in a cellar, and we loaded the boat so full of spoil it was nearly awash when we started upriver, now in much better humor than when we had decended it. The wine helped.

We returned to the manor house and rested a day before setting out for London with the horses. The trip was uneventful for aside from light rains every afternoon, the weather was not bad. We arrived late, bedding down with our horses at the horse fairgrounds. The next day I repaired to the old Roman baths where Arthur had established his court, and Cornu looked for buyers for his horses. I found the court in turmoil, seething with gossip.

Gawaine and his brothers were much in court, even Gaheris, who had been rescued by Guenevere from exile for his killing of Morgause, as a surprise for Gawaine's party. Guenevere now treated the brothers with an airy indifference which galled Gawaine.

"I was wrong about the woman, and I admitted it," he complained to me. "The trial by combat proved it was not her hand that poisoned the apple. What does she want?"

I looked at him with a critical eye. "You are not aware, then, that Aggravain and Gaheris fail to share your feelings in this matter? Cornu has heard Aggravain traduce the queen in tavern after tavern."

"Ah, Aggravain! He has no good word for anyone!" Gawaine grumbled.

"He seems to have fewer good words for the queen than for anyone else," I said. "He swaggers, with Gaheris shadowing him, buying drinks at the taverns for knights and commoners alike. In fact, Cornu tells me, he buys for anyone who will listen to his tales. He has but one theme: King Arthur's wife is a murderer and adulteress. Do not tell me you are unaware of this. Even I already know!"

"I have heard it said," Gawaine admitted, "and I have taxed him with it. He denied it."

"And you believe him? Oh, come, Gawaine! I have known him

almost as long as you have. He was a sneak and a liar from the time he could walk and talk."

"What would you have me do, then? He laughs and says he has no money to buy such quantities of ale. I know that to be true, at least."

"He buys it, nevertheless," I said grimly "Find out where the money comes from. And tell Gaheris to stand clear of him. Take some responsibility here! Gaheris lends credence to Aggravain and it ill becomes him! He was once rescued from exile by Guenevere. The least he owes her is his silence."

"Gaheris never says anything," Gawaine protested. "It was me who set him to watch Aggravain."

"It doesn't appear so," I said, suddenly blazingly angry at his obtuseness. "You would do well to bring your brothers to heel, or I will make it a matter for the clan mothers. If necessary, I will have the three of you bound, thrown into a cart and taken back to Morgan's hold for judgment! Do you think your wailing at her funeral relieves Gaheris from responsibility for the death of Morgause?"

Gawaine was shaken. "I swear on her blood that I do not believe Gaheris intended her harm. He grieves bitterly for his part in her death. He weeps at night when he thinks no one hears."

"If he seeks to fix his hate on something other than himself, he would do well to find another target than the queen," I said. "Guenevere deserves better by him. Wronging her will not make up for his killing his mother."

I could not bring myself to feel pity for Gaheris. If he had not been Gawaine's brother I would have already acted just as I threatened. Only my high regard for Gawaine had protected Gaheris to this time. I led clan Merrick. When I was no longer willing to hold my hand from the throat of Gaheris, not even Gawaine's general popularity would serve to delay justice longer. Even Gawaine would fall in the ruin his brother was preparing, and I was sure Gawaine knew this. He took his leave from me, promising to speak again to Aggravain.

He did, and Aggravain chose to see Arthur as a result, not me.

He was wise, for I would not have been as lenient as Arthur. I had just gone to Arthur to warn him of the trouble I saw coming, but I had not yet spoken when Aggravain was announced. He went straight to Arthur, ignoring me.

"Cousin," he said, looking at Arthur from under lowered brows, "I am here against the advice of my brothers, but I can no longer stand silent and observe Lancelot and Guenevere abuse your trust."

"Have a care, Aggravain," Arthur said. "I hate gossip and will not hear it. I will hold you responsible for what you say."

"I speak the truth, Sire! Lancelot and the queen have had an adulterous relationship for years, and everyone knows it. It is a scandal that threatens the stability of your throne."

"Am I someone?" Arthur asked in a steely voice.

"Of course, Sire!" Aggravain replied, confused.

"For a moment, I wondered," Arthur said in a tone heavy with irony. "I do not know of this relationship and do not believe it exists. I realize you think me old and blind, but in this you are wrong. There are no grounds for scandal."

"Everyone is talking about it, Sire!"

"Truly? I was under the impression that it was you who were talking about it to anyone who would listen. Some of the younger knights who have time on their hands and nothing in their heads may pay attention to you. I will not!"

"But Lancelot and Guenevere do not deny it, Sire!"

"Deny it? How can they? No one has had the courage to accuse them to their faces, through fear of what Lancelot will do. I am surprised you are not afraid of me in this instance, as well."

"I am acting in your best interests, Sire," Aggravain protested.

"Are you? Your brothers have tried to dissuade you from speaking to me on this subject, and you still have the gall to say you are acting in my best interests?"

"They dare not speak, Sire," Aggravain muttered.

"I can well believe it," Arthur said coldly. "Let me tell you what I would tell them if they uttered such treason. I would say that if I ever heard such words again from their mouths I would have them stuffed with earth. Do you understand me?"

"But I am your cousin!"

"True, and you'd still be my cousin, but you'd be my dead cousin. I consider your behavior outrageous, and the only thing that saves you from my retribution this time is the fact that you are my cousin. You have been warned. If this conversation had occurred before any company but this, I could not ignore it so. Be advised," he concluded, and he waved his hand abruptly in dismissal.

Aggravain turned to leave, but his face reflected his mutinous thoughts. I did not trust him.

"Hold a moment!" I demanded.

Aggravain turned back and I let the anger flowing through me surge forth as I stepped forward, locking on him until he quailed and groveled at my feet, squirming to avoid my touch as I came closer.

"Cousin," I said coldly, "I have marked you for my own. It was you whispering in your brother's ear that led him to stab Morgause. I know it past need for proof. I say you will not escape me if aught you have set in motion brings ill to my brother or his queen. I do not have to answer to Arthur's laws, as he himself must. Beware of me, cousin," I said, and I closed my mind against the flow of emotion, so he could rise and stagger from the room.

"Forgive me," I said to Arthur. "I thought it necessary or I would not have spoken after you. I fear, however, it may already be too late. I read treachery in the man."

I was right. That night Cornu awakened me from a sound sleep. A rush torch lighted my quarters, and in the light of it I could see he was carrying Mordred, who was bleeding from several wounds.

"What happened?" I asked, helping Cornu settle the wounded boy face down on my bed while I examined him quickly.

"It's Aggravain," Mordred gasped. "He's trapped Lancelot in Guenevere's rooms and brought a dozen men to seize him there. Aggravain has been plotting with his friends to bring proof of his accusations against the two of them."

"Damn him! This is too much. He will pay for this in dear coin! But, how came this?" I asked as I worked on his wounds.

"I tried to go for help. He stabbed me." Mordred was fainting as he gasped these few words.

Together Cornu and I tended Mordred, whose cuts were bleeding freely. I deemed he was not in danger of death, however. As soon as I could leave him, I picked up my satchel of medicines and ran toward the queen's wing, fearing what I might find.

The torches had been lit in front of Guenevere's door, so it was like day and the easier to see, if not understand, the chaos there. Dead men lay everywhere, some of them nearly cut in half. I went from body to body. Though a few of them yet breathed, nothing could be done for any of them. I had seen no worse on the battlefield.

"Open up!" I yelled, and hammered on the door with my fist. "It's me, Morgan!" I heard the bar lifted from the door and pushed it open. Guenevere and two of her ladies were on their knees, attempting to comfort a man who was fast dying. It was Collgrevance, one of Aggravain's friends. The ladies tried to shut the door again, but it was thrust open violently by Arthur, naked and wild of eye, brandishing Excalibur.

"Gwen!" he cried. At his voice she rose and ran to him to be held. "Are you hurt?" he asked.

She shook her head against his chest, but did not reply. Collgrevance was dead. Arthur drew Guenevere into her sleeping chamber, away from the dead and dying men, and sat down with her, still holding her tightly. I followed but did not question her, waiting for her to recover her composure.

"Oh, Arthur, it was horrible!" she whispered. "Lancelot came to my door with a drawn sword, wearing only a cloak. My ladies let him in on his insistence. When they roused me, he apologized, saying a page had come to tell him I was in frightful danger. I assured him this was untrue, but before he could leave, Aggravain came to the door and demanded Lancelot surrender himself. We hadn't done anything!"

"I know," Arthur said, patting her.

"Lancelot slammed and barred the door and asked me if I had

any armor in my quarters. You know I have nothing like that here. I can't imagine why he thought I would."

"What happened then?" Arthur asked, bringing her back to the point.

"I told him there was nothing, so he unbarred the door, pulled one man through, disarmed him, cut him down with his own sword, and barred the door again, as quickly as I'm telling you about it. Lancelot stripped his victim and donned his clothing to pad the armor, while Aggravain pounded on the door with the butt of a spear. I don't know why you didn't hear it." She tilted her head back to look at him a moment.

I knew the answer to that. Arthur slept very soundly, particularly after a heavy supper and a flagon or two of wine. It may have been later when they got in from a day's hunting, but not too late for Arthur and Pelleas to eat!

"Lancelot said there was a crowd outside," Guenevere continued, laying her head back on his chest when Arthur did not respond to her question, "but he said he would push them back and escape. He said I was to bar the door after him and that I'd be all right. It was him they were after."

"Yes," Arthur muttered, petting her hair to soothe her, but I thought she was wrong. It was she Aggravain wanted. Lancelot was just a way to get at her.

"I did as he ordered when he went out," Guenevere said, in a voice that was beginning to falter. "I heard the most frightening sounds. Is Lancelot all right?"

"I think he escaped," Arthur said.

Bors, Lancelot's cousin, shoved his head into the room as Arthur spoke and inquired breathlessly, "Are you safe, Sire?"

"Yes, both of us. What of Lancelot?"

"He came to our quarters but a moment ago. He was unwounded, but said the queen was in need of aid. You're sure she is unhurt?"

"I am unhurt, Bors, and thank you for coming," Guenevere said.

He nodded and disappeared.

309

I could hear a body being dragged into the hall and the barring of the queen's bedchamber door. I stayed with her and Arthur long enough to give her a sleeping potion from my medicine satchel, then left to watch over Mordred, letting the morrow carry whatever it might bring.

I did not shut my eyes, and in the morning was cheered to find Mordred sleeping naturally without fever. I left Gareth to watch over him and returned to the queen's quarters. There I found the bodies had all been removed and the hall and anteroom cleaned of blood. Bors was sitting on a stool with the air of a man who had been there a long time. Armed knights stood on either side of the door.

"How bad is it?" I asked as he rose to greet me.

"It's difficult to see how it could be worse, my lady," was his blunt reply.

"How many dead?"

"Thirteen. Several lived for hours, but they all bled to death despite our best efforts to save them."

Thirteen, I thought, the Mother save us! Thirteen! "Who were they?" I asked.

The expression on his face became intent as he counted them off on his fingers. "There was Collgrevance, Madore de la Porte, Gyngalyn, Melyot do Logres, Petipace of Winchelse, Galleron of Galway, Melyon of the Mountayne, Ascamour, Gromoreson Rioure, Aggravain, Florence and Lovel." He looked up when he recited the last name with the air of a schoolboy having successfully completed his recitation.

All but the last three were just names to me; I knew only Aggravain, Florence and Lovel, Gawaine's brother and two sons.

"Has anyone told Gawaine yet?" I asked.

"He knows."

"How is he taking it?"

"He said he warned them all not to meddle with Lancelot. He is grieving, but as much for Lancelot and the queen as for his kin."

"Where are the bodies?" I asked.

310

"They lie in state in the great hall. Gawaine is there with them."

"Then I'll go to him," I said.

Leaving Bors on guard at Guenevere's door, I went in search of Gawaine. He rose from his knees to embrace me as soon as I entered the room.

Arthur came right behind me and hugged us both before taking Gawaine's arm and saying to him earnestly, "I am sorry about Aggravain and your sons, Gawaine, but this business must be settled as quickly as possible. Afterward we will grieve together."

"What are you planning, Sire?" Gawaine asked.

"We must act ahead of the mob," he said. "Have a stake set ready for firing. We'll bring the queen to it at daybreak tomorrow, giving her today to cleanse her soul."

"No, Arthur! You'll never burn her!" I exclaimed, horrified.

"Will I not? I'll have her escorted to the stake and tied against it," he retorted grimly. "If no succor comes, she will suffer the penalty of the law or there will be no law hereafter."

"Lancelot will never let the sentence be carried out," Gawaine said.

I recalled Lancelot had arrived at the last moment to champion the queen's cause once before, when she was accused of poisoning the apple meant for Gawaine. It had occurred to Arthur, too.

"So be it," Arthur said. "Will you escort her to the pyre?"

"Never!" Gawaine exclaimed. "I will have nothing to do with it! I swear, on my honor, I believe her to be innocent!"

"Of course she's innocent!" Arthur shouted. "What damned difference does that make now? Are my knights less dead?"

"A trial would show she was not at fault," I said.

"How? She was not at fault to admit Lancelot to her rooms in the dead of night? Lancelot's actions have sealed public opinion against her for all time, regardless of where the truth lies."

Gawaine's face took on the mulish look it always wore when he was proof against persuasion, and Arthur saw it.

"Very well," Arthur sighed, "if you won't escort her yourself, will you ask Mordred to do so?"

"Mordred was trying to bring help to the queen when Aggravain

311

stabbed him," I said. "Mordred will not be walking anywhere tomorrow."

"Dead?" Arthur asked in a stricken voice.

"No, but no thanks to Aggravain. He struck to kill. Mordred was unarmed," I told him.

Arthur turned back to Gawaine and said, "Now you see? I truly need someone from your family to quiet the mob. Ask Gaheris. He owes the queen a debt, for she begged me to lift his exile. Let him come."

"I doubted her once, and I was wrong. I will never doubt her again," Gawaine said, shaking his head.

"I thank you for that," Arthur said, trying not to sound impatient. Sometimes Gawaine could be dense. "But you must ask your brother to act as escort," he repeated firmly. "Both Gaheris and Gareth, maybe? Your family must be represented, or the gesture is futile."

"They will do so if I order it, but they will not like it. If Aggravain had not died in his folly, he might have volunteered, but Gareth, especially, will object. By Mary's eyes, Lancelot knighted him!"

"Even so," Arthur said.

Early in the afternoon Arthur had Guenevere brought before him for trial in the great hall, after she had rested sufficiently for the ordeal. I was surprised at the size of the crowd. I knew that only Guenevere's presence at Arthur's side had kept the Jutes of Kent from overrunning London these many years. She was the granddaughter of their greatest chief, Hengist. I need not have worried. The men in the hall were veterans who had served Arthur in his wars, the London Irregulars he recruited from the docks, the first to proclaim him king three decades ago. These men and their sons and grandsons had prospered under Arthur's rule and had been given preference where it was possible to do so. They were loyal to him.

"How do you plead, my lady?" Arthur asked Guenevere.

"I am innocent, Sire," she said proudly.

Nithe had a firm grip on Pelleas to keep him from scooping up Guenevere in his arms and stalking off. I could barely contain myself and thought ruefully I could use someone like Nithe to hold me back. This was stupid!

"Thirteen men have been slain. What do you know of that?" Arthur asked.

"I saw but one, and he died in my arms," Guenevere said. "Collgrevance! He was so young! I wept for him."

"So did I, Lady, and for the others," Arthur told her. "They were all young, bound together in an adventure they would have been better off not to undertake. They were told they could uncover information damaging to the throne and that, in exposing it, they would be doing me a service."

"Were you well served, Sire?" she asked.

"Never so poorly," Arthur replied. "I have thirteen dead men, three of them kinsmen. The laws I announced to keep the conduct of my knights in decent check have been broken. You, my lady wife, are accused of adultery, and your accusers are dead. The knight to whom your name is linked is known to have killed them and has fled. What can I make of that?"

"I know the facts are black as you relate them, Sire. Do you believe me when I tell you they prove nothing, except that some wretch has tried to destroy my good name?" Guenevere asked, no trace of pleading in her voice.

"He has succeeded, my lady, and died in the effort," Arthur said. "Does it matter what I believe, when every knight and churl in Camelot believes something else? I warned you that you had enemies, and that circumspection was necessary if you were not to fall into the severest trouble. You would not hear me. You bear some measure of fault in this."

"Woe is me, Sire, but if you believe me innocent of the greater charge, I care not what others believe."

"Even if you burn for it?"

"I wish not to burn. I am afraid of fire, my king. Nevertheless, let come what may. I am innocent and will go to my death in the sure knowledge God will find me so and do me the justice denied me among men."

Arthur waved to have her taken away, turned his head from the sight of men, hid his face and wept. I wept openly.

Next morning dawned bright and pleasant with just enough breeze to lift wisps of Guenevere's unbound hair and float it around her face. She was pale but composed. Gareth and Gaheris supported her on either side as she was stripped of her robes down to her white shift. The two led her to the stake and turned her so she faced Arthur, who stood alone. I would not take my place beside him, nor would Nithe, nor Pelleas.

Nithe told me she and Pelleas had gone to see the queen in the chapel where she was praying. The guards attempted to keep them out, but word came from Arthur to admit them. Pelleas offered to take her away to safety, but Guenevere had refused gently, thanking him.

As I watched, it became clear Arthur could not give the order for Guenevere to be bound to the stake, so she gave it herself. Gareth and Gaheris honored her wishes. Then a kern brought a torch to set the fagots ablaze, looking to Arthur for the signal. Guenevere spoke to the man, but he ignored her and continued to look at Arthur. Taking the life of a queen was not done on any authority but one.

I did not know what Arthur might decide, finally: Give the order to set the fire, free and pardon her, or take her down from the stake himself and be damned to everyone. I could not wait to see. I shrugged off Cornu's restraining hand and marched down the grassy slope toward Guenevere's stake, so intent on releasing her I missed the sight of Lancelot and his men bursting from the trees but an arrow-shot from where the stake was set. A trumpet sounded, and I looked to the right at the sound. Twenty men at arms were charging down on me. Cornu and Pelleas, who had both followed me, dragged me back out of the way of the horses, being ridden at full gallop to rescue the queen.

The common people cheered them on, and I was close enough to see Guenevere's face as color mounted to it.

Lancelot rode straight up to Guenevere, swinging his great sword as he came. Oh! Oh! He cut men down like wheat in harvest!

No! They were unarmed! Look! Look out, Gareth! . . . Lancelot struck Gareth! Oh, Lud! Couldn't he see?

I felt I could no longer watch, but I could not look away, either. Cornu held me in his huge hands, squeezing so tightly I would have screamed had I breath left. It was as though Lancelot had panicked. Men died right and left under his blows before he reached the queen. He slashed her bonds, lifted her and swept her to the saddle. She had her arms outstretched to Gareth as blood spurted from gaping wounds in his head and neck. He collapsed beside the stake. He had a look of surprise on his face. . . . I saw his long, fair hair trampled under the hooves of Lancelot's charger. Guenevere hid her face as Lancelot bore her away.

I heard Arthur screaming and saw him start forward, to throw himself on that terrible bloody sword, if need be, to stop the carnage. Knights from his personal guard seized him and sat on him while he raved, and Lancelot rode past. Arthur beat his fists on the ground, yelling, "No! No!" as Gaheris fell to Bors, for Bors followed Lancelot in and out of the melee, cutting a swath as deadly as that of his leader.

The kern with the torch had dropped it into the brush at the stake before he was struck down, and it blazed merrily. His clothes caught fire as he writhed in pain, bleeding from a deep cut in the shoulder. He spurted red until he was pumped empty and stopped moving. I imagined him screaming, but, in truth, I could not make out one sound from another. Cornu held me tightly until it was over, perhaps to prevent me from attacking Lancelot myself.

As soon as the horsemen rode away he released me, and I walked among the knights, some dead, some dying, until I found Gareth, his bright hair dark with clotted blood. He was dead at the hands of the man he idolized, Lancelot. Oh, Lancelot, I thought, how large grows the band of ghosts who await your blood!

Friends and relatives from among the spectators dragged some individuals apart from the other fallen men, and the wailing and screaming came from both the wounded and the bereaved. Cornu brought me my satchel of medicines and bandages, and together we set to work saving what lives we could and passing over those we could not. I did not see Gawaine, but I had not expected to. He had told me he thought executing Guenevere was little better than murder of an innocent. What would he think of this?

Arthur walked by dazed, and someone shouted, "Do you still believe her clean of sin?"

Arthur simply shook his head, not trusting himself to speak.

I went to him, and took his arm, seeing the horror in his eyes. "Damn the law!" he said. "I tried to serve it and only got men butchered like hogs in autumn! Lancelot betrayed me! To think once I called him the foremost knight in the realm!" He was muttering, in shock, and I told his knight attendants to take him away, that I'd be in to see him later.

When finally there was no one standing before Cornu and me waiting for help, I turned and leaned against a wagon. Some enterprising farmer had brought it full of produce to sell, taking advantage of the crowd gathered to watch the burning. I saw that his cabbages were all flecked with blood. Who would buy them now?

"Take me to Arthur," I sighed, and Cornu led me away from the cries of the dying.

CHAPTER
XVII

I joined Arthur's train in his attempt to recover Guenevere. He might have let her go with Lancelot, but Gawaine would not let the matter rest. Cornu went with me, as always, but Pelleus and Nithe returned to their home on the isle of Mona, for Nithe loved both Arthur and Lancelot and did not wish to choose between them.

There were plenty of boats in London, with the king in residence in the city. Arthur commandeered them to transport his men and horses across the Channel to Armorica. It was still summer and the trip over was almost pleasant. I was not at ease on boats. They set us down and sailed off, following their own concerns.

We did not catch up with Lancelot until we reached Joyeuse Garde, his castle in Armorica, and there we could not reach him. Day after day Gawaine stood before his gate and challenged him to single combat, swearing Lancelot owed him a life for killing his kinsmen: his brothers Gareth, Gaheris and Aggravain and his own two sons, Florence and Lovel.

Mounting a siege was boring work. Arthur and I had time to talk, hours and hours, and became close. We talked about our different childhoods, and I told him what I remembered of our mother, stories he seemed grateful to hear. He said they made him feel he knew her, and he wept several times in regret that he had missed so much. I did not tell him of finding Uther in our

317

mother's room, and, indeed, Arthur asked me no questions about Uther.

I had never felt so comfortable with any man before. Arthur had no claims on me, or expectations of me, nor I of him. We could be completely open with one another, barring a few subjects Arthur's tact and my reticence left untouched.

We both worried about Gawaine, whose grief and anger seemed to obsess him past all else. Lancelot sent out heralds to Arthur and to Gawaine pleading to avoid facing Gawaine, fearing he would have more of that family's blood on his hands. Lancelot's own men prevailed upon him, finally, for Gawaine stooped to calling Lancelot names, "coward" and "miscreant" and worse, cutting at the sod with his great sword in frustration. Lancelot's cousins convinced him his honor was at stake, and so, reluctantly, he came out.

Under the rules agreed to, each knight was allowed a squire, and Gawaine chose me, swearing I was the equal of any of Lancelot's men. I think he feared refusal if he asked anyone else, for Lancelot had been much loved by Arthur's knights.

I had expected Bors would stand with Lancelot, but he chose Lavayne, instead, the man Guenevere believed to be his lover. Perhaps it was true. Neither of the men seemed to recognize me, tricked out in a mail shirt and helmet, even when I wound my amulet around my helmet.

Single combat for armored men could be slow and strenuous, and victory was as much due to stamina as to skill. The swords weighed as much as seven or eight pounds and had to be wielded with one hand to allow the other free to hold the shield.

Gawaine, a dozen years older than Lancelot, was soon gasping for breath, and finally Lancelot caught him with a backhanded swipe he was too tired to avoid. It dented his helmet, cracked his skull and laid him on his back like a trussed stoat.

As Lancelot dropped his shield and raised his sword for a two-handed blow, I charged him with my staff outthrust and struck him in the center of the gorget around his throat. He was unbalanced enough to fall over backward, grunting as the wind was knocked out of him. His helmet fell off, and his head was bare to my next blow. Lancelot could never have prevented me from smashing his face before Lavayne reached me. I looked down at him a long moment, then stepped back. Here was the man who had killed my lover Hemiston, Lancelot of Uther Pendragon's line, whose death would pay the blood debt owed my father. And yet I could not kill him.

I took a position of guard over Gawaine, wondering a fleeting moment what squires were supposed to do under these circumstances. Had I the knowledge, I would not have done differently.

Lavayne brushed by, cursing me for interfering while helping Lancelot to his feet, but Lancelot hushed him.

"Who is this, Lavayne?" he asked.

"Some ill-conditioned cur who knows not the rules of single combat or else holds them in light regard. Who are you, knave?" were the words Lavayne addressed to me.

"Knave? Me? I am Morgan, sister to Arthur, High King of Britain," I informed him. "Do you not know your betters?"

"A girl?" Lavayne asked in disbelief.

"Not a girl, Lavayne, a woman. A shield-maiden of old!" Lancelot corrected him. "I am in your debt, Lady Morgan. You stopped me from committing an unknightly act I would have ever regretted. Tell Gawaine I love him well, and hope he has not taken too great a hurt. Tell him also that I will not respond to further challenges, whatever the provocation." And, leaning on Lavayne's arm, he began to limp away.

Men from both sides reached the wounded men and helped move them from the field. Gawaine was taken off on a stretcher. I thought it remarkable there was not open fighting between the opposing forces, but Arthur assured me later it never happens.

"You committed a breach of propriety, though, striking Lancelot, that could only be forgiven a woman," Arthur said.

I looked closely at him, and he was smiling slightly, teasing me. If he had lost Gawaine, I do not know what he would have done. I had not seen him smile since this business began.

The weather turned cold and miserable, for winter was upon

us, and still we sat before Joyeuse Garde doing absolutely nothing that I could see but slowly freezing to death. December in Brittany was the time when all thrifty kerns could be found warming their feet in front of peat fires and warming their bellies with apple brandy. I stared up at the walls of Lancelot's castle, knowing he was as snug before his own peat fire as any kern. I looked back at my pavilion tent and then around at the makeshift shelters the men had devised for themselves. What were we doing here? I wondered, drawing my cloak more tightly about my shoulders.

I made my way over frozen ground, chopped into a rough, slimy surface by the hooves of war-horses. Sentries before my tent, trying to appear military, saluted as I stooped to enter. On my bed lay Gawaine, sunk in drugged slumber.

"How is he?" I asked Cornu.

"The better for fresh food sent from the castle," he responded.

Lancelot worried over Gawaine, holding himself responsible for wounding him in single combat, though how he could have avoided it, short of allowing Gawaine to wound him, I did not know. Lancelot sent us food and rich wines in an effort to save his old comrade. Gawaine was not told the source.

"Ah, my lady," he said as he awoke and saw me. "Every time I open my eyes from sleep I find you standing over me."

"Like a corbie crow waiting to peck your eyes out?" I asked, smiling.

He laughed a little and said, "Can you speak again to Arthur about going home? I would die in my own land."

"Give up the siege?" I asked.

Gawaine had not asked to go back to Britain before this day. His dreams must have become as real to him as his waking hours. Perhaps he had dreamed of asking. I knew Arthur, heartsick for Camelot, had wished to leave for months. Gawaine had objected so strenuously, having sworn to avenge his brothers, that Arthur reluctantly had continued the hopeless effort. It was Arthur who had requested of Gawaine that his brothers stand unarmed with Guenevere; he felt responsible for their deaths.

The effort to take Lancelot was hopeless. If Lancelot mounted a strong push against our puny forces, he could sweep us back into the sea at any time. Perhaps he stayed his hand for the sake of old friendship, or even because Arthur was still his liege lord.

"I will speak to Arthur," I promised Gawaine with a straight face. "With your wishes united with mine, perhaps I can persuade him this time."

Gawaine had a low fever that nothing Cornu and I did could lift, and at times he seemed to forget what had transpired over the past bitter months. I despaired of his ever recovering.

On the way to tell Arthur of Gawaine's request, I relived in my mind the nightmare of Guenevere's rescue at the stake. The same scenes had passed through my mind a thousand times. So many men killed, and for nothing! Arthur had disarmed Guenevere's guards so there would be no bloodshed, and they were helpless before Lancelot. I could still see Gareth as he looked up at Lancelot, confident his hero would stay his hand, once he looked into his face. Gareth had died under Lancelot's sword with a smile on his lips. What had possessed the man?

I recalled the weeks of desperate struggle afterward to find enough allies to attempt the retrieval of Guenevere, though to what purpose? So she could be bound again to the stake?

Gawaine, so calm when his brother Aggravain and his sons Florence and Lovel fell into the trap they themselves had set for Lancelot, was inconsolable when Gareth and Gaheris were cut down by the same hand. I could not find it in my heart to blame him. Gareth and Gaheris had been defenseless, trusting in Lancelot. Armed, either could have given a good account of himself. Together, they would surely have prevailed against Lancelot. Gaheris was a mighty fighter, not graceful, but powerful. Gareth was just coming into his full strength, and promised to surpass even his father, Pelleas, in time. As it was, neither had had a chance.

This kind of thinking was bootless. I had been over it many times, and always was reduced to "might-have-beens." Yet I could not stop. I had long ago settled upon the death of Lancelot, and no other of that cursed line of Uther Pendragon, to quiet my father's ghost. Yet, when I had had the chance, I could not kill him. I could not! At least I had not used my witchy powers to overcome him. I had taken him down as a true shield-maiden. Even he had said so! I sighed, thinking, not for the first time, that my father did me no service, loading my head with stories of avenging heroes. He should have had a son with a taste for blood. I realized all my life I had hated the responsibility he had laid on me as a child. How could he have done such a thing to a young girl? Had Boudicca such a father? I wondered.

This responsibility should not have been mine, but some warrior kinsman's. But who, then? Gawaine plainly was not Lancelot's match, and Lancelot would not fight Arthur at all, though Arthur offered to settle the quarrel between them in single combat. I thought Pelleas might defeat him if brought to face him. I understood why Nithe refused to allow either of them to challenge the other. Lancelot was like a younger brother to her. Pelleas was her very life. So firm was she in her determination not to let them confront one another, she had let neither Pelleas nor his sons join Arthur in his siege of Joyeuse Garde.

I did not blame her. I wished I had not come. There was nothing to keep me here, the Mother knew, except Gawaine's need of skilled nursing. There was also little to draw me back home; Drake was now Lord of Galloway. I would have been honored at Morgan's hold as head of clan Merrick, but not needed. The clan mothers ran clan matters to suit themselves.

I went into Arthur's tent. Arthur dismissed his captains at my request and gave me private audience. "Gawaine has asked me to plead with you to break off this siege and go back home so he can die in peace in his own land," I told him.

Arthur shook his head in weary disbelief. "Will he remember this tomorrow?"

"If you tell him, and I tell him, he will believe he said it. He may deny he meant it," I responded.

Arthur nodded. "It is not as easy as it sounds. We'd have to get Lancelot's promise not to attack while we withdrew, then find boats and finally risk the Channel, which is not the least of the dangers."

I knew that. I worried most about the horses, and whether we should not just leave them on the continent, trading them, perhaps, for the boats. "We will have to do it sooner or later, anyway," I said. "What, besides Gawaine's oath to take vengeance, has kept us here this long?"

"Lud knows," Arthur said wearily. He had been drinking wine sent by Lancelot, but showed no sign of its effect. He was too tired and depressed even to get drunk. "Guenevere has not forgiven me for risking her at the stake. Will I have to marry again to get an heir?" he asked.

I had been present at the bitter interview between Arthur and Guenevere when Lancelot released her, as his confessor had insisted for absolution. Lancelot was a good Christian and could not resist an order from that source. Even so he had exacted a promise from Arthur to send her home and not harm her. I recalled Guenevere's words, "It is ironic that a pledge must be exacted against harsh treatment at your hands, Arthur. A more generous man would never have permitted me to stand trial for a fault known by him not to exist," she had said.

Arthur's reply had been in a similar vein. "A more prudent woman would have heeded her husband when he asked her to avoid the appearance of wrongdoing, if she would protect herself and her reputation. You were willful, and seemingly even now have no regret for the good men dead because of your foolishness."

"My foolishness was innocence," she had replied.

"Your innocence was foolishness," Arthur had retorted.

"And yet I was innocent! Whatever you may think Lancelot was to me, he was something you never were; he was my friend!"

"Queens should know better than to have such friends," Arthur said and turned away, allowing her to leave without further comment.

I had wept to see it. Cold words on both sides, yet I knew they loved each other still. Too much blood had been spilled and too much pain endured for there ever to be ease between these two again.

Lancelot had escorted her to Arthur, and it was to Lancelot,

323

not Arthur, that she bade farewell, giving him her hand to kiss. She was still on the palfrey Lancelot had given her, and his men, not Arthur's, formed a guard of honor for her as she rode off to seek a ship to Britain. She did not speak to me, though she looked at me calmly enough.

Arthur had been thinking, too, while my mind played with the past. He brought me back to the present, saying, "I will send to Lancelot for a parley. I should have done it before, regardless of Gawaine, but I was ashamed. I hold the deaths of Gareth and Gaheris and the others on my head, as much as Lancelot's."

"It was not your hand that struck down unarmed men," I replied.

Arthur merely sighed and sent a page with a message to Lancelot. Instead of returning a page with an answer to Arthur, Lancelot came himself, attended by a number of his cousins, all once Knights of the Round Table.

"I grieve to see you in such straits, Sire," Lancelot said.

"I imagine you do," Arthur replied. "If I had served you so, I would grieve as well."

"I meant no harm to Gaheris and Gareth, Sire!"

"Gaheris and Gareth? There were twenty-six others cut down beside the stake, mostly unarmed. What of them? What prompted you to do it?"

"Some of them were only kerns," Lancelot said dismissively, "but you raise a point on which I have long pondered. Why were the knights not armed?"

"So there would be no resistance when you came for the queen. Did you think I would let her be burned, in sooth? It would be out of character for you not to appear," Arthur replied, an old anger edging his words.

"I wish they had been armed!"

"To what purpose? You might not have overcome them and then the queen would have surely burned. I trusted your chivalry to prevent you from striking an unarmed man. So did all present."

"I was so intent on the rescue, I saw resistance in any who stood between me and the queen," Lancelot said, shaking his head like some creature in torment.

"There would have been no need of rescue, had you not fled from Guenevere's rooms, announcing your guilt to all of Christendom," Arthur said. "Could you not have trusted to the king's justice?"

"How could you believe me, under the circumstances?"

"You? I would believe Guenevere. All she had to say was that her women were with her. Do I not know how modest she is? Have we ever made love within earshot of another person?"

"Can you forgive me, Sire?"

"Do you think me a fool, even now?" Arthur asked in an anguished voice. "Between the pair of you, you and Guenevere have destroyed the Fellowship of the Round Table and laid waste my life's work. How can you ask for forgiveness? I cannot forgive myself for placing trust in one who would abuse it so."

"I misjudged you as well, Sire," Lancelot said, more subdued than ever I remembered him. "I should have submitted to your justice. My guilt overwhelms me, and easy as it would be to overcome you here, I will not give you battle."

"Man to man, you would never overcome me," Arthur grated. "If you'd had the courage to face me after wronging me, many lives of men would not have been wasted. I cannot make you face me, and I have no other interest here. Were it not for debts I owed Gawaine for putting his unarmed brothers before your sword, I would have gone long since."

"How does Gawaine fare, Sire?" Lancelot asked, swallowing the insult with a visible wince.

"He is dying," Arthur said harshly.

"What will you do then, Sire? How can I serve you?"

"If you mean, what will I do when I leave here," Arthur said after a short silence, "I do not know. I have given you my promise not to harm Guenevere, and I will honor that. Beyond that, you have no right to ask. Will you allow us to disengage and leave without hindrance?"

"I will bespeak boats for you," Lancelot said. "Your hand has lain heavily upon my lands, and my people will rejoice to see you gone. I will command them to give you all assistance to make it so."

With that, Arthur nodded, and walked away.

Next morning I was standing in the early half-light with Arthur, planning on steps needed to disengage, when a messenger rode up. He gave Arthur several rolled letters and departed without speaking.

Arthur passed them to me, a gesture of confidence which touched me. I broke the seal on one, held it to the light streaming from the open tent and told Arthur, "This is from Kay." Arthur watched with interest, for letters are no common thing. I offered it to him and read it aloud after he waved it away.

"Arthur, High King of the Britons," I began.

"Skip to the meat of it," Arthur ordered.

I complied, saying, " 'Mordred,' Kay writes, 'pretends to have letters stating you have been killed in battle, and that Lancelot is coming with hordes of knights from Brittany to claim the throne. Mordred has imprisoned Guenevere in London and has informed her he will marry her at his coronation after defeating Lancelot's invading forces. He is raising men among the Picts and Saxons to oppose Lancelot's return. I am attempting to deny the truth of his claims, but he is most persuasive, and I am not believed. Come quickly, Sire, if you would preserve your rule.' "

I rolled the scroll back up. "That's it," I said, "except for more formal words about wishing you a good trip and praying God for your safe journey and so on."

A wave of anger washed over Arthur's face. "Was it not enough," he growled, "that my queen betrayed me with my closest friend, or so it is believed by the meanest of my subjects? Now my bastard son conspires to steal my throne!" He looked at me. "Have you news of this independently?"

I opened the other two letters, one addressed to me and the other to Gawaine, and skimmed them. "Yes, Kay sends separate word to me and to Gawaine, in case the rumors of your death were true," I said.

"That sounds like Kay," Arthur said dryly. "Well, we must hurry our departure. Write to Kay that we will be ashore within the month. Will you look after Gawaine and take care he is not left behind? I will not be able to. I expect we will have battle as soon as we land, for Mordred will have spies out."

"I don't believe this, Arthur," I said. "Mordred would never serve you so. Besides, that part about marrying Guenevere is ludicrous."

"How so? She is still the most beautiful woman in Britain. It was common talk that the boy was besotted with her."

"Perhaps that was true before he laid eyes on Viki, Pelleas' daughter," I said. "All the young men who see Guenevere for the first time imagine themselves in love with her. They get over it after she treats them like the children they are. So she would have done with Mordred, if it's true at all. In any case, he is betrothed to Viki now."

"Why would Kay say so, then?" Arthur argued.

"Kay is devious, Arthur, more so than perhaps you realize," I said. "He does not love you."

"I never thought he did," Arthur said, "but he took oath never to be false to me in matters that affected my rule. To my knowledge, he has never broken that oath."

Arthur would not hear further discussion, so I left to make my own arrangements. Without our requesting it, Lancelot sent a horse litter, so we were able to transport Gawaine to the seashore, where we found a boat had been specially set aside for his use. Lancelot had loved Gawaine and his brothers, I realized. It was disconcerting to find virtue in your enemy.

Gawaine's fever did not subside, but he stayed rational, becoming stronger daily so that it was all I could do to keep him from throwing himself into the loading of boats. I knew Arthur intended to land in London, where he could count on support. The London Irregulars still formed the bulk of his personal troops, but they were sick and weary of the long, cold siege. The Fellowship of the Table was so shattered, first by the quest for the Grail, and then by Lancelot's defection, that Arthur was almost without any heavy

327

cavalry. In any case, mounted men would be useless in close quarters like the dock area of London where he planned to land. Mordred's Saxon and Pict allies would fight on foot wherever we encountered them, with the exception of the few knights he might recruit from the local population.

Horses could take a lot of space, and Arthur ordered that none could be shipped back to Britain, to make it possible for all the men to be transshipped at the same time. I thought Cornu would be devastated, but he merely shrugged.

"We'll start over, Lady," was all he said.

We left the horses for Lancelot, to cover the expense of the ships and to repay for the land we had laid waste during the siege. My own animals had long since become part of Arthur's army and were no longer mine to dispose of one way or another. I could understand Arthur's not wanting to be beholden to Lancelot for anything.

The open water between Britain and the shores of Brittany was predictably rough, but I had not expected to be driven ashore at Dover. As it was, we were lucky to land anywhere. The Jutes of Kent, loyal to Guenevere, resisted us, meeting our boats in small fishing craft bearing ax-men. Each of our boats carried a covered pot of live coals to ignite arrows wrapped in oil-soaked rags. We set fire to the swarming small craft and sailed through their blazing boats with surprising ease.

There were more men assembled on the beach, awaiting us, but they were no match for the Irregulars, who put them to flight before I reached shore. We captured the survivors from the boats and tied them in long strings so they could walk on either side of us, shielding us from ambush. I took stock of our situation when the fighting stopped and found only one casualty: Gawaine.

"Ah, cousin, your wound has opened again!" Arthur exclaimed as he came upon us. Gawaine lay on the beach, and I was attempting to stanch the flow of blood, to no avail. Gawaine's gillies had turned a small boat on its side to shield us from the wind, and his legs were covered by a plaid taken from someone's back.

"Aye, and for the last time, I fear," he replied.

"This is no good," I muttered, glancing up at Arthur.

"Give it over, cousin," Gawaine said. "All you are doing is hurting me." He took my hand gently and pushed it away.

"You can't just die!" I exclaimed.

"Can I not? I think I will. I no longer care, anyhow." He looked at me. "Will you do something for me you may not like?"

"Probably," I said. "I usually do."

"Write to Lancelot then and tell him I forgive him. Tell him of Mordred's treachery and ask him to bring help to Arthur. I do not wish to go to my death hating Lancelot and be forced to haunt him for the rest of his life. I am tired, Morgan."

"I will do it," I said, "but I will not forgive him for hurting you so grievously, even if I have to walk without rest throughout eternity myself." As I said the words I felt a chill, but I would not take them back. I looked up at Arthur again, who shook his head sadly.

"So be it," Gawaine said. He closed his eyes and Arthur rose to other duties which were pressing. I remained with Gawaine, watching the strength slip away from him and planning the letter I must write. He opened his eyes once more. "It is not enough," he announced.

"What would you, then?" I asked.

"Arthur's life is in ruins," Gawaine said. "He would have patched something together with Lancelot, if I had allowed it. I have hurt Arthur as badly as I hurt Lancelot, and I loved them both, Morgan. I would do one more thing."

"Name it," I said. "I swear I will do it, if it is possible at all."

"Let my death carry Uther's blood guilt. Lift the curse you have placed on Lancelot that he might find some peace in this world or the next."

"I find I no longer care about avenging my father," I told him with surprise after considering the request. "I seem to have no taste for revenge. I could have taken my revenge on Uther Pendragon's line by killing Lancelot, and I did not." Oh, Boudicca! What kind of shield-maiden was I?

He continued to eye me steadily, so I said, "Besides, it would not serve. You know the laws of blood debt!"

"Indeed, I do. We are both clan Merrick, but both of us have British fathers, do we not? Do you think my father, Lot, less a Briton than your father, Gorlais, merely because you loved one and hated the other?"

"That isn't the point," I said. "You have no blood connection with Uther. You cannot serve as Uther's surrogate. Lancelot can."

"Uther married my aunt, did he not? Did you know he married your mother, Igraine, by brehon contract and not by Christian vow? I'll wager you did not."

"No, I didn't," I said. Furthermore, I didn't believe it. Uther was a Christian and had required my mother to embrace his religion. Still, Gawaine was dying!

"Do not the people of clan Merrick honor contracts as if they were ties of blood?" he continued with a ghostly chuckle. "Besides," he said, "my grandfather's father was Aurelius Ambrosius, older brother to Uther Pendragon and once High King himself, as I recall telling you before." His voice held a chiding note, but there was a hint of laughter in his eyes.

"I recall your saying it, cousin, not just once, but many times," I said, my voice breaking. It was true, but I had never felt less like teasing.

"Is it a bargain then?" he asked, anxiously. He knew he had but little time left.

"I will make this bargain with you, Gawaine: I will release Uther's line of any wrong done mine if you will do the same. As I once told you, it truly was my hand that struck down your father, Lot, not Balin's nor Pellinore's." I awaited his response, fearing the worst, and was surprised when he grinned at me. It was a weak, lopsided grin, but one that reminded me of the boy I had secretly loved.

"Drake told me of this years ago, Morgan. He offered me single combat as your champion. I refused it, of course, telling him there was no need, but I will take your offer now."

330

His hand tightened on mine as pain took him. He was sweating as he lay on the cold beach.

"Please, Morgan! Let my dying be for something!" he pleaded, taking my hand and drawing it to his mouth and kissing it.

"Ah, love, I will then," I said. Unbinding the golden chain and pendant from my brow, I placed it in his hands, clasping them around it. "Myrddin told me once that only I could free the corbie crow from the net that holds its spirit. I release it into your hands, my love."

The words were barely out of my mouth, before he died, smiling at me. I wept for a few moments, uncontrollably, and heard Cornu's pipe playing a lament of such beauty that I forgot everything but my grief. I wept for Gawaine, and for Guenevere and Lancelot, and for Arthur, and Gareth, and finally for myself. Arthur found me so. He lifted me to my feet and turned me to face him, hugging me tightly.

"He is dead, Arthur," I said, "and I loved him so. I never told him."

"He knew it. You do not always hide your feelings as well as you think you do. Knowing this was one of the things that never failed to give him joy when his black moods descended on him. He told me so. He is the last of my Gaelic knights," he added sadly.

I pushed myself away and looked up at Arthur. "Let me have his gillies," I said, "and I will bury his ashes."

"They are yours. I doubt they would follow me, anyway," Arthur said. "Ironic, isn't it? At the end the only true followers I have are those who came to me first, the London waterfront toughs."

"What will you do?"

"I will go home to Camelot and become a local squire, most likely. The binding that brought Britons, Gaels and Picts together has unraveled and will not be retied while we live."

"Mordred will take your place, unless Kay lies," I said.

"Not with my blessing," he replied.

"So be it," I said, "but remember my warning: Beware of Kay." And I turned back to care for Gawaine's body.

331

His gillies were already there, waiting for me, and Cornu's music carried us through the ritual. When I set the torch to the pyre, I looked around for Arthur, and found him gone. I wondered if I would see him again alive, as Cornu led me away to rest.

Despite my sorrow I felt curiously light, and realized it was the first time since I was a child that the specter of my father's walking ghost was absent from my deepest thoughts. I would sleep on this battlefield more soundly than ever in my bed at home. I trusted the morning to bring me new counsel. Boudicca would see to it.

COURTWAY JONES is a cultural anthropologist and eth-
nohistorian who earned his Ph.D. at Columbia University.
He has taught at Indiana University and Pennsylvania State
University. His bestselling first novel, *In the Shadow of the
Oak King*, began this uniquely lively and original trilogy on
the world of King Arthur, *Dragon's Heirs*.